Birds of Prey

ALSO BY J. A. JANCE

A Novel of Suspense

BIRDS OF PREY

J. A. Jance

WILLIAM MORROW   75 YEARS OF PUBLISHING
An Imprint of HarperCollinsPublishers

HarperCollins books may be purchased for educational, business, or sales promotional use. For information please write: Special Markets Department, HarperCollins Publishers Inc., 10 East 53rd Street, New York, NY 10022.

FIRST EDITION

Designed by Cassandra J. Pappas

Printed on acid-free paper

Library of Congress Cataloging-in-Publication Data
Jance, Judith A.
Birds of prey : a novel of suspense / J. A. Jance.—1st ed.
p. cm.
ISBN 0-380-97407-X
1. Beaumont, J. P. (Fictitious character)—Fiction. 2. Police—Washington (State)—Seattle—Fiction. 3. Seattle (Wash.)—Fiction. I. Title.
PS3560.A44 B57 2001
813'.54—dc21 00-059445

01 02 03 04 05 QW 10 9 8 7 6 5 4 3 2 1

For Pat Hall and Mary Daise

Birds of Prey

Prologue

H IT ME AGAIN," Dr. Kenneth Glass said as the bartender walked past. The man gave Ken a questioning look, and not without reason. There had been cocktails before dinner and wine with. And now he had just finished downing his third after-dinner Glenmorangie. "It's all right," Ken reassured the barkeep. "I'm not driving anywhere."

While the bartender went to pour the next drink, Ken fumbled his cell phone out of his pocket and tried calling home. Again. And still, even though it was well past 2 A.M. back home in Atlanta, Georgia, his wife was not yet home.

"Shit!" Ken muttered as he flipped the phone shut and stuck it back in his pocket.

"Pardon me?" the bartender asked.

"Nothing," Ken said, taking his drink. "I've been calling

and calling, but my wife's still out," he added in explanation. There was no reason to make the bartender think Ken was mad at him. "You work your butt off, and what does it get you? A wife who likes the money you make just fine, but doesn't really give a crap about you."

The bartender nodded sympathetically. "Ain't that the truth," he said, turning to answer a summons from another customer.

Ken pulled the drink toward him and then stared down into the glass as if hoping the liquid gold contents might hold the answer to some of his burning questions. He tried to remember the reasons Faye had given him for not wanting to come along on this trip. Let's see, there was the Buckhead Garden Club meeting, and since Faye Glass was the newly installed vice president, she certainly couldn't be expected to miss their first spring meeting just because her husband was being honored with a dinner at a national convocation of his fellow neurosurgeons. No, Faye's garden club meeting was far more important than that! But it was almost 3 A.M. back home in Atlanta, and the garden club meeting sure as hell wasn't running that late.

Ken took a sip of the single-malt Scotch. Despite the booze he had consumed, he felt he was thinking clearly—maybe for the first time in months. The signs had been there for a long time—all the classic signs of marital discord: disinterest in sex and in almost everything else as well; everything that had to do with Ken, that is. The two exceptions had been the Buckhead Garden Club and Faye's new laptop computer, which had become her constant companion. She took it with her everywhere, stowed in the trunk of her shiny white Lexus. He had finally smelled a rat, or rather, Ken had allowed himself to smell a rat when Faye had refused to come along on this trip with him, even though she knew how important it was to him to be honored by his peers. Ken had done his best to convince her to change her mind. Baboquivari Mountain Resort was one of Scottsdale's newest and finest. Always before Faye would have jumped at the chance to accompany him. This time she had simply refused, and no amount of coaxing had persuaded her otherwise.

What if she's having one of those cyber-affairs? Ken asked himself for the first time. *What if she's picked up some loser on the Internet, and she's going to leave me for him?* The whole idea was almost unthinkable, but Ken forced himself to think about what would be, for him, the worst-case scenario. At three o'clock in the morning, kidding himself about the Buckhead Garden Club just didn't cut it anymore.

"Is this seat taken?" someone asked over his shoulder.

Ken turned to find himself faced with a handsome young man in his mid-to-late thirties. "Help yourself," Ken said.

The young man settled onto the barstool while Ken made one more futile attempt to call home. Still no answer. In returning the phone to his pocket, he swung around slightly on the barstool.

"I'll be damned," the newcomer exclaimed. "Dr. Kenneth Glass from Emory University Hospital? The people at Disneyland are right. It is a small world."

Ken gave the man a bleary, puzzled look. "Do I know you?" he asked.

"Your name tag," the newcomer replied with a grin. "Name tags are always a dead giveaway." He held out his hand. "My name's Pete James. Mindy Hudson is my sister. I know Mindy and Rick have thanked you. But let me do the same. Our whole family is eternally grateful for what you did for Kelsey. Can I buy you a drink?"

Ken Glass didn't need another drink, but he was glad to have the company—someone to talk with who might help take his mind off his troubles. "Don't mind if I do."

Mindy Hudson was one of Ken's patients. She and her husband, Rick, had come to Ken's office pregnant and heartbroken, having just learned that their unborn fetus had been found to have spina bifida. Ken was one of a handful of Vanderbilt-trained neurosurgeons who had taken the school's pioneering in utero surgical techniques back home to Georgia. The Hudsons had come to Crawford Long Hospital at Emory University hoping to find a way to spare their child from the most crippling effects of that disease. And it had worked. Months after undergoing a delicate surgical procedure while still in her mother's womb, Kelsey Hudson had been born. At eighteen months she was now a healthy, normal, and mischievous toddler.

"What brings you here?" Ken asked Pete James. "To Scottsdale, I mean."

"I'm a computer consultant," he said. "My company specializes in Internet security systems. I'm in and out of Phoenix a couple times a year."

"Have you stayed here before?" Ken asked.

"At the Baboquivari?" Pete returned. "No, first time. I told my travel agent that I wanted to try someplace different, and she booked me in here. It's pretty nice, don't you think?

For a hotel, that is. When you stay in hotels all the time, they can get pretty old. What are you doing here?"

"Convention," Ken replied. His tongue was feeling a little thick against the roof of his mouth, and he did his best to enunciate clearly. There was nothing worse than a yammering drunk. He'd been around enough of those in his time that he sure as hell didn't want to *be* one.

"Last one," the bartender said as he set two drinks down on the counter, and followed those with two checks, one for Ken and another for Pete James.

"Wait a minute," Ken said angrily. "What does that mean? That you're cutting me off?"

"Don't take it personally," the bartender told him. "We generally close this bar up at midnight. If you want another drink, there's still the small bar off the lobby that stays open until one."

"Oh," Ken said. "That's all right then."

Pete James paid in cash and left. Ken, on the other hand, downed his drink in one long gulp and then scribbled his name and room number onto the tab, along with a fairly hefty tip. Faye always accused him of being a light tipper. It did his heart good to prove her wrong.

"It's late," he said to the bartender. "S'pose I should hit the hay."

When Ken stood up, he had to grab on to the back of the barstool to keep from tipping over. It was enough to cause the bartender some concern. "You gonna be all right, Dr. Glass?" he asked. "I can get someone from security to help you."

"Don't bother, I'm fine," he said. "Fresh air'll do me a

world of good." Ken looked around for the guy who had bought the drink, whose name he had suddenly forgotten, but he was nowhere to be seen. "Thanks anyway," he muttered.

With that, Ken set off unsteadily across the bar and let himself out through a patio entrance that led past one of the hotel's several pools to his wing of the massive complex. Standing outside in the nippy March weather, he paused long enough to pluck the phone out of his pocket. Once more he tried dialing home, and once more the phone rang and rang in a house where nobody answered.

Damn her anyway! Ken thought angrily. *She's out somewhere whoring around with some boyfriend instead of being here with me. I'll show her. I'll divorce the little bitch and we'll see how well she does for herself out in the open market.*

As Ken fumbled the phone back into his pocket, he heard what sounded like hurrying footsteps behind him. Half-turning and trying to get out of the way of whoever it was, he saw only an upraised arm. There was no time to cry out; no time to defend himself. Ken felt something hard thud against the side of his head, followed by the sensation of falling—of falling into the water. Even drunk, Ken knew enough to hold his breath and to try to rise to the surface, but when he did so, there was something that kept him from reaching air—something that pushed him back down, and not just once, but again and again.

Eventually he couldn't hold his breath any longer. When Ken Glass finally exhaled, water flooded into his mouth and lungs. He struggled for a while after that, but finally there was no fight left in him and he fell still.

Seconds later, the man who had introduced himself as Pete

James climbed unhurriedly out of the pool, toweled himself dry, and then slipped back into the clothes he had left concealed behind a hedge at the pool's far end. Wrapping the wet towel around the police baton he had used to whack Ken Glass on the head, he made his way back to the rental car he had left in the hotel parking lot.

Other than the bartender, no one in the hotel had seen him or even known he was there. As he headed for the Hertz lot at Sky Harbor International, he couldn't help but be proud of himself. This wasn't his first job, but it was certainly his best—clean, trouble-free, and by the book.

"Another one for our side," he said under his breath. "One more down and God knows how many to go."

1

THE BLONDE FIXED ME with an appraising eye that left me feeling as defenseless as a dead frog spread-eagled on some high school biology student's dissection tray. "And what do you do?" she asked.

When the headwaiter had led me through the cruise ship's plush, chandelier-draped dining room to a round table set for six, four of the chairs were already occupied by a group of women who clearly knew one another well. They were all "women of a certain age," but the blonde directly across from me was the only one who had gone to considerable effort to conceal the ravages of time. I had taken one of the two remaining places, empty chairs that sat side by side. When I ordered tonic with a twist, there was a distinct pause in the conversation.

"Very good, sir," the waiter said with a nod before disappearing in the direction of the bustling waiters' station, which was directly to my back.

For the better part of the next five minutes the conversation continued as before, with the four women talking at length about the generous divorce settlement someone known to all of them had managed to wring from the hide of her hapless and, as it turned out, serially unfaithful exhusband. The general enthusiasm with which my tablemates greeted the news about a jerk being forced to pay through the nose told me I had fallen into an enemy camp made up of likeminded divorcées. So I wasn't exactly feeling all warm and fuzzy when the ringleader of the group asked her question. The fact that I was on a heaving cruise ship named *Starfire Breeze* pitching and bucking my way into Queen Charlotte Sound toward the Gulf of Alaska did nothing to improve my disposition.

With little to lose, I decided to drop my best conversational bomb. "I'm a homicide detective," I told the women mildly, taking a slow sip of my icy tonic which had arrived by then. "Retired," I added after a pause.

I had put in my twenty years, so retired is technically true, although "retired and between gigs" would have been more accurate. However, it didn't seem likely that accuracy would matter as far as present company was concerned. So retired is what I said, and I let it go at that.

Over the years I've found that announcing my profession to a group of strangers usually cripples polite dinnertime small talk. Most people look at me as though I were a distasteful worm who has somehow managed to crawl out from under a rock. They give the impression that they'd just as soon I went right back where I came from. Then there are the occasional people who set about telling me, in complete gory detail, everything they know about some obscure and previously unsolved crime with which they happen to be personally acquainted. This tactic always serves to turn dinner into an unpleasant parlor game in which I'm set the lose/lose task of coming up with the solution to an insoluble mystery. No winners there.

Surprisingly enough, the blonde took neither option A nor option B. Instead, she gave me a white-toothed smile that was no doubt as phony and chemically augmented as the rest of her. "My name's Margaret Featherman," she announced cordially, standing and reaching across the table with a jewel-bedecked, impeccably manicured hand. She gave me a firm handshake along with an unobstructed view of a generous cleavage.

"These are all friends of mine," she chirped. "We went to college together. This is Naomi Pepper, Sharon Carson, and Virginia Metz." As she gestured around the table, each of the women nodded in turn. "The four of us are having our annual reunion. And you are?" Margaret prompted, resuming her seat.

She had a gravelly voice that made me want to clear my throat. I pegged her as a smoker or maybe an ex-smoker.

"Beaumont," I told her. "J. P. Beaumont."

I didn't voluntarily elaborate on the Jonas Piedmont bit any more than I had on my employment situation. Nothing was said, but she frowned slightly when I said my name, as though it displeased her somehow. It occurred to me that maybe she had been expecting to hear some particular name, and Beaumont wasn't it.

Although the other three women had been chatting amiably enough when I first arrived, now they shut up completely, deferring to Margaret Featherman as though she were the only one of the group capable of human speech. Whatever it was that had disturbed Margaret about my introduction, she regained her equanimity quickly enough.

"Now that we're out from behind Vancouver Island, the water is a little choppy," she allowed a few seconds later. "I suppose your wife is feeling a bit under the weather." She gave a helpful hint by nodding pointedly in the direction of the empty chair beside me.

"I'm a widower," I said.

Again, that wasn't quite the whole story. If a wife dies in less than a day, is her husband still legitimately a widower? And if a first wife dies years after a divorce and it still hurts like hell to lose her to the big C, are you not a widower then? After all, Karen and I may have been divorced, but we had two children together and were still connected in a way no legal document could ever quite sever. Even now I'm surprised by how much her death continues to grieve me. Maybe if I were still drinking, I'd be in such an emotional fog that I wouldn't notice. But I'm not, so I do, and that wasn't any of this nosy broad's business, either.

"My wives are dead," I added brusquely. "Both of them." So much for winning friends and influencing people.

I expected the comment to shut her up, but I doubt even that would have worked had it not been for the appearance of our white-coated waiter. His name was Reynaldo and his accent was definitely Italian. He came to the table prepared to take orders for the *Starfire Breeze*'s second dinner seating. Like my tablemates, Reynaldo blithely assumed I would know whether or not whoever wasn't occupying the empty chair next to me was coming to dinner.

"Will your wife be joining you, sir?" he asked.

"I don't have a wife," I growled at him.

It was far more of a rebuke than the poor guy deserved. After all, Margaret Featherman was the one who'd gotten my dander up, but Reynaldo was obviously experienced in dealing with cantankerous American tourists.

"Very good, sir," he responded smoothly. "And what would you like for this evening's first course?"

It turns out placing a dinner order on a cruise ship is a complicated affair—appetizers, salad or soup, an entree along with pasta and fish courses, as well as dessert. It was a world away from the greasy grub at Seattle's long-gone Doghouse where they used to fry everything, including the lettuce. On the *Starfire Breeze* the menu was written in assorted European languages with rib-eye steak nowhere to be found. Reynaldo patiently explained each menu item. His English, I'm sure, was fluent enough, but his pronunciation was somewhat opaque. Or maybe his and my failure to communicate had less to do with his accent and more to do with all those years of work-related target practice before anybody came up with the bright idea of muffling ears to shut out the noise and the damage.

What with one thing and another, it took a long time for everyone to place their orders, and I welcomed the breather. As long as Reynaldo was quizzing the ladies over their dining choices, the blonde had no other option but to leave me alone. I knew that once she tackled me again, I'd be forced to admit the ugly truth—that I was on the *Starfire Breeze* for one reason and one reason only: to serve as my newlywed grandmother's chaperon.

"I'd feel so much better if you'd agree to come on the honeymoon with us," Beverly Piedmont Jenssen had said to me a number of weeks earlier. "Lars and I are both getting up there, you know. If anything did happen to go wrong—not that it will, mind you—I wouldn't worry nearly so much if you were along to take charge of things."

"Getting up there" was something of an understatement. When my grandmother stepped onto the gangplank of the *Starfire Breeze,* she clocked in at a spry eighty-six-soon-to-be-eighty-seven. Her new husband, Lars Jenssen, is a year older than she is. My new step-grandfather also happens to be my AA sponsor.

The two of them had met months earlier, doing KP duty after the memorial service for my dead partner, Sue Danielson. That acquaintanceship, struck up over washing and drying dishes, had led to a whirlwind romance. Beverly had lobbied for "living in sin" and not disturbing the social security and retirement arrangements left to her by my late grandfather. Lars, a retired halibut fisherman, had convinced her that he had salted away enough money to take care of both of them in their old age, whenever that might occur. To prepare for that eventuality, they had bought their way into Queen Anne Gardens, a retirement/assisted living place on Queen Anne Hill, only a matter of blocks from my Belltown Terrace condo at Second and Broad.

Beverly and Lars had tied the knot at a simple ceremony in front of a justice of the peace. Lars, who still regretted never having made good on a promise of taking his deceased first wife to see his old haunts in Alaska, was determined to treat his new wife better than he had his previous one. Their honeymoon cruise on the *Starfire Breeze* had been Lars' idea. Having me along as aide-de-camp was Beverly's, although, to give the man credit, Lars never murmured a word of objection.

The very word "cruise" is usually enough to turn me green around the gills. During my college days, I had once tried to earn money by joining up with one of my fellow Ballard High School Beavers as a summertime hand on his father's salmon-fishing boat. We had barely exited the Straits of Juan de Fuca before I became hopelessly seasick, helped along by an old Norwegian salt who had cheerfully advised me that putting a chaw of tobacco under my tongue would help ward off the unpleasant symptoms. I ended up being put off the boat and shipped home from Neah Bay in what could only be termed total disgrace. After that I became a committed landlubber, swearing never again to set foot on a ship or boat. For more than thirty years I had made that vow stick— right up until I went head-to-head against Beverly Piedmont Jenssen about taking my grandfather's ashes on board *The Lady of the Lake* over at Lake Chelan. And now, she was trying to do it again.

"I'd like to help out, but I don't do cruise ships, Beverly," I had told her. "I'm a pitiful sailor. I'd be so sick, you and Lars would end up taking care of me."

"I was afraid you'd say that," she responded brightly. "But I have just the thing." She had opened her capacious

purse and dug through it for some time before extracting her
trump card—a small, rectangular clear plastic container. She
handed the box over for my inspection. On top were the
words "Travel-Aid." Inside the see-through lid was something that resembled two pieces of gray cloth with two button-
sized squares of white plastic stuck in the middle of each piece.

"What's this?" I asked.

"You'll see. Open it up," Beverly ordered.

I did. What emerged from the box turned out to be two
small stretchy bracelets made of knitted cloth tubes over some
kind of elastic. What had appeared to be buttons actually
turned out to be two small squares of white plastic, smooth on
the outside but with a lump of smoothly formed plastic on the
inside. I studied them for some time, then looked back at Beverly. "I still don't get it," I said. "What are they?"

"Bracelets," she declared. "You put them on like this."
Grabbing one of my wrists, she stretched the cloth-covered
elastic until it opened wide enough to admit my big-knuckled
hand. Then she positioned the bracelet so the smooth plastic
knob came to rest between the tendons inside my wrist.
"There," she said, surveying her work with satisfaction.
"That's how you're supposed to wear them. If your watch gets
in the way, you may have to stop wearing it for a day or two."

"I'm supposed to take off my watch and wear this?" I
demanded. "What for?"

"Why, to keep from getting seasick, of course," she told
me with unflinching confidence. "I've checked with several
people, including the pharmacist at Bartell's. They all swear
these things work like a charm."

And although I hadn't been much of a believer, I had to

admit they were working. Once we exited Queen Charlotte Strait, we had hit rough waters. The *Starfire Breeze* was making her way north through the kind of swells that, in days past, would have had me barfing my guts out, but here I was, sitting down to dinner and planning to enjoy myself. All I had to do was survive Margaret Featherman's updated version of the Spanish Inquisition.

Reynaldo swept the table clear of all but one of the menus and then disappeared again. I braced myself for the next assault, only to be spared by the arrival of our missing tablemate. "Sorry I'm late," a male voice said. "I decided to take a before-dinner nap. I must have gotten carried away with the sleeping bit. My name's Marc Alley," he added. "That's Marc with a *c*, not a *k*."

I felt an instant affinity for the guy. Here was some other poor unfortunate soul who, like me, had spent a lifetime having to explain his name to every stranger he met. Across the table from me, Margaret Featherman brightened instantly. I stood and held out a hand in greeting, which is when I noticed that he, too, was wearing the telltale Travel-Aid bracelet. Obviously Marc Alley and I had more in common than trouble with our given names.

"I'm J. P. Beaumont," I told him. "Most people call me Beau."

Stumbling over trying to remember all the women's names, I hesitated for only a moment, but that was long enough for Margaret Featherman to jump in and resume control. "Naomi Pepper," she said, indicating the somewhat plump woman just to my right. Naomi's softly curling brunette hair was flecked with gray.

Marc nodded. "Glad to meet you," he said.

"And this is Sharon Carson." Sharon was an attractive-looking woman with silver—almost white—hair pulled back in a French twist and held in place by an enormous black comb. Her ready smile had an easy grace about it. "How do you do," she said.

I found out later that Marc was in his mid-thirties, but with his fresh good looks and wire-rimmed glasses, he seemed far younger than that. And far too nice. Maybe I was just having a bad day, but considering my initial encounter with the four women, I felt as though I were introducing a guppy into a pool filled with sharks.

"This is Virginia Metz," Margaret continued. Virginia wore her red hair in what would have passed for a military regulation buzz cut. I wondered at the time if her hairstyle had to do with sexual proclivity, extreme fashion slavery, or, as in Karen's case, with the aftereffects of chemotherapy.

"And I'm Margaret Featherman," Margaret concluded with a triumphant smile. "So glad you could join us."

Outside the movies I'd never seen a classic double take until Marc Alley did his the moment Margaret spoke her name. "You're not by any chance related to Dr. Harrison Featherman, are you?" he asked.

"As a matter of fact, I am," she answered with a disarmingly bright smile. "Or at least, I was. Harrison and I were married for twenty-some years. We aren't now, of course. You know him, I take it?"

"Know him!" Marc exclaimed. "He's my doctor. He's the man who performed my brain surgery. I used to have terrible grand-mal seizures, sometimes two or three a day. Since the surgery I haven't had a single one. Dr. Harrison is here on the ship to discuss the procedure and its aftereffects with a group of other neurologists from all over the country. That's why I'm here, too. He dragged me along as his exhibit A, so to speak."

"Are you saying Harrison is on this very ship?" Margaret demanded.

"Yes," Marc told her. "You mean you didn't know that?"

Margaret shook her blond mane. "I had no idea," she said. "What a coincidence."

The other women at the table exchanged discreet but knowing glances. Clearly none of them believed a word of it, and neither did I. Not then. And not now.

DURING DINNER I did my best to hold up my end of the conversation. That wasn't too difficult, since I was no longer Margaret Featherman's principal target. That dubious honor was now bestowed on poor Marc Alley. Casting herself in the role of magnanimous hostess, Margaret saw to it that wine—a high-priced Cabernet—flowed like water. So did the double entendres.

From the moment Marc sat down at the table, I suspected that Margaret had every intention of using him, later that evening, to tick off another notch on her bedpost. By the time the second bottle of Cabernet had made the rounds, I think Marc was picking up on that same message. I don't believe he was particularly happy about it.

The tipsy looks Margaret beamed in Marc's direction were

about as subtle as a fully loaded Mack truck. And about that enticing. Reynaldo and his assistant waiter, an attentive Portuguese named Joaô, were delivering the crème brûleé when Naomi Pepper, the woman sitting next to me, leaned over and whispered, "If Marc hadn't shown up, my money would have been on Joaô to get lucky tonight. As things stand, I'm betting Marc is it."

Startled and struck momentarily dumb by her comment, I glanced furtively in Naomi's direction, only to have her wink at me. That little bit of byplay was enough to draw Margaret Featherman's sharp-eyed attention. "Wait a minute, you two," she said. "What's going on over there? No secrets allowed."

According to my scorecard, Margaret was well on her way to being snockered. I was grateful the only kind of driving she'd be doing at the end of the evening would be in the elevator going back to whichever deck her cabin was on.

"Don't work yourself into a lather, Margaret," Naomi said. "I was just asking Mr. Beaumont here if this was his first cruise."

This was, in fact, a bald-faced lie, but I figured my best tactic was to follow Naomi's lead. "First one ever," I responded brightly. "If this is how they feed us at every meal, no one is likely to starve."

Margaret was looking straight at me when I started to answer, but then her eyes wavered and her glance slid away. The back-and-forth movement of her irises told me she was watching someone make his or her way across the room. From the tightening of her bare shoulders and the down-

turned stiffening of her lips, I could tell that this new arrival
was someone Margaret wasn't thrilled to see.

"Mother!"

"Why, Chloe," Margaret Featherman responded enthusiastically. As she spoke, she rearranged the separate features of
her face into what passed for a welcoming smile. "How wonderful to see you."

I looked up and saw at once that Chloe could be none other
than Margaret Featherman's daughter. She was a blonde,
unreconstituted, and younger, early-thirties version of her
mother, but the resemblance between the two women was
striking. In terms of prickly personality, she was evidently a
carbon copy.

"What the hell are you doing here?" Chloe Featherman
demanded.

"I'm taking a cruise," Margaret returned. "And don't be
so rude. Say hello to my friends. You know this is the time of
year when we always get together. We usually spend the
week in Reno. This time we decided to come cruising on the
Starfire Breeze instead."

Chloe Featherman glanced perfunctorily around the table
and nodded briefly to each of the women seated there. When
her eyes reached Marc Alley, who was fumbling to his feet,
napkin in hand, her jaw dropped.

"Marc!" she exclaimed. "What are you doing here? You
were supposed to sit at the same table with Dad and me and
some of the others. We're upstairs—in the other dining
room."

"I'm so sorry," he stammered uncomfortably. "There

must have been some kind of misunderstanding. When I got to my cabin, there was a message waiting for me about a change in the dining arrangements. The note said I would be at table sixty-three in the Crystal Dining Room rather than upstairs in the Regal."

With her face a study in barely controlled fury, Chloe Featherman swung back to face her mother. "I doubt there's been any misunderstanding," she said pointedly. "And I'm sure I know who it is who left you that message. Stay out of Dad's business, Mother," Chloe warned. "You have no idea what's at stake here."

"Oh, I know what's at stake, all right," Margaret Featherman replied. Her voice dripped ice and so did her eyes. Clearly there was no love lost between this mother-and-daughter duo—in either direction. Moments earlier, Margaret had been flirting with Marc and giggling like a drunken schoolgirl. Now she seemed much older and stone-cold sober.

"It's the same thing Harrison's been chasing all his life," she continued. "Some multimillion-dollar grant, I'll bet, with a skirt or two thrown in on the side. Marc here was telling us all just a little while ago that he's along on the cruise as Dr. Featherman's exhibit A. Which reminds me, how is the lovely Leila? Has she finished up her degree yet? And doesn't it bother you having a stepmother who's three whole years younger than you are?"

Muscles tightened in Chloe Featherman's slender jaw. "It happens that Leila and Dad are very happy together," she said stiffly. "As you well know, whatever makes Daddy happy makes me happy."

"How touching," Margaret returned. "But then you

always were Daddy's little girl. There's certainly nothing new and different about that. However did you know to come looking for me here?"

Chloe Featherman held out her hand. In it was an envelope with the cruise line's distinctive logo on it. "I guess no one in the purser's office thought there might be more than one M. C. Featherman on board the *Starfire Breeze*. Since it's marked 'urgent,' someone brought it to me at our table upstairs. I opened it by mistake."

Margaret took the envelope. Without even glancing at it, she stuck it into her purse. "That's quite all right," she said. "I'm sure you have no interest in my personal dealings."

"You've got that right," Chloe Featherman said. Then, with one final glare in poor Marc Alley's direction, she turned and stalked off. He stood looking longingly after her as she made her way out of the dining room.

"Oh, Marc, do sit down," Margaret Featherman said impatiently. "Obviously we're not going to have the benefit of your company for another meal. Chloe will see to that. So we'd best make the most of the time we have."

Snubbed by the daughter and too polite to tell the mother where to go, Marc sank back into his chair, but he made no effort to return to his crème brûlée. Margaret resumed her role of head honcho. "So what are we doing after dinner?" she said.

"There's a musical in the theater," Naomi offered. "That looked like it might be fun. Or else there's a pianist/comedian in the Twilight Lounge, followed by big band music and dancing."

"I do so love dancing to all that wonderful old music from

the thirties, forties, and fifties," Margaret said. "The Twilight Lounge sounds good to me."

Margaret Featherman made her pronouncement with all the authority of a papal decree and with the obvious expectation that everyone else in the group would agree with her. Naturally, they did so at once, with the single exception of Marc Alley, who had nerve enough to raise an objection.

"I think I'll turn in early," he protested. "I have an interview with a reporter early tomorrow morning. I should probably get some sleep."

"Oh, come on," Margaret insisted. "Don't be such a spoilsport. Besides, you already told us you took a nap before dinner. We're four single women who have happened, through the luck of the draw, to come up with something that's supposedly statistically impossible on board a cruise ship—two eligible bachelors. If you think we're turning either one of you loose that easily, you're crazy."

It looked as though Marc Alley was stuck for the duration, and so was I. And that's how, a half hour or so later, Marc and I ended up at one of the posh, upholstered banquettes in the *Starfire Breeze*'s spacious Twilight Lounge. André Morton, the ship's self-proclaimed pianist/comedian, was six decades and several bushel-loads of talent shy of qualifying as the next Victor Borge. André wasn't nearly as funny as he thought he was, and it seemed to me that he didn't play the piano all that well, either. Victor Borge has always been considered something of a national hero in the Scandinavian-stocked homes of my boyhood in Seattle's Ballard neighborhoods. The old Dane continues to be hilariously funny. Even pushing ninety, Borge plays the piano with a gusto André

Morton will probably never achieve. In other words, I didn't care for the show, and I wasn't much looking forward to the dancing, either.

It's not that I can't dance. When I was in eighth grade, my mother saw to it that I had a year's worth of lessons. Mother was a single parent who raised me alone without child support and without the benefit of any help or encouragement from her parents, either. She was a talented seamstress who did alterations and repairs for several Ballard-area dry cleaners. She also had a regular clientele among Seattle's tight-fisted upper crust, who came to our upstairs apartment with photos of the latest New York and Paris fashions which they had clipped from various magazines. From the photos alone Mother was usually able to create wonderful knockoffs at a fraction of the price of the designer variety.

That's where my dancing lessons came from—Mother's sewing. She whipped off two or three ball gowns for a lady named Miss Rose Toledo who ran the local dance studio. The next thing I knew, I was dressed in a suit and tie and shipped off to dance lessons at four o'clock every Thursday afternoon for nine whole months—the entire duration of eighth grade.

Looking back, I wish I could have found a way to be more appreciative of what Mother was trying to do for me. Instead, I was a typically sullen and lippy teenager. I remember arguing with her that ballroom dancing was so old-fashioned—that nobody danced together anymore, not since somebody invented the twist. But Mother prevailed, and so I went—sulking all the way.

But that particular night, all those years later in the Twilight Lounge on board the *Starfire Breeze*, I was grateful she had insisted because dancing, it turns out, is just like riding a bicycle. I may have been rusty to begin with, but I still remembered the moves.

I confess I had my work cut out for me. I was spread thin over three partners while a much younger Marc Alley only had to deal with one. Admittedly, Marc's was a handful. Margaret Featherman danced with her body glued to his in a way that made it look as though she was ready to seduce him on the spot. I remember Mother warning me about girls who danced that way. Miss Toledo told me much the same thing. Somehow, I don't think anyone ever got around to telling Marc Alley.

I was taking a turn around the floor to the tune of "Dancing in the Dark" with Naomi Pepper, the plumpish woman who had winked at me earlier. We passed close by Marc and Margaret just in time to catch Margaret nibbling on the poor guy's ear.

"Reminds me of *The Graduate*," Naomi said. "How about you?"

"Marc's so young that he's probably never even heard of that movie," I replied.

For me, that's one of the advantages of hanging out with women my own age. They know the same jokes and music. We saw the same movies back when we were kids. The generation gap was something that had driven me crazy about working with my last partner, Sue Danielson. She had been so much younger than I was that we'd had major communication problems. Now, with Sue dead, there was no way those problems would ever be resolved.

"Margaret was after Marc to begin with," Naomi confided, bringing me abruptly back to the dance floor. "Once she saw the stricken look on Chloe's face when she caught sight of him at our table, Margaret went into overdrive. Poor Marc's fate was sealed right then, and he didn't even know it."

"Isn't it a little sick for a mother to be in that kind of overt competition with her own daughter?" I asked.

"Margaret and Chloe have been at each other's throats from the day Chloe was born. Sometimes it happens that way between mothers and daughters," Naomi added with what struck me as a wistful shrug.

"I take it you have kids, too?" I asked.

She nodded. "A daughter, Melissa—Missy. She's more than ten years younger than Chloe—and a hell of a lot more trouble. At least Chloe went to school and got a degree. Missy's getting an altogether different kind of education."

I thought of my own daughter, Kelly. She wasn't a problem now, but as a teenager she had marched to her own peculiar drummer. She had run away from home at age seventeen and had wound up living with a young actor down in Ashland, Oregon. She and her husband, Jeremy, are now the parents of my three-year-old granddaughter, Kayla. My son, Scott, is a newly minted electronics engineer with a good job in Silicon Valley. He had brought his girlfriend, Charisse—also a double E—to his grandmother and Lars' wedding. At the time Scott had told me, on the Q.T., that he intended to give Charisse an engagement ring come Christmastime. In other words, I know that raising kids isn't always all it's cracked up to be.

Next up on my dance card was Sharon Carson. She was elegant, beautiful, and an excellent dancer. I was happy to learn that she was far more concerned about looking good on the dance floor than she was about carrying on casual conversation. As a consequence, when I danced with her, there was almost no talking, and that was fine with me.

Last came the redhead, Virginia Metz. After cruising around the dance floor with Sharon Carson, dancing with Virginia was like dancing with a plywood cutout. She held me at a firm arm's length. "So," she said eventually, "besides your room and board, what else do you get out of this?"

I was stumped. "What do you mean?"

"Come on, Mr. Beaumont. I know what you're after. You cruise dance hosts are all alike. The cruise line lets you travel for free as long as you make yourself available to all the poor, lonely single women on board. Meanwhile, you're hoping to waltz your way into some well-to-do widow's bank account and/or bed," she added with a reproachful and unkind look in Marc Alley's direction.

"I think you're operating under a bit of a misapprehension," I said.

"Really?" she returned sourly. "I don't think so."

I was building up to some kind of smart-mouthed reply to Miss Poisonality's pointed comments when a tall man with a thick mane of white hair came pushing and shoving his way through the couples on the dance floor. He ran full-tilt into Virginia's shoulder, knocking her off balance. I had to use both arms to catch her and keep her from falling. The man, however, didn't pause or apologize.

"Maggie Featherman!" he roared. "Just what in blue blazes do you think you're doing?"

Margaret and Marc Alley were on the far side of the floor. As the man came charging up to them, Marc broke away. The look on his face was one of sheer astonishment. Margaret came up grinning from ear to ear.

"Why, Harrison," she said sweetly. "How good to see you again. What a surprise, running into one another like this! I should have known Chloe would have to run straight back to Daddikins and tattle."

"Surprise, nothing!" he shot back. "You set this whole thing up to embarrass me. You even contacted the cruise company and changed Marc's dinner reservation. You've no right to do that, Maggie. It's stalking, that's what it is, and it's against the law. When we get back home, I have half a mind to take you to court over it. If nothing else, I'll at least get a court order to keep it from ever happening again."

"Come on, Harrison, lighten up. It's not necessary to cause a scene here. People are on vacation. They're dancing and having a good time. They don't need to be exposed to our messy domestic relations."

"There's nothing 'domestic' about it," he replied. "This is war, Maggie. W-A-R. And as soon as we get home, you can tell Joe Reston that he'll be hearing from my attorney."

"My, my. You really are hot, aren't you," Margaret Featherman said with a chillingly superior smile. "And I must say both Joe and I will be shivering in our boots."

Harrison Featherman glowered at his former wife. "You ought to be shivering, you little bitch," he declared. "By God, you ought to be!"

By then, summoned either by the bartender or by the

sound of raised voices, two uniformed members of the *Starfire Breeze* crew entered the lounge and were making their way across the crowded dance floor.

"Sir," one of them said quietly, laying a restraining hand on Harrison Featherman's shoulder. "I believe that's enough now!"

The good doctor spun around and focused his fury in a new direction. "Enough!" he repeated with a snarl. "It most certainly isn't enough—not nearly! I intend to find out who it was at Starfire Cruises who released my confidential travel information to my ex-wife. As soon as I do, I'll have that asshole's job!"

With that, Harrison Featherman shook off the crewman's hand and stalked off across the dance floor. The band, which had let the music die a fitful death during the encounter, seemed to wind back up again, the way my grandmother's old 78-rpm Victrola would rev back up when I'd grab the handle and give it a few spins. Throughout the confrontation, Marc had looked as though he hoped a hole would open up in the dance floor and swallow him down in a single gulp. Instead, as soon as the music began again, Margaret Featherman—looking totally nonchalant—wrapped both arms around his waist and somehow cajoled him into dancing again. Virginia Metz, on the other hand, heaved a sigh of disgust, turned, and flounced off the floor, leaving me no gentlemanly alternative but to follow her back to the table.

Flopping into her chair, she crossed her arms and shook her head.

"What was that all about?" Naomi Pepper demanded. "What's up with Harrison?"

"I tried to warn you that coming on this cruise was a mistake," Virginia replied. "Didn't I tell you there was no such thing as a free lunch, especially not where Margaret Featherman is concerned?"

"You told us, all right," Sharon Carson agreed. "I guess Naomi and I were just hoping you were wrong."

3

AT SIX THE NEXT MORNING I was awakened by a determined knocking. I staggered out of bed and limped to the door on feet that complained bitterly about my previous night's maneuvers on the Twilight Lounge dance floor. Peering out through the peephole, I found Lars Jenssen standing in the carpeted corridor holding two lidless cardboard cups filled to the brim with hot coffee. He was stooping over to put one of them down in preparation for knocking again, when I swung open the door.

"There you are," he said, easing himself into the room and handing me one of the steaming cups. "What are you trying to do, sleep your whole life away?"

"Lars," I said as patiently as possible. "This is a cruise. People are supposedly allowed to sleep late."

"Well, for cripes' sake, it is late. It's after six, you know."

In my jobless state, 6 A.M. was still very much the middle of the night. "Is there a problem? Is something wrong with Beverly?"

Easing himself down on my sofa, Lars nodded his head glumly. "I'll say," he muttered.

I felt a clutch in my gut as my mind went shopping through the vast array of medical disasters that could possibly befall someone my grandmother's age. "What's the matter?" I demanded, sinking down on the foot of my recently abandoned bed. "What's going on?"

"Why didn't you tell me Beverly had a problem?"

In actual fact, during the course of their whirlwind courtship, Lars had never asked me a single question about my grandmother's physical or mental health, nor had he asked for my opinion. Come to think of it, she hadn't asked me about his, either. For a change, I felt totally blameless.

"What kind of problem?" I asked.

"Slot machines," he answered.

"Slot machines?" I repeated.

"Ya, sure. One-armed bandits, or whatever the heck you call them. She seems to love the gosh-darned things. She went into the casino last night right after dinner and it took me the rest of the night to get her back out again. All she wanted to do was sit there on that little stool and throw her money away, one quarter at a time. Of course, they don't take quarters, either. You have to go up to that little window and buy some kind of stupid tokens. When she ran out of tokens, she wanted me to go buy some more so she wouldn't have to move away from that one certain machine, but I told her no way. I told her hell would freeze over before she caught me buying something so she could dump more money down a rathole."

"You woke me up at six o'clock in the morning to tell me Beverly played the slot machines last night?"

"We had a fight over it," Lars admitted sheepishly. "She locked me out of the room. I spent the night out on deck until it got too cold. Then I went upstairs to the buffet. I've been there ever since."

As a veteran of my own relationship disasters, I felt nothing but sympathy. "You're not the first groom to be locked out of a honeymoon suite," I assured him. "And you sure as hell won't be the last. Do you think she's still mad this morning?"

Lars shrugged his shoulders and looked miserable. "Beats me," he said.

"What did she say?" I asked. "Tell me exactly."

"That she'd spent as many years as she was going to living with some stubborn old coot who was forever telling her what to do. She told me that if she wanted to spend her 'mad money' on slot machines, then it was nobody's business but her own. She said if I didn't like it I could lump it—and sleep somewhere else."

In other words, Margaret Featherman wasn't the only passenger on the *Starfire Breeze* who wasn't letting anyone else tell her what to do. I didn't like being cast into the role of marriage counselor, but there I was—caught in the middle.

"What did you say?" I asked.

"I said that earning money was too damned hard to just stand on the sidelines and watch somebody throw it away.

You know, you put the coin in the hole and it goes *chink, chink, chink,* and nothing happens, and no money ever comes back out."

"Look," I said. "Wait until eight o'clock or so, then show up at the door. On the way there, stop by the gift shop and buy something nice. Maybe even some flowers, if they happen to have some on board. Tap on the door. When she opens it, hand her the flowers or whatever, tell her you're sorry, and everything will be fine."

"But I'm not sorry," Lars insisted. "I'm pissed. Couldn't I just stay here with you? You've got a nice big room."

Through some kind of travel agent wizardry I had lucked into a junior suite at the last minute. It was a nice room with a marble-surrounded Jacuzzi tub and a separate shower in the bath. As rooms go, it was more than large enough to accommodate two people, but I sure as hell didn't want to spend the next six days sharing it and my king-sized bed with a disgruntled bridegroom who probably snored like an eighteen-wheeler going up a steep grade.

Thinking about a solution, I stalled for time by taking a tentative sip of my coffee and scalding the top layer of skin on my upper lip in the process. Meanwhile Lars downed the contents of his cup as though the temperature of his drink were less than lukewarm. Watching him, the term "asbestos lips" came to mind.

"I'm sure Beverly will get over it," I offered.

"Nope," he insisted. "I don't think so."

For several moments we sat in stark silence drinking from our respective cups. "So how was dinner?" I asked.

"Dinner?" Lars growled. "Too darned much food. Do you have any idea how much food goes to waste on a ship like this? It's downright criminal."

I waited for him to tell me about the starving children in China. He didn't.

"And all that foreign food on the menu. What's the matter with good old American food? Whatever happened to pot roast? Whatever happened to chicken pot pie? And why on earth would anyone want to eat snails?"

In other words, the escargots hadn't been a big hit.

"How about the people at your table?" I asked. "What are they like?"

Out of deference to the newlywed couple's privacy, we had agreed in advance that Lars and Beverly would eat during the first seating, and I would take the second.

"They hooked us up with a couple of kids," he grumbled. "Max and Dotty. They're here celebrating their fortieth," he added. "As if sticking together for forty years is anything to brag about."

"Look," I said. "I'll go shower. You hang tough. Once I'm dressed, we'll take a turn around the deck. Things'll probably look better in the clear light of day."

"It's raining," Lars said. "It's September. What do you expect?"

I reached over and pulled aside the blackout curtains. Sure enough, outside nothing was visible but a second curtain, this one made up of sheets of falling rain.

Grabbing some clothes from the closet, I disappeared into the bathroom. I came out twenty minutes later—shaved and dressed—to find Lars sound asleep. Snoring softly, he was sitting bolt upright with his now-empty coffee cup clutched in one massive fist. I figured that if he could sleep that soundly having just downed a cup of full-strength coffee, he must have needed the rest. So, recalling that sage advice about letting sleeping dogs lie, I slipped out the door and left him there. After hanging the DO NOT DISTURB sign on the doorknob, I went in search of Beverly Piedmont Jenssen.

The *Starfire Breeze* is no small potatoes. According to company brochures, it carries two thousand passengers and a crew of a thousand. Using my well-worn detective skills, I went first to my grandmother's last-known address—her stateroom on Bahia Deck. The door to her room was ajar, and an attendant was busily making up the bed. "Breakfast," he told me when I inquired. "Mrs. Jenssen went to breakfast."

The ship is fourteen stories tall. It boasts two formal dining rooms—the Crystal and the Regal—as well as a twenty-four-hour buffet up on the Lido Deck. Knowing my grandmother, I tried the buffet first—to no avail. After that, I tried the dining rooms. To the dismay of a full contingent of concerned wait staff, I waved aside all offers of help and went wandering through the white-tableclothed wilderness of the Crystal Dining Room. In a windowed alcove near the back of the ballroom-sized room I came across Marc Alley huddled at a table for two with an early-forties blondish woman armed with a laptop computer as well as a small tape recorder.

He was up and dressed—nattily coat-and-tie-dressed—but he looked more than a little worse for wear. His overused appearance reminded me of some of my nightly debaucheries back in the good old days when I was hell-bent on mis-spending my own youth. Since Marc was obviously busy with the scheduled interview he had mentioned the night before, I was prepared to walk past without interrupting them. To my surprise, he waved me over to the table.

"How's it going, Beau?" he said.

"Fine," I told him. "How about you?"

He gestured toward the woman seated with him. "This is Christine Moran," he said. "She's a journalist. This is Beau Beaumont."

The blonde held out her hand and looked me up and down. "Beau Beaumont," she said. "Isn't that a little repetitive?"

As a cop I've always had a natural aversion to journalists of any kind. Christine Moran's greeting did nothing to make me want to change that position. I smiled back at her. "Let's put it this way," I said. "Given a choice between Beau Beaumont or Jonas Piedmont Beaumont, which one would you prefer?"

She nodded. "You're right. Glad to meet you, Beau."

"Are you with one of the papers?" I asked, thinking of Seattle's two dailies.

Christine shook her head. "I'm a freelancer," she said. "Mostly medical stuff for various popular-science and health-type journals. I'm covering the neurology meeting on board. I'm also interviewing Mr. Renaissance Man here as a sidebar to a feature article I'm doing on Dr. Featherman."

"Renaissance?" I asked.

Marc shrugged. "That's how I feel," he explained. "Once I had the brain surgery and my seizures stopped, I felt like I'd been reborn, like Dr. Featherman had taken a terrible monkey off my back and given me back my life. I could have called myself Lazarus, I suppose, but I prefer Renaissance."

I caught sight of the outer edge of a hickey peeking out from under the collar of Marc's starched and pressed white shirt. If Harrison Featherman had dealt with one part of Marc's being reborn, Dr. Featherman's ex-wife had evidently made her own contribution to his sense of well-being, if not necessarily his health.

I took another look around the dining room to ascertain that Beverly Jenssen wasn't to be found among the other diners. "If you're trying to do an interview, I'd better let you get on with it."

"Wait," Marc said. "Do you have plans for later on today?"

"It's an at-sea day," I told him. "Barring a helicopter ride, I don't suppose I'm going anywhere."

"I'd like to talk to you for a little while," he said. "I need your advice on something. What time would be convenient? I'm busy with the conference all morning. How about one o'clock?"

I couldn't imagine what kind of counsel Marc Alley would want from me. If it was some kind of advice to the lovelorn, I knew I was out of my league. "Sure," I said. "Where should we meet?"

I would have liked to suggest my stateroom, but I had no idea whether or not I'd still be dealing with Lars. "How about right here?" Marc returned. "We can have lunch."

"Right," I said. "That'll be fine."

Nodding to Christine Moran, I skedaddled out of the Crystal and took the atrium's glass elevator two floors up to

Regal. And that's where I found Beverly Piedmont Jenssen, delicately slicing her way through a thick piece of syrup-drenched French toast.

"Well," she sniffed as I took a seat at the table. "I suppose Lars came crying on your shoulder, and now he's sent you here to try talking some sense into me, right?"

"Something like that," I admitted.

"But he didn't offer any kind of an apology, did he?"

"No, but—"

"No buts," Beverly interrupted. "If he wants to talk to me, he'd better come on his own two feet, and he'd better be carrying his hat in his hand."

"It's just that he didn't like you gambling, Grandma," I said. "For some reason, it really upset him."

"I noticed that without having to be told," she replied.

"Don't you think you could tone it down a little?"

"Jonas," she said. Beverly Jenssen was already sitting bolt upright in her chair, but when she said my name, she seemed to gain in stature—the way an angry cat can seemingly double in size by standing its fur on end. "I was gambling with my own money," she said. "And what I choose to do with my money is my business."

"Lars just hates to see you throwing your money away."

"Who's throwing it away? At last count, I was up two hundred and eighty-six dollars, so I don't see what he's complaining about. But the money's beside the point. In fact, it has nothing to do with money, nothing at all."

"It doesn't?" I asked.

"No. Lars wants to be able to tell me what to do, and that's not going to happen. It turns out I don't even like slot machines all that much, but as soon as he told me we were leaving, I decided I would sit on that stool the rest of the night—until hell froze over, if necessary."

"Look, Grandma," I argued. "This is your honeymoon. What would it hurt to just go along with things?"

"It would hurt a lot," she retorted. "That kind of bossiness has to be nipped in the bud. If Lars had said he was tired and asked me couldn't we please go back to the room, I would have gone along in a minute without a complaint. But he *told* me we were going. There's a big difference."

Beverly Jenssen finished polishing off her French toast and pushed her plate away. An alert buser swooped over to collect it. "Will you be having breakfast, sir?" he asked, with a coffeepot poised over the clean cup in front of me.

"No, thanks," I told him. "I'm just visiting."

"Very good, sir," he replied, and disappeared with Beverly's plate in one hand and the coffeepot in the other.

"You were at our wedding, weren't you, Jonas?" she asked.

"Yes, of course I was."

"And do you remember my saying anything about love, honor, and *obey*?"

"Well, no."

"Right," she said. "That's because I had the judge leave out the 'obey' part. We said love, honor, and cherish. Not obey. You see," she added, "obey was in my first wedding ceremony. I'm a person who keeps my word. Since I made the promise, I kept it. But keeping that vow to your grandfather,

Jonas, cost me far more than I ever would have thought possible. I lost my daughter over it, and I almost lost you, too. I'm not going to live that way again."

Beverly set her cup back in the saucer with enough force that coffee slopped out over the top. She used her napkin to brush away a mist of tears that suddenly veiled her eyes. That's when I understood that this lover's quarrel really had nothing to do with slot machines and everything to do with my grandfather—Jonas Piedmont, my biological grandfather.

My mother was pregnant with me when her boyfriend, my father, was killed in a motorcycle accident on his way back to his naval base in Bremerton. Jonas Piedmont had disowned his pregnant teenaged daughter. All those years she struggled to raise me on her own, he had never so much as lifted a finger to help her. Not only had he turned his own back on my mother, he had forced his wife, my grandmother, to do the same. It was long after my mother's death from cancer and only when my grandfather had been crippled by a stroke and was at death's door himself that I had reestablished contact with them.

No, as far as Beverly Piedmont Jenssen was concerned, there were far bigger issues at stake than an evening spent plying the handle of a one-armed bandit.

"Lars is in my room sleeping," I said. "I think he spent most of the night sitting outside in a deck chair."

"Silly old fool," Beverly murmured. "He'll probably catch his death of cold."

"Don't you want to go talk to him?"

Beverly sniffed and dabbed at her nose with a lacy handkerchief she had fumbled out of her pocket. "I don't think so," she said. "I'm just not ready to talk to him yet. I don't know what I'd say. In fact, I think I'll go back to the cabin and lie down for a while myself. The truth of the matter is, I didn't sleep very well last night, either."

"Come on, then," I said, helping her up and offering my arm. "I'll walk you to your door."

Her hand on my arm was almost bird-boned, and she leaned against me as we walked. The gale had yet to blow itself out, and I was happy to be there to steady her as we made our way down the long, narrow corridor to their cabin on the Bahia Deck.

"I'm glad to see you're wearing your bracelets," she said when we stopped in front of her door and while I waited for her to extract the room key card from her pocket.

"They saved my life," I told her. "In this kind of rough sea, if I weren't wearing them, I'd probably be flat on my back in bed."

I held the door open for her and walked her as far as the freshly made-up bed. "You're sure you don't need any-thing?" I asked.

"No," she said. "I'm fine. I'll just take a little nap. And if I do need something, the attendant is right outside."

"All right, then," I said, backing toward the door. "Sleep well."

"Jonas?" she said.

"Yes."

"Are you going to tell Lars what I said?"

"Do you want me to?"

"I don't think so. If he's as smart as I think he is, he'll fig-ure it out on his own. That's what I'm hoping, anyway."

"Okay," I said. "Mum's the word."

I went out and closed the door. As I walked back up the corridor carpeted with a distinctive strewn-seashell design, I was struck by a fit of despair. Lars and Beverly were both pushing ninety, for God's sake, and the two of them still couldn't make heads or tails of the battle of the sexes. If with a combined total of over seventy years of experience with marriage they couldn't make it work, then there sure as hell wasn't much hope for the rest of us.

4

AFTER DEPOSITING BEVERLY in her cabin, I returned
to mine. Lars was still asleep, only now he was
sprawled crosswise on my rumpled bed. Because of that, I
didn't hang around. Instead, I went down and tried walking
around on the Promenade Deck. When that proved to be far
too wet and blustery, I went up to the Lido Deck's buffet and
drowned my sorrows in a couple of cups of coffee.

It turns out I did have some sorrows to drown. I've never
been one for great feats of introspection, but now, retired
from Seattle PD, I found that self-examination had caught up
with me anyway. I'd be fine as long as I was preoccupied with
whatever was going on around me, but as soon as I was left to
my own devices, waking or sleeping, a single image invaded
my being.

In my mind's eye I would once again see Sue Danielson, wounded and bleeding, lying propped against the living-room wall in the shattered ruins of her apartment. She would be clutching her weapon and waving me down the hallway toward where her ex-husband was hiding. And then, moments later, I would once again be standing in the bare-bones waiting room at Harborview Hospital. The doctor, still in surgical scrubs, would come through the swinging door. He would catch my eye over the heads of Sue's two bewildered young sons and give me the sign—that slight but telling shake of his head—that said it was over. Sue Danielson hadn't made it.

No matter how many times I relive those wrenching scenes, they don't get any better. I've been to the departmental shrink. Dr. Katherine Majors tells me that I'm suffering from post-traumatic stress. She claims that's why I keep having flashbacks. Not the kind of flashbacks that makes broken-down vets think they're back in 'Nam and under attack by the Vietcong, but close enough. Close enough to keep me from sleeping much at night. Close enough to make me wonder if I'm losing my grip. Close enough to make me postpone accepting the attorney general's offer to go to work on her Special Homicide Investigation Team based down in Olympia.

It's not as if this kind of stuff hasn't happened to me before. I was there years ago when Ron Peters was hurt and later on when Big Al Lindstrom got shot, but those incidents didn't affect me quite the same way. Ron may be confined to a wheelchair now, but he's reclaimed his life. He has his daughters, Heather and Tracy, and a new wife. And now Ron Peters is the proud father of a recently arrived son who also happens to be my namesake.

As a result of his injuries, Big Al Lindstrom was forced to take early retirement, but as far as I can tell, he and his wife, Molly, are both enjoying the hell out of it. The AG's office made Big Al the same offer they gave me, and he didn't even think twice about saying thanks, but no thanks. Molly probably would have killed him if he had tried to go back to work.

With Sue Danielson, though, it's different. She's dead. Her sons are orphans, and no amount of psychobabble from Dr. Majors is going to change that. No amount of talking it over and "getting it out of my system" will alter the fact that Sue won't be there to see her boys graduate from high school or college. She'll never be the mother of the groom at a wedding or have the chance to cradle a newborn grandchild in her arms. I continue to blame myself for all those things—to feel that, justifiably or not, there must have been something else I could have done that would have fixed the situation and made things turn out differently.

And, Lars and Beverly's honeymoon aside, that was the other reason I was on the *Starfire Breeze*—because I hadn't yet figured out what to do with myself or how to forget.

"Is this seat taken?"

I looked up to find the beaming face of Naomi Pepper, my seatmate from dinner the night before, smiling down at me. She was holding a cup of coffee in one hand and a plate piled high with fresh fruit and melon in the other.

"No," I said. "Help yourself."

"You're the only familiar face I saw," she continued. "I hope you don't mind."

"No, really. It's fine."

Naomi settled down across from me. "Everyone else

seems to be sleeping in." She grinned. "I'm the only early bird."

"Does that make me the worm?" I asked.

Her smile disappeared. "Are you always this surly?" she returned.

Her question took me aback. I had been making a joke that didn't strike me as particularly surly. "What do you mean?"

"How about, 'My wives are dead. Both of them'?" Naomi continued mockingly. "For somebody who's supposed to be a fortune hunter, you don't have much of a knack for it. That's not what I'd call getting off on the right foot. In fact, you made it sound as though you personally were responsible for knocking them both off, which isn't a very high recommendation when you're shopping around for wife number three."

With Anne Corley, the term "knocking her off" was far closer to the painful truth than I wanted to come, although the exonerating words of the official determination had labeled her death "justifiable homicide." Rather than say so, however, I went on the offensive.

"Fortune hunter!" I exclaimed indignantly "Whatever gave you the idea that I'm a fortune hunter?"

"Isn't that what dance hosts do?" she asked. "They prowl through cruise-ship passenger lists looking for wealthy widows or divorcées. Which I'm not, by the way," she added, slicing into a piece of watermelon and forking some of it into her mouth. "Far from it."

I may have sounded surly before, but now I was truly offended. "Look, once and for all, I am not a dance host—never have been. I don't know where you women get that idea."

"Oh," she said. "You're such a good dancer. That's why,

when we girls talked it over later, we all assumed you were one."

"Thank you," I muttered, feeling somewhat mollified by the compliment. "About the dancing, I mean. My mother's the one who insisted I take lessons," I added.

Naomi smiled brightly. "You certainly got her money's worth."

We sat in silence for a while during which Naomi worked her way through several pieces of melon. As she did so, I noticed for the first time that Naomi Pepper was wearing a wedding band.

"Will you be joining us for dinner tonight?" she asked a few minutes later. "Or did we scare you off? I've heard tell that as a group we can be a pretty intimidating foursome."

"I'm tough," I said. "I think I can handle it."

She smiled back at me, and it seemed that the earlier unpleasantness had been entirely forgotten. "For years, Harrison Featherman was the only male in the bunch who could put up with all of us as a group, but then even he bailed. Now we're back to the way we started some thirty-five years ago when we were all college roommates over at Wazoo. Now it's just the four of us."

In the state of Washington, natives speaking shorthand refer to the University of Washington in Seattle as the U Dub and to its cross-state rival in Pullman, Washington State University, as Wazoo. As a former Husky, I couldn't help falling into the old collegiate rivalry. Unlike a few other things I could name, it doesn't seem to diminish with time.

"So you were all Cougars together way back when?" I asked.

"Not *that* long ago," Naomi returned with a slight lift of her eyebrow. "But, yes, we all went to school over in Pullman. And, yes, we're all Cougars to the core."

"I take it you're roommates here, too?" I asked. "On the cruise, I mean."

She smiled again. "Three of us are. Margaret has her own cabin, but no one's complaining. After all, since she's the one paying the freight, beggars can't be choosers."

I knew how much I had paid for my junior suite. "That had to be a fair piece of change."

Naomi nodded. "Margaret's always been generous about throwing Harrison's money around, but inviting us on a cruise did seem a little excessive, even for her. I wondered about it right up until Chloe showed up at dinner last night. Her temper tantrum pretty well let the cat out of the bag. Margaret is here and she brought all of us along in hopes of zinging Harrison one more time—for old times' sake, I guess. But that doesn't mean the rest of us can't go ahead and have fun, does it?"

"No," I said. "I suppose not."

Naomi flagged down a waiter. I waited while he poured more coffee for both of us. "So where do you and your husband live?" I asked.

"My husband's dead," she said flatly. The shoe was on the other foot now, and the abruptness of her answer surprised me.

"Sorry," I stammered. "It's just that the ring . . ."

She glanced down at her left hand for a moment as if considering whether or not she should say anything more. "Gary and I were separated when he died," she said. "We had started divorce proceedings, but then he got sick—liver cancer. He came back home expecting me to take care of him, and since there wasn't anybody else to do it, I did. He died four months ago—on Mother's Day, as a matter of fact. I've been meaning to take the ring off ever since, but somehow I just haven't gotten around to it."

Naomi hadn't said that much, but all of what she did say hit home. I, too, had lost a former wife to cancer. It's one thing to be married to someone when they die. It hurts like hell, but at least there's a template of acceptable behavior for the survivor to go by. There are expectations about what to do. People know that you'll attend the funeral. People send flowers and condolences, and they know what to say. When you're no longer married or—as in Naomi's case—not quite divorced, all bets are off. The rules go out the window, and the person who's left is stuck figuring out his or her own answers to all those tough questions.

"My former wife and I had been divorced for years before Karen died of breast cancer," I said quietly. "People seemed to think I shouldn't have been affected. *I* thought I shouldn't have been affected, but I was. It hurt like hell. It *still* hurts like hell."

That sudden admission on my part surprised me, and it seemed to surprise Naomi, too. Her eyes filled with tears which she quickly wiped away. "Thank you for saying that," she said. "It helps to hear it from someone who's been there."

She was still grappling with regaining her composure when Margaret Featherman found us. "So someone is up and around after all," she said, sidling up to our table and, uninvited, taking one of the empty chairs. "I hope I'm not interrupting anything."

Margaret's eyes darted back and forth from Naomi's face to mine. Since we both must have looked suitably guilty, she gave us a conspiratorial smile. "Of course. I can see that I *am* interrupting. Maybe I'd better shove off and give you two a little privacy. I was just looking around to see if anyone wanted to join me in the exercise room. I tried calling your cabin, but all I got was voice mail."

"Stay where you are, Margaret," Naomi told her impatiently. "You're not interrupting anything."

"What about Marc Alley?" Margaret asked. "Has anyone seen him this morning?"

Naomi shook her head. So did I, and it seemed to me the lie was justified. The last thing Marc Alley needed right then was to have his neurologist's ex-wife show up in the middle of his interview and introduce herself to the nice lady writing an article about Harrison Featherman's almost miraculous surgical exploits for the readers of some popular medical journal. No, that wouldn't do at all.

"So what have you two been up to?" Margaret asked pointedly. She didn't ask right out whether or not Naomi Pepper and I had spent the night together, but the snide implication was there all the same.

"Sitting and talking," Naomi answered before I had a chance to. "We considered going for a walk on the Promenade Deck, but it's a little too blustery out there for my money."

"Mine, too," Margaret said. "That's why I'm opting for the treadmill in the gym. Care to join me?"

"No, thanks," Naomi told her. I didn't bother to answer, since the question clearly hadn't been directed at me.

Margaret stood up then. "That's all right," she said. "But you're forgiven. I can see why you might find Mr. Beaumont's company more stimulating than mine."

I waited until she was out of earshot. "That woman is irritating as all get out."

"Isn't she though," Naomi Pepper agreed.

I turned on her in amazement. "But I thought you were friends."

"You don't know much about women, do you," Naomi observed.

That was absolutely true, and it worried me some that my state of mystification was so blatantly obvious to the casual observer.

"Just because someone's a royal pain in the ass doesn't mean you stop being friends," Naomi continued. "I suppose you've heard about unconditional love?"

I nodded. "I'm aware of the concept," I replied.

"Well, this is unconditional friendship."

"I see."

About that time Lars Jenssen came wandering into the buffet. He spotted me from the doorway and came straight to the table without bothering to collect a tray or food. His two-hour-plus nap on the bed in my cabin appeared to have done him a world of good. He was chipper and cheerful.

"Beau," he said. "There you are. Where've you been hiding?"

Right here in Grand Central Station, I felt like saying. "I've been having coffee and waiting for you to wake up so I could have my cabin back."

I caught Naomi Pepper's puzzled look. "This is my grandfather," I explained hastily. "Or rather, my step-grandfather. Lars Jenssen. He and my grandmother got married a few weeks back. They're on their honeymoon."

"And who's this lovely young woman?" Lars asked, leering ever so slightly.

"Naomi Pepper," I said. "We're seated at the same table in the dining room at dinner."

"Good for you," Lars said. "I was hoping you'd find someone your age to hang around with. It yust wouldn't do for you to be eating with Beverly and me. Where is she, by the way?"

"In your cabin the last I saw her."

"Still upset?" he asked warily.

"You could say that."

"Dang," Lars said, shaking his head. "I still don't know what I did that made her so mad, but I was hoping she'd be over it by now."

Beverly had instructed me not to tell Lars what the score was. Since I didn't want her mad at me, too, I kept all elucidating comments and explanations to myself. "Maybe you'd better go ask her," I suggested. "And, as I said before, you might consider taking her a little something from the gift shop when you do."

"As a bribe, you mean? Well, all right," he agreed. "That's probably a good idea."

With that he turned and went back the way he had come. Several steps away, he stopped and returned to the table. "I almost forgot," he said. "You had a phone call. That's what woke me up."

"Who was it?" I asked.

Lars shrugged. "Beats me," he said. "Some guy. Didn't

leave a name. Must not have been that all-fired important. Said he'd be seeing you later anyway."

Giving Naomi a mock salute, Lars went on his way. I wondered who might have called. The only person I had made arrangements to see later was Marc Alley. Maybe he needed to cancel our lunch date.

"What a perfectly dear old man!" Naomi exclaimed as Lars disappeared from sight.

"He's dear, all right," I said. "That's what last night's lovers' quarrel was all about. Beverly, my grandmother, was evidently having a blast dropping money in the slot machines in the casino. Lars got all burned up about it. He thought she was throwing away his hard-earned cash which she, on the other hand, claims was her hard-earned cash. The upshot is the bride locked the groom out of the honeymoon suite. He ended up on my doorstep at six o'clock this morning. So much for my short-lived reputation as a fortune hunter. I agreed to come on the cruise to handle things in case one or the other of them got sick or hurt. I didn't think I'd end up having to serve as an on-site marriage counselor."

My explanation caused Naomi Pepper to break into peals of laughter. "You mean you're here as a chaperon?" she managed when she was finally able to speak again.

I didn't think it was nearly as funny as she did. "That's right," I told her.

She reached over and touched my arm. "I think that's one of the sweetest things I've ever heard." She stood up then. "I have to go. See you at dinner?"

"I guess," I told her. "Unless I get a better offer."

"Good. See you then."

With that Naomi left. I waited for a few moments before I headed back to my cabin. There I treated myself to the luxury of a long soak in the Jacuzzi, which I had missed when I first woke up. From the damp steam in my bathroom I assumed Lars had treated himself to a shower of his own, but by the time I got back to my stateroom, my ever-vigilant room attendant had already replaced one set of wet towels with new dry ones.

Standing in my bathroom I was just putting my wristlets back on when the phone rang. "Hello."

"You're back," Marc Alley breathed. "I don't want to be a pest, but I need to talk to you right away."

"About?"

"He fired me."

"Who fired you?"

"Dr. Featherman. There was a message waiting for me here in my cabin after I finished up with the interview. He said that as soon we get back to Seattle I need to find myself a new doctor."

"Good riddance, if you ask me," I told him. "From what I saw on the dance floor last night, the guy strikes me as a complete jerk."

"But I didn't do anything," Marc countered. "I had dinner with his ex-wife, and I danced and necked with her, but that's all. And I'm not the one who changed the dinner reservations. When we left the lounge, all I did was walk her back to her stateroom. Period."

I remembered the hickey I had spotted on Marc's neck. Despite his protestations, I still suspected Marc's woebegone look that morning had something to do with sexual over-indulgence.

"That scene on the dance floor really embarrassed me," he continued. "And then there's Chloe."

"Dr. Featherman's daughter."

"Right. She works in his office, you see. I was sort of under the impression that she liked me. In fact, I was building up to asking her out on a date, but now I suppose I've blown that as well."

"Don't be so hard on yourself, Marc. I think Chloe's mother blew it for you. But you said you needed advice. What kind of advice?"

"What do I do about dinner?"

"Dinner?" I asked.

"Should I ask the maître d' to put me at another table or in another dining room or what? From the sounds of it, I don't think I'm going to be eating dinners with Dr. Feather-man and Chloe."

"Who paid for your trip?" I asked.

"Dr. Featherman," Marc replied.

"And what do you have to do in return?"

"The interview, for one thing, and I've already done that. And then I'm supposed to be part of a panel discussion on our next at-sea day—Friday, I think. If any of the other attendees want to talk to me, I'm supposed to make myself available, but that's about it."

"So kick back and enjoy yourself," I advised him. "I'm sure you're right. After what's gone on, you're not going to get to first base with Chloe Featherman. You could just as well forget about her and keep your options open. Margaret herself may be a handful, but the rest of the women at the table aren't that bad."

"That was why I asked to talk to you later when I saw you in the dining room. What do you think about Margaret, Beau? I mean, it seemed like she really liked me. You strike me as a man who's been around. Do you think she was just putting on an act, or do you think she's truly interested in me?"

The poor sap. *She's interested, all right.* That's what I wanted to say, but I didn't. "If you want advice to the lovelorn, you're barking up the wrong tree," I told him. "Ask Dear Abby. Ask Ann Landers. But don't ask me. As far as Margaret Featherman is concerned, I wouldn't even hazard a guess."

5

SOMETIME DURING THE AFTERNOON, the wind died down, the clouds rolled away, and the sea turned relatively calm. Late in the afternoon, shortly after we turned into Chatham Strait, an announcement came over the intercom that a pod of whales had been sighted off the port bow.

Ralph Ames, my attorney and good friend, is an experienced cruiser. He had insisted that I invest in a tux for the cruise. While I was dressing for that night's formal-night dinner, I realized that the ship wasn't rolling nearly as much anymore, and it gave me hope that we were in for some smooth sailing.

This was my first cruise, and I was starting to learn that I'm not much good at doing nothing. Considering the efforts cruise directors make to keep people occupied, I'd guess my fellow passengers weren't any better at it than I was. In the course of that first seemingly endless at-sea day, in addition to dodging seasickness, I had also managed to avoid the art auction in the Promenade Deck Sea Breeze lobby bar.

Ralph, who is as much an old hand at purchasing original art as he as at cruising, had advised me in advance that cruise art auctions are seldom a good idea. On my own, I had opted out of entering the Trivia Tournament or trying my hand on the golf simulator. But I knew better than to think I'd be able to dodge that evening's formal dinner. Bored as I was, by the time evening rolled around, dressing for dinner almost seemed like a good idea. Based on the way people looked that night, most of the other folks apparently felt the same way. Other than getting all gussied up, there wasn't much else to do.

Cruise ships are a world unto themselves. I had quickly picked up on the prevailing photo-op mentality. Ship's photographers were all over the place. Pictures were posed and snapped at various set times—coming on board in Seattle, for example, or being attacked by pirates or drinking champagne at the Captain's Welcome Aboard party. The photos are then displayed (for sale, of course) in a long interior gallery on one side of the Promenade Deck. Figuring Lars would balk at the idea of actually purchasing any of the pictures with more of his "hard-earned cash," I went down to the gallery prior to the first dinner seating. I wanted to locate Lars and Beverly's "Welcome Aboard" photos. I was also hoping that I'd catch sight of the two of them dolled up in their evening-dress finery. I figured the once-in-a-lifetime chance of seeing

Lars Jenssen decked out in a tuxedo was worth the price of admission.

There were lots and lots of photos—hundreds of them, in fact—arranged in row after neat row. It took a while for me to locate the specific ones I was searching for. In the process I came across one of Harrison Featherman. The good doctor was part of a trio, the other members of which were two young women. I recognized his daughter, Chloe, at once. The other was an olive-skinned woman whose almond-eyed beauty stood in stark contrast to Chloe's blond good looks. I estimated both young women to be in their early thirties. They stood on either side of Harrison, posed on a hokey set that had them all standing in front of a life ring imprinted with the cruise ship's logo. Harrison was grinning for the camera and looking enormously pleased with himself.

A closer examination of the picture revealed why he might possibly have been so proud. The two young women were both lovely. As far as Chloe was concerned, her natural beauty was far more apparent when her lips weren't curled into a sneer and when the white heat of anger toward her mother hadn't robbed her cheeks of all their natural color. Even though I remembered Margaret Featherman mentioning Harrison's new wife, I couldn't recall her name as I examined the photo. Her exotic beauty was more subtle than Chloe's, and seemed to come from the inside out. On further study I realized that not only was the new Mrs. Harrison Featherman a looker, she was also pregnant—very pregnant. If my memory of such things served, she had to be at least eight months along. I wondered if going on a cruise that late in her pregnancy had been recommended or approved of by her ob-gyn.

I glanced back at the white-haired Dr. Featherman, who had to be a decade or so older than I am. *Harrison, you randy old devil, you!* I said to him silently. *Fathering a child at your age! But I'll bet having a wailing newborn baby in the house, or better yet, a terrible-twos toddler, will wipe that smile off your face in a hell of a hurry.* I walked away from the picture grateful that I wasn't standing in Harrison Featherman's shoes.

Several sections of pictures away, I finally caught sight of Beverly and Lars posed in front of the selfsame logo-emblazoned life ring. Pulling the photo from its place, I went on to peruse the collection of pirate pictures.

"You're not buying any of those crazy pictures, are you?" Lars asked, coming up behind me and standing at my elbow just as the clerk slipped my purchases into a bag. "They cost an arm and a leg."

"I wanted one of your 'Welcome Aboards,' " I told him. "And I really got a kick out of the one of you and the lady pirate."

"It's yust so much foolishness," he grumbled. "Some other danged excuse to take your money."

Not surprisingly, Lars hadn't sprung for a tux. He was wearing a pill-covered tweed sport coat with leather patches at both elbows. His trousers had grown shiny and crease-free through years of wear. His one concession to formality was a tie—a brand-new one that had Beverly's touch written all over it.

"Where's your lovely bride?" I asked.

Lars shook his head dolefully. "Still getting all fixed up," he said. "She rented one of those fancy dresses from that store right next door to the jewelry shop. She wanted me to rent one of those monkey suits, too, just like the one you're wearing, but I told her no way was I getting in one of those. She yust came back from the beauty shop a few minutes ago. She had her hair done in some god-awful thing she called an upsweep. If you ask me, her hair looks like the fender of a fifty-seven Cadillac."

"You didn't tell her that, I hope," I told him.

"Are you kidding? Do I look dumb or something?" Lars laughed and gave me a playful punch to the shoulder. "I don't want to be locked out of the room two nights in a row."

Lars and I waited for Beverly Piedmont Jenssen near the entrance to the dining room and caught sight of her riding down in the glass elevator. Looking fetching and festive in her black, long-sleeved gown, she waved at us from the elevator. Someone in the beauty shop had given her a hand with her makeup. She looked twenty years younger than she had the last time I saw her that morning. Lars might complain about the cost, but he sure couldn't gripe about the results. That was the good news. The bad news, unfortunately, was that her hairdo really did resemble the fender on a '57 Cadillac. When I stepped forward to kiss her hello, I noticed the silver-and-tanzanite brooch at the base of her throat.

"Nice pin," I said as she regally offered me her cheek.

"Lars gave it to me," she said.

Just out of Beverly's line of vision, Lars nodded, winked, and gave me a thumbs-up sign. The wily old turkey had followed my advice after all.

"Will you be joining us for dinner tonight, Jonas?" she asked.

"No. I just wanted to get a look at the two of you all duded up. Are you going to have pictures taken on the way into the dining room?"

"Yes, we are," my grandmother declared determinedly. "And whether Lars likes it or not, we're going to buy some of them to take home with us."

To his credit, Lars seemed to know when he was licked. He was prepared to be agreeable, but not so much as to appear out of character. "If that's what you want," he muttered. "But I still think they charge way too much."

Once the pictures were taken and Lars and Beverly proceeded into their dining room, I wandered out on deck. It was a cool, brisk evening. I strolled around on the Promenade Deck for a time, then I went indoors and sat in one of the artfully arranged seating areas. All the while I was observing the other formally dressed, party-going folks, I struggled with my own case of pre-party jitters. I kept coming back to my shrink's parting words. "Go and have a good time," Dr. Majors had said to me. "It's going to be a wonderful trip, Beau. Try to savor every moment."

Right about then, I was dreading dinner rather than savoring it. In the old days I would have screwed up my courage with several stiff shots of MacNaughtons and gone into the dining room in a warm, boozy haze. Because I'm still on the wagon, I marched into the Crystal Dining Room much later, having ingested no artificial morale boosters other than a single cup of dreadful coffee in the Sea Breeze Bar.

Part of my problem was concern that this dinner would be

a repeat performance of the previous evening's grilling session. I have to admit I wasn't looking forward to that. For my money, a little bit of Margaret Featherman's company went a very long way. By the time I entered the dining room, I had decided that if the situation didn't improve, I'd do whatever I had to the next morning to make alternative seating arrangements for the remainder of the cruise.

I've heard it said that ninety percent of the things people worry about never happen. That's how it turned out to be with that night's dinner. All my advance concerns proved to be groundless. After a somewhat awkward start, the whole affair—dinner, right on through the show and dancing afterwards—wound up being a rousing success.

Marc Alley and I were the first to arrive. He was dressed in one of those stylish double-breasted tuxes favored by the younger set. He seemed to be in much better spirits than he had been earlier in the day. "I take it you're over the shock of being deemed unworthy to be counted among the honorable Dr. Harrison Featherman's lucky patients?"

"I guess," he replied with a wry grin. "Maybe it's the same way a trout feels when the fly fisherman throws him back in the water. Lucky, but still wondering why I wasn't good enough to keep."

"Don't worry," I told him. "I'm sure there are plenty of other doctors in Seattle who'll be only too happy to take you and your money."

The women—two of them, anyway—arrived about then. Sharon Carson and Virginia Metz, dressed in long gowns that did them proud, had evidently stopped in the bar long enough to be in a party mood. And now that word was out that I wasn't a "dance host," Virginia was noticeably less hostile. When she and Sharon took seats on either side of Marc Alley, my heart fell.

Great, I thought. *That means I'll be stuck in the hot seat between Naomi Pepper and Margaret Featherman.*

I expected the two latecomers to arrive together. Instead, Naomi showed up alone. She was dressed in a black suit that passed for formal attire but wasn't nearly as dressy as the clothing the other women were wearing. I was hoping we could just take up our conversation where we'd left off at the buffet that morning, but that didn't happen—at least not at first. Naomi seemed to be in a bad mood. She was downcast and disinclined to talk. I wondered if it was something I had said or done. It wasn't until she was halfway through her first glass of wine that she seemed to come alive.

Reynaldo took orders for drinks and then stalled for a while. He seemed to be waiting for Margaret, the table's last missing diner, to arrive before taking our food orders. Eventually, though, the waiter could delay no longer. As he started around the table, I realized that I was enjoying not having to deal with the snide biting commentary that passed for Margaret Featherman's dinnertime conversation. And to be honest, no one else seated at the table appeared to miss her all that much, either.

By the time we had finished appetizers and moved on to soup, conversation was flowing freely. Even Naomi's flagging spirits seemed to have made a remarkable recovery. The only people who remained anxious about Margaret's continued absence appeared to be the wait staff. In the course of the meal, all the servers—everyone from Joaô, up through the headwaiter—made polite inquiries. Would Madame Featherman be joining us? Was she perhaps feeling unwell? Marc and I answered the queries with genuinely puzzled shrugs. The women rolled their eyes and exchanged knowing smirks. I wondered if the wait staff received extra points or a bonus of some kind based on the number of bottles of wine served per table. In that case, Margaret would be sorely missed since, without her in attendance, per capita wine consumption went way down.

Finally, finished with my entrée, I suggested that perhaps someone from the group should be dispatched to phone Margaret's room to check on her and make sure she was all right. Immediately thereafter, Naomi Pepper leaned over to set me straight. "Remember this morning how you said you'd see us at dinner unless you got a better offer?" she inquired in a discreet undertone.

I nodded.

"Margaret probably did just that," she added. "Got a better offer, I mean. That's par for the course with Margaret. The four of us would plan for weeks to do something together, but then something unexpected would come up— usually a male something—and Margaret would bail on us. We're used to it."

"Fair enough," I told her. After all, if Margaret's best chums were prepared to turn a blind eye to her flaky behavior, who was I to object? Besides, without having her in attendance, everyone else seemed to be enjoying themselves immensely. Sharon Carson and Virginia Metz remained totally focused on Marc Alley. Laughing and chatting away, he was apparently rising to the occasion.

All during dinner the ship's photographers worked the room, taking pictures right and left. Just prior to dessert, they showed up at our table. We shifted chairs around so Marc and I could stand behind the three ladies. The resulting photo shows the women wearing dazzling, white-toothed smiles. Marc and I, on the other hand, are wearing a matched pair of inane grins. We both look as though we have no idea about what to do with our hands—which, in actual fact, we didn't.

When it came time to deliver the dessert menus, the reason for the wait staff's continuing concern over Margaret Featherman's absence became clear. The headwaiter himself—a heavyset man named Angelo—came to the table to make an official and suitably ceremonial pronouncement.

"I am so very sorry Madame Featherman was unable to join you tonight. She spoke to the head chef earlier today and made a special dessert request for your table's dining pleasure this evening. I'm happy to report that the kitchen staff has been delighted to comply. And so, unless there is someone who wishes to choose from the regular dessert menu, Reynaldo will be serving raspberry soufflés all around."

After that, no one bothered giving the standard dessert menu a look-see. Not wanting to appear ungrateful, we all told Reynaldo that we'd be happy to sample Margaret Featherman's specially ordered soufflés.

When the soufflés arrived, they were wonderful. As soon as I lifted the first steaming spoonful to my mouth, my nostrils were assailed by the aroma of hot fruit rising from the steamy sauce. Instantly I was transported back to my child-hood and to my mother's small kitchen in Seattle. There, every summer, the aromas of hot fruit would fill the entire apartment as Mother dutifully canned peaches and apricots and put up raspberry and blackberry preserves.

I've heard it said that remembered smells linger longer in memory than do recollections from any of the other senses. One whiff of that steaming raspberry sauce made a believer of me. Naomi must have caught the faraway look on my face.

"Where'd you go?" she asked.

"Back to my childhood," I told her. "This sauce takes me back to when I was seven or eight and used to help my mother do canning."

"Really," she said. "The only thing *my* mother knew about canning was to use an opener on a can of Del Monte peaches. But this is wonderful," she added.

I looked around the room, where other diners were enjoy-ing their non-specially-ordered desserts. "How do you sup-pose Margaret pulled this off?" I asked. "How do you go about getting a cruise ship kitchen to agree to whip up a spe-cial command-performance dessert like this?"

"I understand that nicer ships are happy to comply with special requests," Naomi answered. "But I'm sure it helps if you go in waving around the promise of a very large tip. From the looks of him, I'd guess Angelo is worried about whether or not the tip will actually materialize, since Margaret herself wasn't here to sample the kitchen's impeccable delivery. The sad thing is, the way tipping works on cruise ships, no gratu-ities actually change hands until the very last day. In other words, the staff won't know whether or not Margaret stiffed them until it's too late for them to do anything about it."

"Would she?" I asked. "Stiff them, I mean."

Naomi sighed. "Probably. It's happened before."

After dinner we once again repaired to the Twilight Lounge. This time the pseudo-comic/pianist was missing. Instead, we were treated to the talent of an African-American torch singer named Dahlia Lucas who specialized in Billie Holiday ballads and wasn't half bad. As Marc Alley had done all during dinner, when the dancing started up again, he assumed responsibility for Virginia and Sharon, leaving me in charge of Naomi. We danced some, but mostly we listened to the music and watched.

"Are you having fun?" I asked.

"On the cruise, or tonight?"

"Both."

Naomi nodded. "More than I thought I would," she said.

"Me, too."

"And what about your grandparents?" she asked. "Are they having fun, too?"

"I think so," I told her. "They seem to have gotten over last night's spat. I'm sure everything will be fine as long as Lars doesn't tell Beverly what he really thinks of the way she's wearing her hair tonight."

"Which is?" Naomi asked.

"He told me it looks like the fender of a fifty-seven Cadillac. The sad truth is, he's absolutely right."

Naomi laughed. I liked the sound of it. Her laughter seemed to bubble up from her toes. It made me want to laugh right along with her.

"What's the story with her?" I asked, nodding toward the dancers as Marc Alley led Virginia Metz onto the floor.

"She's a breast-cancer survivor," Naomi answered.

"I figured as much," I said.

"What makes you say that?"

"The short hair," I said. "That's always a dead giveaway."

"You're wrong there," Naomi told me. "Virginia's a ten-year survivor. During chemo, she got used to wearing her hair short and never let it grow back. Dick probably had something to do with that."

"Who's Dick?"

"Her husband. He left her two weeks after she had her mastectomy. Told her he couldn't handle the stress."

Hearing that, I couldn't help thinking about Dave Livingston, my first wife's second husband. He had cared for Karen with unstinting devotion and patient loving kindness all during her ultimately fatal battle with breast cancer. It was no coincidence that although Kayla Cartwright, my three-year-old granddaughter, has no grandmother on her mother's side, she does have the benefit of two doting grandfathers—Grandpa (me) and Papa Dave. Obviously Dick Metz didn't play in the same league as Kayla's Papa Dave.

"Sounds like a hell of a nice guy," I said. "And what about Sharon? Did she fare any better than the rest of you as far as men are concerned?"

Naomi shook her head. "Not much. She had one of those husbands you hear about from time to time, the ones who think they're wired for two-twenty. In fact, Leonard Carson is on his second twenty-something right now. Sharon lasted until she was forty before he traded her in. The second Mrs.

Carson only made it to thirty-five. He's on number three at the moment, but now she's getting a little long in the tooth as well, so I doubt she'll be around much longer, either."

I shook my head. "You ladies sure do know how to pick 'em," I said with an uneasy laugh.

Naomi nodded. "That's why we all stick together. We encourage meaningless relationships whenever possible in hopes of keeping the others from making any more stupid mistakes." She glanced around the room. "Speaking of which, I'm surprised we haven't seen them yet."

"Seen who?" I asked.

She laughed. "Margaret and her current man of the hour. Make that man of the moment. She loves to brag. Gloating in solitary splendor isn't her style. I'd think she would have let her current hunk out of bed long enough to bring him around so the rest of us could get a look at him. That's what she would have done back in the old days."

"Maybe they're having too much fun," I suggested.

"Maybe," Naomi agreed, but her dubious tone made it sound as though she didn't really believe it.

Ever since we'd come into the lounge, I had been toying with a plan. Considering the way the conversation had gone for the last little while, there didn't seem to be much point in mentioning it. But finally, about the time the orchestra took a break, I worked up enough courage to ask, "Are you going into Juneau tomorrow?"

"I guess so," Naomi said.

"Would you care for some company?"

She looked at me and smiled. "I think I'd like that. We're

supposed to dock around seven-thirty. Want to disembark with the early birds?"

I was so surprised by how easy that was that I almost forgot to answer. "Sure," I replied. "Why don't we meet upstairs at the buffet about six-thirty or so, grab some breakfast, and then be ready to go ashore with the first wave of shore-bound passengers?"

Naomi nodded. "Sounds good to me." After a pause she added, "What about your grandparents?"

"What about them?"

"Will they be going ashore, too?"

"Probably."

"Wouldn't it be a good idea if we took them along so we could more or less keep an eye on them?"

That didn't seem like an especially good idea to me, but I could see resistance was futile—like being assimilated by the Borg on that "Star Trek Voyager" series.

"Beverly and Lars are a couple of early birds," I told her. "I'll check with them first thing in the morning and see what they say."

Since we hadn't finished eating dinner until after ten, it didn't take long for the remainder of the evening to turn into a late night. Not only that, thanks to Lars' previous early-morning wake-up call, I was running on empty while everybody else in the group was acting as though the night were still young. Finally, around midnight—about the time the rest of the group was heading for the buffet and the all-you-can-eat chocolate fest—I opted out of the party in favor of getting some sleep.

In my stateroom, with its dimmed lights and turned-down bedding, I could hardly wait to strip off my tie and peel out of my tux. Then, donning my robe, I went outside onto my private balcony. I was close enough to the back of the ship that I could see the glow of phosphorescence churned up in our wake. I stood there for some time, smelling the sea and listening as the ship's bow cut through the water.

For a time I could barely believe that I had done it—that I had actually asked someone out on a date. Finally, it got too cold to be standing barefoot on an outside lanai in nothing but a robe and a pair of briefs. I went inside, where I called the purser's desk and asked them to leave a message for Lars and Beverly Jenssen to call me first thing in the morning if they were interested in having company on a day trip to Juneau.

After that, I crawled into bed. Gradually water and wind got the best of me and I drifted into a sense of peace—the first real peace I had felt in months. Lying in bed, I could easily imagine that I had left the world of murder and mayhem far behind. In actual fact, that couldn't have been further from the truth. Murder was alive and well two decks down, in a mini-suite at the end of the corridor where, although nobody knew it yet, Mrs. Margaret Featherman had gone missing and would soon be presumed dead.

6

BEVERLY AND LARS JENSSEN must have been up and taken their phone message at the crack of dawn, since they returned it shortly thereafter. They were upstairs in the buffet and finished with breakfast by the time I showed up. Naomi appeared a few minutes later, and I made introductions all around. Once Naomi and I brought our coffee and food to the table, Beverly had her daily planner opened and laid out on the table. She was ready to roll.

Beverly had taken the whole idea of this cruise as a serious challenge. She wanted to see as much as possible without wearing Lars or herself out. She had pored over the shore-excursion options, narrowing down the choices to what she thought the two of them couldn't afford to miss and what they could do without. In Juneau she wanted to take the cable-car ride up the side of a mountain overlooking the city. For someone who lives in downtown Seattle, calling Juneau a city is using the term loosely.

I have to say I wasn't terribly enthusiastic about the idea. I didn't see much point in riding up through trees and looking down on a bunch of ragtag buildings, but I didn't object. After all, my whole purpose for being there was to see that Beverly and Lars saw and did what *they* wanted. I did my best to go with the flow and keep my mouth shut. Naomi, on the other hand, gave every appearance of enjoying the outing.

In the process of standing in line for the cable car, Beverly and Naomi struck up a conversation with another pair of *Starfire Breeze* passengers. Beverly's new friends, Claire and Florence Wakefield, were a few years younger than my grandmother—somewhere in their seventies, I'd say. They were retired spinster schoolteachers who hailed from New York City. As they were happy to tell us, this was their first trip "out west."

Despite my preconceived notions, the cable-car ride was actually a pleasant surprise. The sky overhead was a clear, limitless blue. The air was cool and surprisingly brisk. The few deciduous trees that were visible were already alive with beginning hues of fall color.

The line for tickets was relatively short at that early hour of the morning, and the trip up and down the mountain didn't take nearly as long as I had anticipated. As a consequence, we were finished with that and ready to return to the ship long before the *Starfire Breeze*'s shuttle was due to come collect us. In the interest of preserving energy, our traveling companions were lobbying for a speedy return to the ship, so I flagged down a passing cab. Fortunately it was a lumbering old station wagon that's probably put into service only during cruise-ship season—and we all clambered into that. Lars and Beverly sat in front and the Wakefield sisters took the middle seat while Naomi and I scrambled into the far back.

"So," Florence Wakefield said to me once we were settled. "You live in Seattle?"

I nodded. "That's right," I said. "I live in a downtown condo."

"We're planning on staying in the city for several days after the end of the cruise," Florence continued. "Where would we have the best view of the pin?"

I had no idea what she was talking about. "The what?" I asked.

"You know," she said impatiently. "The pin. Seattle's pin."

"You mean the Needle?" Naomi asked, trying to suppress a smile. "You want a view of the Space Needle?"

"That's it," Florence said. "Where's the hotel with the best view of the Space Needle?"

"Don't tell us," Claire interrupted. "Once we get to town, we'll catch a cab and have the driver take us around until we find someplace that suits us."

Juneau isn't all that big, and by then we were back at the cruise-ship dock. As we approached the gangplank, I was surprised to see Marc Alley down on the dock at the base of the gangplank. He was pacing back and forth. As soon as he caught sight of Naomi and me, he seemed overjoyed to see us.

"She's gone!" he announced.

"Who's gone?" I asked.

"Margaret Featherman. Dr. Featherman and the first officer came to my cabin early this morning. They pounded on
the door so hard I thought there might be a fire or something.
When I opened it, Dr. Featherman pushed his way inside,
demanding to know where she was, since her room attendant
had reported that Margaret hadn't been in her room at all
overnight. I told them that I had no idea where she was. I told
them I hadn't seen her since the night before last, when I
walked her back to her room. I don't think they believed me.
They said something about doing a room-to-room search of
the entire ship. What should I do, Beau? Whatever's happened
to her, they seem to think I had something to do with it."

Naomi was standing beside me. I heard her sharp intake
of breath when Marc first announced Margaret was gone. As
for Marc, he looked so upset and agitated that I felt sorry for
the guy. And all the while he spilled out his tale of woe, Beverly, Lars, and the two Wakefield sisters hung on every word.
As tactfully as possible, Naomi and I herded the others up
onto the ship, then we came back down to where Marc stood
waiting.

By then Naomi seemed to have recovered somewhat from
the distressing news that her friend was missing. "Did all this
happen before or after the ship docked?" Naomi asked.

"After," Marc replied. "At least by the time they came to
my cabin and woke me up, we were docked."

"So maybe it's all right then," Naomi said reassuringly.
"My guess is they're just pushing panic buttons. I know it
says in the book that we're all supposed to swipe our room
key cards as we get off and on the ship. But I can tell you Margaret Featherman has been breaking rules all her life. Or

maybe they just missed hers somehow. She's probably off in Juneau spending an armload of money."

"Have you seen either one of your dance partners from last night?" I asked.

Marc nodded. "I tracked down both Virginia and Sharon before they got off the ship to go into town. Dr. Featherman had been by to see them, too. They told him they hadn't seen Margaret since the night before last, either. In fact," he added miserably, "it sounds as though I may have been the very last person who did see her."

"Not true," I told him, hoping to ease his worries. "Naomi and I both saw Margaret yesterday morning. We were upstairs in the buffet, and Margaret was on her way to the exercise room."

Marc heaved a sigh. "Well, that's a relief anyway."

"Don't worry," Naomi said. "Just wait. Margaret will turn up at the last minute. Since she's always late, it'll probably be just before they raise the gangplank. My guess is she'll arrive with a new coat or some piece of artwork. The galleries around Juneau are supposed to be great, and Margaret wouldn't be above buying a new fur coat if she wanted one. She's been a fan of fur for as long as I've known her. I've always said that if any of those anti-fur protesters outside Benaroya Hall ever tried to take on Margaret Featherman, they'd end up getting far more of a fight than they bargained for."

Smiling grimly, Marc Alley allowed himself to be led back up to the top of the gangplank, where we were all very careful to make sure our room key cards were properly swiped by the crewmen waiting there. Once on board, Marc said he was going back to his room. Naomi and I repaired to the Sea

Breeze Bar for more of their dreadful coffee. We sat there without speaking for a fairly long time. And the longer we didn't speak, the lower Naomi's spirits seemed to go. She may have been able to lend Marc Alley some calming reassurance when he needed it, but she wasn't able to accept any of that comforting solace on her own behalf. She had successfully convinced Marc that Margaret Featherman was off enjoying herself on a shopping spree. Naomi herself didn't believe that for a moment.

"What if something bad really has happened to her?" Naomi asked at last.

That's how people in America talk about the unthinkable. We don't say, "What if she's dead?" We say, "What if something bad's happened?" Maybe if we don't actually mention the word "death" or "dying," we can somehow dodge the bullet and keep death from happening to us or to the people we care about. After spending almost twenty years on the homicide squad, I'm not much good at using euphemisms. I'd rather have all the cards—even the worst ones possible—out on the table.

"You mean, what if Margaret Featherman is dead?" I asked bluntly.

Naomi bit her lip and nodded.

"Then the cruise line calls in the FBI to investigate," I told her.

That news seemed to jar Naomi more than I expected it would. "The FBI?" she asked. "Really?"

I nodded. "In the past several years, cruise lines haven't exactly been forthcoming about unpleasant incidents on board their various ships. There were instances of theft and sexual assault and at least one mysterious death that were all 'under-reported,' I believe is how they termed it. In other words, they tried to sweep their problems under the rug in hopes of sparing themselves any bad publicity. If it didn't happen, there was no need to report it. Finally, there was enough of an uproar that the feds stepped into the breach. My understanding is that if a ship visits American ports or if American citizens are involved as victims, then the FBI is called in to investigate regardless of where the problem occurs."

After that, frowning and lost in thought, Naomi Pepper seemed to drift far away from me. "Look," I said finally in an effort to bring her back. "I'm sure you're worried about Margaret. That's perfectly understandable. But I'm also sure that she's fine. It'll probably turn out to be exactly the way you said it would. She'll come back on board tonight having failed to swipe her card as she disembarked. Or else she's stowed away in somebody else's cabin right now, screwing her brains out. Eventually, though, she and her current Lothario are going to have to come up for air or food or both. Unless I'm mistaken, the ship's security tapes will probably be able to lead us to wherever she's holed up."

"Security tapes?" Naomi asked. She looked shocked— even more so than she had appeared earlier when I mentioned the FBI. "You're saying this ship has security monitors?"

Something that continues to amaze me about women and men is the difference in what they observe. Ubiquitous ceiling-mounted security cameras had been one of the first things I had noticed after coming aboard the *Starfire Breeze*. Naomi Pepper had missed them entirely.

"How could you not notice?" I asked. "Little video cameras are everywhere on this ship—in all the corridors and all the public areas. In fact, we're probably showing up on somebody's monitor even as we speak."

This time when Naomi raised her eyes, the look on her face was one of pure panic. "You mean everything that happens on board is on tape?"

"Most likely."

At that point, all color drained from Naomi's face. Her breathing sped up. For a moment I thought she was going to hyperventilate.

"I saw Margaret later," she admitted softly. "I mean, I saw her after you and I ran into her upstairs in the buffet. I was with her again late in the afternoon."

I've spent a lifetime asking questions. It's one of those old work habits that's virtually impossible to break. "Where?" I asked.

"I went to her cabin. If that shows up on the tapes, then they'll probably come looking for me as well, just like they did with Marc. They'll be looking and asking questions."

"Of course they will," I agreed. "That's the way investigations work. If the worst happened and if Margaret Featherman does turn out to be dead, the authorities will be in touch with everyone who talked to her or had any contact with her in the past few days. That includes you and me and everyone else at our table. There's no reason to be upset about it."

"But I am upset," Naomi returned. "What if they want to know what Margaret and I talked about?"

"That's simple," I replied. "You tell them. End of story."

Naomi said nothing. "So what did you talk about?" I asked finally after another long pause.

Naomi grimaced. "It was . . ." She paused. "It was very unpleasant."

Talk about being slow on the uptake. That was when I finally realized that Naomi and Margaret must have had some kind of quarrel. Whatever the topic of discussion had been, it was something Naomi didn't want to share with me any more than she wanted to tell it to some note-taking FBI operative. And that's when I had the first tiny glimmer that maybe Naomi Pepper knew far more than she was pretending to about Margaret Featherman's unexplained absence. That would explain her obvious reluctance to discuss it. It would also explain her virtual panic at my mention of security cameras in the ship's corridors.

Those thoughts entered my mind, but I immediately pushed them aside. If she was involved in what had happened to Margaret, I didn't want to hear it. After all, Naomi Pepper and I had spent several very pleasant hours together in the course of the last few days. She was someone I was comfortable with; someone whose company I could see myself enjoying; someone I could like. Surely I couldn't be that unlucky. Surely lightning wouldn't strike me twice in exactly the same way. Cops—even ex-cops—aren't supposed to become involved with people who turn out to be homicide suspects— or worse.

As I said before, questioning people is a hard habit to break. Even though I didn't want to know the answer, I couldn't keep from asking, "How unpleasant was it?"

We were sitting in the Sea Breeze Bar on the Promenade Deck. Throngs of people came and went, talking and laughing. Naomi's gaze settled into one of those distant thousand-yard stares that excluded me and left her blind and deaf to everything going on around us.

"Naomi?" I prompted.

Her eyes strayed back to me. "It happened such a long time ago," she said in a strangled whisper. "Why would anyone want to bring it up this many years later?"

"Bring what up?"

"My daughter," she said. "Missy."

"What about her?"

For the longest time Naomi averted her eyes. Once again she bit her lower lip and didn't answer.

"Missy is Harrison Featherman's daughter," she murmured finally in little more than a strangled whisper. "She's Harrison's and mine."

That got me. With those few words, my opinion of Naomi Pepper plummeted several notches. Dr. Majors is forever telling me that feelings aren't right or wrong. They simply are. At that point, I had no reason to feel betrayed—certainly not the way Margaret Featherman must have felt betrayed when she learned about it. And, as far as I'm concerned, maybe *betrayed* is the wrong word. *Disappointed* might be closer to the mark. I had thought Naomi Pepper to be a better person than that.

"You're telling me you had an affair with the husband of one of your best friends? That the two of you had a child together?"

"It wasn't like that," Naomi said quickly. "Not an affair. It wasn't like that at all."

Right, I thought. *And the moon is made of old green cheese.* "Just how was it then?" I asked.

"We were all friends back then, Beau, good friends. By that time everyone else had managed to have their kids. Gary and I kept trying and trying, but nothing happened. I wanted a baby so badly that it broke my heart every time I saw a pregnant woman in a grocery store or at the mall. It seemed like everyone in the whole world could get pregnant at the drop of a hat—everyone but me. Finally, Gary and I went to see a specialist—a fertility expert—to have ourselves tested and to find out what the problem was. The doctor told us straight out that Gary's sperm count was so low that we'd probably never have kids.

"I was so upset by the news that I didn't know what to do. I went into a state of total depression—clinical depression. It was all I could do to get out of bed in the morning. I spent all day every day lying there like a lump watching one useless television program after another. Gary would come home from work at night and I'd still be in my nightgown and bathrobe. The previous day's dirty dishes would be in the sink and there'd be nothing cooking for dinner. Gary tried what he could to get me to snap out of it, but nothing worked. I just kept sinking deeper and deeper." She paused.

"And then?" I prompted.

"Finally, one Saturday afternoon, the four guys were all out playing golf together. They got together a couple of times a year, for old times' sake. Dick Metz and Leonard Carson were in one cart, and Harrison and Gary were in the other. It was at a time when I was really low, and I'm sure Gary must have been at the end of his rope. He wound up telling Harrison about what was going on with us. He asked for advice— not as a doctor and patient, but as a friend. Harrison told him we could either blow twenty or thirty thousand bucks on a fertility expert and try artificial insemination, or we could get someone else to help us out."

"Meaning Harrison Featherman was offering to stand stud service?"

Naomi blushed in the face of my indelicate question. She blushed but she answered all the same, meeting my eyes as she did so. "So you see, it wasn't an affair at all. We only did it that one time, and that's all it took. It wasn't because of me that we couldn't get pregnant. It was just like the doctor said. So you see, it was Gary's problem and Gary's solution."

"I'm assuming you never got around to telling your good friend Margaret about any of this," I offered.

Naomi nodded. "Right. I never told anyone. Gary knew, and so did Harrison, of course, but they wouldn't have told her. And I wouldn't have either. Didn't."

"But she did find out."

"Somehow, but not until yesterday."

"Who told her?"

"I have no idea. I was alone in the room in the afternoon, taking a nap. She called and lit into me on the phone. How could I have done such a thing when all this time she thought I was her friend? She was screaming and ranting and raving so loud I'm surprised the whole ship didn't hear her. Fortunately, I was the only one in our cabin at the time. I tried explaining to her that what happened had nothing to do with our friendship. She demanded that I go to her cabin right then to talk about it, and so I did. I didn't want Sharon and Virginia to come into the room and hear what was going on. After all, it was bad enough Margaret knew my awful secret. I didn't want the rest of the world to know about it as well, although now I'm sure word will get out anyway."

I have to admit I was skeptical that no one had known about all this earlier. "You mean to say no one ever figured any of this out on their own? Doesn't Missy resemble her biological father?"

Naomi shook her head. "Fortunately she looks just like me—sort of the same way Chloe looks like Margaret."

"In other words, Harrison Featherman turns out to be your universal sperm donor. He can sire kids all over the place and no one comes back on him about it because the offspring all look like their various mothers instead of like their father."

Naomi swallowed before she answered. "If Melissa had resembled Harrison—if people had noticed—I suppose I would have had to say something. But she didn't. And all my friends knew I was so overjoyed at getting pregnant and having a baby that they just celebrated with me."

"So who spilled the beans yesterday?"

Naomi shook her head. "I have no idea, and Margaret didn't say. She just asked me straight out whether or not it was true. I told her yes, it was. I didn't want to lie about it."

"You mean, you wanted to stop lying about it."

"Yes," Naomi said quietly. "I suppose that's right."

"What time of day was this?"

Naomi shrugged. "It was late in the afternoon when she

called me—around four-thirty or five o'clock. I'm not sure. And it must have been between five and six when I left her cabin."

"Where did you go then?"

"I didn't want to go back to the room. I had been crying, and I didn't want to have to face Virginia and Sharon looking like that. So I went up to the spa. Fortunately, they'd had a last-minute cancellation, so I was able to get in for a massage. After the massage, I spent some time in the hot tub and didn't go back down to the room until I figured Virginia and Sharon would already have left for dinner.

"While I was upstairs in the spa, I kept trying to figure out what to do. I thought about just skipping dinner altogether, but then I thought, no. Since Margaret knew, I made up my mind to go to dinner and face the music. I was sure she was going to bring it up regardless of whether or not I was there. The only thing I could do was be there to defend myself."

"You thought she was going to tell?"

Naomi nodded. "In fact, that was the last thing she said to me as I left her room—that if I thought she was going to keep this dirty little secret a secret any longer, I was crazy. So when I went to dinner, I felt like a prisoner being led to execution. I was determined that when she brought it up, I'd tell every-body the truth and get it over with once and for all. And if Virginia and Sharon decided to write me off, then I planned to leave the ship, go to the airport in Juneau and catch the first plane back to Seattle. But then, when Margaret didn't show up at dinnertime, I was grateful. I felt as though God had given me a reprieve."

I nodded, remembering how Naomi's flagging spirits had

gradually revived during the course of dinner. Of course they had. Every moment Margaret delayed putting in an appearance meant one more moment of respite for Naomi before Margaret blew the whistle, which she no doubt would have done. My few dealings with the woman had shown quite clearly that she was absolutely ruthless and that she thrived on public humiliation—other people's public humiliation.

"And so you made up the story you told me about Margaret probably having found some new boy toy who was keeping her too preoccupied to come to dinner?"

"It sounded plausible enough," Naomi returned.

Just then Virginia Metz and Sharon Carson came cruising through the lobby bar on their way to the elevators. Catching sight of the two of us sitting there, they descended on our table in a flurry of questions and shopping bags.

"Did you hear what's happened?" Virginia demanded at once. "Margaret is missing."

"We heard," Naomi said.

"Have they found her yet?" Sharon added.

Naomi shook her head. "Not that I know of."

"Maybe we should go talk to the first officer and find out what's happening," Sharon Carson suggested. "He told us that if we had any questions or concerns, we should come see him right away."

"No," Naomi said quietly. "Not just yet. The three of us have to talk. There's something I need to tell you."

I've wised up enough in my old age to know when to take a hint. "If you ladies will be good enough to excuse me," I said, standing up, "I believe I'll head on back to my cabin."

7

ON THE WAY THROUGH the ship, I was still stunned by Naomi's admission. I couldn't imagine a woman being so desperate for a baby that she'd go to such lengths to conceive one. Why not use an anonymous donor? And the fact that her husband had helped hatch the plan was downright astonishing. As for Harrison Featherman—in my book he was beneath contempt. It seemed to me that Margaret Featherman had every right to be pissed as hell at both of them—at her friend Naomi Pepper and at her ex-husband as well.

I expected I'd be able to go back to my cabin and have some time to relax and think things over. Naturally, that turned out to be an unachievable goal. There's a little clear

Plexiglas mailbox on the wall next to the door for each cabin on the *Starfire Breeze*. Mine was stuffed full of messages. When I opened the various envelopes, the messages were pretty similar. In steadily increasing levels of urgency I was told to contact the purser's office ASAP.

The message light on my phone was blinking furiously as well. I listened to the messages, but they turned out to be the same thing—see the purser. Obviously, whoever wanted me to contact the purser wasn't taking any chances on my not getting the word.

"This is Mr. Beaumont," I said, as soon as someone answered the phone. "I have several messages saying I should contact the purser's office at once. Do you have any idea what this might be concerning?"

"Of course, Mr. Beaumont. If you'll just stay on the line, I'll put your call right through."

To where? I wanted to ask, but naturally whoever had answered left me hanging without giving me a clue. I wondered if maybe I was next on the list to have a door-pounding visit from Dr. Harrison Featherman and his traveling henchman, the first officer.

"Dulles here," a cool female voice announced in my ear.

"Would that be Ms. Dulles, Mrs. Dulles, or Miss Dulles?" I asked.

"That would be Agent Dulles," she responded even more coolly. "Agent Rachel Dulles."

Agent Dulles didn't bother to add "of the FBI." She didn't have to because I'd already figured that out. *Typical fed,* I thought. *No sense of humor.* But then, I supposed, if you're posted as agent in charge of an end-of-the-earth outpost like Juneau, maybe your sense of humor disappears right along with the transfer papers to your new territory.

"Is this Mr. Beaumont?" she asked.

I find that humorless FBI agents always bring out the worst in me. I had to rattle her chain just a little. "Any relation to John Foster?" I asked.

If there was a hint of a smile at that, no trace of it leaked into her strictly business telephone voice. "We're distant relations," she said icily. "My grandfather and John Foster were second cousins."

Great, I thought. If her grandfather and John Foster Dulles were second cousins, that meant I was dealing with a young and humorless female FBI agent.

"The purser's office said this was Mr. Beaumont," Agent Dulles continued. "Is that correct?"

"Yes," I said. "J. P. Beaumont."

"As in Jonas Piedmont, retired Seattle homicide detective? How kind of you to call me so promptly."

I didn't point out that I was responding to a whole series of urgent messages, but it did cross my mind that even though Agent Dulles might be young, if she knew that much about me, she had done her homework.

"I understand you left the ship today in the company of one Naomi Cullen Pepper," Agent Dulles resumed. "Is that also correct?"

"Yes," I replied. "Ms. Pepper and I, along with a number of other passengers, took a shore excursion and rode the cable car in Juneau."

"Two of those other passengers would be your grandparents, Mr. and Mrs. Lars Jenssen, I believe."

I could feel my hackles rising. "That's also correct," I told her curtly, "although I can't imagine why you'd be interested in involving my grandparents in all of this."

"In all of what?"

I wasn't about to be sucked into playing that kind of game. "In whatever it is you want to talk to me about," I growled back at her. "My grandparents are on their honeymoon. I expect them to be left undisturbed."

"That remains to be seen," Agent Dulles responded. "I'd like to speak to you in person at your convenience. We could do that in the privacy of your cabin, if you wish, or someplace more public if you'd prefer. I'm at your disposal."

Like hell you are! I thought. "Name your poison," I told her.

"How about if I come to you, then," she offered brightly. "It might be a little less awkward."

"Suit yourself," I told her.

"Good. I'll be right there."

She was, too, in less than five minutes and without needing to be told where my cabin was. As soon as I opened the door and found her standing outside, I recognized her as someone I had seen before, although I couldn't place her. She was tall and slender with wide-set gray eyes. Her hair, brunette with flecks of gold, was trimmed in one of those chiseled cuts where the back is cropped close to the skull and the front and sides swing free. I doubted a single hair on her head ever had nerve enough to be out of place.

"Mr. Beaumont?" she asked. "Or should I call you Beau?"

Since she wanted to play the game as though we were old pals, I decided to string along. "Beau will be fine," I agreed grudgingly, beckoning her into the room.

"And I'm Rachel," she returned, smiling and holding out her hand. It was while we were shaking hands that I noticed that her gray eyes, like her hair, also contained flecks of gold.

"Won't you have a seat?"

She walked over to the sofa that was part of the junior suite's sitting-room area. She was wearing one of those cruise-type pantsuits—dressed-up navy-blue sweats made of some kind of silky material with appliquéd anchors and other seafaring items sewn on in gold. As she walked away from me, however, I noticed the slight but distinctive bulge that revealed the presence of a small-of-back holster. She might be dressing the part, but Agent Dulles was no casually cruising tourist.

She sat down, crossed her legs, and turned on a surprisingly warm smile. "You didn't sound especially overjoyed to hear from me on the phone," she said. "But I couldn't be happier that you're here. I've come to ask for your help."

I was thinking about everything Naomi had told me earlier in the afternoon—about her relationship with Harrison Featherman and about her last confrontational conversation with the missing Margaret. If Agent Dulles asked me questions about that, I would be obliged to answer even if the information I gave resulted in the investigation turning its microscopic focus on Naomi Pepper.

"Sue always spoke highly of you," Rachel added.

"Sue?" I asked stupidly.

"Sue Danielson," she returned. "Your former partner."

"You knew her?"

"Yes, I knew her. You probably don't remember me because there were so many other people at her funeral, but that's where I met you. We were actually introduced. I saw you again at the Fallen Officers Memorial when you were there with Sue's boys. That was a very nice thing to do, by the way, making sure they were able to attend."

So that's where I had seen Rachel Dulles before—at Sue Danielson's funeral. And that's also why I hadn't remembered her name. Funerals for murdered police officers bring together law-enforcement folks from all over the country, who attend in order to pay their respects. Those two separate events had been attended by hundreds of people, most of whom I hadn't known personally. But I have to admit, hearing Sue's name mentioned right then rocked me. I had come on this cruise hoping to escape my nightmarish memories, yet here she was cropping up in casual conversation.

"How did you know Sue?" I asked the question while trying to gather my wits about me.

Rachel Dulles smiled. "I know, I know. It's a tradition. FBI agents and local cops are always supposed to be at each other's throats, right? People may think that old adage 'Sisterhood Is Powerful' went out of fashion right along with bra burning, but when it comes to women in law enforcement, there still aren't all that many of us. And, no matter what jurisdiction or agency we work for, we're all fighting the same battles for respect and acceptance. Several years ago, a group of us from various agencies in the Seattle area—"

"You're from Seattle?" I interjected. "I thought you were based somewhere up here—in Juneau, maybe."

"No, Alex and I are both based in Seattle."

"Who's Alex?"

"Alex Freed. My partner. He's young, straight out of the academy, and useless as far as I'm concerned. He was playing cool, macho dude and couldn't be bothered with taking his Dramamine. Said it would make him sleepy. As soon as we hit rough water, he turned green. He tried taking the Dramamine then, but it was too late. He was up all night long, puking his guts out. I didn't get much sleep."

"You mean you're staying in the same cabin? That's not the way partners used to work back at Seattle PD."

"This is the new FBI, remember?" she returned with a smile. "Alex Freed and I may be in the same cabin—it's an inside one and not nearly as nice as this, by the way—but don't think there's any fooling around between us. My husband would definitely not approve. On board Alex and I are known as Kurt and Phyllis Nix, husband and wife."

"I see," I said.

"But getting back to Sue," Rachel Dulles continued. "Several years ago a few of us started getting together informally once a month or so, to network and talk things over. Sort of like Footprinters, but for women only and with no dues. That's where I met Sue Danielson. We became acquaintances if not close friends. What happened to her was . . . tragic," Rachel added after a pause. "It also should have been preventable."

That, of course, was my position, too. That Sue's death should have been entirely preventable. That I—J. P. Beaumont—should have done something to prevent it. My thoughts must have been written on my face. Or else Agent Dulles was a first-class mind reader.

"I don't mean you," she said quickly. "I mean we as a society should have prevented it. Domestic abuse kills people. After years of suffering, it's so easy for women—even strong women like Sue—to get sucked back into all the old patterns and fall for the same old lies. She never should have agreed to see Danielson on her own."

"That's true," I said. "I wish to God she hadn't."

"One Saturday morning, not long before she died, Sue and I were having a second cup of coffee after the rest of the group had gone," Rachel continued. "That in itself was unusual because most of the time Sue would have to go rushing off early to get her boys to or from soccer or Little League or something. But that particular morning, for some reason, she had some extra time. We got to talking about partners. I remember her mentioning you in particular. She said that of all the partners she'd ever worked with, you were by far the best. Her exact words were that you were 'good people.' Later, when I saw you with Sue's boys at the funeral and again at the memorial service, I knew what she meant when she said it. I also knew it was true. You *are* good people."

Rachel's compliment caught me totally unawares. "Thanks," I mumbled, forcing the word out over the fist-sized lump that had formed in my throat.

"And that's why I'm here. Because you're good people, and we need help."

"We who?" I asked.

"Alex and I," she returned. "The Agency."

"With Margaret Featherman's disappearance?"

"No," she said. "Not that exactly. The agent working her disappearance hasn't come on board yet, although he's scheduled to arrive sometime later today. Alex and I are working another case right now. He's pulling shore duty at the moment, which suits him just fine. We've been on board the *Starfire Breeze* since she left Seattle. A handful of people—high-ranking officers—know we're working a case. As far as everyone else is concerned, we're a pair of ordinary passengers, one of whom isn't a very good sailor."

"Get Alex a pair of these," I said, reaching for my Travel-Aid box off the bedside table where I'd left it. "You can buy them in the gift shop, and they really do work. I'll be putting mine back on as soon as we pull away from the dock."

She examined the box for a moment and then handed it back. "These work?" she asked.

"They do for me," I told her. "But getting back to business—you're telling me that the case you're working has nothing to do with Margaret Featherman's disappearance?"

"May have nothing to do with it," she corrected. "Our main concern right now is that what's happened with her may compromise what we've already got going. As I said before, there'll be another agent coming on board later today who'll be assigned to the Featherman disappearance. Alex and I won't be making contact with him for fear of blowing our own cover. If it turns out there is a connection, we'll cross that bridge when we come to it. In the meantime, what Alex and I need is for someone to act as an informant for us, someone who's actually inside Margaret Featherman's circle of friends, someone who can keep us up-to-date on what's happening with them. From the looks of things, you appear to be the most likely candidate—if you'll agree, that is."

Acting as an informant without any kind of official credentials didn't sound like a good idea to me. "I'm not agreeing to anything until I have some idea what this is all about and until I get a look at your badge."

Nodding, she pulled a thin ID wallet out of a zippered pocket and passed it across to me. After examining it, I handed it back. "Looks legit to me," I said.

She smiled and tucked it back away.

"So what's the deal?" I asked.

"Have you ever heard of an organization called LITG—Leave It To God?"

"I've heard of 'Leave It to Beaver,' " I told her.

She gave me a blank look. I had the sudden sense that once again, just as with Sue, Rachel Dulles and I were standing on opposite sides of a yawning generation gap. "You know," I added lamely. "The TV series."

"Never saw it," Rachel resumed. "But you do know about right-to-lifers?"

I nodded. "I have heard about them," I told her.

"Most right-to-lifers are perfectly ordinary and decent folks," Rachel continued. "They also don't happen to believe in women having abortions."

For obvious reasons, I'm glad my own unwed mother didn't take the then-illegal-abortion way out of her predicament. But I don't think of myself as a right-to-lifer, either.

"But beyond those regular people, there's the lunatic fringe," Agent Dulles went on. "They're the people who blow up abortion clinics and use sniper rifles to pick off abortion-performing doctors as they back their cars out of their driveways on their way to work. The Leave It To God folks qualify as the lunatic fringe of the lunatic fringe. They're opposed to progress in everything from genetically bred corn to computer chips. They call themselves Leave It To God, but as far as we know, they're not related to any church or church-affiliated organization. They refer to themselves in their manifesto as Secular Humanists."

"What the hell is that?"

"Right-to-lifers are opposed to doctors who perform abortions. Members of Leave It To God are opposed to doctors who save lives."

"What do you mean?"

"Their position is that God put sickness and disease on this earth as a lesson in suffering for everybody. Sort of as a device to keep us in our place. As cutting-edge techniques become available, doctors are saving lives that would otherwise have been lost. Leave It To God believes that's wrong. Their members maintain that God and God alone should decide who lives and dies. They don't approve of someone like Dr. Featherman, for example. He's invented a new surgical technique that allows patients who would otherwise be crippled by grand-mal seizures to return to living productive lives."

"Like Marc Alley," I breathed.

Rachel nodded. "Exactly."

"You're telling me these Secular Humanists are targeting Harrison Featherman?"

"That's right," she said. "The Agency received a tip to

that effect. The problem is, Marc Alley may be targeted as well."

"Why, because he didn't die?"

"Correct," Rachel replied. "Marc Alley is back to living a normal life. In LITG's book, that's wrong. He isn't bearing his assigned cross and serving as an example of suffering for everyone else. That qualifies him as a target, too."

"That's crazy," I said.

"It *is* crazy," Rachel agreed. "But it's happened before—four times that we know of so far. Dr. Aaron Blackman was a cancer researcher at Sloan. Blackman allegedly committed suicide. Two weeks later, one of Blackman's patients—a woman whose supposedly incurable brain-stem tumor had gone into remission after Blackman's tumor-shrinking treatment—was fatally creamed in a crosswalk by a hit-and-run driver. And one of a team of Atlanta doctors using a new in utero surgery for spina bifida drowned in a swimming pool at a resort down in Scottsdale. His death was initially ruled accidental. Then one of the first babies he helped with those surgical techniques was snatched out of a grocery cart at a Wal-Mart in Savannah. The child was found dead in a ditch two days later. It was after that last incident that the Agency received a letter—the manifesto, as it's called—from Leave It To God in which they take credit for all of those incidents. After the letter, the investigations into the deaths of the two doctors were reopened. Both are now listed as homicides."

"What makes you think Featherman will be targeted?"

"A list of names accompanied the letter. It contained the names of one thousand doctors from all over the country, including six in the Seattle area—two at Swedish, one at the

U Dub, and three at Fred Hutch. Featherman was one of the two from Swedish."

"Does he know about it?"

Rachel Dulles nodded. "All the doctors have been notified."

"And the patients?"

She sighed. "No. My superiors decided that letting all the patients know about the situation might cause wholesale panic. It would involve far too many people—far more than we could handle or protect. We're doing what we can to keep all targeted doctors under surveillance, but even that is leaving the Agency spread pretty thin."

"This is rich. Some smart doctor figures out a way to save people from dying or being crippled by some appalling disease and then somebody else comes along and knocks the patients off because they had nerve enough to get well?"

"That's the way it works. Dr. Featherman isn't exactly keeping his ground-breaking treatment under wraps. Neither was the spina bifida guy. He was in Scottsdale at the conference for the express purpose of expounding upon and expanding use of techniques that originally came from Vanderbilt University Medical Center in Nashville. And since Marc Alley is such an outspoken supporter of Dr. Featherman's treatment, we're assuming that makes him a likely target as well."

"And you're expecting the same kind of thing might happen here?"

Rachel nodded. "As soon as we learned about the shipboard conference, we tried to talk Dr. Featherman out of coming on the cruise, but he wouldn't hear of it. He has a big grant from the National Institutes of Health riding on this conference. He was afraid if he backed out of attending, the grant sources would dry up."

"So what are you and Alex doing about all this?" I asked.

"Starfire Cruises gave us a list of all passengers and crew members. While we're on board, the Agency is running checks on all of them, but that takes time. So far nothing has turned up on any of them, but we did learn from the purser's office that Margaret Featherman received two separate faxes. One was delivered to her the night before last, and another one yesterday afternoon. When the agent from Juneau comes on board, we're expecting he'll have a court order giving him and eventually us access to the text of those two faxes."

"You're thinking Margaret Featherman may have been involved in this plot to target her ex-husband?"

"There is an outside chance of that," Rachel Dulles said. "From what I've learned about the former Mrs. Featherman, she could be capable of almost anything."

That's how she struck me, too, I thought.

Just then there was a knock on the door. I looked through the peephole and was dismayed to find Lars Jenssen standing there. "What is it?" I asked, opening the door.

"Can I come in for a minute?"

I glanced back at Rachel Dulles, who shook her head. I have a feeling Lars got a glimpse of her at the same time. "It would probably be better if you didn't," I told him.

Lars gave me a lopsided grin, along with a conspiratorial wink. "So it's like that, is it," he said. "Ya, sure. I yust wanted to tell you that there's a Friends of Bill W. meeting getting together in the library in another half hour or so. Beverly's on her way to high tea with the Wakefield girls, which means I'm free to go to my meeting. I was wondering if you'd like to come along, but I can see that's a bad idea. I'll yust go on about my business."

Right, I thought. *And go straight back to Beverly and tell her that her grandson couldn't come to the AA meeting because he was entertaining a woman in his cabin.*

Lars started down the hall.

"Where did you say the meeting was again?" I called after him.

"In the library. Four o'clock."

I closed the door and turned back to Rachel Dulles. "What exactly is it that you want me to do?"

"Keep an eye on Marc Alley."

"Like I kept an eye on Sue Danielson, you mean? I didn't do her much good, did I? What makes you think I'd have any better results looking after Marc?"

Rachel Dulles let that one pass. "Why was he waiting for you at the bottom of the gangplank earlier today?"

"To tell us—Naomi Pepper and me—about what had happened to Margaret Featherman, that she had disappeared."

"And why do you suppose he told you?"

"I give up."

"Because he trusts you, Beau. And so do I."

She glanced at her watch and stood up. "I have a meeting, too," she said. "So I'd best be going. Here's my cabin number," she said, pressing a card into my hand. "And remember, as far as the ship is concerned, I'm Phyllis Nix. Call me right away if Marc mentions anything unusual or disturbing."

"What about telling him what's up?" I asked.

Agent Dulles shrugged. "I may be under orders not to warn the patients," she replied, "but that doesn't mean you are."

I opened the door for her. Once she was out in the corridor, Agent Dulles turned and offered her hand. "Thanks for the help, Beau. And by the way," she added, "most of my friends call me Rachey."

I watched her go until she turned into the elevator lobby, then I closed the door and shook my head. I might not have taken the attorney general up on her offer to go to work for the Special Homicide Investigation Team, but one way or another, it looked as though J. P. Beaumont was back in the game.

8

THERE ARE ALMOST as many reasons for going to AA meetings as there are meetings themselves. That day I went because I wanted to prove to Lars Jenssen that there was no hanky-panky going on between me and the attractive young woman he had spied sitting in my stateroom. I arrived at the *Starfire Breeze*'s book-lined library only a few minutes after he did. With Lars there's no such thing as presumption of innocence, but even he had to admit that I couldn't possibly be that smooth or fast an operator.

"Another woman from your table, I suppose?" Lars asked when I sat down beside him.

"No," I said with no further elucidation.

Lars sighed. "If I'da only known this was what cruises

were like, I would have taken them years ago when I was a lot younger."

"What does Beverly have to say about your wanting to play the field?" I asked.

"Who's playing?" Lars asked. "Since when does it hurt to look?"

Because we were still in port, the library was officially closed. Glass doors had been pulled shut and fastened over the shelves, locking the books inside. Upholstered chairs and love seats had been moved into a loose semblance of a circle which was gradually filling with people. When the library doors were finally pulled shut several minutes later, there must have been twenty-five or thirty people gathered in the room, about the same number of attendees that show up for most AA meetings on land.

Lars had called this a Friends of Bill W. meeting. In AA circles that means it's an open meeting where anyone involved in a twelve-step program is welcome to attend. Sobriety is a catch-all term that can apply to any number of issues. Looking at the attendees gathered in that room, I noticed that a few of the older guys sported bulbous, thickly veined noses that spoke of years of hard drinking and hard living both. During introductions, a couple of the younger people mentioned that they were involved in Narcotics Anonymous. Several others came from the Al-Anon side of the spectrum.

Al-Anon is a separate organization with its own twelve-step program designed for people involved with drinkers and druggies. It helps members gain tools to maintain enough serenity that they don't resort to killing or leaving their loved ones or end up falling into the same trap of drinking and drugging themselves. One woman, a grandmotherly type in her sixties, announced that she belonged to Overeaters Anonymous. OA must have worked for her because she looked great, although it occurred to me that dealing with a food addiction on board a cruise ship had to be a very real kind of hell.

On dry land, AA, NA, OA, and Al-Anon sort themselves into separate meetings. On the *Starfire Breeze* we were all part of one group. We had finished introductions and someone was reading from the Big Book when a latecomer burst into the room and dived into the first available chair. Her tardy arrival created a small stir. I judged her to be a woman in her seventies—sturdy but a little stooped at the shoulder. Once seated, she seemed to have a difficult time sitting still. Her hands fluttered nervously in her lap. She shifted back and forth in her seat and checked her watch time and again. Of all the people in the room, she was the one who seemed most in need of a meeting.

When it was time for sharing, some people spoke, some didn't. When the group leader nodded at the woman, she launched into her story.

"My name's Lucy," she said. "Me an' Mike have been married for almost fifty-five years. Twenty-five of those we was both drunk. We sobered up on our twenty-fifth anniversary, and we've both been straight ever since. But now . . ." She faltered and shook her head. It took several seconds for her to gather herself again.

"Now things is different," she said. "It's not like Mike has fallen off the wagon or nothin'. It's worse."

In AA nothing is supposed to be worse than falling off the wagon, but from the grim set of Lucy's mouth, I knew what was coming would be bad news.

"It started with him just forgetting little stuff. At first we both sort of laughed about it together and more or less ignored it. But it's a lot worse than that now, and I've been hidin' it—keepin' things to myself because I didn't want to worry the kids none. There's nothin' nobody can do about it anyways. Nothin' that'll make it better."

By then everybody in the room knew what Lucy and Mike were up against. If developing Alzheimer's isn't everybody's worst nightmare, then it's got to be right up there, close to the top. I glanced at Lars. Unsmiling, he nodded. He probably knew more than anyone in the room about what Lucy and Mike were dealing with. Alzheimer's disease was what had killed his first wife, Aggie, eight years earlier.

"The kids pooled their money to send us on this trip," Lucy continued. "I didn't have the heart to try talkin' 'em out of it. I thought I could handle things same as I do at home, but all of a sudden it's taken another turn for the worse. Mike won't so much as come out of our room or even get dressed. He just sits there in his underwear or not all day long watchin' that damned TV set, excuse my French. And he's not watchin' on one of the channels where there might be a program worth watchin'. Oh, no, it's the same stupid channel, hour after hour, the one that shows what's happening off the back of the boat. That's all he watches.

"Mike says he's scared. He's afraid if he leaves the room they'll probably throw him overboard, too. I keep tellin' him they won't—that nobody's throwin' nobody off the back of the boat, but that don't make no difference. He won't listen. I feel like I'm in a jail cell instead of on some hoity-toity cruise. This afternoon, I wanted a drink so bad I could taste it. After thirty years, that's what I wanted to do today—go out and get fallin'-down drunk. That's why I'm here. I gave the room attendant fifty bucks and asked him to watch Mike for me till I got back. I knew if I didn't come to a meeting today, I was gonna lose it."

Lucy's words had tumbled out so fast that when she finally stopped speaking, she was almost breathless. She sank back into her chair. Spent with effort, her fluttering hands lay still for the first time.

"We're glad you're here," the self-appointed leader said after a moment's pause. "And if you want to hang around for a little while afterwards, maybe some of us can give you a hand with Mike, help take a little of the pressure off."

There were nods of assent and murmurs of agreement and encouragement all around the room. Before I came into AA I thought it was going to be a bunch of deadbeat, down-at-the-heels drunks sitting around a room complaining about not being able to drink anymore. What I didn't realize at first is that AA is a fellowship. People who go there end up caring for one another. Strangers don't stay strangers for long.

"Thanks," Lucy mumbled. "I'd really appreciate it."

The meeting went on for several more minutes, but I had fallen off the track, stopped cold by the implications of what Lucy had said—that her husband was afraid someone *else* would be thrown off the ship. Did that mean that he had already seen someone go overboard? Was that real, or was it simply a figment of his unraveling imagination?

When had it happened? I wondered with that old familiar catch in my gut that always used to tell me when separate pieces of a case were starting to fall into place. *About the same time Margaret Featherman disappeared? Did that mean that Mike possibly had witnessed what had happened to her?*

The bad part of all this was that I had learned about this potential witness in the course of an AA meeting. That second A stands for anonymous. What's said during meetings is strictly confidential. Without Lucy's full agreement in the matter, there was no way anyone in the room could reveal a word of what she had said there—me included.

Once the meeting finally broke up, Lars Jenssen was the first to approach Lucy with his offer of help. Several others did the same, saying they'd be glad to come sit with Mike from time to time during the cruise in order to give Lucy a break so she could go to the dining room for dinner or have some fun on one of the shore excursions. I hung back because I wanted to talk to Lucy alone. That was easy to do since I knew Lars would pick up all pertinent information, including the location of her room as well as her last name.

"Mike and Lucy Conyers are second seating," Lars told me as we started toward the elevators. "I told her Beverly and I will come sit with Mike tonight so she can have a little break—dinner and maybe a show later. I don't think Beverly will mind, do you?"

"No," I assured him. "I'm sure she won't."

Lars sighed and shook his head. "Ya, sure," he added

solemnly after a pause. "It's a hell of a thing when they get so bad you can't leave 'em alone. It's like having a baby all over again, only worse. The person you knew isn't there anymore. You can't reason with 'em. Can't get 'em to understand. And you can't leave 'em alone for even a minute because they'll get lost or set fire to the house or take too many pills.

"And I know why he keeps looking off the back of the ship. Aggie did that, too. Sat in the car looking out the back window instead of the front. Like she didn't care at all where we were going. She just wanted to remember where she'd been."

Lars knew what Lucy Conyers was going through, all right.

"What deck are they on?" I asked.

Lars plucked a piece of paper out of his shirt pocket. "Aloha seven-six-three," he told me. "Are you going to help out, too?"

"I'll try," I said. "There may be something I can do."

Lars is usually bolstered by attending meetings, but this time that wasn't true. Hearing about Lucy and Mike Conyers' tribulations and revisiting his own bad old times seemed to have sapped the stamina right out of him. He looked as though he could use a boost.

"Want to stop off in the buffet for a cup of coffee?" I asked.

Lars shook his head. "I think I'll head back to the room. Don't much feel like shooting the breeze," he said.

That surprised me. Lars has a weakness for coffee. Under most circumstances, an offer of free coffee would have been downright irresistible for him, but since he turned me down,

I didn't stop off at the buffet, either. Instead, I went straight to the Aloha Deck and parked myself in the elevator lobby nearest 763. It was only a matter of minutes before Lucy Conyers showed up.

"Hi, Lucy," I said, introducing myself and falling in step beside her as she started down the corridor toward her stateroom. "I'm J. P. Beaumont. People call me Beau. I didn't get a chance to meet you during the meeting. Lars Jenssen is my grandfather."

"What a nice man!" she exclaimed. "He offered to bring his wife and come watch Mike this evening so I can go up to the dining room for dinner."

"It sounds as though you can use the break."

She stopped in front of the door to the cabin marked 763—an inside cabin with no way to see out. Mike and Lucy's kids may have paid for their parents to go on the cruise, but they hadn't sprung for an outside cabin with a lanai or even so much as a window. No wonder Lucy Conyers felt as though she was locked in a jail cell. She was.

Lucy stood in front of the cabin door making no move to insert the key card in the slot. It struck me that she was savoring this last bit of freedom before facing up to whatever awaited her inside.

"Just gettin' away long enough to come to the meetin' was a big help," Lucy said. "You have no idea!"

"I'm sure I don't," I agreed. "It must be rough."

She nodded. "But I'm feelin' better somehow. Not quite as hopeless as I was before, and not wonderin' where my next drink is comin' from. It's so nice of all you people to worry about me. I'm very lucky."

That made me feel like a first-class turkey. I wasn't there chatting with Lucy Conyers because I was a kind, concerned human being. Behind the nice-guy mask, I was actually pumping her for information.

"You mentioned during the meeting that your husband was afraid someone might throw him overboard, too. Is that correct?"

"Yes."

"You also said he'd been watching TV since we first set sail."

"That's right."

"So when did he first start worrying about being thrown overboard?"

"That didn't come up until last night," Lucy answered. "I was in the bathroom. He came and pounded on the door and told me I had to come out quick and see what was on TV. When I came out, there was nothin' to see but more of what he'd been watchin' all day long—waves and water and nothin' else. But Mike was all excited, pacin' back and forth and wavin' his arms. He kept sayin' that somebody had thrown Peggy off the ship and that they'd be comin' for him next."

"Who's Peggy?"

Lucy shrugged. "Beats me. The only Peggy I know any-thin' about is Mike's mother, but she's been dead for thirty years, and she didn't drown, neither."

"What time was this?"

"When I was in the bathroom? It must have been around six or so, although it could've been earlier. All I know is by the time I got around to looking at the TV set, it was still light

enough to see. I tried tellin' Mike that he was mistaken—that
Peggy was dead and he was just makin' things up as he went
along. I suppose it could be that there was a log in the water
that looked like it was a person. I don't know. I can't tell what
the man saw or didn't see, but I can tell you for sure that I
didn't see nothin'. 'Sides, sometimes Mike's like that. He
imagines things that aren't real. He sees and talks to people I
can't see or hear, people who aren't there at all. When Mike's
seein' things like that, there are times I think I'm gonna go
stark ravin' crazy myself."

"Maybe he wasn't seeing things this time," I suggested
quietly.

Lucy Conyers' jaw dropped. She peered up into my face.
"What do you mean?"

"Most people on board the ship don't know about this yet,
but a female passenger is missing. The last time anyone saw
her was late yesterday afternoon. She didn't come to dinner
last night, and she wasn't in her cabin overnight. Since Mike
was watching the view from that stern camera, I think he
actually may have seen her go overboard."

Lucy's eyes widened. "Is that possible?"

"It is."

"What should I do?"

"Go find the ship's first officer and tell him what's happened—that your husband may have seen someone go off the
ship into the water late yesterday afternoon. Then the authorities can review the tapes from the ship's security cameras and
see if they picked up any sign of what happened."

Lucy dropped her eyes and glanced at her watch. "I can't,"

she said. "I told the attendant I'd be back in an hour, and it's almost that now. Could you maybe do that for me? Talk to the ship's first officer, I mean."

"I'll be glad to, but since the subject came up in the course of a meeting, I can't do that unless you give me permission."

"Actually, me and Mike would be really grateful if you did," Lucy said. "You see, it would be such a relief for me to know that Mike really did see somethin'—that he wasn't just imaginin' things for a change. Meanwhile, if you'll excuse me, I'd best be goin' inside. I'd invite you in, but I can't never be sure of what I'll find. Mike don't always cover up properly, if you know what I mean. It's embarrassin' as all get-out for me, although it don't seem to bother him none. Not in the least. And that's the strange part. Back when we was young, Mike was always sort of modest-like. In fact, years ago, you wouldn't have caught the man wearin' a pair of shorts, or swimmin' trunks, neither." She laughed. "He hated his legs then, and they're a whole lot funnier-lookin' now."

Shaking her head, she put the key card in the slot, and the door clicked open. As it swung in on its hinges, I caught sight of a totally naked man sitting sprawled on the love seat. As soon as the door opened, a uniformed room attendant—a male—appeared from some other part of the room and bolted toward the door.

"So glad you're back, Mrs. Conyers," he muttered as he pushed past me into the hall. "But I must go right away."

"Of course, Ricardo," Lucy Conyers said to him. "Thank you so much."

Then she stepped inside and closed the door behind her,

shutting both Ricardo and me in the hallway. Ricardo didn't pause to exchange pleasantries. Two doors down the hall he ducked into a service lobby while I headed back toward the elevator. From there I went straight to the purser's desk.

Among the hired help, there seems to be a caste system on board cruise ships. At least that was true on the *Starfire Breeze*. Sailors who did grunt labor on board were mostly of Far Eastern extraction—mainland Chinese and Korean. Room attendants, kitchen help, and servers in the buffet areas tended to hail from the Philippines. In the dining room, the wait-staff personnel seemed to be Portugese or Italian, with the supervisors—headwaiters and maître d's—all Italian. The young folks in crisp white uniforms who worked behind the counter at the purser's desk and the people who manned the cash registers in the concessions—the gift shops and bars—tended to be Brits or Americans, while the captain and other top-echelon officers were Italian.

At the purser's desk I waited in line with other American tourists trying to sort out their various travel concerns. At last, when I reached the counter, I said to the young man who greeted me, "I'd like to speak to the first officer, please."

"You are?"

"J. P. Beaumont," I told him.

"And what would this be concerning?" he asked.

"It's about Margaret Featherman," I replied.

That announcement had no effect at all on any of the other passengers who were also at the counter being waited on just then, but the reaction among the uniformed crew was an instantaneous dead silence. It reminded me of driving across a bump with a CD playing in a vehicle. After that moment of utter silence, cheerful smiles were reapplied and conversations resumed.

"Won't you come this way, sir," the young man serving me said. He showed me into a small office. "Please have a seat," he told me. "First Officer Vincente will be with you as soon as possible."

That proved to be true. First Officer Luigi Vincente arrived within a matter of minutes. He was a tall, unsmiling man with a close-cropped head of curly, slightly graying hair. "I understand you have information concerning Margaret Featherman?" he asked.

"That's correct. The videos that are filmed off the stern of the ship—how long do you keep them?"

He shrugged. "The security tapes taken of each voyage are kept for a month-long period. After that, the tapes are reused. Why?"

"Would it be possible to review the tapes made by the stern camera last night between five and six?"

"This is not so easy, but I am sure it would be possible," First Officer Vincente told me. "Why do you want to see them?"

"Because I have reason to believe someone on board saw a woman fall into the sea. It seems likely to me that woman would be Margaret Featherman."

First Officer Vincente's face turned red. "Someone fell off the ship? Impossible! Who says they saw such a thing?" he demanded. "And how? Was he there when this happened?"

"The passenger who saw it was in his cabin," I replied.

"It's an inside cabin on the Aloha Deck. He was watching the video display of the ship's progress on his television set."

Vincente considered the implications. "This seems quite unbelievable," he said. "Preposterous, in fact. How is it that no one else noticed such a thing?"

"Humor me," I said. "Take a look at the tape."

I expected to be summarily dropped and told to go mind my own business. Instead, after a moment's consideration, First Officer Vincente made up his mind. "Come with me," he said.

He led me through a maze of back-of-the-house corridors and into a staff-only elevator. Once on the elevator, we dropped far into the bowels of the ship, where he once again led me through a trackless maze of interior corridors.

I wondered about it at the time. I was sure this territory was usually off-limits to fare-paying passengers, yet after only one initial objection, he led me on. In the process he ignored questioning looks from several of his fellow officers who let us pass without comment. Obviously, on the *Starfire Breeze,* if Luigi Vincente thought I was all right, so did everybody else.

9

EVENTUALLY FIRST OFFICER VINCENTE motioned me into a darkened room lined with dozens of glowing video monitors. Inside, a uniformed crew member snapped to attention the moment we appeared. If I had studied the arm-patch guide on my television monitor, I would have known the technician's exact rank from what was on the sleeve of his uniform. As it was, all I knew about him was what his name tag said—Antonio Belvaducci. After an urgent consultation conducted entirely in Italian, the crewman hurried back to his computer console and punched a series of commands into a keyboard.

"There," Antonio said in English after several minutes had passed. "I will run the tape on the monitor at the far end."

First Officer Vincente led me to the last of the monitors.

Someone hastily pushed two chairs in our direction, and we took seats. When the tape came on the screen, the time stamp in the bottom right-hand corner showed 17:15 /03 SEP. Because we were watching in real time, viewing the tape was a whole lot like watching grass grow—and just about that exciting.

I admit that my mind strayed eventually. I reached the point where I was watching but not seeing. Suddenly, in his chair beside me, First Officer Vincente stiffened. "Wait," he commanded. "Go back."

At the computer console, Antonio froze the image and then turned it back several frames, and there she was. At precisely 17:47 a female figure, arms flailing, came tumbling past the lens of the camera and plunged silently into the sea, where she disappeared from view. Antonio rewound the tape and played the frames again. This time, it was possible to see how she windmilled her arms in a desperate attempt to right herself, as if hoping to enter the water feet- rather than head-first.

"Can you get closer?" First Officer Vincente demanded.

It took a few moments for the computer to enhance a small area of one particular frame. When the image reappeared, a cold chill passed over my body as though someone had doused me with a bucket of ice water. From the nose down, Margaret Featherman's face was shrouded in a layer of duct tape. No wonder she hadn't screamed aloud. No wonder no one had heard her cries for help. Her mouth had been taped shut.

"This is terrible," Luigi Vincente said. "If you will excuse me, Mr. Bowman, I must go at once and inform the captain. When you are ready, one of my officers will return you to the purser's desk. And perhaps, if it is not too much trouble, you would be so kind as to inform Dr. Featherman of this unfortunate occurrence."

I tried to object. "Wait a minute," I said. "Shouldn't that kind of information come from someone on the crew, someone with official standing . . ."

But First Officer Vincente was already out the door. I turned back to the computer operator. "Can you tell me where we were right then?"

Nodding, Antonio picked up a phone and called what I assumed to be the bridge. For my benefit, he conducted the phone call in faultless English. "Where was the ship at seventeen hundred hours forty-seven last night?" he asked.

I turned again to the monitor. "Can I see the whole picture again?" I asked, while he waited on hold.

After a few moments the picture expanded. Now, with my vision no longer focused entirely on the falling woman, I could see a narrow band of shoreline running along one side of the screen. So, rather than in mid-ocean, Margaret Featherman had gone into the water while the *Starfire Breeze* was somewhere close to land—near enough to see it, anyway.

"Could someone swim that far?" I asked.

Antonio gave me what struck me as a continental shrug. "That depends," he said. "On how far she fell, how hard she hit the water, whether or not she was conscious when she hit, and whether or not she was a good swimmer. The water aft is broken up by the wake of the ship, so that is better for her than if she fell into it when it was flat. Still, it is very difficult to say. The water is cold. Even a very good swimmer would not survive for long."

On my own, I knew that the duct tape which had probably been intended to stifle Margaret's screams might well have worked in her favor. For one thing, when she hit the water, the tape over her mouth would have prevented a reflexive intake of breath that would have flooded her lungs with icy water.

The crewman's next comment was directed into the telephone, then he turned back to me. "The bridge reports we were just off Port Walter," he said. "They say we reduced speed for some time in order to allow passengers to observe a pod of whales."

I remembered then the announcement that had come over the loudspeakers urging all interested passengers to come to deck 14 to observe the whales off the port bow. In other words, at the time in question, all eyes on the ship had been glued there instead of aft. The only exception had been poor Mike Conyers, who had been watching his television monitor instead.

"Yes," Antonio was saying on the phone. "I will tell him."

"Tell me what?"

"When you speak to Mrs. Featherman's family, Captain Giacometti wishes you to say simply that she is currently missing. Missing but not presumed drowned. The U.S. Coast Guard has now been notified and is sending Search and Rescue teams to her last-known position."

Right, I thought. *Too bad they're twenty-four hours too late.*

While waiting for someone to come fetch me, I remembered all those other security cameras stationed in strategic places all over the ship. I also remembered how it's always easier to ask forgiveness for something after it's done than it is to ask permission before doing it. Since First Officer Vincente himself had brought me here, maybe he wouldn't mind all that much if I viewed one more tape. The operative phrase here is: Give me an inch, and I think I'm a ruler.

"Would it be possible for me to see the security tape on Mrs. Featherman's deck for that same time period?" I asked.

"Which deck is that?"

"Aloha," I told him, casually passing along information I had gleaned from First Officer Vincente on our long walk though the ship. After another expressive shrug and what seemed like a long, several-minute wait, the image of a long empty corridor appeared on the same screen where, a little while earlier, Margaret Featherman had tumbled toward the sea.

"Where do you want to start?" Antonio asked.

"At five," I said. "But would it be possible for you to fast-forward it?"

The people who appeared and disappeared up and down the long corridors moved along with high-speed bouncing gaits that put me in mind of silent movie days. Because Margaret's Aloha Deck stateroom had been at the very back of the ship, most of the people traversing the corridor stopped well short of her door, which was just to the right of the camera's ceiling-mounted position. Only when someone came all the way down the hallway did I have Antonio slow the action.

At 17:01 Naomi Pepper appeared. Her arrival right then squared with what Naomi had told me earlier. In the tape,

Naomi appeared to knock on the door, which opened to allow her inside. After that, nothing more happened until 17:37, when Naomi emerged. Just outside the door, she paused and then fled, almost running, down the hallway. She had barely disappeared into the elevator alcove when someone else—a uniformed attendant of some kind—appeared in the hallway in front of Margaret's door. Since the man was carrying a tray laden with glasses, silverware, and a covered plate, I assumed he came from Room Service. All I could tell about him was that he seemed to be of fairly slender build. Unfortunately, he held the tray in such a manner that it totally obscured his face from the camera's probing view.

Reaching the door, he made as if to knock. Then, finding the door unlatched, he disappeared inside. As the door closed behind him, the date stamp read 17:43.

"Where the hell did he come from?" I asked. "He just appeared out of nowhere."

"From across the hall," Antonio informed me. "That's a service door with access to the staff elevators."

"Go back several frames," I told him.

One at a time we scrolled through a series of individual frames. The service door opened slightly a full minute after Naomi Pepper entered the room. Then it remained partially ajar until after Naomi disappeared down the hall. Only then did it open far enough for the waiter to step out into the hallway.

After that nothing happened for the next several minutes. At 17:50 the door to Margaret Featherman's room opened once more. Again the man with the tray appeared. Once again

he held it in a strategic-enough fashion that it totally concealed his face. It looked to me as though he was well aware of
the camera's position and had taken care to counter it. Only
as he pulled the door shut behind him did I notice he was
wearing a pair of gloves. Then he dodged into the service door
and disappeared, closing that one behind him as well.

"This is very serious," Antonio breathed. "I will report it
at once."

"I'm sure you will," I said. "What about the staff-access
corridors? Are they subject to video surveillance as well?"

Antonio shook his head. "Too expensive," he said. "The
cameras are located in passenger areas only."

"Too bad," I told him. "It looks to me as though some of
the ship's company is in it for more than just wages and tips.
Thanks for the help."

By then another crewman was standing by to take charge
of me and deliver me back to the purser's desk. Once there, I
was mystified as to what to do next. I resented the idea of the
cruise-ship officers dodging the responsibility for making the
official notification to Margaret Featherman's family. Not
having to deal with grieving family members is one of the
better benefits of being a retired police officer. Nonetheless,
since First Officer Vincente had drafted me for the job, I figured I'd better get started.

"Dr. Harrison Featherman's cabin, please," I said.

This time there was a young woman behind the counter.
"If you would please step to a house phone . . ." Before she
could go any further into the standard security spiel, my uniformed escort whispered a few discreet words in her ear. She
nodded and, without another word, tapped a few swift key

strokes into her computer terminal "Of course, Mr. Bowman. Dr. Featherman's suite is on Bahia eight-four-eight."

My name's Beaumont, not Bowman, I wanted to growl at her, but I didn't. Instead, I dutifully headed for the elevator lobby and for Dr. Harrison Featherman's stateroom. Official or not, here I was cast in the unpleasant role of bearer of bad tidings. When Margaret went overboard, the *Starfire Breeze* might have been close enough to land for her to swim to safety, but that didn't strike me as a very likely outcome. Vincente wanted me to say Margaret was "missing" only, not "missing and presumed drowned." But it seemed to me that, after hearing the news, Margaret's relations would be obliged to draw their own conclusions. And maybe, as far as Harrison Featherman was concerned, the loss of a troublesome ex-wife wouldn't be such bad news after all.

Predictably, when I reached Harrison Featherman's cabin, the doctor himself was out. However, the current Mrs. Featherman—the beguiling and exceedingly pregnant Leila—was in. For some reason, the name I couldn't recall the day before when I was looking at the gallery of pictures on the Promenade Deck came back to me now as soon as I heard her voice.

"My husband isn't here just now," she said, opening the door far enough to peer out at me. "Can I help you?"

"My name is Beaumont," I said, barely managing to suppress the recently amputated "Detective" part. "J. P. Beaumont."

"What is this concerning?" Leila asked.

Behind me two couples, returning from shore and laden with bulging shopping bags, came crowding noisily down the corridor. "It's private," I murmured. "May I come in?"

Leila opened the door and beckoned me into a junior suite that was somewhat larger than mine. On a table in the corner the remains of a solitary lunch awaited the arrival of a Room Service attendant who would eventually come and retrieve the tray. Mrs. Featherman wore a long, flowing caftan made of some kind of gauzy turquoise material that drifted around her as she moved, softening her ungainly, pregnancy-imposed waddle. Motioning me onto the sofa, she used the bedside table for support before taking a seat on the edge of the rumpled bed.

"What's so private?" Leila asked.

"First tell me if you know where your husband is and when he's expected back. My business is really with him."

"He was planning to go ashore. Since I'm not at my energetic best these days, I decided to stay on the ship. I would have just slowed him down."

"Slowed him down?" I asked.

Leila nodded. "He was looking for someone," she said.

"For his former wife—for Margaret?"

Leila nodded again.

"Do you have any idea when he'll be back?"

"We're due to sail soon. I'm sure he'll be back on board before then."

I knew from reading that morning's *Starfire Courier* that our expected departure from the dock in Juneau was at 6 P.M.—eighteen hundred hours—with all passengers due back on the ship at least half an hour prior to that.

"He may already be back on board," Leila continued. "But just because he's on the ship doesn't mean he'll come straight here. We don't eat dinner until the second seating. He likes to spend these pre-dinner hours visiting with some of his fellow physicians. They may be hanging out in one of the bars. They tend to congregate in the cigar lounge. The warnings about smoking and health don't apply to them, you see," she added with a smile.

Her casual use of irony surprised me. An ironical view of the world usually comes only with advancing age. It's something I would have expected from someone far older than Leila Featherman.

"Wouldn't he call to let you know he was back on board?" I asked.

"We don't find it necessary to keep track of each other's every movement," she replied. "The two of us don't have that kind of relationship."

If past behavior is any indication, you probably should, I thought.

"You still haven't told me what this is about," Leila pointed out.

"Where was your husband last night between five and six?"

"I have no idea. As I told you before, we're second seating. I run out of energy so easily these days that I decided to get some rest before dinner. I closed off the door between the bedroom and the sitting room, put on my night-blinders, and went to asleep. Harry was here when I went to sleep, and he was here later on, when I woke up. I would imagine he was here the whole time, but I have no way of knowing that for sure. He may very well have nipped out for a smoke. Why?"

While I considered whether or not to tell her, Leila figured it out on her own. Realization spread slowly across her face. "Wait a minute," she said. "Does this have something to do with Margaret's disappearance?"

Once put that way, there was little point in dodging the issue. I had been sent to deliver the bad news, and so I did—to Leila Featherman rather than to Harrison himself.

"We have reason to believe that Margaret Featherman fell overboard late yesterday afternoon."

"Overboard," Leila echoed. "You mean she's dead then?"

"We don't know that for sure," I said. "It appears that we were fairly close to shore at the time it happened. If she was conscious when she hit the water, she may have managed to swim to safety. Or, barring that, someone may have spotted her and picked her up."

"But if she'd been found, wouldn't we have heard by now?" Leila asked. "Wouldn't someone have let us know?"

I nodded, and it was true. News stories of daring rescues at sea are usually blared around the world within a matter of minutes.

Leila's hand went to her mouth. "Margaret dead," she repeated. "It's hard to believe."

"Remember," I cautioned. "At this point, we're not positive she's dead."

Leila sighed. "Personally, I can't say that I'm sorry. But this is going to be tough on Harry. Very tough. And on Chloe, too, especially after the big scene at dinner the other night. Have you spoken to her?"

"To Chloe? No, I came looking for Dr. Featherman first."

"Well, she's right next door," Leila said. With the help of

the table, Leila pushed herself to her feet. "I'm sure she'll want to know what's happened. Wait here while I go get her."

Leaving the cabin door propped open with the dead bolt, Leila went out into the corridor. I heard a knock, followed by the unintelligible exchange of murmuring voices. Moments later, Leila and Chloe came into the room where I was. Seeing the two young women together, it was difficult to imagine how one could be the other's stepmother.

Chloe came straight to where I sat and stared down at me in wide-eyed disbelief. I thought she'd recognize me as one of the people who had been seated at her mother's table two nights earlier, but there was no visible sign of recognition.

"You say my mother is dead?" she demanded. Her skin was flushed. Her breath came in short hard gasps, as though she'd just finished running the thousand-yard dash.

"As I told Mrs. Featherman, your mother is missing. We don't know for sure that she's dead. From the point where she went overboard, it's possible she could have made it to shore safely."

"But how can you know where that was?"

"Because we know the exact time she went into the water, and the ship's GPS—global positioning system—keeps track of where the ship is at any given time. The Coast Guard has been notified and is launching search-and-rescue missions toward Port Walter, your mother's last-known position. If she's still alive, they'll find her."

"What if she's dead?"

"They'll find her then, too. It's entirely possible that she'll wash up on shore."

"From the middle of the ocean?"

"As I said, we weren't in the middle of the ocean," I responded. "We were near land. It was after we entered Chatham Strait and while the ship had slowed to whale-watch. Was your mother a swimmer?"

Chloe nodded. "She swam very well. She did two miles every morning in the lap pool at her condo."

If Margaret was a two-mile-a-day swimmer, that made it more likely that she might possibly have made it to shore. "Well, then," I said. "Let's hope for the best. To me it didn't look all that far."

"You're saying you saw it happen?" Chloe demanded. "Were you there?"

"No, I wasn't. Your mother's fall was captured on film by the ship's security camera. I've just come from seeing the video."

"And you're sure it was Mother?" Chloe asked.

"I'm sure," I said.

Chloe paled. Reaching out, she grasped Leila's arm and allowed herself to be guided over to the bed. "If she fell off the ship, she must be dead," Chloe whispered. "But I can hardly believe it's true, that something like this could happen. It sounds like a terrible practical joke."

"It's no joke, Chloe," Leila said gently. "The first officer sent Mr. Beaumont to tell us. To tell your father, really. But since Harry wasn't here, I thought you'd want to know about it right away."

I had seen Chloe Featherman two nights earlier with her eyes narrowed in fury, trying to stare down her mother. Now, for a brief period at least, Chloe Featherman managed to achieve the look of a grieving daughter. She spent the next several minutes weeping inconsolably while Leila Featherman held her and comforted her as best she could. At last, Chloe quit crying long enough to take a ragged breath.

"Tell me again," she managed. "When did it happen and how?"

"We don't know the how of it," I told her. "Not yet, at least. There'll be an official investigation, of course. We do know when it happened. There's a time stamp on the security camera film that gives the exact moment. She went overboard late yesterday afternoon—at seventeen forty-seven."

"What time is that in real time?" Chloe asked.

"Five forty-seven P.M." I said.

"Was there a note?"

"A note?"

"A suicide note."

It hadn't occurred to me that Margaret Featherman was suicidal. Mean as hell, but not suicidal. People intent on killing themselves generally look for privacy. They don't knock themselves off while visitors are popping in and out of the room. And I've never yet known a suicide who donned a layer of duct tape before pulling the trigger or driving into a bridge abutment. But suicide was Chloe's first assumption, and I was kind enough to let her keep it for the time being. Besides, when it came time for a wholesale homicide investigation, use of that duct tape might well be a detail the FBI would want to keep as a holdback.

What followed was an astonishing transformation in Chloe Featherman's demeanor. Her tears dried up as abruptly as if she had turned off a faucet. Pallor was replaced by flush as uncompromising anger displaced Chloe's initial spate of grief.

"That bitch!" she exclaimed. "That incredible bitch! Mother's gone and killed herself, and what better place could she have chosen than on a cruise ship where my father is involved in a major conference? Just think of the audience— some of Dad's most prestigious colleagues, noted neurologists from all across the nation. Think of the headlines that'll grab! And when better to do it than when Dad is on the verge of nailing down a stupendous grant? There's bound to be a scandal after that kind of thing, and everybody in the business knows that people who write checks for grants are scared to death of scandals. They're petrified of even the whiff of a scandal.

"Now that I think about it, the whole thing makes perfect sense. It's exactly the kind of stunt Mother would pull. She hates Dad so much that she'd do anything to hurt him, to discredit him. After all, that's why she came on this ship in the first place. She was looking for anything she could find that would make the grant proposal blow up in Dad's face."

"Come on, Chloe," Leila Featherman said gently. "I'm sure you don't mean that."

That one kind remark was enough to make Chloe turn the full force of her anger on Leila. "Don't you start, too. I'd have thought you'd be the last person to jump to Mother's defense."

"If she's dead, she's dead, Chloe," Leila responded patiently. "I can't imagine that she would do such a terrible thing just to spite your father. Yes, I know Margaret was a troubled person, but she wasn't crazy. I don't believe even she would go to such lengths just to mess up one of your father's business deals."

"You may not be able to imagine it, but I can," Chloe returned grimly. "She's my mother. I happen to know her a whole lot better than you do. Where's Dad?"

Leila sighed. "I don't know. He went ashore early this afternoon—looking for your mother. He thought she might have slipped off the ship and gone to some of the galleries. I'm sure he's back on board by now. My guess is he stopped off in the cigar lounge to have a smoke."

Chloe leaped to her feet. "I'm going to go find him," she declared. Leila reached out to stop her, but Chloe shrugged away from Leila's restraining grasp.

"Dad deserves to know about this sooner rather than later," Chloe continued determinedly. "I'm sure the whole ship is alive with gossip. I'm going to find him and tell him now, before somebody else does."

"Really, Chloe. Do you think that's wise?" Leila asked. "Wouldn't it be better to wait here until he comes back? That way we could all be together when he finds out, and that way he'll be able to hear the news in private rather than in one of the bars, with everyone around him being able to hear whatever's being said. I'm afraid this is going to be very hard on him."

"What do you want to do?" Chloe returned. "Wait long enough so he can read all about it in tomorrow morning's *Starfire Courier*? No way! I'm going to find him and tell him now. Do you want to come along?"

Leila shook her head. "I'll wait here," she said.

Chloe left, slamming the door shut behind her. Having accomplished my mission, I stood up too and made as if to follow. "I'd best be going then as well," I said.

"Oh, no, please, Mr. . . ."

"Beaumont," I supplied.

"Please stay, Mr. Beaumont. In case Chloe doesn't find Harry, I'd like to have someone official here to tell him. I don't want to be the one to have to do it."

I couldn't blame her there. That was probably the time when I should have told Leila Featherman that I wasn't really official at all—that I'd been drafted off the street and sent to do the cruise ship's dirty work because First Officer Vincente hadn't wanted to soil his own lily-white hands performing the job himself. But I didn't say anything of the kind. My mother's fondest hope was always that I would grow up to be a "good boy." I tried being a good boy right then, and did as I was told. Even though my instincts warned me to get the hell out, I sat back down, put my hands in my lap, and waited for Harrison Featherman to return.

10

FOR THE LONGEST TIME after Chloe left, Leila and I sat in the gathering darkness without exchanging a word. Leila was the one who broke the silence, speaking musingly, as if talking more to herself than to me.

"What I said is true. Margaret's a very troubled woman. Troublesome, too, although I suppose that's what all second wives say about first wives. Still, I can't believe that she'd go so far as to commit suicide just to spite Harry. What do you think?"

I remembered the duct-tape mask that had covered the lower part of Margaret Featherman's face as she tumbled toward the sea and the two people who had been in her stateroom at or near the time of her fatal plunge. "I'm of the opinion that she didn't commit suicide," I said.

"Her death was an accident then?" Leila asked.

"More like murder," I replied.

Leila gave a sharp intake of breath, followed by another period of thoughtful silence. This time I was the one who broke it.

"You mentioned that you thought learning about Margaret's death would be hard on your husband," I said finally. "Why? Is it because of what might happen to Dr. Featherman's pending grant as a result of the adverse publicity, or is it because he still cares for her?"

Leila laughed ruefully. "Harry still cares for Margaret, all right," she said. "Just the fact that they continue to drive one another crazy is proof enough of that. People assume that hate and love are opposites, Mr. Beaumont, but they're really very closely related. Love and indifference, maybe, but not love and hate. If you don't care one way or the other—if you're really over a relationship—the other person can no longer hurt you."

I was struck by the wisdom in Leila's observation. To all outward appearances the second Mrs. Featherman was just another youthful trophy wife. But there was more depth to her than I had first supposed.

"You're saying Margaret could still hurt Harry?" I asked.

Using Harrison Featherman's pet name gave me pause. Everyone else who mentioned the man referred to him as Harrison. They all seemed dazzled by the Harrison persona or else by the title of doctor. Only his second wife, this young and very pregnant second wife, had burrowed under the formal name and title to excavate a man named Harry who seemed to live a hidden existence beneath the formal pomp and circumstance.

"Yes," Leila answered. "Margaret was forever taunting Harry. She specialized in showing herself off with men who were far younger than she was. Initially, I think I was Harry's way of getting back at her for that. Tit for tat, you know." Leila smiled. "But I knew going into the relationship that there was still unfinished business between them. It doesn't bother me, and it doesn't mean I love Harry any less or that he doesn't love me. Harry's been very good to me, Mr. Beaumont. Even now, when there's so much going on and he's under such awful stress, he's still made every effort to see to it that if anything were to happen to him, the baby and I would be well provided for. Chloe, too, for that matter."

"If anything were to happen . . ." I said. "What exactly do you mean by that?"

It was too dark to see Leila's face across the room, but I heard wariness creep into her voice. "You know," she said softly. "If Harry were to die or something."

She hadn't come right out and said it, but I was pretty sure I knew what she meant. "As in, if something terrible happened to Harry the same way it has to some of the other doctors on the list."

Leila breathed an audible sigh of relief. "I'm glad to hear you know about that," she declared. "It really wears me down to be worried sick about him and to have to keep pretending that nothing is the matter. At night I toss and turn and can hardly sleep. I jump at every sound. Even here on this ship. Especially on the ship," she added softly. "I know they told us that there'd be people on board to protect him, but still . . . It's such close quarters that I can't help but worry."

"How long have you known about this?" I asked.

"About the list? Not long," she answered. "For only three weeks or so, but it feels like forever. Harry's been so brave about it, but he's also mad as can be that someone is interfering with his life and his wishes. He's a doctor, you know, and he's determined to carry on and do everything just the way he did before and act as though nothing is the matter. He refuses to give in to those people—refuses to be intimidated by them. It scares me to death, but it makes me proud, too."

The white-haired guy I had seen ranting on the dance floor had struck me as an overbearing jerk, but Leila Featherman saw her husband as a hero and loved him to distraction. Jerk or not, Harrison was incredibly lucky to have a wife who was smart enough to recognize that he had feet of clay and loyal enough to love him in spite of them. Right at that moment, I had no doubt that Leila Featherman loved her husband with every ounce of her being—loved him so much that she even worried about how he would handle the disturbing news of his ex-wife's apparent death.

"Have any more died?" Leila asked. "Any more of the doctors on the list? That's what you FBI guys are supposed to be doing, isn't it—protecting the doctors?"

I guess I'm a little slow on the uptake sometimes. It wasn't until then that I finally realized Leila Featherman had somehow jumped to the erroneous conclusion that J. P. Beaumont was an agent with the FBI. I was about to tell her otherwise when there was a click in the lock and Harrison Featherman let himself into the room, turning on the light as he did so. He smiled at Leila. "Why are you sitting here in the dark?" he asked. As soon as he saw me, the smile faded.

"Who are you?" he asked.

"It's Mr. Beaumont, Harry," Leila answered for me. "He's with the FBI. Did Chloe find you?"

"Chloe? No. Why? Was she looking for me?"

"Please sit," she said, patting the bed beside her. "Something terrible has happened."

Harrison Featherman did as he was told and sat on the edge of the bed next to his wife. "What?" he asked, then paled. "Not Marc. Please, God, don't tell me something awful's happened to Marc Alley."

"Not Marc, Harry," Leila said gently. "It's Margaret. She fell overboard late yesterday afternoon. Mr. Beaumont here came to give us the news. He seems to think it's likely that she's dead."

Harrison Featherman whole body shuddered as though he'd received a physical blow. "Margaret dead?" he rasped. "What do you mean, she fell off the ship?"

"Just that. Mr. Beaumont said she went overboard at five forty-seven yesterday afternoon."

"You're saying she drowned?"

"We don't know that for sure," I hedged. "Depending on what kind of swimmer she is, she may have made it to safety."

"Margaret's an excellent swimmer," Harrison Featherman declared. "But that doesn't mean much when you go overboard while you're at sea."

"We weren't at sea," I told him. "We were in Chatham Strait, just off Port Walter, when it happened."

"You're saying people on this ship know exactly where we were when she fell in?"

"Yes."

"Then why the hell didn't they do something about it at the time—like send out lifeboats or call in the Coast Guard. Why are we hearing about it now, more than twenty-four hours after it happened?"

"Because none of the ship's crew was aware of what had happened until today, when they were reviewing the security tapes. Her fall was captured on one of them."

Harrison stood up and strode over to the desk, where he picked up the telephone. "This is unbelievable!"

"What are you doing?" Leila asked.

"I'm going to call the Coast Guard and ask for a search team. We've got to try to find her."

"Please, Dr. Featherman," I assured him. "Captain Giacometti has already handled that. Search and Rescue units are already on their way."

Sighing, Harrison Featherman put down the phone and returned to the bed. He sat down beside Leila, who leaned against him and began rubbing his back. Two fat tears dribbled down the man's cheeks. He brushed them away with a single angry swipe.

"Margaret can't be gone," he said. "She may have been a royal pain in the ass, but she still had so damned much to offer." Then another thought crossed his mind. He looked at me and frowned.

"She was messing around with Marc Alley. Is there a chance someone was really after Marc and got to Margaret by mistake? I saw her dancing with him. I'm sure she was going to take him to bed. That's what she usually did with her young studs." Harrison Featherman's voice cracked as he said the words.

I could see that Leila was right. Margaret's death did grieve the man, but so did the fact that his ex-wife had been dancing with Marc Alley and was maybe about to get it on with him as well. In fact, listening to Harrison Featherman right then, I couldn't tell which of the two situations bothered him more. The fact that he was upset and complaining about Margaret's possible dalliance with Marc in the presence of his own young wife didn't escape me, but it was evidently lost on him.

About that time there was a loud knock on the door. Not the gentle, polite tap of an arriving room attendant, but the firm, in-your-face kind of knock administered by cops the world over. I recognized it. I've used that knock myself time and again.

"Todd Bowman," a voice in the corridor announced as soon as Leila Featherman opened the door. "I'm with the FBI. Is Dr. Featherman in?"

As soon as I heard the name it all made perfect sense. Beaumont and Bowman. First Officer Vincente had misheard my name and had assumed that I was the FBI agent sent to investigate Margaret Featherman's disappearance. No wonder he had treated me like visiting royalty. No wonder he had taken me, no questions asked, into the bowels of the ship and made me privy to that initial viewing of the security tape. No wonder he had asked me to notify Dr. Featherman of his ex-wife's possibly fatal mishap. It was all a case of mistaken identity, and I was in deep water.

Without even glancing in my direction, Bowman turned

his attention full on Harrison Featherman. "I'm so sorry . . ." he began.

"Don't bother. I know all about it," Harrison said impatiently, waving in my direction. "He already told me."

Bowman turned to me. "And you are?" he asked.

"Beaumont," I said. "J. P. Beaumont."

"Don't you two know each other?" Leila Featherman asked. "I mean, you do work together, don't you?"

"No," I said. My voice sounded very small. "We don't."

"You don't?" Leila looked puzzled. "But I thought . . . When you came to tell us . . ."

"When he came to tell you what?" Todd Bowman asked.

"About Margaret. I just assumed he was with the FBI. I mean, he knew about the list and everything."

Todd Bowman sighed. "Oh," he said. "That's all right then. I'm sure he's working the list detail. First Officer Vincente told me there were other agents on board, but I didn't think we'd be running into each other like this." He offered me his hand. "Glad to meet you, Beaumont. And since you've already made the official notification, then there's no need for me to do it."

"Right," I agreed. I stood up and sidled toward the door. "But now that you're here, I'll be going. It's probably best if I don't hang around."

Bowman nodded. "You're right. I'll catch up with you later in case we need you."

On my way down the corridor, I broke into a cold sweat. In my own mind, I hadn't been impersonating a federal officer, at least not intentionally. But I didn't see how I'd be able to convince a federal prosecutor that was the case. Not in a million years.

Back in my stateroom I went out onto the lanai and stood there. It was dark, and I could see the phosphorescent glow of water kicked up and disturbed by the ship's passing. Despite myself, I couldn't keep from imagining what that horrific plunge must have been like for Margaret Featherman. My cabin was on the Capri Deck. Hers had been on Aloha—three decks closer to the water. Still, even from Aloha, it was a very long fall into the sea—the same as falling off the top of a building that was four or five stories tall.

So who was responsible? Instinct told me that neither Leila Featherman nor her husband had anything to do with Margaret's fall or death, whichever it was. I regard myself as a fairly good judge of human behavior and character. The news had rocked them both. And they had both grasped eagerly at any suggestion that Margaret might still be alive. I had been only too glad to leave them with that small glimmer of hope. It was true, the Coast Guard might still find her, but in the privacy of my own mind a happy outcome didn't seem likely. I was pretty well convinced the only thing successful searchers would bring home with them would be Margaret Featherman's body-bagged mortal remains.

I considered Harrison's initial reaction, before he knew the bad news was about Margaret. His first concern had been that whatever had happened might have had to do with Marc Alley. And then, later on, even after he knew Margaret was the victim, he had wondered if perhaps Marc had been the killer's real target. As far as I was concerned, the duct tape pretty well ruled that out. This wasn't a case of mistaken identity. Whoever had wrapped Margaret's face in tape had known the person they were dealing with or at least the person they *thought* they were dealing with.

There was a possibility that with three separate parties named Featherman on board the ship, the hit man—I was convinced the person carrying the tray had been male—might have gotten the staterooms confused. He might have gone to Margaret's cabin thinking it was Harrison and Leila's cabin and had thrown the woman he found there into the water believing Margaret was Harrison's current wife rather than his first one.

How likely is that? I wondered.

Well, cases of mistaken identity seemed to be running rampant on the *Starfire Breeze*. There was my current Bowman/Beaumont problem, for one thing. And then I remembered how, on that first night, a fax addressed to Margaret Featherman had mistakenly been delivered to Chloe, her daughter. If someone from the ship's crew could make that kind of error, couldn't a killer mix things up as well? Besides, anyone who still thinks crooks are smart hasn't spent the last twenty-odd years dealing with them.

If that was what had happened—if the Leave It To God folks had mixed up whose cabin was whose—Marc Alley was still in danger and still out of the loop. I tried calling Rachel Dulles' cabin to discuss the situation with her and see what she thought, but there was no answer, and I didn't feel comfortable leaving a message for her on voice mail. *I'll tell Marc at dinner*, I told myself. *That'll be soon enough.*

Later, when I was getting ready to go to dinner, Beverly

called me. The sound of her voice reminded me that now, through their own kindness, they too were involved in something far more serious than simply being good Samaritans. The question was, should I let them go ahead and become involved, or should I warn them away? I felt I had a moral obligation to be straight with them. Besides, Lars had been at the meeting as well. He had heard Lucy's story at the same time I had.

"Lars and I are getting ready to go down and stay with Mike Conyers right now," Beverly was saying cheerfully. "Lucy's about to leave for the second seating in the Regal Dining Room, so we need to be at their cabin as soon as possible."

"Wait," I said, making up my mind. "Let me come down and talk to you before you go."

"I don't see why that's necessary—"

"Believe me, Beverly, it is. Just wait for me, please. I'll be there in a couple of minutes."

The elevators were crowded with people going to dinner. I hustled down the stairway instead. "So what's this all about?" Lars asked when he opened the door to let me into their stateroom.

"If you're going to get involved in this, you should know that Mike Conyers wasn't making it up," I told them. "He really did see someone fall in the water. Her name was Margaret Featherman, and it happened at five forty-seven yesterday afternoon, about the time everyone else on board was looking at that pod of whales. Her fall was captured on one of the ship's video cameras, but no one other than Mike actually saw what happened until today—this afternoon, when we reviewed the tape."

"Why, forevermore!" Beverly breathed. "I can hardly believe it."

"Where'd it happen?" Lars asked.

"In Chatham Strait," I said. "Near Port Walter."

"That's good, then," Lars said at once. Suddenly he was all business and know-how. "The shipping lanes through there aren't all that far from shore. If she's a halfway decent swimmer, she might have made it to land. I remember there's an old cannery at Port Walter with a bunch of old buildings where she could have gone inside and dried off. And then there's the fish-and-game station. That's a year-round outfit. She could have gone there for help, too. Has anyone contacted them yet?"

"The captain's been in touch with the Coast Guard on that," I said.

Lars nodded. "Good, good," he said. "What was she, drunk? Had a few too many and fell off her balcony?"

I took a deep breath. Not only had I impersonated an officer, here I was about to divulge supposedly confidential pieces of a homicide investigation. "It wasn't an accident," I said.

"You're saying it's murder then?" Beverly asked.

I nodded. "I saw her fall," I said. "Someone had covered her mouth with duct tape."

"Ya, sure," Lars said. "Sounds like murder all right."

"And here's my concern," I added. "There were a lot of people in that meeting this afternoon, Lars. Eventually word is bound to get out that someone really did go overboard about the time Mike said he saw it. Once that happens, someone else may make the same connection I did. What if word gets back to the killer that there's a witness? They'll have no way of knowing all Mike saw was someone falling past the camera."

"I get it," Lar's said. "You're thinking the killer may think Mike Conyers saw all of what happened and come after him as well."

"You mean Mike Conyers could be in danger as well?" Beverly asked. "But I've talked to his wife. The poor man's not even all there. He couldn't possibly testify, could he?"

"No. But the killer may not be aware of that."

"Should we warn Lucy?" Lars asked.

"I don't know," I said. "She's already got a whole lot on her plate. How much more do you think the woman can stand?"

"Women are a whole lot tougher than men realize," Beverly interjected. "She needs to know exactly what she's up against. If one of you men won't tell her, then I will."

Lars nodded. "Beverly's right," he said. "We should tell her."

"Go ahead then. Except for the duct tape. I'm sure the FBI is going to want that as a holdback."

"A what?" Beverly asked.

"It's a detail of the crime known only to the investigators and to the killer. I probably shouldn't have told you, either. But I have."

"We'll keep it quiet," Lars said grimly. "Won't we, honey bun."

Beverly smiled at him and nodded. I noticed she was wearing a different dress, but she was once again wearing her new peace-offering brooch.

"I'll let you get going, then," I said, backing toward the

door. "But wait a minute. You called me a few minutes ago. Was there something you needed?"

"Oh, that's right," Beverly said. "A bunch of us are going to go on that narrow-gauge White Pass train ride in Skagway tomorrow. We were wondering if you'd want to go along."

I didn't know there was a narrow-gauge train ride in Skagway. "I hadn't really given it much thought," I admitted.

"Lars wants to do that, and so do the girls . . ."

"The girls?" I asked.

"You know, the Wakefield girls, Claire and Florence. We're going to see if Lucy and Mike would like to go, too. I know she's worried about Mike being a problem, but if we're all along to lend a hand, we should be able to handle whatever comes up."

I glanced at Lars, who nodded. "Might be a good idea," he agreed. "Just in case."

With both of them asking, there wasn't much chance of my turning them down. "Sure," I said cheerfully. "That's what I'm here for—the just-in-cases."

"Good," she said. "Once we talk to Lucy, I'll go right up to the tour desk and purchase the tickets so we won't have to worry about that in the morning. I'll leave a message about departure times. I understand the train runs several times a day. I'll try to get us on one of the earlier ones."

No surprises there. "Good," I said. "See you in the morning."

"But wait," Beverly said, before I managed to make it out the door. "What about that nice woman who was with you this morning in Juneau. What was her name again?"

"Naomi Pepper."

"Right," Beverly said. "Will Naomi be joining us? She's more than welcome to, you know."

"I doubt it," I said. "I imagine she's already made other plans."

I went back up to the Promenade Deck and wandered once again through the photo gallery, picking up copies of Lars and Beverly's formal-dinner pictures as well as a copy of the one taken at Margaret Featherman's table, the one where Margaret wasn't there.

Sitting in the Sea Breeze Bar and waiting for the dining-room doors to open, I studied the picture closely. By the time the photographer had shown up, dinner was over and we were all about to enjoy our specially ordered raspberry soufflés. By then Margaret Featherman had long since taken her terrible plunge into the drink, and somehow, knowing that made me feel incredibly sad. Treating us all to those soufflés had been Margaret Featherman's one last chance to show off. Too bad she hadn't been there to enjoy it.

Marc and I both looked uncomfortable and stupid. The three women all looked great. Beverly was right when she said women were tough. Less than four hours had elapsed since Naomi's awful confrontation with Margaret. According to her, she had fled Margaret's room in tears, but here she was smiling for the camera and looking completely at ease. I looked up and glanced around the room, hoping to catch sight of Naomi or Virginia and Sharon and wondering how they had all fared after Naomi's afternoon revelation.

Slipping the pictures back in the plastic bag, I sat and thought about Naomi Pepper some more. I remembered how upset she had been when I had first mentioned the presence of the security cameras. And I remembered, too, her pause just outside Margaret Featherman's door before she had retreated down the hall.

She hadn't pulled the door all the way shut, and that open door had allowed the man waiting across the hall to have unannounced access into Margaret's cabin. Had that been a deliberate act on Naomi's part, or was it simply an oversight? I wondered. It was possible that she had been so upset that she had simply failed to notice that the door hadn't closed and that had turned out to be a waiting killer's lucky break. Or had she known someone was lying in wait just across the corridor and left the door open on purpose?

Much as I didn't like it, I had to admit that was a possibility. And by the time they finally opened the doors to the Crystal Dining Room, I went in along with everyone else, but I wasn't the least bit hungry.

11

IN THE CRYSTAL DINING ROOM, Margaret Featherman's table was set for six, but it was totally empty
when I arrived. Marc Alley came rushing in a few minutes
later. He was flushed and out of breath.

"Did you hear what happened?" he asked, as Reynaldo
passed him his linen napkin. "To Margaret, I mean?"

I played dumb. I guess I wanted to know how much Marc
Alley knew without my having to tell him. "What?" I asked.

Marc waited until Reynaldo turned away. "They say she
fell overboard yesterday afternoon," he confided in a whisper.
"I overheard two of the ship's officers talking about it just
now, out in the lobby. They were speaking Italian. I don't
guess it ever occurred to them that one of the American
passengers might actually *understand* Italian. They seemed

pretty shocked when I asked them about it directly. As soon as I did, they clammed up and said they weren't allowed to discuss it."

Joaô, Reynaldo's assistant waiter, came around, poured Marc's water, and took our drink orders. "And where are the lovely ladies this evening?" he asked with a smile. "Will they be joining you?"

The news about Margaret Featherman may have been common knowledge among some members of the crew, but it must not have filtered down to the dining-room staff. "I have no idea," I told him. "No idea at all."

Shaking his head, Joaô went on his way.

"What could have happened?" Marc asked as soon as Joaô was out of earshot. "Do you think it was an accident?" he asked. "Or do you think she may have committed suicide?"

"If Margaret Featherman is dead, I doubt it was either an accident or suicide," I told him.

"Murder then?" Marc asked. I nodded. Marc had lifted his water glass to his mouth. Now he set it back down on the table without taking a drink. "Why do you say that?" he asked.

"I saw the tape," I said. Then, realizing that could be taken either way, I added, "The videotape."

"Of her falling?" I nodded. "But how did you see it?" he demanded. "And how come, when I asked you a little while ago if you knew what had happened, you pretended to know nothing about it?"

"I was trying to mind my own business," I told him. "As for seeing the tape, it doesn't matter how I saw it. The point is, I did."

"And you don't think it was suicide? Why? Who would have wanted her dead?"

It was time to take the bull by the horns. "Marc," I said. "Not only do I think Margaret was murdered, I also have reason to believe that the same people who killed her may try to kill you as well."

Marc's eyes widened in surprise, but before he could say anything, Reynaldo turned up with menus and our drinks—a glass of Cabernet Sauvignon for Marc and a tonic with a twist for me. By now, most of the other tables were full. Some of the early-arrival diners were already starting in on their appetizers.

"If you don't mind," I said to Reynaldo, "Mr. Alley and I will go ahead and order. The ladies seem to be delayed this evening. If and when they arrive, they'll have to fend for themselves."

Even in the glowing chandelier light of the dining room, I could see Marc's face had turned ashen. "What on earth are you talking about?" he demanded as soon as the two of us were alone once more. I told him what I knew, explaining about Leave It To God in as understandable a manner as I could, although explaining the unexplainable is never easy.

The end of my story was followed by a period of utter silence. I thought Marc was coming to grips with everything I had said, but it turned out I was wrong. Rather than taking what I said into consideration, he rejected it out of hand.

"That's utterly preposterous!" Marc announced when I finished. "You say all the information about Leave It To God and their so-called plot came from the FBI?"

I nodded.

"Well, they probably made up the whole thing," Marc said. "It's the most farfetched story I've ever heard. What a crock!"

Dismayed by his reaction, I tried to argue him out of it. "Nobody made anything up, Marc. You've got to listen to reason. This is a serious situation—a deadly serious situation, and you may be in danger."

"Wait a minute," he said. "Have you ever been down to the Experience Music Project?"

Located at Seattle Center, Microsoft co-founder Paul Allen's baby, a state-of-the-art rock and roll museum, is only a matter of blocks from my Belltown Terrace condo. But Janis Joplin artifacts have never been high on my list of must-sees. "Never," I said.

"Well, I have," Marc returned. "As it happens, I've seen the facsimile edition of the FBI's file on 'Louie, Louie.' That alone runs to well over a hundred pages. If the FBI was dumb enough to try to prove that an indecipherable song was really a far-reaching communist conspiracy, then they're probably also dumb enough to fall for all this crap about somebody called Leave It To God. What I find hard to believe is that you fell for it, too."

"Marc, all I'm asking is that you take this seriously."

"And do what?"

"Keep your eyes open, I suppose," I said. "Don't do anything risky. Don't hang out with anyone you don't know. You could be in danger."

"I've been in danger," Marc Alley replied coldly. "Having

three and four grand-mal seizures a day is dangerous. I could have fallen down in the street and been run over by a Metro bus. Having brain surgery is dangerous. Living life is dangerous. Don't think I'm going to put my new life on hold because some fiction-writing jerk down at the FBI has dreamed up a crazy conspiracy theory about a group of kooks bent on killing doctors and their patients. If any of this were true, don't you think someone from the FBI—someone official—would have told me about it?"

I didn't want to have to come out and tell him the truth—that the FBI had determined that patients were expendable, while their high-profile physicians were not. Meanwhile, Marc's voice had risen in volume so much so that people from nearby tables were glancing curiously in our direction.

"What do you expect me to do about this?" Marc continued without bothering to lower his voice. "Am I supposed to lock myself in my cabin and stay there until we get back home to Seattle? Go from being a passenger to being a prisoner? Not on your life!"

"Marc, all I said is for you to be careful."

"I've spent a lifetime being careful, and I'm sick of it," he retorted. "If somebody from Leave It To God wants to come looking for me, they're welcome. In the meantime, I'm not changing a thing. Now, if you'll excuse me, I don't feel much like eating right now."

With that, he tossed his napkin down over the remains of his half-eaten appetizer and stalked off through the dining room.

Reynaldo appeared at my shoulder. "Was something

wrong with Mr. Alley's food?" he asked with a concerned frown.

"Mr. Alley's food was fine," I told him. "It was the company he found objectionable."

I ate the rest of my meal in solitary splendor, well aware of the sidelong glances from neighboring diners, who were probably wondering by then if I was a kind of Typhoid Johnny carrying some horrible germ that had sickened all my companions. I had about decided to forgo dessert and leave when Todd Bowman came striding into the dining room. With help from the maître d', the FBI agent zeroed in on my table. The thunderous expression on his face told me things were about to go from bad to worse.

Todd's was a formidable presence. He's one of those weight-lifting characters with a twenty-inch bull neck that comes with a set of massive shoulders and biceps to match. Glowering at me, he looked pissed as hell.

"Did you get a charge out of impersonating a federal officer, Mr. Beaumont?" He took a seat without bothering to observe any of the social niceties like saying hello or waiting to be asked.

"Look," I said in what sounded to me like a calm, placating fashion. "What happened was simply a matter of mistaken identity. When I told the attendant at the purser's desk who I was, he must have heard Beaumont as Bowman. It's an easy mistake. No harm done."

"No harm?" Bowman snarled. "How can you say 'No harm'? I've just come from speaking to Captain Giacometti. He's torqued beyond belief and of the opinion that the FBI is an agency made up entirely of morons. He's quite unhappy that someone who wasn't a sworn FBI agent was allowed access to highly sensitive material. He bristles at the idea that an ordinary passenger was made privy to the ship's security tapes. I personally am ticked off that you, Mr. Beaumont, took it upon yourself to notify Margaret Featherman's family about the nature of her disappearance. Where the hell do you get off, and who do you think you are?"

Bowman was big, and he was also young. Like Rachel Dulles, he couldn't have been much older than his late twenties or early thirties. Sitting there bristling with anger, he looked more like a petulant high school football player than like a self-respecting FBI agent. *When did FBI agents get to be so young?* I wondered. *Or else, when did I get so old?*

"First Officer Vincente asked me to make the notifications, so I did," I told him.

"Of course he did," Bowman replied. "He asked you because he was under the mistaken impression that you were a member of the FBI. And it sounds to me as though you did nothing at all to disabuse him of that notion. Did it ever occur to you that the way he was treating you was rather unusual?"

The truth was, it had occurred to me at the time it was happening. It had seemed odd that First Officer Vincente was treating me like visiting royalty and taking me to parts of the ship that should have been off-limits to fare-paying passengers. But even if I had understood what was happening at the time, I doubt I would have mentioned it. At that moment, I had been far too intent on finding out exactly what had happened. First Officer Vincente and I both had wanted to know for certain what Mike Conyers had witnessed. Had he seen a real body go overboard, or had he made up the whole story?

Not wanting to get as worked up as Bowman was, I took a calming breath before I answered. "I went to First Officer Vincente because I was in possession of vitally important information concerning one of the ship's passengers who had been reported missing," I replied. "At the time I felt Vincente's treatment of me was entirely warranted—that it was completely in line with the caliber of information I was providing."

"How is it that you happened to be the one in possession of that 'vitally important' information in the first place?" Bowman demanded. "Did you yourself witness Margaret Featherman's fall from the ship?"

"No," I replied. "I did not."

"Who did, then, and how did you find out about it?"

Siccing the likes of Todd Bowman on someone as fragile as Mike Conyers or as stressed out as Lucy Conyers seemed like the last thing on earth I wanted to do, but I didn't see any way around it. Morally and legally I was obligated to tell the FBI investigator everything I knew about the case under investigation.

"Would you care for something to eat, sir?" Reynaldo's timely interruption couldn't have come at a better time.

"No," Bowman growled back at him. "No, thank you," he added as if remembering his manners.

"Something to drink, perhaps?"

"No. Nothing."

"What about you, Mr. Beaumont? Could I interest you in some bananas Foster?"

"Why not?" I said. If Agent Todd Bowman was going to wring my neck, at least I'd die happy.

The waiter moved away from our table while giving his head a regretful shake. I'm sure that, in view of the dwindling number of diners in his section, Reynaldo was seeing his opportunity for generous tips on this cruise disappear as well.

"It's too bad you didn't get here earlier," I said. "If you had, you could have met Marc Alley."

"Who's he?"

"Dr. Harrison Featherman's patient, and, and in the opinion of some ship's gossips, Margaret Featherman's one-night fling on the first night of the cruise. As near as I can tell, the cutting-edge brain surgery techniques Dr. Featherman used to cure Marc's epilepsy were enough to put both of them on the map as far as Leave It To God is concerned."

Todd Bowman's tie looked as though it were about to burst under the pressure of his bulging neck. "How the hell do you know about that?" he demanded.

I decided now was the time to be straight with him. Any delay and anything less would serve only to make matters worse. "Rachel Dulles told me," I said. "She and Alex Freed are working the list detail. She was good friends with my former partner, Sue Danielson. I'm a retired Seattle police officer, Agent Bowman. When Agent Dulles found out I was on the ship and happened to be sitting at the same table with Marc Alley, she contacted me and asked me to help out. And, as far as that's concerned, it looks as though you guys need all you can get."

"What's that supposed to mean?"

"What if LITG let themselves into Margaret's room

thinking it was actually Harrison Featherman's cabin? Just because they made one mistake doesn't mean Featherman is out of danger. I don't think Marc Alley is in the clear, either."

"Dulles and Freed are under orders to protect Dr. Featherman."

"Yes, I know. Protect the doctors at all costs and leave the patients to their own devices. That doesn't sound like such a fair deal to me, and maybe it didn't seem fair to Agent Dulles. Maybe that's why she called me in on it. And I'm serving notice, Agent Bowman. You do what you have to do, but I'm taking it on myself to protect Marc Alley."

"If you interfere any more—"

"Think how it's going to look if this ever comes out—and it will come out eventually—that the FBI saved the doctors and left their patients twisting in the wind. Believe me, John Q. Public is going to be royally pissed. This may be the new FBI, Agent Bowman, but I never heard anyone say that only the rich and powerful are worthy of being protected from domestic terrorism. You can call what I'm doing interference if you like, but in protecting Marc Alley I'm saving the FBI's bacon. Including yours, now that I think about it."

Bowman was one of the new breed of post–O. J. FBI agents. He had been thoroughly trained in procedures, and in spin-doctoring as well. He knew that public relations are everything. My oblique threat to let the FBI's internal policy loose in public was enough to make him back off a little.

"Did I understand you to say that you think Marc Alley and Margaret Featherman had something going?"

"May have had something going," I corrected.

"What about you and Ms. Featherman?"

"Me and Margaret Featherman? Don't make me laugh. She wasn't my type. She couldn't stand me from the moment she laid eyes on me."

"How come?" Bowman asked.

"Why didn't she like me?" I returned. "Probably because I was too old for her. I'm sure she would have liked you just fine. Harrison Featherman told me she went for the studly type. By the way, any word from the Coast Guard?"

Bowman glared at me. For a moment he didn't answer. Finally, with a sigh, he did. "Not yet," he said. "I went back to security with Captain Giacometti and looked at the tape in question one more time. Margaret Featherman took a hell of a fall. You left her former husband with the impression—or the hope, let's say—that she might have survived it. I doubt that's true."

"I doubt it, too," I said. "So at least we agree on something."

"Did you tell Marc Alley about what had happened?" Todd Bowman asked.

"No, I didn't," I replied. "I didn't have to. He's the one who told me. He had heard it from some of the officers on board. They were talking about it in Italian, which Marc happens to understand."

"Great," Bowman said. "Another one of those wonderful little coincidences—similar to the way you found out about the video?"

I ignored his pointed gibe. "What about Margaret's friends? Have you told them?"

"I talked to two of them—Sharon Carson and Virginia Metz. In fact, I was in their cabin up until a few minutes ago.

I waited around for their third roommate, Naomi Pepper, but she never showed up."

There were several very good reasons why Naomi Pepper might have chosen to make herself scarce around their three-women cabin and at the dining-room table as well. What she'd had to tell her friends earlier that afternoon didn't paint a very pretty picture of what close friends do to close friends. Neither did what I had seen of her in the security tape before she ran from Margaret Featherman's doorway and disappeared down the corridor.

Abruptly, Todd Bowman changed the subject. "You still haven't told me how you heard about that videotape," he said.

"At an AA meeting," I told him. "One of the women there, Lucy Conyers, has a husband who's an Alzheimer's patient. He's been sitting glued to his cabin's television set ever since he came on board. He's the one who saw Margaret Featherman go in the water, but since the man's not in total possession of his faculties, his wife assumed he was making things up. She didn't believe him. He claimed someone had thrown Peggy off the ship and would come for him next."

Bowman frowned. "Isn't Peggy a nickname for Margaret? Did he know Margaret Featherman?"

"No chance. According to his wife, the only Peggy he knew was his mother, and she's been dead for years. But he kept harping on the incident and driving his wife crazy. Finally, Lucy, his wife, was so upset about what was going on that she mentioned it at the AA meeting this afternoon. As soon as I heard the story, I was sure there was some connection between what Mike Conyers claimed to have seen and what had happened to Margaret Featherman. I thought right away that the poor guy might not have made it up."

"AA?" Bowman asked. "Isn't that as in drunks? And isn't the stuff that goes on in those meetings supposed to be kept secret?"

Contempt suddenly crept into his voice. I heard him speak with the arch superiority of someone who figures he's forever above needing the services of such mundane things. And right along with his arrogance came something else as well—the babelike innocence of someone who assumes nothing bad will ever happen to him. He naively believed that no evil he might encounter could possibly take such a bite out of his mental resources that he'd choose to dive into the nearest booze bottle looking for relief. And it certainly never occurred to him that later on, once he'd drowned his sorrows, he, too, might be brought low enough to go looking for support meetings in hopes of getting his head screwed back on straight.

For a moment, I envied Agent Todd Bowman both his innocence and arrogance, but it didn't take long for me to get over it. I knew from firsthand experience all the bad stuff that goes along with that killer combination. I was also well aware that in my years in AA I've encountered more than my share of both burned-out cops and burned-out FBI agents.

"I met with Lucy Conyers after the meeting," I told him patiently, giving him a quick lesson in twelve-step ethics. "She gave me permission to talk to the authorities about what her husband had seen. That's the only reason I've told you about it."

By then Todd Bowman had pulled out his notebook, the

same kind of ragged spiral job I used to use myself. "The Conyerses' cabin number?" he asked, holding a stubby pencil at the ready.

"I wouldn't bother trying to see them right now," I added, once I gave him their number. "I'm pretty sure Lucy's at dinner at the moment, up in the Regal Dining Room. But when I saw her earlier this afternoon, she was stretched so thin she was about to fly apart. I understand she made arrangements for someone to look after Mike this evening so she could get out for a while, and I doubt talking to Mike by himself would do anybody any good."

I didn't mention that Mike Conyers' adult baby-sitting service was currently being supplied by my own grandparents. There didn't seem to be much point in telling Todd Bowman that. It would only have made matters worse.

"Anything else?" he asked.

"What if whoever threw Margaret Featherman overboard learns there's a possible witness and comes looking for Mike Conyers?"

"You said yourself the man's not all there, and he wouldn't be much of a witness. There's nothing at all on the tape that reveals the killer's identity."

"The killer doesn't know that," I said.

"Maybe," Todd Bowman allowed dubiously. "What else?"

Here it was. If Leave It To God was responsible for Margaret Featherman's death, then whatever had gone on between her and Naomi Pepper before her death was nothing more than bad coincidence. But if someone else was involved—

someone who was connected to Naomi Pepper and her daughter—then Todd Bowman needed to be aware of what had happened.

"Did you talk to Sharon Carson and Virginia Metz together or individually?" I asked.

"Together. Why?"

"Did they give any reasons as to why Naomi Pepper might not have been with them in their room right then?"

Bowman frowned. "Not really. They just said she was out. Neither one of them seemed to have any idea about where she was or when she'd be back."

"So they didn't mention anything to you about Naomi Pepper's daughter?"

"No. Should they have?"

"Well, since Margaret Featherman's husband, Harrison, also happens to be the father of Naomi Pepper's daughter, they probably should have."

"You mean Margaret was Harrison Featherman's second wife?"

"No. Margaret was Harrison's first wife."

"So where does Naomi Pepper come in? Was she wife number two and Leila is number three?"

I shook my head. "Dr. Featherman evidently fathered a child with Naomi, one of Margaret's closest friends, while he and Margaret were still married. That baby, a girl, is in her late teens now. From the way it sounds, Margaret didn't know a word about this until sometime yesterday afternoon— shortly before she died."

"How shortly?"

"I'd say within a couple of hours. And Naomi was in Margaret's room talking about it within minutes of Margaret's fall."

"How do you know that?"

"Naomi told me so herself."

"How old is the daughter?"

"Eighteen or so—over ten years younger than Harrison and Margaret's daughter, Chloe."

"I suppose you found out about all this by attending another meeting?"

"No," I said. "I'm just the kind of guy people like to confide in."

Agent Bowman rolled his eyes at that. "Sure you are," he said. He pushed his chair back and stood up. By now the dining room was practically empty. Most of the tables had been cleared and reset for breakfast. Reynaldo and Joaô lingered impatiently in the background, waiting to finish clearing our table.

"I guess I'll go see if I can track down Lucy Conyers," Bowman said. "You're probably right. It doesn't sound as though there's much to be gained by talking to her husband. Where will I be able to find you in case I need you?"

"I'll be in my cabin," I said, giving him the number. For that evening, at least, I didn't figure anyone from Margaret Featherman's table would be making the scene in the Twilight Lounge.

"And one more thing," I added as Bowman turned to leave.

"What's that?"

"Did Captain Giacometti say anything to you about a

Room Service attendant visiting Margaret Featherman's room late yesterday afternoon?"

"No."

"If I were you, I'd go back to him and have him show you the Aloha Deck security tape between five and six. You may find it very interesting."

Bowman's eyes narrowed. "I take it you've already seen this tape?"

"I just happened to," I said.

"Another coincidence, I suppose?" he asked.

"Oh, no," I said. "That was no coincidence. I asked to see the tape on purpose, and their security guy was kind enough to show it to me. I can't imagine why they didn't offer to show it to you."

"I can," Todd Bowman muttered. With that he abruptly rose and abandoned the table, leaving me to breathe a sigh of relief at having successfully handed Agent Bowman another likely target for his wrath. Even with the FBI on board and actively pursuing a case, Starfire Cruises was still trying to get away with "under-reporting."

Not a good idea, I told myself. *Not for them, and not for me, either.*

12

I T WASN'T THAT LATE when I got back to my room, but I was bushed. Although the cable-car ride in Juneau had happened during the morning hours of that same day, it now seemed like weeks ago. There had been too many people crammed into the day, too many stories, too much happening. Cruises are supposed to be leisurely. Instead of a vacation, my time on the *Starfire Breeze* was beginning to feel just like work. I stripped off my clothes and lay down on the bed. Closing my eyes, I tried to sort through the jumble of the day's people and events.

By then my concerns about being prosecuted for impersonating a federal officer had pretty well been put to rest. Todd Bowman may have been young and inexperienced, but it seemed to me that he had accepted my explanation and no longer thought what had happened represented deliberate malice on my part. And, other than the last bit about the unauthorized security tape, he had seemed happy with the added information I'd been able to pass along to him. He hadn't even seemed too outraged by learning that Rachel Dulles had tapped me in her effort to keep Marc Alley out of harm's way.

Marc Alley himself was another problem altogether. He hadn't appreciated my warning, and he wasn't likely to pay any attention to it, either. Instead of hearing me out, he had marched off in a huff. What could I do to get back in his good graces? As Marc had stalked away from our table in the Crystal Dining Room, he had clearly been deeply offended. He had undergone an extremely risky surgical procedure in an effort to escape the cocoon imposed by his previous physical disability. I was afraid that my suggestion that he play it safe would yield exactly the opposite effect of what I had intended—that I'd push him into taking more chances rather than fewer.

Good work, Beaumont, I groused at myself. *What do you do for an encore?*

And, with barely a pause, the requested encore appeared in the guise of Naomi Pepper. She had entrusted me with a closely guarded family secret, which I had been obliged to pass along to Todd Bowman. It would have been nice if someone other than me had blown the whistle on her and the fact that Harrison Featherman had fathered the child who had been raised as the daughter of Gary and Naomi Pepper. No such luck. Agent Bowman had said that he had talked to Sharon Carson and Virginia Metz shortly before coming to the dining room looking for me. His obvious surprise at hearing about Melissa Pepper's unorthodox paternity told me that Sharon and Virginia had kept their mouths shut on that score. I probably should have done the same.

What puzzled me was why Sharon and Virginia hadn't mentioned it. Was it because Naomi had lost her nerve that afternoon and hadn't gotten around to telling them her secret? Did they know and were they keeping quiet out of loyalty, or was it because they thought the paternity issue had nothing at all to do with Margaret's going overboard?

I disagreed with them regarding the latter position. Much as I might have liked to blame what had happened on Leave It To God, I knew that Margaret Featherman had taken her plunge within hours of learning of her husband's dalliance with Naomi. No, dalliance wasn't the right word. That implied a level of romantic involvement on one or both sides that Naomi Pepper claimed hadn't existed. According to her, what had passed between her and Harrison Featherman had been little more than a friendly favor.

As soon as that thought crossed my mind, I wondered if it was true. Had Gary and Naomi Pepper paid Harrison Featherman a "stud" fee of some kind in exchange for his sperm donation? Or had he selflessly performed that so-called service strictly out of the goodness of his heart? *Fat chance,* I thought. Tears over his ex-wife's mishap notwithstanding, good old Harrison didn't strike me as a milk-of-human-kindness sort of guy.

Which led me to thinking about Gary Pepper. According to Naomi, her husband had willingly gone along with the whole program. He himself had suggested it. But was that true? How many men would have stood still for, much less encouraged, that kind of a cure for his own infertility and his wife's resulting depression? And how had Gary Pepper felt about the baby once Melissa was born? Had he regarded her as his own and treated her with loving, fatherly pride, or had he dealt with her as an interloper—as someone else's child and not his own? And how much did Harrison Featherman's involvement in their lives contribute to Gary and Naomi Pepper's eventual marital breakup all those years later?

Lying there on my bed, I suspected that the same seeds that had implanted Missy Pepper in her mother's womb had also doomed Gary and Naomi's marriage. Had they known what was coming, they might have realized that paying for artificial insemination using an anonymous donor could have spared them untold grief rather than accepting Harrison's so-called friendly offer.

As I mulled the intertwining fates of those four people, two of whom I had never met, I fell asleep. I had drifted into a deep sleep when the telephone on the bedside table startled me awake. It was pitch-dark in an unfamiliar room. While I fumbled to locate the receiver, I felt a momentary panic. No doubt the caller would report some kind of medical crisis having to do with either Lars or Beverly.

"Beau?" The plaintive female voice that greeted me definitely didn't belong to Beverly Piedmont Jenssen. By the time I located the bedside lamp and managed to switch it on, I had sorted out Naomi Pepper's trembling voice. She was sniffling and sounded as though she'd been crying.

"Can I come see you?" she asked. "Please?"

I had been lying on the bed naked except for a pair of shorts. Once I could see the clock, I saw it was twenty of one.

"Now?" I asked, not very graciously. "It's the middle of the night."

"I've got to talk to someone," she said. "And not on the phone, either. I'm standing here in the lobby by the purser's desk. People are staring at me."

There was a part of me that wanted to say, *So go back to your room.* But I didn't. Naomi sounded far too upset to be given that kind of advice.

"Where are you?" she asked.

"Capri, four-five-four," I told her.

"Good," she said, sounding instantly better. "I'll be right down."

I jumped off the bed and straightened the wrinkled covers. Then I pulled my shirt and pants back on. I was just tying my shoelaces when Naomi Pepper knocked on the door. Some women can cry and look good at the same time. Naomi wasn't one of them. She looked like hell. Her face was red and puffy; her eyes were bloodshot; her makeup, smeared under her eyes, had left a smudgy trail down both cheeks.

When I opened the door, she fell into my arms and sobbed against my shoulders. "What's the matter?" I asked.

I led her into the room and eased her down on the love seat. Then I filled a glass with ice from the ice bucket and poured her some bottled water out of my fridge. If I'd had something stronger, I would have offered her that. She looked as though she could have used it. She gulped the water gratefully and then subsided against the back of the couch while she waited through a full-blown case of hiccups.

"What's wrong?" I asked again when the hiccups finally stopped.

"They told," she said simply.

"Who told what?" I asked.

"Virginia and Sharon," Naomi said, as tears once more welled in her eyes. "I told them about Harrison and me this afternoon, and I swore them to secrecy. But they told anyway. I just spent two hours with an FBI agent named Todd Bowman. He saw the security camera video of me leaving Margaret's room right about the time she went in the water. He didn't come right out and say so, Beau, but I think he believes I killed Margaret. He thinks I had one of the waiters from the ship help me do it."

"Did you?" I asked.

"Of course not. How can you even ask such a thing?" she demanded indignantly.

There were two answers to that question—the short answer and the real one. The real one had to do with a woman named Anne Corley—a woman as lovely as she was dangerous—who had walked into my life one afternoon at a cemetery on Queen Anne Hill and had thrown my whole world into a tailspin. Of all the killers I've ever met, she was the one who absolutely blindsided me. I fell in love with Anne Corley too hard and too fast. At the time there were plenty of red flags, all of which I blithely ignored. I ended up betting everything on Anne's presumed innocence. When I lost, I lost big.

I chose to give Naomi Pepper the short answer. "I'm an ex-cop," I explained. "I spent most of my career at the Seattle Police Department interviewing homicide suspects or murder victims' grieving family members and friends. Someone who admits to having had a serious confrontation with a homicide victim within an hour or so of the time of death and who was seen in the victim's presence at around the same time is bound to be high on any list of possible suspects. Although, if you are a suspect, Agent Bowman should have read you your rights. Did he?"

Naomi shook her head and then blew her nose.

"Or offer you access to a lawyer?"

"No, but how could he? Where would I get a lawyer on a cruise ship in the middle of the night?"

I thought of my friend and lawyer, Ralph Ames, who wouldn't be above hiring a float plane and/or a helicopter if he had felt that kind of extreme measure was necessary. "It can be done," I told her. "Until you have an attorney present, you probably shouldn't agree to talk to Bowman again."

That was good advice, but I doubt she heard it. "Why would Sharon and Virginia go and tell like that?" Naomi resumed. "When I told them about Harrison and me, I begged them to keep it quiet. They both promised that they wouldn't say a word. How could they betray me like that when they're both supposed to be my friends? You can see why I don't want to go back to the room, can't you? How can I face them knowing what they've done?"

"They may not have done anything," I said quietly.

Naomi Pepper frowned. "What do you mean?"

Here it was—fess-up time. "Sharon and Virginia didn't spill the beans about you and Harrison Featherman," I told her. "I did."

She looked stunned. "You? But why?"

"Because I had to, Naomi. The law compels me to. Todd Bowman is conducting a homicide investigation. It's against the law for anyone to withhold information in that kind of case, but that rule is far more stringently applied when the person doing the withholding happens to be a police officer or an ex-police officer. Civilians may be able to keep their mouths shut and get away with it, but judges don't look kindly on it when cops and ex-cops try to pull the same stunt."

Naomi looked even more stricken. "That means you must think I killed her, too, don't you!" she said accusingly.

"I didn't say that."

She shook her head and rose from the couch. "You didn't have to," she replied. "I'll be going then and leave you alone. Maybe I can find a place to sit in one of the lounges and wait for the sun to come up. Once we get to Skagway, I'll decide what to do."

"Sit," I ordered. "Sit and listen."

"Why should I?" she demanded in return. "So you can read me my rights, too?"

"I used to be a cop, Naomi, and I may be one again, but right now I'm a civilian the same as you—a civilian who's trying to be your friend. What exactly did Agent Bowman say?"

For a time Naomi stood uncertainly in the middle of the room. Finally she sat back down. "He said that I'm not allowed to leave the ship without checking with him first. He made it sound like I'm under house arrest or something. How can that be? Margaret was my friend. I'd never kill her."

"She disappeared within hours of hearing about the relationship between you and her ex-husband," I said evenly. "Think about how that looks. Everything is going along more or less smoothly. Then, as soon as she learns that one critical piece of information, she's out of here. I'm sure Todd Bowman believes there's a connection, and I don't blame him because so do I. How did Margaret find out?"

Too worn down to argue, Naomi huddled more deeply into the couch. "I don't know," she said.

"Margaret must have given you some idea."

Naomi shook her head. "When I talked to her she was a raving lunatic and not making much sense. She said something about Harrison rewriting his will, but I can't imagine what that would have to do with me."

It was like a camera lens shifting into focus. For the first time I saw what had happened in an entirely different light. "Wait a minute. Has Harrison Featherman been giving you money?" I asked.

Naomi looked at me briefly, then her eyes shifted away. She nodded. "Yes," she said softly.

"Why?" I asked. "For how long?"

"Harrison knew how difficult things were for me. And after Gary died, it was that much worse. I really had to struggle. Gary never believed in life insurance, you see, so there wasn't any of that—not a dime. And the medical bills were appalling. I took in roommates in order to meet the mortgage payments. Otherwise, Missy and I would have lost the house and been thrown out on the street. When we split up, I did manage to get Melissa on the reduced-price lunch program at school. I even went so far as to apply for food stamps once, but they wouldn't give them to me. They said I had too many assets."

"And so Harrison helped you."

Naomi nodded, but when her eyes met mine, what I saw

in them was defiance. "Yes, he helped me. Missy is his daughter, too. He wasn't about to let her starve."

"And when he gave you this help, how did he do it?"

"What do you mean?"

"Did he write you checks?"

"Of course not. Those would have shown up in his checkbook. Margaret or Chloe would have seen them."

"But Harrison and Margaret were already divorced by then. How would she have had access to his checkbook?"

Naomi bit her lip. "He was helping me before they were divorced."

"And before you and Gary separated?"

She nodded.

"So you're saying Chloe doesn't know about any of this, either?"

"I don't think so."

"What about Melissa?"

"There was no reason for her to know."

"So how did Harrison manage to pull this off and give you money without anyone else knowing about it?"

"He made cash deposits to my checking account from time to time. That's all."

"And you paid taxes on this money?"

"Well, no. Not really. What he gave me I considered gifts."

"How many gifts?" I asked. "How much money?"

She shrugged. "I don't know exactly. A couple thousand a year, probably. More when Missy needed counseling."

"And now?" I persisted.

"What do you mean?"

"Didn't you tell me that Missy was living away from home?"

Naomi nodded. "She is now."

"And is Harrison Featherman still helping out?"

"Only a little."

I sighed and shook my head.

"What's that supposed to mean?" Naomi demanded. "Are you judging me? Have you ever been poor, Mr. Beaumont, so poor that when you got to the check stand with your groceries you didn't know how much food you'd have to put back on the shelves because you didn't think you'd have enough money to pay for all of it?"

When I was a kid living with my single-parent mother, we would have gone hungry from time to time if it hadn't been for the kindhearted baker downstairs who made sure whatever baked goods he didn't sell somehow made their way upstairs to our apartment. But I was the kid then, not the parent. My mother would have known far more about Naomi Pepper's side of the charitable-donation table than I did.

"I've been that poor," I said. "But it was when I was a kid growing up in Ballard. I wasn't the parent worrying about feeding my child in those days. All I wanted to know back then was what was for dinner. I may be in no position to judge you, but Todd Bowman is."

"Todd Bowman?" Naomi asked. "What does he have to do with any of this?"

"Did you tell him about the money?"

"No. Why?"

"Because Todd Bowman works for the FBI. When he

finds out about Harrison Featherman's cash-only deposits—
and he's bound to find out—he'll come to only one conclusion."

"Which is?"

"Blackmail, which happens to be a very good motive for
murder. When you talked to her, did Margaret Featherman
threaten to blow the whistle on you?"

"You mean, was she going to tell Chloe? The answer to
that is yes. In fact, that was the last thing she said to me—that
she was going to tell. I told her to go ahead. I told her that if
she wanted to wreck her daughter's life, that was up to her,
but I didn't kill her, Beau. I swear to God I didn't."

"When you came out of her room, why didn't you close
the door?"

"Close it?" Naomi asked. "I thought I did. But I was so
upset, if it wasn't closed properly, I must not have noticed."

"Did you see anyone else in the corridor?"

"No, no one. The hallway was empty all the way from
Margaret's room to the elevator. Why?"

"Did you notice anything about the service door directly
across from Margaret's room?"

"No. I didn't even know there was one."

"So you didn't see that it was slightly ajar?"

"No. Are you saying someone was hiding there?"

"Yes."

"Then that must be the killer, the person Todd Bowman
thinks is my accomplice in all this. Is that right?"

I nodded. "Let me ask you something, Naomi. In addition
to Virginia and Sharon, is there anyone else on board this ship
that you know?"

"Chloe and Harrison, of course. And I know Leila by sight. Do they count?"

"Yes."

"But aside from them, there's no one else. At least, no one else I'm aware of so far. Why?"

"Is there anyone else who might have known about the payments to you from Harrison Featherman? Anyone at all?"

"It's not something I'm proud of," Naomi said quietly. "It isn't the kind of thing one goes through life bragging about."

"You mentioned Margaret said something about Harrison Featherman rewriting his will. What exactly did she say?"

"She told me she had found out about the rewritten will and that Melissa was being treated on a par with Chloe and the baby Leila is expecting. That threw me for a loop because I knew nothing about it. Harrison never mentioned a word of it to me."

"How did Margaret find out?"

"I have no idea. She didn't say. Maybe she bribed someone who works for the estate-planning lawyer who did the work. Anyway, then she asked me straight out if Melissa was Harrison's child, and I said yes. Then she said, 'I thought so,' and how could I do that to her and how could I betray her that way? I tried to explain to her that I was desperate to have a baby, that Gary and I had tried and tried. After that she got real quiet, then she said, 'I suppose you think you're the only one who ever wanted to have a baby?' I don't know what she meant by that. I mean, she and Harrison had Chloe, didn't they? Then it was like she just went haywire. Nuts! She started screaming obscenities at me and throwing things—her shoes, her purse. She told me to get out, and I did."

"Chloe is an only child?" I saw at once that was the wrong question. "I mean, she was raised as an only child."

Naomi nodded.

"Did Harrison and Margaret try having another child after Chloe was born?" I asked.

"I don't know," Naomi answered. "They may have. We never talked about it."

"But I thought you were good friends."

"Just because women are friends doesn't mean they talk about everything," Naomi returned. "And I know men don't talk about a lot of that stuff, either," she added. "Some things are too painful to mention."

Naomi Pepper had me there.

"You said she threatened to tell Chloe. What would that have accomplished?"

"I'm not sure," Naomi replied. "I think Margaret thought it would drive a wedge between Harrison and Chloe. The two of them have always been incredibly close from the very beginning, from when Chloe was just a toddler. I think Margaret was terribly jealous of the way they got along. And then, to have Chloe and Leila end up being friends as well . . ." Naomi shook her head. "That just drove Margaret wild."

"Do you think it was the fact that Harrison was making financial provisions for all his children that upset Margaret so? Would what he did in rewriting his will have had any adverse impact on Margaret's income, for example?"

"I doubt it," Naomi said. "Margaret always claimed that she had the best divorce attorney her husband's money could buy. When they did the property settlement, it was supposedly a clean, cut-and-dried deal. Margaret said she didn't want to be in a position of having to wait around for the mailman to know whether or not the support check was going to show up. And as far as I know, she never had to worry about that.

"At the time of the divorce I remember Harrison was stretched pretty thin financially. He had a couple of tough years, but eventually he worked his way out of it. Whatever settlement Margaret got, it must have been substantial, and I'm sure she invested it wisely. As far as I know, money or the lack of it has never been a problem for her."

"She didn't have to work?"

"She worked, all right," Naomi conceded. "But it was because she wanted to, not because she had to."

"Doing what?"

"I don't know, really. About the time Chloe went off to kindergarten, Margaret went back to school and got a Ph.D. in something from the U Dub. Genetics, I think. I was a liberal arts major, so all that hard science stuff leaves me cold. I don't understand it at all. And that was something else the four of us never talked about—work. It wasn't all that happy a topic for any of us. When we got together, it was to have fun."

"What did you talk about then?"

"Old times," Naomi said wistfully. "About the times when we were young and beautiful, and didn't have a care in the world. Back then everything was ahead of us and nothing was impossible."

"You were telling me about Margaret's divorce attorney. What about you?" I asked. "Did you have one?"

"Not really," Naomi said. "There was the guy who was supposedly handling my divorce but then I had to stop the proceedings because Gary moved back home. He's really the only one I've ever used, and he wasn't particularly good. At the time, Margaret suggested I use hers, but of course I never could have afforded him."

"Do you have any criminal defense attorneys in your circle of friends?"

"No. Do I need one?"

"In my opinion, yes. What's your plan for tomorrow?"

Naomi shrugged. "We dock in Skagway in the morning. We had all planned to take that narrow-gauge railroad trip up White Pass, but since Todd Bowman told me I can't get off the boat without his permission and since I'm damned if I'll ask him, I guess I won't be doing that."

I reached over to the bedside table, picked up my wallet, and shuffled through it until I found one of Ralph Ames' cards. The card was one of his new ones that listed both his Seattle and his Scottsdale numbers.

"Once we dock, you might want to give this guy a call," I said, handing the dog-eared card over to Naomi. "Ralph's a friend of mine, and he's very good."

"Is he expensive?"

"Yes, but he's also well worth it. I'm sure you and he will be able to work something out."

Naomi stood up then. "Where are you going?" I asked. "Back to your cabin?"

She shook her head. "Not tonight. After everything that's happened, I just can't face Virginia and Sharon. Maybe tomorrow I'll be tough enough, but not tonight."

"Where are you going to sleep then?"

"Like I said, I'll hang out in one of the lounges."

"No, you won't," I told her. "That's silly. Why don't you sleep here? You can have the bed. I'll sleep on the floor."

Naomi tried to object to this arrangement, but she didn't stand a chance. After all, I worked my way through college selling door-to-door for Fuller Brush. I know how to overcome objections. When she finally said yes, I flagged down my room attendant and laid hands on an extra blanket, a few extra pillows, and a roll-away bed. Sleeping on the paper-thin mattress of a roll-away cot wasn't how I had envisioned spending nights aboard the *Starfire Breeze*. But that was hardly surprising. Nothing about this cruise was working out the way I expected.

13

WHEN I LAY DOWN on the cot, it wasn't with much hope of sleeping. Naomi hadn't undressed, and neither did I. For one thing, I fully expected that Todd Bowman would come knocking at the door any minute and wake us both up.

Lying in the dark, I became more aware of the ship's up-and-down movement in the water. I also noticed that, since the previous night, I hadn't bothered to put my wristlets back on. To my amazement and relief, I no longer seemed to need them.

"Are you asleep?" Naomi inquired from across the room.

"No."

"Me neither. You must think really badly of me. It's not just what I did to get pregnant, but what I did afterward. I thought Gary and I would be bringing the baby into a stable, loving home. I didn't expect that our marriage would blow up in our faces. I never meant to ask Harrison for help, and I didn't ask, either. Not really. It's just that when he offered, I didn't have the strength to turn him down. Gary never was worth much when it came to supporting the family. He loved to gamble way more than he liked paying the bills. Harrison offered me a lifeline; I took it."

"Why?"

"Why did I take it?"

"No. Why did he offer?"

"I don't know. All he said was he wanted to make sure Missy was taken care of. That she was his responsibility as much as she was mine."

"Does Melissa know any of this?"

"No."

I tried to square this view of Harrison Featherman's self-less generosity with the guy who had charged onto the dance floor with the express purpose of bitching out his ex-wife. Not that Margaret hadn't deserved bitching out. Still, staging that kind of confrontation in public showed less-than-gentlemanly behavior on Harrison's part. For that matter, so did screwing around behind his wife's back.

"But I wasn't blackmailing him, Beau. That may be how it'll look to everybody else, but that isn't what was going on."

"Nobody's judging you," I said.

"That's not true. You were," she said. "So was Margaret, and the same goes for Sharon and Virginia. They judged me without my even telling them about the money. I'm sure other people will think the same thing, especially if and when Todd Bowman gets around to arresting me for Margaret's murder."

"He hasn't done that yet, and he may not. Murder is damned hard to prove, especially if there isn't a body," I told her. "The evidence would all be circumstantial, and that doesn't go very far when a homicide is involved. You'll just have to take things one step at a time. One step and one day," I added.

After that, Naomi subsided into silence, and so did I— silence but not sleep. Here I was again, making the same mistakes I had made once before. Not that I was in love with Naomi Pepper—not even close. But still, I was *involved* with her. I had taken her in despite the very real possibility that she was the prime suspect in a murder investigation. At least when I fell for Anne Corley, I had no idea she might be a suspect.

With Naomi Pepper, I wasn't the least bit sure she wasn't a viable one.

Finally, I fell asleep. Some time later, I dreamed about Anne Corley. That's not surprising. It happens fairly often. What was different about this dream was that she was on board the *Starfire Breeze* and seated at the same table in the Crystal Dining Room along with the rest of us—with Margaret Featherman and Naomi, Sharon Carson and Virginia Metz. Marc Alley was nowhere to be found. It was just me and those five women. As usual, Margaret Featherman was running the show.

"What is it that makes men so stupid?" she asked.

"That's simple," Anne Corley told her. "All you have to do is lead them around by the balls, and they forget they have a brain."

I tried to say something in my own defense, but it was useless. Anne's stinging remark was greeted by such gales of gleeful laughter that it was impossible for me to be heard. The laughter seemed to go on forever. They were all still hooting and giggling when I finally managed to escape by waking myself up.

By then, it was five o'clock in the morning. The *Starfire Breeze* was docking in Skagway, and my back hurt like hell. I never have been any good on roll-away beds or on hide-a-beds. They all have metal cross-support bars that hit me right in the lower ribs. Feeling as if somebody had been punching me with his fists, I got up, let myself out of the room, and went upstairs to the computer lounge. There I used my key card and one of the ship's computers to log onto the Internet and send Ralph Ames an E-mail.

Whenever Naomi Pepper managed to get in touch with him, I wanted Ralph to have some idea of what was going on. That was only fair. Friends don't blindside friends—not if they can help it.

By the time I finished with the computer, it was still too early for the dining rooms to be open for breakfast, so I went upstairs to the buffet. Naturally Lars Jenssen was already there.

"You're up bright and early," he said when I put down my coffee cup and pulled out a chair at his table.

"How're things?" I asked.

He shrugged. "Last night was rough duty," he said.

"Being around Mike was just like having one of them—what is it they call them again, when it's like you're living in what you lived in before?"

"You mean a flashback?"

He nodded. "That's it. A flashback. Geez! I can't help feeling sorry for Lucy. I feel sorry for both of them."

Beverly showed up just then. "Are you going to the train dressed like that?" she asked. "Your clothes look like they've been slept in."

I wasn't about to tell my grandmother the real reason behind my messy state. Having to sleep in my clothes because there was a strange woman in my bed wasn't something I wanted to explain to my octogenarian grandmother.

"I'm not a very good packer," I said, and let it go at that.

By eight-thirty that morning, it was pouring-down rain. In a bedraggled little group we made our way from the *Starfire Breeze* across the dock to where a White Pass and Yukon excursion train stood waiting to take on passengers. Lars led the way, taking Mike Conyers by the elbow and covering both their heads with a huge umbrella provided compliments of the cruise ship's stewards, who were stationed at the top of the gangplank. The crewmen alternated between swiping key cards and offering disembarking passengers the use of loaner bumbershoots.

The women—Beverly and the two Wakefield "girls"—clustered around Lucy Conyers in a tight, clucking little group. All of them were muffled in long coats that would have served them well in a Siberian blizzard, but not one of them had accepted one of the proffered umbrellas. Instead, to a woman, they walked through the rain wearing identical rain

caps—those ugly little fold-up jobs that elderly women are
forever producing out of the depths of their purses. To me they
resembled a group of nuns who had traded in old-fashioned
wimples for clear-plastic headgear. The rain caps may have
protected their beauty-shop hairdos from the downpour, but
they seemed to offer scant protection from the cold.

Looking out for stragglers, I brought up the rear. Being
your basic cool, macho dude and a Seattleite to boot, I didn't
stoop to carrying an umbrella. As far as coats were concerned,
I figured a slightly damp tweed jacket would keep me warm
enough in what I envisioned as an uneventful excursion in an
overheated train car.

Knowing what I did about Mike Conyers and remembering what Lars had told me about his first wife constantly
looking backward, I wasn't at all surprised when Lars headed
for the last car on the train. Count on Lars to be considerate.
If Mike Conyers was determined to see where he had been,
then riding in the last car would make looking back that much
easier.

As we stood in line waiting to board, I noticed Marc Alley
hurrying past with a group of passengers headed for cars
closer to the front of the train. I nodded in his direction, but
he didn't acknowledge or return my greeting. He seemed to
be caught up in a conversation with the medical reporter I had
seen him with several days earlier. I wondered at the time if
he really was that fully involved in conversation, or if he had
ignored me on purpose as part of a deliberate slight.

Once aboard the train, it took no time at all for the group
to settle in. The women whipped off their rain hats, shook

off the moisture, and stowed them back in their individual purses. Then, before the train even left the platform, they took from those same purses a cornucopia of edible delights— apples, bananas, pears, sweet rolls, and muffins—that had been liberated from the morning's breakfast buffet and brought along to ward off starvation.

The bounty of what Beverly termed our "forenoon coffee" resembled the New Testament parable of the loaves and fishes. It turned out there was more than enough food to go around. Several people in the car who weren't in our own group to begin with joined in the impromptu feast. And, in the absence of a miracle, I suspect they must have brought along supplies of their own.

For a change, I had the good sense to keep any sarcastic comments to myself. For one thing, they were feeding me. For another, every passenger in the car except me had lived through the Great Depression. All of them had probably experienced some degree of hardship back then. A few may well have endured times when they had no idea where their next meal was coming from. If that kind of powerfully imprinted memory had resulted in their raiding the *Starfire Breeze*'s buffet line, then it was a defense mechanism best not questioned or criticized. When Beverly handed me a bruised, overripe banana, I accepted it meekly and ate it the same way.

As the train eased through town, I got a kick out of the fleet of tourist buses. They looked like refugees from 1920s and 1930s national parks.

"That's where the museum is," Lars explained, pointing. "That's where they have the display of what the gold rushers had to bring along with them. Wait till you see it," he added. "We'll run over there this afternoon, after the girls are back on board the ship. You won't mind going, will you?"

It wasn't the first thing on my list, but I did my best to muster some sincere-sounding enthusiasm. "Sure thing, Lars," I said. "I'm looking forward to it."

As we headed out of Skagway, the rain was so thick there wasn't much to see. That's about the time Lars Jenssen started spinning yarns, and everyone else in the car leaned forward to listen. I suppose all those years of entertaining his fellow fishermen in the fleet had added to Lars' gift of gab, but I suspect he was simply a natural-born storyteller to begin with. He started off with tales about the building of the White Pass railway itself. As the train moved higher up the mountain, the rain lifted slightly, leaving the mountainsides draped in blankets of cloud and the canyons lost in drifting banks of fog. Then, as the sun started burning through, Lars pointed out a faint path that seemed to climb straight up a perpendicular cliff that was so wet and shiny it looked like it was made of glass.

"See that?" he asked. "That's the Chilkoot Trail. Before they built the railroad, that was the only way to get to Lake Bennett from Skagway. My dad's older cousin, Olaf, was a gold rusher, and that's the way he and his buddies went over the mountain. Partway up they came across a young fellow who'd been beaten up and robbed. Somebody'd stolen his packhorse and the thousand pounds of supplies each prospector had to bring along. The young fella had been hurt and was bleeding pretty good, except when Olaf went to help him, it turned out he wasn't a he at all."

"A woman gold rusher?" Claire Wakefield exclaimed. "I never heard about any of those."

Lars nodded. "Her name was Erika, and she hailed from northern Minnesota. Seems her twin brother, Erik, had planned to go to Alaska, but when he was killed in a threshing accident, she took his papers, dressed herself in his duds, and went in his place. It might have worked fine if she hadn't fallen in with a bad bunch in Skagway. Halfway up the mountain, they beat her up, took her stuff, and left her to die. And she would have, too, if Olaf and his bunch hadn't happened across her when they did.

"They patched her up and took her with them. Almost to White Pass, Olaf knew that if the Canadian Mounties saw that the group was short one set of supplies, they'd send one person back down the mountain. So Olaf made arrangements to meet up with the group at Lake Bennett before they rafted down the Yukon. Then he took off on his own and entered Canada illegally."

"Did he make it?" somebody asked when Lars paused briefly. The questioner turned out to be a man who hadn't been part of our group originally but who had been drawn in by both the food and the storytelling.

"Ya, sure," Lars said.

"What happened, then? Did your cousin strike it rich?"

"Rich enough," Lars answered. "And he married Erika, of course."

"Why 'of course'?" Florence Wakefield asked huffily. "Some women get along perfectly fine without getting married," she added.

"They did all right together," Lars told her. "Went back to

Minnesota and bought a farm in what's now pretty near downtown Minneapolis. Their kids made a ton of money when they sold it years later. The last I heard, one of their great-great-grandsons was serving in the state legislature. For all I know, maybe he's governor by now."

"Good for him," Claire said. "In fact, good for the whole family."

As if for emphasis, watery sunshine now burst through the cloud cover, leaving the surrounding cliffs awash in blinding glare. Here and there through the mist we caught sight of more traces of that fabled Chilkoot Trail. Seeing it zigzag its way up the mountainside, it was impossible not to be impressed by the brave if foolhardy men and women who had followed it and their dreams in an often fatal and usually unsuccessful search for gold.

As the sun came out, Lars seemed to run out of steam. When that happened, Mike Conyers grew increasingly restless. Up until then, he had sat patiently enough, listening quietly, as Lars regaled the group. Now, though, it was clear he had reached the end of his limited attention span. For a while Lars and Lucy both attempted to keep him occupied and in his seat, but then he broke into a low, keening wail—an eerie howl that was somehow reminiscent of the wolflike sound effects in one of my favorite childhood programs, "Sergeant Preston of the Yukon and His Wonder Dog, King."

"Mike wants to go outside," Lucy explained. "He wants to stand on the back."

There was a small observation deck on the very back of the train. There was also a sign posted on the door that said NO PASSENGERS ALLOWED BEYOND THIS POINT. Unfortunately,

Mike Conyers had moved beyond the ability either to read or mind a posted sign. He reminded me of a grocery-cart-imprisoned two-year-old whose mother has just told him he can't have a candy bar. The more Lucy said no, the louder Mike wailed. Finally, shaking her head in exasperation, Lucy stood up and retrieved both their coats.

"I'll take him out," she said. "Otherwise, it'll only get worse."

Lars came to her rescue. "No, no," he said. "I understand what's going on. You stay in here and keep warm. I'll be glad to go outside with him."

With a grateful nod, Lucy helped her husband on with his coat, then she returned to her seat, while Lars took Mike by the elbow and guided him out onto the balcony. I expected that alarms would sound somewhere in the train the moment the forbidden door was opened. I waited for an irate conductor to come flying through the car and order Mike and Lars back inside. None of that happened. There was no alarm, no conductor came, and no one objected to the fact that Lars Jenssen and Mike Conyers were doing something that was supposedly expressly prohibited.

With Lars outside, there was no one to continue giving a blow-by-blow description of the building of the railroad. I remembered that Lars had said there was a tunnel somewhere on the track, but during the better part of two hours, despite the incredibly steep grade, we had yet to pass through it. There were occasions when the switchbacks were so tight that we could see the front of the train rounding a curve long before the back of the train ever reached it. Down in the steep ravines far below us, where dregs of fog still drifted here and there, we sometimes caught sight of waterfalls sending torrents of water hundreds of feet off rockbound cliffs. It was spectacularly beautiful—breathtakingly beautiful. Despite my natural reserve and my cop's detached if not blasé attitude, I was becoming more and more impressed.

Then, just as we neared the top of the grade, the door at the far end of our car swished open, and Marc Alley came marching down the aisle. I nodded to him, thinking that perhaps he had come looking for me in order to bury the hatchet. No such luck. With an oversized camera bobbing around his neck, Marc hurried right past me and out onto the back of the train, where Lars and Mike Conyers stood leaning against the rail. No alarms sounded when he went out, either.

I saw Marc position himself right in the middle of the observation deck. With his feet spread to maintain his balance, his elbows extended on either side of his head as he focused his camera. Then, as the door at the front of the car swished open once more, the car was plunged into total darkness as the train entered what I would later learn was called Tunnel Mountain.

As the train roared into the tunnel, I caught one final glimpse of Marc Alley, standing there with his attention focused entirely on his camera. I heard the door to the observation platform swish open and closed once more. In the darkness, I hoped that meant Marc was coming inside. Just then, I saw a flash go off, not once but twice. Worried that someone else had come down the aisle and bumped into Marc without seeing him, I started out of my seat to go check. Just then I heard the observation platform door swish open one more time. As I stepped into the aisle, someone crashed into me with enough force that it knocked the wind out of me and sent me sprawling back into my seat.

Struggling to regain my breath, I heard a long, piercing scream. The sound ended abruptly as the observation platform door slid shut once again. Heart pounding, I staggered back to my feet and charged down the aisle. I reached the observation platform just as the train burst out of the far side of the tunnel and into blinding sunlight.

Out on the platform, Marc Alley was on his hands and knees, scrambling to regain his footing and his camera. He crawled over to the rail and pulled himself unsteadily to his feet. Lars, clinging to the guardrail, was holding Mike Conyers' coat and pointing back through the tunnel. As for Mike Conyers? He was nowhere to be seen.

"What happened?" I shouted, over the clatter of iron wheels on the track.

"Someone hit me," Marc shouted back at me. "They hit me from behind. And when I fell . . . Oh, my God!" The dawning horror of realization washed over Marc's face. "Where is he?" he demanded. "Where's the other man who was standing right here?"

"He fell," Lars shouted back. "I caught hold of an arm of his coat, but it came away in my hands. It happened just as we went into the tunnel."

"But is he all right? We weren't going all that fast. Maybe he landed on the track and he's okay or just bruised up a little. Somebody stop the train! Pull the emergency brakes! We've got to go back and check."

Lars reached over and laid one hand on Marc Alley's shoulder. "He didn't fall on the tracks." Lars said the words quietly. Despite the din of the moving train I heard every word as distinctly as if he'd been speaking with a microphone from the pulpit of a deathly still church. "He fell a long way— a long, long way."

Just then someone did yank the emergency brake. The sudden slowing sent Marc, Lars, and me tumbling into one another and grabbing desperately for the rail to keep from falling ourselves. By the time the train finally stopped, the conductor came careening through the door.

"What's the meaning of this?" he demanded, his voice trembling with righteous anger. "What the hell is going on here? Can't you read the sign? It says no one's allowed beyond this point!"

"Someone fell," I said.

"Fell!" he repeated. "You mean someone fell off the train? When? Where?"

"Back there," Lars told him. "Just on the other side of the tunnel."

Behind us the door opened again. Lucy Conyers staggered out onto the observation platform. "What happened?" she asked.

"Go back," the conductor ordered. "No one's allowed out here!"

But Lucy wasn't listening to him. She looked from Lars to Marc to me with a questioning, horrified expression that none of us wanted to answer.

"Where's Mike?" she demanded. "Tell me. Where did he go? He was right here a minute ago. Where is he now?"

The conductor's face passed through a myriad of expressions—angry, impatient, outraged—before settling on one of concern. "You know this man?" he asked with surprising gentleness. "You know the man who fell?"

"Fell!" Lucy repeated. "Mike fell off the train?" She ran to Lars and grabbed his jacket by the lapels. "Is it true?"

Shaking his head, Lars handed her Mike's coat. "I tried to catch him," he said. "I caught the arm of his coat, but he fell right out of it. I'm sorry."

Lars looked as though he himself were about to burst into tears, and I knew exactly how he felt.

"How far did he fall?" Lucy demanded.

"I'm not sure," Lars told her. "It seemed like a long way."

"You mean he's not all right then."

"No, he won't be all right."

The conductor turned on Lars. "You all know each other?" Lars and I both nodded. Marc said nothing. "All of you stay here," the conductor continued. "Don't touch anything. The engineer and I will decide what to do."

Lucy, with her face buried in Mike's coat, fell into Lars' arms and sobbed her heart out against his chest. Since he was busy comforting her, I turned my attention on Marc Alley, whose face had turned pasty-white.

"Are you all right?" I asked.

He shook his head. "Somebody pushed me," he said. "They tried to kill me."

"You're sure it was deliberate?"

He nodded. "You warned me something like that could happen. You told me those people were going to try to kill me. But did I listen? No, I did not, and now my stupidity has cost that poor man his life. I fell, and as I did, I must have shoved him. I couldn't see anything, but I'm sure that's what happened. What am I going to do, Beau? A man is dead, and it's all my fault."

"You're sure this was done on purpose?" I asked. "I mean, someone could have just come through the door and bumped into you by accident. It was dark enough that they wouldn't have been able to see anything, either."

Marc shook his head grimly. "No," he declared. "Whoever hit me did it on purpose."

"How do you know that?"

"Because I felt two hands on my back. They hit me right at the base of my ribs, just above the belt and hard enough to knock the breath out of me. I was standing close to the door because I wanted to get a shot of the canyon that would be framed by the walls of the tunnel as the train went inside. But because I was standing so close to the door, I fell to the floor and landed inside the rail instead of falling over it. I felt someone against me then, as I fell. That must be when I hit Mike. Oh, my God. I'm the one who knocked him off the train. But even if I didn't, it's still all my fault. Whoever came after me caused this to happen. You warned me to play it safe, and I didn't pay any attention. It doesn't really matter who pushed Mike. What's happened is all my fault."

That's when I remembered the person who had come mowing down the aisle from the observation platform and who had knocked me aside as easily as if I'd been a ninepin. Whoever it was had to be the killer, but when I was hit, the train had been engulfed in total darkness. I never caught a glimpse of the person.

"Did you see who it was?" I asked.

Marc shook his head. "By the time I landed, we were in the tunnel. I couldn't see a thing."

The door opened again. The conductor stepped back outside. "Everybody inside," he said. "We're going to back through the tunnel and see if we can see where he landed. I've notified the Alaska state troopers. They'll be sending a pair of investigators up from Skagway. We'll try to catch sight of the victim and see if there's a chance he's still alive. We've asked for a Search and Rescue team."

As ordered, we made our way back inside. I returned to my seat and motioned Marc Alley into the empty place beside me. Then, moving almost imperceptibly, the train began to inch backward. It took a long, long time for it to back into the tunnel. It took even longer for us to creep through Tunnel Mountain until finally we eased back into daylight on the far side.

"Come on," the conductor said to Lars and Marc. "Show me where it happened."

I wasn't officially invited on this little excursion, but I tagged along anyway. Once back outside the tunnel, we all stood hanging on to the guardrail and peering down at the floor of the canyon a good thousand feet below us. Naturally, hawk-eyed Lars was the one who spotted what was left of Mike Conyers.

"There," he said, pointing. "See him? Right there next to the stream."

After several minutes I, too, was able to sort out exactly where it was Lars was pointing. By then, someone on the train had produced a pair of field glasses and passed them along outside. As soon as I took a look at the limp figure sprawled across a man-sized boulder, I knew it was all over.

I passed the binoculars along to someone else and went back inside to where Lucy Conyers was curtained off behind a protective barrier of womanhood. My grandmother caught my eye and raised her eyebrows. When I shook my head, she stepped aside and allowed me access into that inner circle. Inside, Lucy Conyers turned her tear-filled eyes on me, and for the second time in two days, retired or not, I had to pass along the bad news.

"Did you see him?" she asked.

I nodded.

"And?"

"Mike's not moving, Lucy," I told her. "It looks as though he landed on a boulder. Search and Rescue will go retrieve him, but I doubt he's alive."

Lucy Conyers nodded and stiffened her shoulders. "Okay," she said quietly. "If that's the way it is, okay. At least now poor Mike doesn't have to suffer anymore."

And neither do you, I thought. At least I had the good grace not to say it aloud, and neither did anyone else, although I'm sure I wasn't the only person who connected those dots. Mike Conyers was the one who was dead, but at least death had ended the inevitable erosion of his faculties. For Lucy, no matter how much grief she felt, this final loss would be a blessing. However it had come about, at least she would no longer be trapped into trying to hold the line between the person Mike Conyers had once been and the child/man entity and stranger he was gradually becoming.

Beverly leaned down and touched Lucy's shoulder. "Are you going to be all right?" Beverly asked.

Lucy looked at my grandmother and then back at me. "Yes, thank you," she said. "I'll be fine."

I knew then that she would be.

14

AFTER SOMETHING LIKE THAT happens, people go into a form of shock. They talk in hushed tones. They compare what they saw or thought they saw and try to make sense of what has happened. Marc Alley went back to his own car. Lucy was protected by my grandmother and the Wakefield "girls." Lars, standing alone out on the observation platform, was the one I worried about.

"I should have caught him," he said. "When I was younger it was nothing to grab a two-hundred-pound halibut and heave him into a boat single-handed. If I could have caught his arm instead of his coat . . ." He sighed.

"You did what you could," I told him. "And the thing is, if you had caught his arm, there's a good chance he would have pulled you off the train right along with him."

"I almost wish he had," Lars said hopelessly.

I wanted to console him, wanted to make him feel better. "You know more than anybody what he and Lucy were going through. Don't you think he's better off?"

Lars closed his eyes and shook his head. "That's not for you or me to say, Beau," he said. That comment was the nearest thing to a rebuke I ever had from Lars Jenssen, and I knew I deserved it.

"You're right," I said. "Sorry."

We stayed on a siding at the top of White Pass long enough for the Search and Rescue helicopter to arrive, then the train headed back down the mountain. Two hours later and only halfway back to Skagway, the train pulled over and stopped. Moments later a pair of Alaska state troopers came aboard.

Detectives Sonny Liebowitz and Jake Ripley were an unlikely-looking and-sounding pair of partners. Sonny was short and wide and sounded as if he had just stepped off the El in downtown Chicago. Jake, on the other hand, was tall and scrawny. He looked like an American Indian, but he spoke with a distinctly Southern drawl. It might have been interesting to have an opportunity to chew the fat with them and find out just how it was that both of them had ended up in Alaska, but by then it was almost three and my mostly geriatric fellow passengers were growing restless and cranky.

These were folks accustomed to three square meals a day plus occasional snacks. By three o'clock in the afternoon, even those who had partaken of Beverly's picnic-style "forenoon coffee" were famished and more than ready to be back on board the *Starfire Breeze*. They weren't at all happy with the prospect of further delays. I heard grumbling as soon as Detectives Liebowitz and Ripley announced that no one would be allowed to disembark until after they had completed their interviews. As a fellow detective, I applauded any plan that included interviewing all the passengers on board the train, since Mike Conyers' killer was bound to be among them. As primary caretaker of a covey of aging passengers who had missed lunch and were in danger of missing dinner as well, I was more than a little concerned about how long the questioning process would take.

First the detectives worked their way through our car, taking names and asking general questions about who was in the car and who was sitting where. After half an hour to forty-five minutes of that, they went into a more detailed mode. For that, they conducted people off the train. Lucy Conyers was the first person designated for that treatment, and her solo interview took the better part of an hour. When Jake Ripley came to collect the next interviewees, Marc Alley and Lars Jenssen, Lucy Conyers didn't return to the train.

At the time I noticed her absence and thought it odd, but I didn't give it all that much consideration. It occurred to me that, after what had happened, maybe she had chosen to spend some time alone. It was possible that the constant attentions of Beverly and the Wakefield "girls" were beginning to get on her nerves. It was also possible that she had found access to a telephone and was using that private time to notify her children of their father's death. That's a hurtful job best done without benefit of an audience.

Once Liebowitz and Ripley had finished with Lars and Marc, I wasn't the least bit surprised that I was next on their list. They led me off the train and into a small guard shack which came equipped with a desk, a noisy but effective electric heater, and three rickety folding chairs. Sonny Liebowitz, seated behind the desk, motioned me into one of the two remaining chairs. Jake leaned his lanky frame against the door and stayed there, making me wonder if he was keeping me inside or keeping others out.

"So, Mr. Beaumont," Sonny Liebowitz said. "You're the retired cop Mr. Alley was telling us about?" I nodded. "What's this about the FBI and some off-the-wall murder plot?" Sonny continued. "Any truth to that, do you think?"

"If you want official confirmation, you'd be better off contacting the two FBI agents assigned to the case, Rachel Dulles or Alex Freed. They're registered as ordinary passengers on board the *Starfire Breeze* under the names of Phyllis and Kurt Nix."

Sonny seemed surprised at that news. "So Alley wasn't making this up? There really are two FBI agents on board the ship?"

"By actual count there are three," I told him. "You may know Todd Bowman."

"You mean that young, fat-necked baby fed from up in Juneau?" Jake Ripley asked.

From my point of view, Todd Bowman wasn't all that much younger than Jake was, but age, like beauty, is relative. "That's right," I said. "Bowman's on board, too. He's investigating the death of Margaret Featherman."

"That's the lady who supposedly fell overboard day before yesterday?"

I took exception to the way Sonny Liebowitz spoke and to

the question itself. I didn't like his use of the word "supposedly." Margaret Featherman was gone. There was no "supposedly" about it.

"That's right," I said.

Sonny clicked his tongue. "Sounds like this cruise has been nothing but a barrel of laughs. I guess the *Love Boat*'s leaving fantasyland. You wonder why people around here are tired of cruise lines and all the people and shit they drag up here? I'll tell you why. They dump their raw sewage and garbage and bilgewater into our waterways and figure it's no big deal. As for the passengers, some of them decide they're back in the Wild West and think anything goes. Wrong!"

Obviously Detective Sonny Liebowitz wasn't a card-carrying member of the Alaskan Tourism Board. Furrowing his thick brows, he studied his notes for some time before he spoke again. "So, from what you're saying, I'm assuming that the FBI is taking this whole situation seriously. What about you, Mr. Beaumont? Do you think someone came through the car, ran out onto the observation platform, and pushed Mike Conyers over the side when what they really meant to do was off Marc Alley?"

"That's what I believe happened," I said. "When we went into the tunnel, I know Marc was standing right in front of the door, lining up his camera to take a picture. Then, in the dark, I remember hearing doors open and close."

"You say doors. As in at both the front and the back of the car?"

I nodded. "That's right, and it worried me. Marc was out there, and I was afraid that in the dark someone might stumble into him without seeing him. I was on my way to check when someone coming back up the aisle—back from the observation platform—crashed into me running full-tilt. The blow was hard enough that it knocked the wind out of me and sent me flying ass-over-teakettle right back into my seat."

"But you didn't see who it was?"

"No, it was dark."

"Any chance this unknown assailant might have been Lucy Conyers?"

"Lucy?" I repeated in surprise. "Of course it wasn't Lucy."

"Why not?" Sonny returned. "It's happened before. Some old person goes off his rocker. Next thing you know, it gets to be too much for the relatives—you know, for whoever's supposed to be taking care of him. Matter of fact, we had an incident just like this a little over a year ago. Middle of August last year, a woman pushed her husband out of their motor home and left him stranded in the middle of nowhere on the Al-Can Highway. Claimed they stopped along the road to take some pictures and she drove off without knowing he was out of the vehicle.

"That was a damned lie, of course. After we questioned her long enough, she finally broke down and told us what really happened. She said her husband was so hard to deal with that she just couldn't take it anymore, that she couldn't handle all the responsibility. According to her, she thought the bears would take care of the problem for her. They didn't, of course. Somebody found him first, but then he caught cold and died of pneumonia anyway. Now we've got his grieving widow in the slammer. She's serving seven to nine, man-two.

"When we talked to Lucy Conyers a little while ago, I got

the same feeling from her that I did with this other dame. Relief that poor Mike wouldn't be suffering anymore. Made me wonder if maybe sweet little Lucy hadn't done something herself to help 'poor Mike' along."

Everything in me said he was wrong. "It wasn't Lucy," I declared.

"What makes you say that?"

"Because Lucy was sitting closer to the door than I was. Whoever knocked me down did so while rushing back through the train to one of the other cars. You need to talk to the passengers in those cars and find out who all left their seats during the time the train was in the tunnel."

"But Lucy Conyers wasn't in her seat when it happened," Jake Ripley said quietly.

"She wasn't?" I asked in surprise.

"No. She claims she was in the rest room in the next car when the lights went off. According to her, she stayed put the whole time because she was afraid of trying to walk on the moving train in the dark, afraid she might stumble or fall."

"I would have been afraid of the same thing," I said.

"And maybe that's exactly what happened—she did fall," Sonny theorized. "Coming back down the aisle from the observation deck, she lost her balance in the dark. She fell against you hard enough that she knocked you back into your seat. There's no apparent bruising, but it's a little early for that."

"In other words, you've already made up your minds as to what happened, and Lucy Conyers is it?"

Sonny Liebowitz beamed and nodded. "In a manner of speaking," he agreed. "Lucy brought her ailing hubby on the cruise and train ride hoping for an opportunity that would allow her to unload him before he had a chance to get any worse. Up here, we believe in letting nature take its course— in not rushing things along; know what I mean?"

"Sounds just like Leave It To God."

"If that's what floats your boat," he returned with a shrug.

"That's not a philosophical position," I told him. "That's the name of the organization I believe is targeting Marc Alley."

"You got any proof of that?"

"No. But talk to the FBI suits. They're on the ship charged with protecting a guy by the name of Harrison Featherman. He's the neurologist who did Marc Alley's brain surgery. Leave It To God is made up of kooks who go after cutting-edge doctors. They target the guys who are doing stuff that's just one step above experimental—the ones using advanced, court-of-last-resort techniques on patients who otherwise would die. Then, when the patients defy the odds and make it, Leave It To God goes after them, too. Their position is that since it was God's intention for those people to die, they take it upon themselves to make sure that happens."

"In other words, the patients are damned if they do and damned if they don't."

"Right."

"And Marc Alley is one of those guys who's supposed to be dead one way or the other. So what's the FBI doing about all this?"

"They have their hands full protecting the doctors. They have a list of targeted doctors from all over the country, and

Harrison Featherman is evidently on the list. Once we were on board, Agent Dulles contacted me and asked me, unofficially, of course, to keep an eye on Marc Alley."

"The FBI's so short-handed these days that they've got to deputize retired cops?" Sonny Liebowitz shook his head and grinned. "Maybe if you'd been doing a better job of it, Mike Conyers wouldn't be splattered all over that boulder back up the mountain."

I let that one pass. "Look," I said. "Whoever did this must have known the train's route and the whole program. He or she knew that as soon as the train entered the tunnel, the lights would go off and stay off until we reached the other side of Tunnel Mountain. The killer counted on being able to make his move, hot-foot it to the end of the train, push Marc off, and then dash back to his place without anyone being the wiser. He or she left in the dark and returned in the dark. The only thing he didn't count on was the fact that Marc Alley wasn't alone out there on that platform."

Sonny Liebowitz held up his hand. "That's stretching it some, isn't it—the idea of planning in advance to do the whole deal in the dark? That would be very premeditated. My guess is that this was more a crime of opportunity. Lucy saw her husband standing out on the balcony. As soon as the lights went out, she realized that was her chance to get rid of him once and for all, and she took it. End of Mike. End of story. We're just damned lucky another person—Marc Alley, for instance—didn't get hurt or killed in the process. Thanks for your help, Mr. Beaumont. That'll be all."

"What do you mean, that's all?"

"I mean we're done here. We have your name, address, and phone number back home in Seattle. If there's anything more we need from you, we'll be in touch."

"And what about Lucy Conyers?"

He grinned. "What about her? I think she'll be staying over for a while. Extending her vacation, so to speak, compliments of the state of Alaska."

"But she didn't do it," I objected.

"In your opinion. Jake, go let Fred and Louie know they can head on into town now. I'm pretty sure we've got everything we need. You should also let him know that Mrs. Conyers will be riding down with us." Nodding, Jake Ripley left the room.

"Who are Fred and Louie?" I asked.

"The engineer and the conductor."

"You're telling them to take the train and leave? Does that mean you're not going to interview anyone else?"

"Why should we?" Sonny asked with a shrug. "Lucy already told us that she's got a fifty-thousand-dollar life insurance policy riding on poor Mike, double that if he dies of anything other than natural causes. She gets rid of the trouble and aggravation of having a sick husband on her hands, and she gets fifty thousand to a hundred thousand bucks in his place. Not bad. That gives us motive and opportunity both. I've known murders where what was at stake was a hell of a lot less than fifty large, and I'll bet you have, too. Not only that, I have a feeling once we have a chance to discuss this with Mrs. Conyers in more detail, that she'll straighten up and tell us everything we need to know."

"As in confess?" I asked.

"Right," he grinned. "Save us the trouble of having to convict her."

"But she didn't do it."

"Sez you," Liebowitz returned. "Let me give you some advice, Mr. Beaumont. Go get on the train. It's a damned long walk from here, even if it is all downhill. And then there's the bears, you know. They're pretty damned hungry this time of year—getting ready for winter and all."

"You're a sorry son of a bitch," I told him.

"Really. Well, I may be a sorry son of a bitch, but I also happen to be in charge. FBI or no FBI, you've got no standing here, Mr. Beaumont. In fact, as an ex-homicide dick from the big city, you've got less than no standing. If I was you, I'd make tracks for that train, fella. And don't let the door slam on your butt on the way out."

As if to underscore Sonny's statement, the train whistle gave two short, shrill blasts. Obviously Fred and Louie had taken Jake Ripley at his word. Not wanting to be left behind to hoof it, I jogged over to the train and pulled myself up onto the last car just as it started to move.

Beverly was waiting right inside the door. "Where's Lucy?" she demanded.

"She's riding into town with the two detectives."

"Why? Is she under arrest?"

"I don't know that for sure, but I'd say it's likely."

Beverly was aghast. "They think Lucy killed Mike?"

"That's my impression."

By now Claire and Florence Wakefield had joined Beverly. "Preposterous!" Claire announced. "That's the most ridiculous thing I've ever heard."

"Where are they taking her?" Lars asked.

"Into Skagway."

"What are you going to do about it?" Beverly asked.

"I don't know," I told her. "There isn't a whole lot anybody can do. She needs a lawyer, of course."

"You have a friend who's a lawyer, don't you?" she asked. "What's his name again? He's always seemed like a very nice man."

"Ralph Ames is a nice man, Beverly," I said. "He just doesn't happen to be here."

"But couldn't you call him?" she asked. "You really must do something about this, Jonas. You're the one who knows how these things work."

I know how they're supposed to work, I thought with a shake of my head. "With someone like Detective Liebowitz running the show, all bets are off."

"He's from Chicago," Lars put in from the sidelines. "Said he came here because he wanted clean winters for a change. Didn't like him much. Didn't seem to have all that much on the ball. That young Indian kid, though, he struck me as being pretty sharp."

"What about Ralph Ames?" Beverly insisted. "Couldn't you at least call him?"

She was putting the squeeze on me again, using the same kind of tactics that had brought me along on the cruise in the first place.

"I suppose I could," I agreed. "I'll try calling as soon as we get back on board the ship."

Florence Wakefield reached into her purse and pulled out a cell phone with the face of Minnie Mouse on the cover. "No sense in wasting time," she said. "Why don't you go ahead and call right now?"

And so I did. I called Ralph from a cell phone on a train in the middle of nowhere in the middle of Alaska, and it worked. Once he was on the phone, I explained that I was calling at my grandmother's behest.

"Is this the lady you sent me the E-mail about?"

"No," I told him. "That's Naomi Pepper. Lucy Conyers is somebody else."

"You're saying a second passenger on the cruise ship is also being accused of murder?"

"Right. Different victim," I replied.

"You must be a jinx, Beau," Ralph said with some amusement. "I've been on several cruises, but nothing like that has ever happened."

"I'm just lucky, I guess. So what do you suggest?" I asked. "The one woman, Naomi Pepper, has simply been advised to stay on the ship unless the FBI agent in charge grants her permission to leave. With Lucy Conyers, though, I'm pretty sure she's under arrest, or she will be shortly, once they get her into Skagway and book her."

"And you don't think she did it?"

"No. I'm convinced it was someone from one of the other cars, but the detectives hit on Lucy and they didn't bother looking any further. I don't think they even interviewed any passengers from the other cars. I'm worried they're going to put pressure on Lucy and buffalo her into confessing in order to cover up their own sloppy police work."

Ralph thought about that for a second. "So she needs help immediately if not sooner."

"Right."

"Let me go to work on this," he said. "What's your number? I'll get back to you."

"This isn't my phone," I said. "Somebody lent me a cell phone so I could call you from here. I don't have the foggiest idea about the ship's number."

"I'm a big boy," Ralph Ames said. "If the *Starfire Breeze* has a number, I'll be able to find it and get back to you. Now, what are the names of those two detectives again?"

"Sonny Liebowitz and Jake Ripley," I told him.

"And the woman's name?"

"Lucy Conyers. Her husband's name was Mike."

I heard the scratch of pen on paper as Ralph jotted down the names. "Good enough," he said. "Now get off the phone and let me go to work. Tell Beverly not to worry."

"I will," I said.

Having heard the words straight from Ralph Ames' mouth, I knew that I wouldn't worry as much, either. I just hoped Lucy Conyers wouldn't have a nervous breakdown before Ralph could protect her from what I was ashamed to think of as "the law" in Skagway.

15

WE ARRIVED BACK in Skagway in brilliant late-afternoon sunlight. But even though the weather had changed, the group that trudged back up the *Starfire Breeze*'s gangplank was more bedraggled than they had been when we left during the morning downpour. Without Mike and Lucy Conyers along, the people in our little group were feeling mighty low. They were all terribly grieved by what had happened—grieved and taking it personally. Then, too, none of us had eaten a full meal since forenoon coffee all those hours ago.

"I don't think we'll be coming down for dinner tonight, Jonas," Beverly told me quietly as we stood in the crowded elevator lobby along with everyone else who had been on the ill-fated train ride. "Lars isn't quite up to facing the dining room. We'll just order from Room Service and have a little something sent up to our room."

I didn't need her to tell me that Lars was hurting. His weathered face sagged. The spryness was gone from his step. His usual hale-and-hearty coloring was tinged with gray. In all the years I've known him, I don't ever remember having seen him look worse.

"Do you think maybe he should go to the Infirmary and see the doctor?" I asked. "Or would you like me to come along up to the room and help?"

"Oh, no. I think he's better off working through this on his own. We'll be fine, Jonas. You do whatever it is you need to do. Hopefully that nice Mr. Ames will be back in touch with you and we can start getting this awful mess straightened out."

"I'll do my best," I assured her. *Whatever that might be.*

Back in the stateroom I was glad to see that the rib-killing roll-away bed had been removed. I located Rachel Dulles' business card and phoned her in her cabin. "What's up?" she asked when I identified myself.

"Did you hear what happened on the train?" I asked.

"Something about an old man falling off."

"His name is Mike Conyers," I told her. "And he didn't fall; he was pushed. The problem is, the detectives on the case are convinced his wife did it. They've taken her into Skagway for questioning."

"So?"

"I don't believe Mike Conyers was the real target," I told her. "I think they were after Marc Alley and missed."

There was a pause. "Where are you?"

"In my room."

"I'll be right there," she said.

Hector, the room attendant, was out in the hallway with his cart when I opened the door to let Rachel Dulles in. He smiled and gave me a knowing nod. *It's not what you think,* I wanted to say to him. Instead, I followed her inside and closed the door behind us.

"What happened?" she asked, and I told her.

"What's your theory?" Rachel wanted to know when I finished.

"I think whoever did it, under the cover of darkness, followed Marc down the aisle, shoved him hard enough to knock him over the guardrail, and then raced back to his seat."

"Without anyone realizing he'd been gone," Rachel added.

"Right."

"Only, Marc was knocked off-balance. He fell, all right, but inside the guardrail instead of over it. In the confusion, Mike Conyers is the one who actually went over the top."

"So the LITG operative is one of the passengers on the train. That narrows the field a little because the train doesn't hold all the passengers at once and crew members don't generally take those trips at all. I'll check with the purser's office and get a printout of the people who did sign up for the train."

"Thanks," I said. "At least somebody seems to be listening. That's more than I can say for the detectives on the case. The problem is, just because whoever it was missed getting Marc this time doesn't mean they won't try again. And an innocent old woman whose husband of fifty-five years has just died stands accused of murdering him."

Rachel wasn't particularly interested in Lucy Conyers' plight. "Marc knows about all this then?"

I nodded. "I told him last night, but he didn't take me very seriously. After what happened this morning, all that is changed."

"You're right," she said. "It is changed. I appreciate your help, Beau, but from now on, I'm taking charge of the Marc Alley problem myself."

"You're firing me?"

Rachel Dulles smiled. "I'm advising you to quit," she told me. "Obviously Leave It To God has upped the ante. If innocent civilians are getting killed, I can't in good conscience have you involved."

I figured I knew how to take care of myself, but I also knew she was doing what was necessary to keep the Agency from incurring any further liability if something did happen to me. Not only that, I was happy to be let loose of the responsibility. Lars Jenssen may have lost his grasp on Mike Conyers' coat, but I was the one who had dropped the ball. When Marc Alley went outside, I should have gone, too.

"Fair enough," I said. "I quit."

"I'd better be going then," she said, starting for the door. "I think I'll go introduce myself to Mr. Alley."

"Let me warn you in advance. He's not enamored of FBI agents."

"Who is?"

"Wait," I said. "Before you go, tell me, what's been happening here?"

Rachel resumed her seat. "Well, Harrison Featherman chartered a float plane. He left Leila and Chloe here and flew over to meet up with the Coast Guard crews who are looking for Margaret. Just to be on the safe side, Alex went along with him."

"Anything else?"

She shrugged. "Not too much. Todd Bowman managed to get copies of Margaret's two faxes. Not much there, I'm afraid. One is from a friend of hers, a guy named Grant Tolliver, who works for a company called Genesis, the same company Margaret worked for. He said things were looking good for the stock sale and that he'd let her know what happens. The other fax was more interesting. It's a draft copy of Harrison Featherman's new will. In the event of his death, half his assets would go to his new wife and any surviving children from that union. The remainder of his estate would be divided between Chloe Featherman and Melissa Pepper, in equal shares or survivor."

"Someone sent Margaret a copy of her ex-husband's new will? Who?"

"I have no idea. The fax came from a Kinko's. We've got someone trying to trace the fax, but whoever sent it evidently paid cash."

"In other words, whoever sent it didn't want to be found."

Rachel nodded. "I suspect it came from someone in the lawyer's office—a legal secretary maybe, or else just a lowly clerk who jumped at the opportunity Margaret offered to make a quick buck. The draft copies are numbered, but whoever did this was smart enough to remove the number before they made their copy."

"And when did that arrive?"

"Here on the ship? It was clocked in at three-ten. I have no idea what time it was delivered to Margaret."

"But as soon as it was and she had a chance to read it, that's when she went ape-shit and called Naomi Pepper to raise hell."

"Right. Which is why Todd is focusing his investigation on her and whoever the guy is who helped her," Rachel explained. "And I can't say I blame him. Friends may not let friends drive drunk, but they don't screw around with their friends' husbands, either."

I was tempted to repeat what Naomi had told me about the motivation behind her engaging in sexual relations with Harrison Featherman, but I didn't. There wasn't much point. Defending Naomi to an FBI agent who wasn't even directly involved in the investigation of Margaret Featherman's disappearance seemed like a bad idea.

This time when Rachel Dulles got up and started for the door, I made no attempt to stop her. She had barely stepped into the hallway when my phone rang. "Beaumont here," I said, picking up the receiver.

"My name's Carol Ehlers. Ralph Ames is a friend of mine."

I've come to believe Ralph Ames wrote the book on networking. I've yet to find a place where he doesn't have a contact or an acquaintance he can call on to pull a few strings or do whatever needs doing.

"This is about Lucy Conyers?" I asked.

"One and the same," she replied. "I'm up in Juneau, but I practice all over southeast Alaska. I have my own plane, a Turbo Beaver, and could fly there from Juneau. The problem is, I have no idea whether or not Mrs. Conyers will actually want my help when I get there, to say nothing of whether or not she'll be able to pay for it. Is she indigent and likely to need a public defender?"

My mind stuck on the Turbo Beaver part. DeHaviland Beavers are top-of-the-line bush-pilot float planes, and they don't come cheap. If Carol Ehlers had her own and piloted it, too, she was not only someone to reckon with, but she was definitely the high-priced spread. Of course, since she was a friend of Ralph's, I shouldn't have been surprised.

"I don't know about the public-defender bit," I replied. "Lucy's not indigent, I don't think, but she's not loaded either. But, if you don't mind, Ms. Ehlers—"

"Please call me Carol," she interjected.

"And I'm Beau," I told her. "If you don't mind, I'd be more than willing to pay for you to fly down here and do an initial consult."

"Skagway is actually up from Juneau, not down. And that's very generous of you—more generous than you know, since my hourly rate is quite steep. Are you sure you want to do that?"

"Lucy Conyers is a friend of my grandparents," I explained. "My grandmother, Beverly Jenssen, is the one who insisted that I call Ralph looking for help. She's not going to stand for it if I end up telling her, 'Sorry. Nothing I could do.' No, compared to that, paying whatever you charge will be a bargain."

Carol Ehlers laughed aloud at that. "All right. Is there anything else I should know?"

"Lucy Conyers' husband was an Alzheimer's patient. From what I can tell, she's been caring for him all by herself for months, if not years. So, in addition to being in a state of shock at her husband's death, the poor woman is worn down—right to the nub. I'm afraid the detectives on the case are going try taking advantage of her weakened state and bamboozle her into incriminating herself."

"Who are the detectives?"

"One's named Jake Ripley. He's probably all right. The one I'm really worried about is an Alaska state trooper named Sonny Liebowitz."

"Great," Carol Ehlers said. "Mr. Missing Miranda Liebowitz himself."

"You know him then?"

"When Sonny Liebowitz chose to leave his native Chicago behind in favor of coming here, in my opinion, Chicago's gain turned out to be Alaska's loss. Yes, I've had my share of dealings with Detective Sonny Liebowitz. So has every other criminal defense attorney in southeast Alaska. What's going on?"

"The last I knew, Liebowitz and his partner were hustling Lucy into a patrol car and were about to drive her into Skagway."

"If Sonny Liebowitz was calling the shots, they probably ended up driving into town the long way."

I remembered seeing only a single road. "There is a long way?" I asked.

"That's a joke, Mr. Beaumont," Carol Ehlers told me. "Sorry. Sonny's well known for obtaining patrol-car-based confessions which, likely as not, end up being thrown out of court. Actually, having Detective Liebowitz on the case could end up working in our favor. So what's the deal here?"

I told her as much as I could, alluding to the fact that there was a good chance Marc Alley had been the killer's intended target. I would have gone into more detail, but she cut me off in the middle of a sentence.

"Sorry to interrupt," she said, "but all this talk is taking too much time. If I'm going to be there soon enough to do any good, I'll need to head home, get the Beaver warmed up, and file a flight plan. I'll be in Skagway as soon as I can. I'll let Mrs. Conyers know that I'm available if she needs my help. After that, it's up to her. She'll either retain me or not. One way or the other, you'll be off the hook, Beau. What time is the ship due to sail?"

"Six P.M."

"And where do you go tomorrow?"

"Glacier Bay. I haven't paid that much attention to the itinerary. I figure once I'm on the ship, I go where it goes."

"I doubt Lucy Conyers is going to be on board by the time you sail," Carol Ehlers returned. "But I'll do my best. If Mrs. Conyers does retain me, I'll need to be in touch to get the names of all the people who were on the train when it happened. I'll want to conduct my own investigation rather than simply relying on Sonny Liebowitz's say-so as to what went on."

"Call anytime," I told her. "I'll be here."

Once off the phone, I went into the bathroom and splashed my face with cold water. For someone who was supposed to be on vacation and taking it easy, I looked pretty damned haggard.

I lay down on the bed and closed my eyes, thinking I'd give myself the benefit of a short nap. I may have actually dozed off, but it seemed to me the light tap on my door came within seconds of my closing my eyes. When I opened the door, Naomi Pepper was standing in the corridor. "Hi," she said. "Anybody home? And are you still taking in strays?"

I glanced up and down the hall and was relieved to see that Hector, my room attendant, was nowhere in sight. I motioned Naomi inside, where she took a seat on the sofa. "What's going on?" I asked.

"I feel like I'm trapped in some other dimension. Everything I thought I knew has gone out the window. Margaret's dead. Sharon and Virginia aren't speaking to me. I refuse to go beg Todd Bowman for a permission slip, so I feel like a prisoner. The *Starfire Breeze* is a very nice ship, but as soon as you can't come and go as you please, it starts feeling like a jail—nice to look at, but a jail nonetheless. I've been going stir-crazy all day. I really wanted to take that railway ride up to White Pass, although I heard something went wrong on that today, too. There was a delay of some kind. Two trains never left at all."

"Calling what happened a delay is a bit of an understatement," I allowed and then went on to tell her about what had happened to Mike Conyers, including the fact that Mike's widow was most likely in the process of being booked in connection with his death.

"Things like this aren't supposed to happen on cruises," Naomi commented sadly when I finished relating the story. "It's supposed to be all beautiful sunsets and romantic dinners, not murders and disappearances."

Her view was so close to my own that it made me laugh, although it really wasn't a laughing matter. Two people—two *Starfire Breeze* passengers—had died in the course of this cruise. Although the ship's crew members were evidently aware of what was going on, most of the passengers were not. The *Starfire Courier* came out daily and dutifully reported that day's schedule of events as well as arrivals and departures, but no mention was made of more serious matters. As far as passengers were concerned, there had been only a "delay" in the White Pass and Yukon excursion train schedule. No one cared to make any kind of official announcement that a man—one of their fellow passengers—had fallen hundreds of feet to his death. As far as I could tell, regardless of FBI involvement, this particular cruise line was still very much in the "under-reporting" business.

"I thought it would be a lot more peaceful myself," I told her.

A period of silence followed. I assumed Naomi had come to see me because she wanted to talk, but her pump seemed to need priming. "So what all has been happening on board today?" I asked.

Naomi Pepper bit her lip before she answered. "I talked to

Harrison before he left to go look for Margaret," she said finally.

"And?"

"I know how Margaret found out about Missy."

"How?"

"Harrison told me that they found a draft copy of Harrison's brand-new will in Margaret's stateroom. It had been faxed to her that afternoon, just before she called me. No wonder she was upset." Naomi shrugged. "I guess I would have been, too, if the shoe had been on the other foot."

"Did Harrison have any idea where it came from?"

"None at all. He's furious about it and convinced that someone in his attorney's office must have leaked it to Margaret the same way someone in his travel agency leaked the travel plans. He thinks Margaret bribed them."

"But he has no idea who it might have been?"

"No."

"Did Harrison say anything about the other fax, the one that came in at dinner that first night and was mistakenly delivered to Chloe?"

"He said it's about the IPO."

"As in 'initial public offering'?" I asked.

"Right. He said Margaret's company was getting ready to do one of those this week, but I don't know any of the details. I don't follow monetary affairs very well. Talk about securities and stocks and all of that bores me to tears. My eyes just glaze over. Gary was always excited about IPOs—said they were a great way to make money. As far as I could see, it was just another way of betting on horses—corporate ones rather than those with four legs. He never made any money on those, either."

Again Naomi fell silent. She plucked at a loose thread on the arm of the couch. Something was going on with her, and I had no idea what it was. "Did you talk to Ralph Ames?" I asked.

She nodded. "He was nice and very reassuring. He told me not to talk to Todd Bowman at all. Ralph said that as long as I say I want to have my attorney present, Bowman will have to leave me alone at least until after we're back in Seattle. After that, who knows?" She gave a hopeless shrug.

"What's wrong, Naomi?"

Tears spilled out of her eyes and down both cheeks. "What's wrong?" she sobbed. "Everything. My life is a shambles. My daughter hates me. Two of my best friends aren't speaking to me, and I'm a suspect in the death of a third one. I'm stuck on this goddamned boat for another three days and two nights, and I don't even have a place to sleep or shower or change clothes. What's wrong? You tell me— what's right?"

I've always been a sucker for damsels in distress. If a woman is crying, I tend to jump in and do whatever's necessary to make her stop. The offer was out of my mouth before I could help myself. "You can stay here with me," I said.

"No," she mumbled into her hanky. "I couldn't do that," and kept right on crying.

I waited until I couldn't stand it anymore. "Look," I said impatiently. "Have you had anything to eat today?"

"No," she sniffled. "I wasn't hungry."

She was still wearing the same clothes she had been wearing when I saw her last—the same clothes she'd worn the night before.

"What about a shower? Did you have one of those?"

"I already told you. I tried going back to the room, but I couldn't stand it. I don't want to see Sharon and Virginia. I don't have any idea what I'll say to them."

I stood up, went to the closet, and pulled out a clean, still-plastic-wrapped terry-cloth bathrobe. "Here," I said, handing it over to her. "One of the nice things about having a junior suite is that there's a wonderful Jacuzzi tub in the bathroom. I want you to go in there, strip down, and have a nice long soak. While you're doing that, I'm going to call Virginia and Sharon and ask them to pack up your things. I'll send my room attendant down to pick them up and bring them here. Then, after you're decent again and feeling a little better, I'm going to order a Room Service dinner to be served right here in the room."

"Really, I couldn't . . ." she objected.

"You can," I told her. "You have to, and you will. Now what's your cabin number?"

After a few more increasingly indefinite nos, I finally won that round. In the end, she never did say an actual yes. She simply took the bathrobe from my hand, disappeared into my bathroom, and shut the door behind her. As soon as I heard bathwater running, I picked up the phone and dialed Naomi's soon-to-be-former cabin. Virginia Metz answered.

"It's Beau," I told her. "Beau Beaumont from the dining room," I added. "Your tablemate."

"Sorry," she said. "With everything that's happened the

last couple of days, dinner in the dining room seems eons away. What can I do for you?"

"Naomi's here with me," I said. "And she'll probably be here for the rest of the cruise."

"So?" Even over the phone, the distinct coolness in Virginia's one-word response was enough to lower my room's temperature by a good two or three degrees.

"She needs her things," I added quickly. "Would you mind packing them up for her? I'll be glad to send my room attendant down to pick them up in a little while."

"After what Naomi did to Margaret, you expect us to pack up her suitcases for her?"

I didn't know if Virginia was more upset about Naomi's having a child with Margaret Featherman's former husband or if her attitude derived from suspicions that Naomi might be involved in whatever had happened to Margaret on board the ship. Either way, I could see why Naomi felt that returning to her cabin was out of the question.

"Well," I said. "It doesn't sound as though you're any more eager to be around her than she is about seeing you at the moment. But if you'd rather, I suppose I could come down and do her packing myself."

"Don't bother," Virginia said curtly. "How soon will you be sending someone to get her things?"

"Say fifteen, twenty minutes? Would that be long enough?"

"We'll have her suitcases packed and waiting outside the door. Tell her we want our room key back, too." With that, Virginia Metz slammed the receiver down in my ear.

Taking my own room key, I went in search of Hector. I found him out in the hallway, using his cart to deliver fresh ice and clean towels to my neighbors two doors up.

"Do you require something?" he asked.

"Yes," I said. "A lady is going to be joining me in my cabin from now on," I told him. "If you wouldn't mind, I'd like you to go down to her old cabin and bring her luggage up here. Her name is Naomi Pepper, and her suitcases will be waiting outside the door." I gave him the deck name and cabin number.

A conspiratorial grin spread across Hector's broad face. Clearly having passengers change cabins wasn't unheard of aboard the *Starfire Breeze*. Hector appeared to be enjoying the idea immensely.

"Of course, Mr. Beaumont," he said quickly. "I'll be only too happy to do that."

I reached for my wallet, expecting to offer him a tip. "No need," he said. "I'll take care of it right away."

Back in the cabin, I tried to sort through all the ramifications of what was going on. Virginia Metz wanted Naomi's room key back. On land that would have been a simple transaction. On board the *Starfire Breeze*, it was somewhat more complicated. On board a cruise ship, those little plastic key cards mean everything. Not only does it allow passengers in and out of their rooms and off and on the ship, it's also necessary for buying even so much as a tube of toothpaste from the gift shop. If you're on a cruise ship without a key card, you don't exist. You're in almost as bad a shape as the poor guy in that old social studies movie they used to show at my elementary school back in Ballard. I think the film was called *The Man Without a Country*.

Naomi was still soaking in the tub, so I picked up the phone and dialed the purser's office. "Supposing a passenger wanted to change cabins," I said. "Would it be possible to turn in one key and have all the charges for that key transferred to another cabin, along with getting an additional key to the new room?"

"It can be done," the crisp-voiced young woman told me. "But of course, there's an additional charge."

"That's understandable," I agreed. "So how does one go about it?"

"Both people have to come to the purser's desk together. That way, new key cards can be issued to both of them at once."

"I see," I said.

The job would have to be done in person. We'd have to go and stand in line in public to do it, and I was sure the fresh-faced young people at the purser's desk would all jump to the same conclusions Hector had. It wasn't something I looked forward to with eager anticipation.

The bathroom door opened. Naomi emerged wearing the robe and with a towel wrapped turban-style around her head. Free of smudged makeup, she looked refreshed and even a little relaxed. I handed her the Room Service menu. "Order something for both of us," I said.

"But it's early," she objected. "Don't you want to wait?"

"There's nothing magic about eating dinner at eight-thirty. Besides, I ended up skipping lunch today, too. We'll eat now. Then we'll go down to the purser's desk and make arrangements to trade in your old key card for one to this room."

Naomi was talking on the phone to Room Service when there was a tap on the door. Hector, still grinning, stood in the hallway carrying two suitcases. "Come in," I said. "Just put them on the bed."

He did so, but I caught him taking a discreet look at Naomi in the process. He was surprised, I think, to discover that the woman in my room wasn't the same one he had seen me with most recently. Once again I made as if to tip him. Once again he declined.

"No, thank you," he said. "I hope you and madame have a very pleasant trip." With a courtly bow, he let himself out and closed the door.

Naomi finished up with Room Service. "Thank you for getting my things. It's so nice to finally get out of those grubby clothes."

"You're welcome," I said. "But why don't you go ahead and unpack? That way, when our dinner comes, there will be room enough to maneuver the dinner cart."

"Where should I put things?"

"Help yourself. Use whatever you need—the closet, the inside bedside table."

I didn't add that I hoped she'd also get dressed. It was bad enough to have half the ship's crew snickering at us. My worst fear, though, was that Lars or Beverly would show up at the door unannounced.

Naomi Pepper and I may not have had any overtly dishonorable designs on one another, but that didn't mean our reputations wouldn't suffer—especially if my grandparents got wind of what was going on. I had come along to chaperon them, but the way things were going, they might well feel obliged to chaperon me.

16

THE GRILLED HALIBUT STEAKS Naomi Pepper and I had for dinner that evening were among the best I've ever eaten, and that includes meals prepared at some of the tonier seafood restaurants in downtown Seattle. There may have been a few things about cruising that didn't measure up to expectations, but the food on board the *Starfire Breeze* was more than living up to advance rave notices.

When we finished eating, Naomi pushed away from the table and smiled. "I really do feel better," she said. "I must have been running on empty."

"My mother always said, 'Food for the body is food for the soul.' Not terrifically profound, but true anyway."

"Is your mother still alive?" Naomi asked.

"No. She died of cancer years ago."

"And the grandmother who's on the ship? Is she your mother's mother or your father's?"

"I never met my father," I told her. "He died before I was born. Beverly is my mother's mother, and she's outlived her daughter by decades."

"That doesn't seem fair," Naomi said. "It's supposed to be the other way around. Parents are supposed to die first."

"Life isn't fair," I told her.

Naomi glanced at her watch. It was only a little past seven. "Since we've already eaten dinner, what do we do with the rest of the evening?"

"First we go down to the purser's desk and straighten out the key-card situation."

"Now?"

"Why not? If we go now, we may be done before the first-seating dinner crowd gets out of the dining rooms and before the second seating shows up."

"Good idea," she said. "As far as I'm concerned, the fewer people we run into, the better."

As we stepped into the corridor, Hector's cart was parked two rooms away from where it had been before. Leaving Naomi standing in the hallway, I poked my head into the room where he was working. "Ready for your dinner service to be removed?" he asked.

"Yes," I told him. "That would be fine. And another thing. Does the king-sized bed in my suite break apart into two singles?"

"Yes."

"When you do our turndown service, would you mind

doing that—turning them into two separate beds? I'd really appreciate it."

A look of complete consternation crossed Hector's face. Madame and me in twin beds wasn't how he had read the situation. A guy with women running in and out of his room wasn't supposed to ask for separate beds when it came time for sleeping arrangements. I could see from his frown that he was disappointed in me—that he was taking what he saw as my lack of sexual prowess personally. His words, however, belied the frown.

"Of course, Mr. Beaumont. Right away."

The people at the purser's desk disapproved of the new roommate arrangement as well, but we muddled through. When we finished, I asked Naomi what she wanted to do next. The first-seating crowd was now beginning to trickle out of dining rooms and back into the atrium and lobby areas. Since we wanted to avoid people as much as possible, we opted for the cardroom, where the two of us played a hard-fought game of Scrabble. I've been an inveterate worker of crossword puzzles all my life. As a consequence, Scrabble is one board game—the only board game—I'm fairly good at. Unfortunately, Naomi was better than I was, although not by much. I was leading right up to the last word, then she moved ahead by ten points.

After leaving the cardroom, we took a turn around the Promenade Deck before the chilly breeze and misty rain drove us back inside. After that, we returned to the room—our room—where Hector had done my bidding. Where before there had been a single king-sized bed, there were now two twins, both neatly turned down and with a mint resting on each freshly fluffed pillow.

I've never been much of a believer in twin beds. I felt as though we'd fallen through a time warp and landed in the middle of a 1950s-era situation comedy. Lucy and Ricky Ricardo had been married for years before she turned up pregnant, but I don't ever remember seeing them in anything other than twin beds. The same goes for Ozzie and Harriet. I always wondered if they alternated beds for sex or just did it on the floor.

"Are you responsible for that?" Naomi demanded as soon as she saw the newly revised sleeping arrangement. From her tone of voice, it was impossible for me to tell if she was mad about it or pleased.

"Hector's the one who actually did it," I told her. "But I'm the one who asked him to. I hope you don't mind. Roll-away beds hurt my ribs. After last night, I figured we both needed some decent rest."

To my amazement, Naomi promptly burst into tears again. They leaked out of her eyes and dribbled in muddy streaks down her cheeks. "Thanks," she murmured. "I've been worried about it all evening, but after you were nice enough to let me stay here, I didn't want to mention it. I mean, after what happened between Harrison and me, I was afraid you'd just laugh if I told you I wasn't that kind of girl."

"Who's worried about you?" I asked with a grin. "I'm not that kind of boy."

Leaving her to mull that, I turned to the telephone, where the message light was blinking furiously. There was only one message on voice mail—a call from Carol Ehlers.

"I'm staying over in Skagway with friends tonight," she said. "Give me a call on my cell phone when you can. Here's the number."

In attempting to return the call I endured several impatient minutes as I sorted my way through the ship-to-shore hassle. I could see that leaving my own trusty cell phone at home in Seattle had been a mistake. Florence Wakefield had told me that her cell phone had been working perfectly ever since the *Starfire Breeze* had entered Alaskan waters. When Ralph Ames had first urged me to buy a cell phone, I had argued with him about it and then griped incessantly once I finally knuckled under and bought one. Now here I was, a few years later, complaining because I didn't have one in my hand. There's no pleasing some people.

At last Carol Ehlers answered her phone. "Beau," she said pleasantly when she heard who it was. "Thanks for returning my call. I thought you'd want to be brought up-to-date. Lucy Conyers has retained me, and she insists that she'll pay all my initial consultation costs as well. That means you're free and clear on that score, and everything here is under control."

"That's good," I breathed. "How's Lucy holding up?"

"All right, all things considered," Carol told me, "but they did book her."

"On what little that twerp Liebowitz had going?" I asked. Carol sighed. "I'm afraid so."

"She didn't confess, did she?"

"No, Lucy didn't do that. She told me she's watched *Law and Order* enough that she knew she needed to keep her mouth shut."

"There you are, then," I said. "I guess television is good for something after all."

"We'll see about that," Carol said with another infectious laugh. "We'll be doing an attorney-present interview with Liebowitz and Ripley bright and early tomorrow morning. That's why I'm staying over tonight. I was waiting at the station when they finally came driving into town. And I was right about Sonny taking his own sweet time to get her here. I'm sure he was working on her the whole way. It's a miracle she didn't cave."

In my homicide days I had cleared more than a few cases by way of patrol-car-induced confessions, so I knew the drill. This time I was glad the ruse of chatting up the suspect hadn't worked. Lucy Conyers had been under terrible emotional stress. I was sure she felt responsible for the fact that Mike had been in harm's way in the first place. It wouldn't be too difficult for an underhanded cop to take advantage of that sense of responsibility and make whatever she said sound like an out-and-out confession.

"I know it meant a lot to Lucy to have me there," Carol Ehlers continued. "She said for me to say thank you."

"She's welcome," I said.

"Where's the *Starfire Breeze* going after Glacier Bay?" Carol Ehlers asked.

I fumbled around until I located my previously unread copy of the *Starfire Courier*. "Sitka is the day after tomorrow. The next day we head back to Seattle."

"So you're not in port at all tomorrow. All right. I'll have my investigator, Jack Hedges, meet up with you in Sitka. I'll want him to interview everyone who was in the train car with Mike and Lucy Conyers."

Great, I thought. *Once Carol Ehlers' detective joined the parade, there would be almost as many investigators on board the* Starfire Breeze *as there were ordinary passengers.*

"Talking to the people in the car isn't going to cut it," I told her. "The person who did this came from one of the other cars. I tried explaining all that to Sonny Liebowitz, and now I'm telling you the same thing. The intended target was a guy by the name of Marc Alley."

"How do you know this?"

Although my face was turned away from her, I could feel Naomi Pepper's eyes drilling into the back of my head. "I can't say right now," I said. "It's confidential."

Carol didn't miss a beat. "I get it," she said. "Someone must be there with you. I'll make sure Jack speaks to you about this in private."

"You might suggest that he contact a pair of passengers named Kurt and Phyllis Nix."

"Were they on the train?"

"No, but they know something about it. Tell Phyllis I gave you her name. That should help."

"Good."

Carol had definitely picked up on my tone of voice. "Don't worry about Lucy Conyers," she assured me. "I'm very good at what I do—just ask Sonny Liebowitz. He wasn't thrilled to see me turn up in her corner, I can tell you that. But speaking of what I do, Ralph mentioned there was some other problem on board the *Starfire Breeze*—that some other passenger might also be in need of my services. Do you know about that?"

More than I should and not nearly enough, I thought, but with Naomi Pepper sitting right there on the sofa, my answer had to be circumspect. "For the moment that all seems to be under control."

"Good. Let me know if anything changes."

"Thanks. I will."

I hung up. When I turned back to Naomi, she was staring at me with a puzzled frown. "Marc Alley?" she asked. "The guy from dinner?"

"Right."

"Why would someone want to kill him?"

"I can't say," I said. "It's part of an ongoing investigation. I'm not allowed to talk about it."

"So you're still a detective after all. You aren't retired at all."

"I am retired," I told her. "I got roped into all this by accident."

"You say Marc was the real target, but they arrested the man's widow?" Naomi asked. I nodded. "What's going to happen to her?"

I shrugged. "Who knows? One of Ralph Ames' friends, a defense lawyer named Carol Ehlers, has ridden to the rescue for the time being. No matter what, they won't charge Lucy Conyers with first-degree murder. To do that, they'd have to prove premeditation. There's no way Lucy could have known that as soon as the train entered the tunnel, the whole place would go black."

"Why not?" Naomi said. "It's on the video."

"Excuse me?" I asked. "What video?"

"The video of the train trip," Naomi replied.

"Are you kidding? You've seen one of those?"

"Sure," she said. "They probably have it for times when the weather's too bad for people to see anything. There's one of Glacier Bay, too. I watched the Skagway one today, since I wasn't able to get off the ship myself. It shows the museum with all the gear the people had to carry with them. Then it follows most, if not all, of the train trip. It shows the cars going completely dark when the train heads into Tunnel Mountain. It even talks about how long it takes for the train to make it all the way through. I think it's something like six and a half minutes."

I was stunned. If Lucy Conyers had watched the video, she would have known about the tunnel. Any other passenger on board the *Starfire Breeze* would have known the same thing. There went my pet theory about no possible premeditation. Whoever had killed Mike Conyers had known exactly how much time would elapse between the time the train went dark and the time people could see again.

"Am I going to need one of those?" Naomi's voice brought me back to the present.

"One of what?"

"A defense attorney."

"Maybe," I said.

"How expensive is your friend, the one I talked to today?"

"Ralph's expensive, but he's also one of the best."

"What if I can't afford him?" she asked despairingly.

"How about if we cross that bridge when we get to it?" I suggested.

After that, neither Naomi nor I seemed to have much more to say. There were several movies to choose from on the television set, so we settled on one of those and watched it. By the time the movie was over, Naomi was curled up on her bed, buried under a mound of covers, and sound asleep. Unfortunately, I was wide awake.

Back in my homicide days, I used to lie awake at times as well. When I couldn't sleep, instead of tossing and turning, I'd use that middle-of-the-night time and mentally sort through various aspects of whatever case I was working on. Sometimes, in the dark of night, pieces of a case that had blown in all directions during the day would suddenly slip into place. So I did that now. I closed my eyes and tried to focus all my thoughts on what had happened on the train ride—on exactly what had been said and who had been where at any given moment.

I tried to remember how it was that Lars had ended up taking Mike Conyers outside instead of Lucy's doing it. How had she reacted? I couldn't recall that she'd appeared to be anything other than grateful when Lars took the responsibility off her hands. And when exactly had she left her seat to go to the rest room? Was it before Marc Alley had come through our car or after? Maybe someone else would know— Beverly, perhaps, or maybe Florence or Claire Wakefield. I took a notepad and pen off the table and jotted a blindly written reminder to ask them each that question the next time I saw them.

And what about Marc? I remember seeing him standing poised with his camera in hand just as the train car entered the tunnel. I recalled one flash for sure, but then, as I lay there, I wondered if maybe there hadn't been two, a second one slightly after the first. On a fresh piece of notepad I scribbled another reminder, telling me to check with Marc Alley to find out whether or not he'd gone to the photo center to have his pictures developed.

The whole exercise took me back to a story I remember reading in a high school literature book. It was about a man who had spent his whole adult life delivering milk with a horse and wagon. One day, the man dropped over dead without ever getting into the wagon, but the horse still ran the whole route, stopping and waiting in front of each house just the way he would have if the man had been getting in and out to deliver milk.

Here I was doing the same thing. I wasn't a homicide cop anymore. Rachel Dulles had "fired" me from my stint as unpaid FBI informant. I had no business asking questions, worrying about suspects, or questioning alibis. And yet I couldn't help myself. No matter how I tried, I couldn't *stop* doing it. It's one of those lessons late in the learning, but being a detective doesn't come with an off/on toggle switch. The city fathers can give you your gold watch and show you the door, but just because they put you out to pasture doesn't mean you can quit. Once a detective, always a detective, plain and simple.

I was finally dozing off when the phone rang. Hector's room rearrangement had left the phone on the far side of both beds—on Naomi's side of both beds. "It might be your grand-mother," Naomi mumbled, stirring sleepily. "You'd better answer."

I hotfooted it out of bed. Feeling self-conscious, I paused long enough to put on a robe, then headed around the beds in the dark. On the way I stubbed my little toe on the bed frame hard enough to jam it and maybe even break it. Groaning, cussing, and hopping on one foot, I made it to the phone and picked up the receiver in time to hear a woman's voice say. "If he's not there, just hang up," followed by a distinct click.

"Hello," I said into the mouthpiece. "Hello? Hello?" But it was too late. Whoever was calling had hung up. All I heard was the dial tone.

"Who was it?" Naomi asked, sitting up and switching on the light.

I stood staring at the phone, trying to decide if the whole thing was a dream. No, my toe hurt too bad for it to have been a dream. And I thought I knew who the caller was—knew the person the woman sounded like. The deep-throated, smoky voice sounded as though it belonged to none other than Mrs. Margaret Featherman. But that was utterly impossible, since Margaret Featherman was dead. Or, if she wasn't dead—if she was alive and capable of making phone calls—why would she be calling me, of all people? The only thing the two of us had in common was a bad case of mutual antipathy.

No, her calling me didn't make any sense at all. *Maybe it was someone who sounded like Margaret Featherman,* I told myself finally. *A close relative or something. A sister, maybe.*

Without any further information—without some solid form of identification—it would have been wrong for me to say anything at all. It would have been inhumane to pass along that unsubstantiated information to Naomi Pepper, raising possibly false hopes that her friend—her former friend, most likely—was still alive and that Naomi herself was no longer a homicide suspect.

Not wanting to sound like a nut case, I lied. "I have no idea who it was," I told Naomi. "It must have been a wrong number. Forget about it."

Naomi waited until I was back on my own side of the bed to turn out the light. Within minutes she had rolled over on her side and was snoring softly. Not me. I lay awake for the next several hours, wondering what the hell was going on. I turned the question over and over in my mind. If through some incredible miracle Margaret Featherman was still alive, what the hell did she want with me? No matter how I looked at it, I couldn't come up with an answer that made any sense.

I went from wondering about the call to thinking about Margaret Featherman herself—Margaret and her two ship-board faxes. Had she bribed someone in her husband's law firm to deliver a copy of his will to her? If so, why? And what about this company she worked for, the one that was suppos-edly about to go public? What was the name of it again? I remembered that when Rachel Dulles had mentioned the name, it had struck me as something biblical.

It took several minutes for me to dredge Genesis out of the old random-access memory. So what the hell was Genesis and what did it have to offer that made selling stock possible or profitable? Supposing the IPO had happened, and Margaret Featherman had come out of it a wealthy woman? Would that offer enough motivation for some other killer? Originally, the fax had been mistakenly delivered to Chloe, and presumably she had read it. Despite her daughter's being a so-called Daddy's girl, I couldn't imagine Margaret Featherman leaving her estate to anyone other than Chloe.

In the end, though, I came back to the name—Genesis. Was there a possible connection between a company called Genesis and a shadowy organization that went by the name of Leave It To God? The very idea was enough to send me spinning right back to square one. This wasn't a night when late-night ruminations were going to give me the kind of answers I needed.

Sometime along the way, I'm not sure when, I realized that I wasn't alone in my room. That probably sounds silly, of course, since I knew Naomi Pepper was there. It was more than her simply being there. It was the realization that someone else was sharing the room with me—sleeping side by side on a bed that was less than a yard from mine. I heard Naomi's slow, even breathing and caught the faint scent of her shampoo and perfume in the air when she turned over in bed or rustled her covers. It was an odd sensation.

Most of the time I'm alone without really thinking about it. It's the way things are, and it would be far too much trouble to make any substantive changes in that solitary state. It had been years since Karen and I had slept together, sharing a room and a bed on a nightly basis. Anne Corley wasn't a part of my life long enough for us to get used to sleeping together, and during the course of my several-months-long affair with a lady named Alexis, we had hardly ever slept over at each other's places. One or the other of us was forever getting up in the middle of the night, dressing, and going home to our own separate condos.

And yet, the simple knowledge that I was sharing my stateroom on the *Starfire Breeze* with another human being soothed me somehow. It felt as though a coil that had been wound too tight in my chest was letting go. My body relaxed. My own breathing smoothed and deepened.

I barely knew Naomi Pepper. Some of the things she had done appalled me, but I liked the sound of her laughter. And I liked the fact that she could beat me—barely—at Scrabble. What the two of us shared could hardly be called a relationship, and yet I was glad she was there in the room with me. Glad she was lying next to me. I was still alone, only not quite as profoundly alone as I had been before.

That realization, pleasant as it may have been, still didn't make me fall sleep. The last time I checked the clock, it was a quarter to four. So much for another restful night on board the *Starfire Breeze*. When it came to cruising, getting your beauty sleep wasn't high on the agenda. I guess that's why people are glad to come home from vacations. It's only when they're back in their own beds that they finally have a chance to rest up.

17

ONCE I FELL ASLEEP, I really slept. I woke up at nine-thirty only because the phone was ringing, which is the story of my life. I've never needed an alarm clock because the telephone never lets me sleep late anyway.

I glanced over at the other bed and discovered that Naomi Pepper was already up and out. The bathroom door was shut. Once again I grabbed up my bathrobe and raced to the phone. On the way I discovered that the toe I'd bumped the night before was black and blue and hurt like hell.

"Hello."

"You are there," Ralph Ames said. "I thought I was going to end up leaving a message. How are you doing?"

"Other than having broken a toe from running after the phone, I'm fine."

"Sorry about that," he said.

I could have told him that my injured toe had nothing to do with him—that I had damaged it while trying to answer somebody else's middle-of-the-night phone call. But since Ralph was willing to accept full responsibility, I let him.

"I'm about to go into a meeting," he said. "But I wanted to check with you first and see how things are going up there."

"Thanks for calling Carol Ehlers," I said. "She's on the job, and it sounds as though Lucy Conyers is in good hands. As for Naomi Pepper, Todd Bowman seems to be leaving her alone for the time being, so I guess she's all right, too."

"The search still hasn't turned up any trace of Margaret Featherman?"

"That depends," I replied.

"What do you mean?" Ralph asked.

"I may have had a phone call from her last night."

"From Margaret? What's going on, Beau? Have you fallen off the wagon or started channeling or what?"

"It was a real phone call, Ralph."

"What did she say?"

"I'm not one hundred percent sure it was her—maybe it was someone who only *sounded* like her—and she hung up before I had a chance to say anything."

"Assuming Margaret Featherman is alive, and after this much time that's doubtful, why would she be calling you?"

"I have no idea."

"When did the call come through?"

"Last night, after I was in bed."

Ralph sighed. "Well, if someone plucked her out of the

water before she drowned, no one here knows anything about it. Seems to me that it would have been broadcast over all the news media by now."

"It's on the news?"

"Sure. Margaret Featherman's disappearance is a big deal down here in Seattle—front-page headlines for both papers, the works."

What makes for headlines always astonishes me. "It is?" I asked.

"Sure. Why wouldn't it be? Margaret Featherman gets turned into a paper multimillionaire one day, and the next day she's missing or dead and most likely the victim of foul play."

"Did I hear you say multimillionaire?" I asked.

"I haven't checked the stock prices this morning, but as of close of business yesterday, that Genesis IPO had gone through the roof. By last night, I'd say Margaret Featherman's net worth was right around twelve or thirteen million, give or take. Since she's one of Genesis' primary researchers, it'll be bad for them if she's out of the picture permanently. The stock could take quite a hit. There's always a chance, if it drops like a rock, she'll end up being worth next to nothing after all."

"Did I hear you say twelve or thirteen million is Margaret Featherman's share?"

"That's right. At the moment."

"And what the hell is Genesis?"

"It's one of Seattle's booming bio-tech genetic-engineering firms," Ralph replied. "What else would it be?"

What else indeed. "And what exactly do they engineer?"

"From what I've read, they believe they've designed a patch—a genetic patch—that can be downloaded into a damaged fetus in utero to correct Down syndrome."

"In utero. They correct the problem before the baby is born?"

"Right. And before the fetus is that badly damaged."

"How do you know all this?" I asked.

"I read it in this morning's paper—*The Times*—front page, right alongside the article about Margaret's disappearance."

"It sure as hell isn't front-page news in the *Starfire Courier*," I grumbled. "Could you fax me the articles, Ralph? I need to see them—all of them. The main article and all the little sidebars as well."

"Sure," Ralph said. "I'll have my secretary do it right away. But other than that, everything is fine? How are your grandparents doing?"

"They were more than a little blue about what happened on the train yesterday. Mike and Lucy Conyers had become friends of theirs. They took Mike's death pretty hard. Lars thinks he should have kept hold of Mike and prevented him from falling. If Beverly's discovered that they've put Lucy under arrest, I'd imagine she's on the warpath this morning."

"Tell Beverly that Carol will do a good job."

"I'll try," I said. "But so far as I can tell, nobody's ever had much luck *telling* Beverly Jenssen anything."

"No," Ralph agreed with a laugh. "I suppose not. All right. If you want that fax, I'd better make arrangements to send it before I disappear into my meeting."

The bathroom door was closed. I hadn't heard any sounds coming from inside, but that didn't mean Naomi wasn't there.

As soon as I got off the phone, I went over and tapped lightly on the door. When there was no answer, I eased it open. Evidence in the bathroom was consistent with her having already showered before leaving the stateroom. Concerned that Naomi might return and catch me half dressed, I locked myself in the bathroom and showered as well.

As the hot water cascaded over my body I was stunned by what Ralph had told me. The whole time I had been under the impression that Margaret Featherman was living off the proceeds of her divorce settlement from her ex-husband. From things Naomi had said about her, it sounded as though her friends had believed much the same thing—that if she had worked, it was because she wanted to do something with her time rather than because she needed a paycheck. Now, though, it sounded as though there was more to Margaret Featherman and her job than any of us—her good friends included—had suspected.

By the time I finished showering, dressing, and shoving my complaining toe into a too-tight shoe, there was still no sign of Naomi. That was just as well. I may have mentioned the late-night phone call to Ralph, but his reaction convinced me I had been right in not discussing it with Naomi. And, without seeing her, it was easy not to say anything about the possibility that Margaret Featherman might still be alive.

I paused by the phone and considered calling Lars and Beverly to see how they were doing. I went so far as to pick up the receiver, but I put it back down without dialing. If I talked to them, they would want to know what, if anything, I had heard about Lucy Conyers. I wasn't at all eager to tell them that the woman had been arrested. No, that was another conversation I was better off dodging for as long as possible.

When I stepped into the hall, Hector and his omnipresent cart were both there. It made me wonder if *Starfire Breeze* room attendants ever had any time off or if they worked round the clock, seven days a week.

"Good morning, Mr. Beaumont," he said as I walked past his cart. "Madame said to tell you she was going up to the buffet."

"Thanks, Hector," I returned, but instead of taking the hint and heading for the Lido Deck and Naomi, I went straight to the purser's desk and asked if they had a fax for me.

"That was fast, Mr. Beaumont," the young woman told me as she handed over a fat envelope with my name typed on the outside. "I only just now finished leaving you a message about this."

I went to the Sea Breeze Bar and ordered a cup of coffee. I tore open the envelope and pulled out a stack of faxed pages. Unfortunately, the resolution on the paper wasn't very good. I could read the headlines fine, but I found myself scowling and squinting as I tried to decipher the text of the articles.

"Try these," someone said.

I looked up to see a smiling Naomi Pepper standing over me offering me the use of a pair of reading glasses. I don't consider myself vain, but I've always taken pride in the fact that I've never needed to wear glasses of any kind.

"Try them," she urged again. "They won't bite."

Reluctantly I put them on. To my dismay, the print resolution in the faxes improved immeasurably.

"Thanks," I said. "Where do you get these things?"

"Any drugstore," she said. "Those cost nine ninety-eight a pair at Bartell Drugs. What are you reading?"

For an answer, I returned the reading glasses along with the first article, a two-column piece topped by a glamorous photo of Margaret Featherman that discussed her disappearance from the *Starfire Breeze* and the fact that the FBI was investigating. It also detailed the progress of the so-far-unsuccessful search the Coast Guard was conducting in Alaska's Chatham Strait just off Port Walter. The article included the information that the loss of Ms. Featherman's considerable talent could possibly cast a cloud over the future of the long-awaited Genesis IPO. The offering had been met with unbridled enthusiasm, but there was concern that news of Margaret Featherman's death might scare away other potential investors.

Naomi Pepper read through the article with a deepening frown forming on her forehead. "Did you know anything about that?" I asked when she finished. "About Genesis, I mean."

"I knew Genesis was the place where Margaret worked," Naomi said. "Just like she knew I work for The Bon, Virginia works for Boeing, and Sharon for the City of Seattle. But I thought it was just a job. I had no idea about her being what it says here—a key researcher."

"What was her training?" I asked. "What did she study in school?"

"Originally, she wanted to be a doctor, but you know how things were back then, when girls were supposed to be nurses, not doctors. Besides, Margaret was too much of a party animal. Her grades weren't good enough. She ended up with a degree in biology and eventually she got a teaching certificate. She could have taught high school biology, but as far as I know, she never did. Harrison didn't approve of having a working wife. Doctors' wives' careers were to be doctors' wives. It wasn't until after the divorce that she went back to school. First she got an advanced degree and then she went to work for this outfit. I know she worked long hours, but there was nothing to stop her since she didn't have to worry about taking care of Chloe."

"Harrison got custody?" I asked. Naomi nodded.

"How long ago was it that Margaret went to work for Genesis?"

Naomi shrugged. "It must have been about the same time Frederick and Nelson closed down and I went to work for The Bon."

The Bon Marché and F & N started out in Seattle as neighboring but competing department stores. The Bon was now the sole survivor of that mercantile rivalry. Frederick and Nelson's demise in the early 1990s was now ancient retail history. It surprised me to know that despite having been divorced that long, Margaret and Harrison Featherman were still caught up in each other's lives. But then I thought about Karen Beaumont Livingston and me and knew I shouldn't have been surprised at all.

"Which Bon?" I asked, returning to the conversation.

"Downtown," Naomi replied. "I sell small household appliances. By the way, could I interest you in a coffee grinder or a blender?"

"I already own one of each, but I don't use them often," I told her. "I'm not much of a cook."

"Who is these days?"

"Let me have your glasses again," I said. She handed them over, and I read the next several faxes before I passed them and the glasses back to Naomi. One of them was evidently from the Business section of the paper. In it Grant Tolliver, president and CEO of Genesis, offered reassurances that even if Margaret Featherman proved to be out of the picture permanently, her pioneering research had placed Genesis firmly in its position as leader of the pack.

"Twelve or thirteen million! I never would have imagined Margaret could end up being worth that much. When it comes right down to it, she's probably worth a lot more than Harrison is," Naomi said thoughtfully. "And for her to be called a pioneering researcher, I feel like there was a whole side to Margaret that I never even suspected."

I was polite enough not to point out that the reverse had been just as true.

"Did Margaret ever mention this Grant Tolliver to you?" I asked.

"The CEO from Genesis?" Naomi shook her head. "No, never."

"Remember that fax that Chloe delivered to the table that first night—the one that was first delivered to her by mistake?"

"Yes," Naomi replied.

"That one came from Tolliver."

"How do you know that?"

"Once a detective, always a detective," I told her. "I have my sources. But how smart is Chloe? If she was aware of what was happening with the IPO, she might have guessed or hoped that her mother would end up being worth a fortune."

"Wait a minute. You're thinking Chloe might somehow be responsible for Margaret's death?"

"With that much money at stake, sure. If you're a suspect, Chloe should be even more of one."

"I don't think so," Naomi declared. "Yes, she and Margaret didn't get along very well. Still, I can't imagine Chloe murdering anyone, least of all her mother. And it's so sad for Margaret, too," she shook her head. "That day when she should have been anticipating a wonderful triumph at work; instead she ended up finding out about Harrison and me and Missy. I never meant for her to find out about that, Beau. You've got to believe me."

"Does Missy know Harrison Featherman is her real father?"

"No. At least I never told her."

"Well, you'd better say something soon," I advised her. "Too many people know about it now. It won't be long before somebody spills the beans. Better you than having her end up reading about it in *The Times* or the *Seattle P-I*. That would be bad."

"I know," Naomi said. "I'm worried about that myself. I tried calling her at work yesterday when the ship was docked in Skagway. She knew Margaret was a friend of mine, and I wanted to let her know what was going on. I left a message, but of course she didn't return the call."

"Missy has a job? I thought you said she's on the streets."

"Was on the streets," Naomi corrected. "She ended up at

one of those shelters over in the University District, one for homeless street kids. I mean, I resent her being homeless or telling other people she is. Missy has a home; she just won't live there. Anyway, the shelter took her in and gave her a place to sleep. They helped her get back on track, too—better than I ever could. She had to be clean and sober, or they wouldn't let her stay. And they told her she had to get a job. With nothing but a GED and with nose rings and earrings out the kazoo and God knows what other kinds of tattoos and piercings, jobs didn't exactly fall into her lap. But she did finally land one at one of those copy places. She's been there a couple of months now, and she's supposed to be moving into her own apartment soon."

"A copy place?" I asked. "Which one?"

"A Kinko's," Naomi replied. "In downtown Seattle. I've never been there. I didn't think I'd be welcome."

A Kinko's! I remembered Rachel Dulles telling me that the fax containing the draft copy of Harrison Featherman's new will had been sent to Margaret Featherman from a Kinko's. Was Melissa Pepper the one who had sent it? I hoped my face didn't betray my consternation. If Missy had sent Margaret a draft copy of Harrison's new will, how had she come to be in possession of the document, and what was her motive for sending it? These were questions Todd Bowman would need to answer, but if I took him this new piece of information—that Melissa Pepper worked for Kinko's—he wasn't likely to view it kindly. Bowman already thought me an interfering doofus. I'd be better off routing this latest tip through Rachel Dulles. She had removed me from the Marc

Alley detail, but she, at least, might be willing to listen to what I had to say.

"Would Harrison have talked to Missy?" I asked. "Would he have told her?"

"Why?" Naomi asked. "What would be the point?"

That was a question I was in no position to answer. Just then I heard my name being announced over the ship's paging system. "Mr. Beaumont, Mr. J. P. Beaumont, please call the purser's desk for a message."

"Excuse me," I said. "I'll be right back."

The nearest phone was the one next to the purser's desk, where there was a long line. I picked the phone up and dialed the message number. "This is J. P. Beaumont," I said. "You have a message for me?"

"Yes, Mr. Beaumont. Beverly Jenssen would like you to report to the Infirmary as soon as possible."

My heart went to my throat. The Infirmary! Something was definitely wrong. I slammed down the phone and ducked to the front of the line.

"Where's the Infirmary?" I demanded.

"Here on the Emerald Deck," I was told. "Go down this corridor all the way aft. You won't miss it."

I stopped by the table in the Sea Breeze Bar long enough to tell Naomi where I was going, then I headed for the Infirmary. I made tracks—as fast as my injured toe would allow. It felt as though it had swollen to twice its normal size inside the confines of my shoe, making me wish I had abandoned my loafers for a pair of tennis shoes. The toe hurt like hell, but what caused my heart to thunder in my chest was won-

dering what catastrophe had now befallen either Beverly or
Lars.

In the waiting room of the Infirmary a somber Beverly
Jenssen sat in a plastic-backed chair dejectedly thumbing
through a dog-eared magazine. When she looked up at me, I
was dismayed to see she was wearing what would, over time,
blossom into a first-class shiner of a black eye.

"What happened?" I demanded.

"Oh," she said. "It's so silly, I don't even want to talk about
it. It's just that the nurse won't let me leave without having
someone come walk me back to my cabin. Lars had such a bad
night that I didn't want to bother him. Once he finally fell
asleep, I wanted him to get as much rest as possible."

"What happened to your eye?"

"I turned it up too high," she said. "It got away from me."

"Turned what up too high?" I asked.

"The treadmill up in the gym."

I was astonished. "You're eighty-six years old. What were
you doing on a treadmill?"

"Walking," she returned. "That's all it is—walking. The
girls—Claire and Florence—asked me to go with them this
morning. They go to the gym every day, you know. Lars is a
good one for walking, but only if you're going somewhere.
Since he doesn't have to worry about going to the beauty shop
or getting his hair wet, he doesn't mind about the weather. He
disapproves of gyms and all that expensive equipment, but
Claire and Florence don't. They go and have a good time, and
they said it helps them get over things—like what happened
to Mike and Lucy yesterday. They said the endorphins make
you feel better. Since Lars was sound asleep when they

invited me, I thought it would be fun to go, too. You know, while the cat's away and all that."

"And then?" I urged.

"Well, we went up to the gym. I watched Claire and Florence get on the treadmill first. It looked perfectly simple, and it was. But then I turned it up too high. I fell and smacked my face on the handle. I'm just lucky I didn't break my dentures. I could have, you know."

I looked around the waiting room. There was no sign of the two harebrained sisters who, in my opinion, had led my grandmother astray. "Where are Claire and Florence now?" I asked. "Still in the gym?"

"Oh, no. They came down with me right after it happened, but I sent them away. I didn't want them spending their whole morning in the waiting room here when it was nothing serious. I told them it was nothing. Then, after they left, the nurse told me I couldn't leave without having someone here with me. That's when I called you. You don't mind, do you, Jonas?"

"No," I said. "I don't mind."

Except that wasn't true at all. I *did* mind. Not that she was hurt or that she had called me. What I disapproved of was her pulling such a damn-fool stunt in the first place.

"What were you thinking?" I demanded. "You don't have any business getting on a treadmill to begin with, for God's sake! Not at your age!"

I must have sounded like an outraged father chewing out a teenaged daughter who has shown up a few minutes after curfew. Beverly's eyes filled with tears. She turned away from me and hid her face behind the magazine.

My back was to the door, so I didn't see Naomi Pepper until she crossed the room and knelt down beside Beverly. "There, there," she said consolingly. "Don't listen to him. He's just being a bully. If you want to get on a treadmill, that's entirely up to you—no matter what your age. I fell down the first time I tried one, too. And once that black eye of yours has a chance to ripen, I think it may be even better than mine was."

For some reason, that seemed to perk Beverly right up. "I've never had one before," she said, giving Naomi a tentative smile. Then she turned to me and glowered. "Even at *my* age," she sniffed. "Well, as far as I'm concerned, if you don't try new things every now and then, you could just as well be dead."

With that, Beverly held out her hand to Naomi, who obligingly hauled my grandmother to her feet. It was Naomi, not I, who walked Beverly Jenssen down the corridor to the elevator lobby and then down the hall to her stateroom on the Bahia Deck. I followed behind them at a safe distance while steam continued to pour out of both my ears.

At Beverly's stateroom, she swiped her own key card to let herself inside. "Naomi, thank you so much for coming to my aid," Beverly said before she closed the door. She said nothing to me. All she gave me for my trouble was a scowl.

"What does that make me, chopped liver?" I demanded once the door had slammed in my face. "And as for you," I said to Naomi, "what gives you the right to interfere in a private family problem?"

Naomi looked up at me. "Biology, maybe," she said. "It was a situation that needed a woman's touch. But if I'm not supposed to interfere in your private family problems, maybe you should think about taking some of your own advice and not interfering in mine."

With that, Naomi thrust the fax envelope back in my hand. Then she turned on her heel and marched away, heading off for parts unknown. All I could do as I watched her go was wonder what the hell I'd done wrong this time. Managing to start a before-breakfast quarrel with both my grandmother and my new roommate was a new all-time record— even for me. And it wasn't just a matter of women sticking together. Naomi had a point. After all, I had come into her life and had no qualms about asking questions about Naomi's relationship with Harrison Featherman and with her daughter, Melissa. Turnabout was only fair.

Way to go, J. P., I told myself disconsolately. *No matter how old you get, you're never going to learn.*

18

NURSING MY BRUISED EGO, I went upstairs to the
Lido Deck and availed myself of the buffet. Outside
the floor-to-ceiling windows, the world was awash in a misty,
dripping rainstorm that cut visibility to less than half a mile—
not the best possible day for viewing glaciers. I tried to take a
positive view of the situation. Since we weren't due in Glacier
Bay until afternoon, there was always a possibility that the
weather would improve the same way it had during the train
ride up the mountains from Skagway to White Pass.

When I went looking for a table, I located one that was
directly beneath a light fixture. Then, after finishing my
cafeteria-style scrambled eggs and toast, I removed the faxes
from the envelope and perused them once more. Even in better light, I found myself wishing I still had the use of Naomi

Pepper's damnable reading glasses. I was deeply engrossed in studying the faxes when Marc Alley dropped by my table with his reporter pal, Christine Moran, firmly in tow.

"Mind if we join you?" he asked.

"Sure," I said. "Help yourselves."

As they took seats, I moved the faxes out of the way and made to return them to the envelope. "Aren't those the articles about Margaret Featherman from this morning's Seattle papers?" Marc asked.

I nodded. "Do you want to read them?"

"We already did," Marc told me. "Christine got them off the Internet earlier this morning."

Christine Moran nodded. "It's driving me crazy," she said. "Here I am a reporter stuck in the middle of not one but two murders. Can I get any information? Not on your life. Other than downloading somebody else's articles off the Internet, I can't find out anything even though, by rights, I'm at ground zero on this story. No one on the ship will say a word. It's stonewall time from the captain right on down."

"I thought you specialized in medical stories."

"I'm a freelancer," she replied. "I can write about whatever I please, and, as I'm sure you know, murder happens to sell. I'm due at the next symposium meeting in half an hour, and I'll be there, but as far as I can see, this on-board neurology stuff is small potatoes compared to everything else that's going on. And if I happen to stumble into another story along the way while I'm covering the symposium, then I will. There's no law saying I can't. Besides," she added after a pause, "this is murder with a medical twist, isn't it?"

I tried changing the subject. "So the meetings are going forward even without Harrison Featherman?" I asked.

"Oh, no," Christine answered. "I understand he's back. A float plane brought him back, and they used a tender to pick him up a little while ago. He's this morning's keynoter. Naturally, Marc here is supposed to be in attendance."

"As in the show must go on?" I asked.

Christine smiled. "I guess," she replied. A somber Marc Alley said nothing.

"Any word about whether or not they found Margaret?" I asked.

Marc shook his head. "No one said anything to me about it. From the dead silence on the subject, I'd say she's a goner."

I wanted to ask Marc if he had received any calls from someone with a voice that sounded remarkably like Margaret Featherman's, but I didn't—not with Christine Moran sitting there hanging on every word. In the meantime, Christine continued to study me with undisguised interest. Her unblinking gaze made me fidget in my chair.

"From what Marc says about you, Beau, I'd say you're not having any trouble keeping your hand in—I mean, you being an ex-cop and all. According to him, you've been right in the thick of everything that's gone on."

I glanced in Marc's direction and wondered exactly how much he had told her. I hadn't sworn the man to silence, but I was a little dismayed that he had spilled his guts to someone who also happened to be a reporter. But then, my relations with the Fourth Estate had never been what I'd call cordial. My years as a cop had caused an initial distrust to ratchet up to a case of genuine paranoia.

"Just a matter of being in the wrong place at the wrong time," I told her.

Even though I had made no derogatory comments, Marc seemed to sense my disapproval. "I had to talk to someone," he said defensively. "I barely slept at all last night. It's not easy to drop off when you realize someone is out to get you and the only reason you're still alive is that the killer missed and took someone else out instead."

Obviously Marc's recent near-death experience on the observation platform of the White Pass and Yukon had left him a changed man. His initial determination not to allow the Leave It To God threat to alter his way of life had taken a direct hit.

I tried changing the subject. "What about those pictures you were taking on the train yesterday?" I asked.

"What about them?"

"Have you had the film developed?"

Marc shook his head. "Didn't have a chance," he said. "There are still a few more frames on that roll. I'll probably finish it off in Glacier Bay this afternoon—if it stops raining long enough to take pictures, that is." He fell silent and then shook his head and sighed.

"What's wrong?" Christine asked.

"Thinking about the pictures," he said. "I'm sorry I missed that shot yesterday—the one off the back of the train. It could have been spectacular, with the canyon outside framed by the entrance to the tunnel. I blew it, though. I forgot to turn off the flash. And when the guy hit me from behind—"

Christine Moran zeroed in on that statement like a hawk

falling out of the sky to strike some unsuspecting prey. "Guy?" she asked at once. "Are you saying you think who-ever hit you in the back was a guy? Did you see his face?"

Marc sighed. "No, I didn't see his face."

"What makes you say 'he,' then?"

"I've been thinking about it all night. It seems to me there was a lot of power behind that shove. Whoever did it meant business. They wanted me to go flying over the railing. Call me an old-fashioned sexist if you want, but I have a hard time thinking of women as muscle-bound hit men. I mean, aren't they supposed to use poison or something?"

Marc had come to the table carrying a tray laden with food. Now, having eaten almost none of it, he stood back up and glanced at his watch. "We'd better be going," he said to Christine. "I can't to be late for Dr. Featherman's speech."

"You go on ahead," Christine said. "As soon as I finish my breakfast, I'll join you. Save me a seat."

Nodding and preoccupied, Marc Alley set off.

"He's such a nice man," Christine commented as she watched him walk away. "What I don't understand is why he continues to be so loyal to Harrison Featherman. I sure as hell wouldn't be. The way that man's treated Marc the last few days is downright criminal. I've never heard of a doctor firing a patient, have you?"

"No," I said. "In my book, Dr. Featherman is breaking new ground as far as doctor-patient relations are concerned."

Moments later, Christine put down her fork and pushed her plate aside, but she didn't get up and follow Marc to the symposium. Instead, she sat back in her chair and regarded me speculatively over a raised coffee cup. "What do you make of all this?" she asked.

"All what?"

"Look," she said. "Let's not be coy. Marc told me enough about Leave It To God that I know I may be on the trail of the biggest story of my career. On the one hand, LITG sounds scary as hell and dangerous besides. It sounds as though they want to roll medical progress back to where it was in the Middle Ages. Forget about penicillin. Forget about the polio vaccine.

"But I can also see where else they may be coming from. What about all those invasive, code-blue lifesaving procedures that are inflicted on people who don't necessarily want to be saved? What about people who are put on life support and left in vegetative states when that's not what they wanted?

"There's a lot at work here, and I want to get to the bottom of it. I have every intention of writing this story, but before I do, I need some straight answers. It would be nice to hear what you have to say."

A reporter with her nose on the scent of a story is about as single-minded as a homicide cop on the trail of a killer—and about as easily deflected.

"The truth is, I don't have anything to say," I told her. "This isn't my case. It's not my place to comment one way or the other."

"Marc told me there are FBI agents on board. He says they're here to protect him and Dr. Featherman as well. Is that true?"

Not in that order, I thought. I said, "Miss Moran, I'm here as a passenger, just like everyone else aboard the *Starfire Breeze*. If you want information about an ongoing FBI investigation, you know the drill. You'll have to ask them."

"Sure," she said, with a short derisive laugh. "So they won't tell me anything, either? Do I really look that stupid?"

I was trying desperately to remember exactly how much I had told Marc Alley about Leave It To God. Having a half-baked story hit the wire services in the middle of the FBI's investigation would be a blow to whatever it was Rachel Dulles and Alex Freed were trying to do. Having the story appear would probably also land both of them in hot water.

"And what makes you so sure Harrison Featherman was the target?" Christine Moran continued. "After all, Margaret Featherman is the one who's dead. From what I read in those articles I took off the Internet this morning, maybe Margaret is the one who should have been on LITG's hit list. Marc might not agree, but compared to Margaret Featherman's research, Harrison's accomplishments look almost superficial. Isn't it possible the FBI is every bit as old-fashioned as Marc Alley claimed to be just now? Given two people with the same last name, naturally the feds assume that the man is the more important of the two, that he's more valuable."

I felt sick to my stomach. If Christine knew about the list, obviously I had told Marc Alley far too much. "Miss Moran—"

"Call me Christine."

"Christine, please. I'm not going to tell you anything. Just drop it."

She stood up then. "I won't drop it," she returned. "You

can tell me to buzz off all you want. So can the FBI, but I'm going to follow this story wherever it leads."

"If you go off half-cocked and publish the story prematurely, you're liable to jeopardize an entire investigation."

"Too bad," she snapped and marched away.

Shaking my head, I watched her go. *When it comes to women*, I told myself, *old Ladies' Man Beaumont is certainly batting a thousand.*

I left the Lido Deck Buffet and headed for my stateroom. In the elevator, I punched the button for my own deck, Capri. Then reconsidering, I punched Dolphin as well. It was time to stop by and give Rachel Dulles a heads-up. Since the symposium was under way, I more than half expected Rachel and her partner would both be off looking out for the safety of one Harrison Featherman. I ignored the DO NOT DISTURB sign posted on the door to the stateroom in question. A muffled male voice responded to my knock.

"Who is it?"

"Beaumont," I said. "J. P. Beaumont."

The door opened a crack. Behind it stood a young man wearing a pair of blue-and-white-striped silk pajamas. I gave up wearing pajamas about the same time I gave up my BB gun, and those were flannel—not silk. My long-held position was that I would never wear pajamas, but then I wasn't having much luck with saying never. Besides, given my own roommate situation on board the *Starfire Breeze*, maybe PJs weren't a half-bad idea.

"Whaddya want?" Mr. Pajamas asked groggily.

"Mr. Nix?" I asked.

He nodded.

"I'm Beau Beaumont—a friend of your wife's."

"Phyllis isn't here," he said.

"That's all right. May I talk to you for a minute?"

I wasn't sure if Alex Freed would recognize my name. Or, if he did, I wouldn't have been surprised if he had told me to get lost. After all, Rachel had already terminated my tenuous connection to the case. Instead, Alex pushed open the door wide enough to admit me. I walked into a stateroom that was even smaller than the one that had housed Mike and Lucy Conyers. There was just barely room enough to maneuver around the outside edge of two twin beds. Instead of a love seat, this room held a single easy chair. Alex motioned me into that. When he did so, I noticed he was wearing his two Travel-Aid bracelets.

"Are those things helping?"

"Some," he said. He was blond and well-built. To my amazement, he looked even younger than Todd Bowman.

"That's right," he said. "Now I remember. You're the guy who told Phyllis about these gadgets. Thanks for the suggestion," he added. "I really appreciate it. Wearing these things saved my life, but do you mind getting to the point? I just pulled an all-nighter and I need to grab some sleep. What is it you want?"

"Is Rachel around? I could probably tell her."

Tired as he was, Alex Freed had been prepared to go on with the Kurt and Phyllis charade. He blinked when I used Agent Dulles' given name, then he shook his head. "She's covering the symposium," he said. "Tell me."

"I've just found out that a reporter on board, a woman

who's here covering the neurology symposium, has made friends with Marc Alley. Now she's hot on the trail of what's been going on with LITG."

"Great," Alex Freed groaned. "That's exactly what we need. Somebody else mucking around in all this and screwing things up. What's her name?"

"Moran," I replied. "Christine Moran."

Alex went over to what was meant to be a dressing table. Instead of toiletries, it was covered with portable office equipment—a laptop computer, a tiny fax machine and printer, and a stack of papers. He sifted through the pile of papers until he found what he was looking for.

"Christine Abigail Moran. She's here on assignment for a magazine called *New World Health*. She was pretty much a last-minute addition to the cruise, so we haven't had time to pick up more than just basic information on her. What's her story?"

"She knows about the list."

"How?"

"I told Marc. Rachel told me that if I thought it was necessary, I could go ahead and warn him, and so I did. It just didn't occur to me that I should swear him to secrecy."

"Damn. And now I suppose this Moran woman is threatening to take the existence of the list public?" Alex Freed asked.

I nodded. "That's right. You can maybe work out some kind of deal with her—offer her first dibs on the story if she agrees to go along with you and not break it until you're ready for the story to go public."

"Agent Dulles and I aren't authorized to make those kinds of deals."

"You may not be, but somebody at the FBI is," I said. "And you may want to get hold of that person so he or she can get cracking on this right away. Christine Moran is off on some wild women's rights tangent that claims Margaret Featherman to be a more likely target for Leave It To God than her ex-husband was. And, in view of what happened to Margaret, maybe Christine Moran is right about that. Did you see the actual list—the original one, I mean?"

"No. Why do you want to know?"

"I was wondering if it came complete with both first and last names."

"I don't know about that for sure, but I don't believe it did. My understanding is that the agency worked with the American Medical Association to track down the most likely fits for each of the listed surnames. They sorted out the doctors doing the leading-edge stuff that they thought were the most logical targets for LITG."

"Doctors, as in physicians, but not doctors as in Ph.D.s," I said. "You do know what Margaret Featherman did, don't you?"

Once again Alex Freed shuffled through his stack of papers. I took that to mean the printout contained dossiers on each passenger and crew member on board the *Starfire Breeze*. I couldn't help wondering what it said about me.

"Margaret Catherine Featherman, Ph.D.," Alex Freed read aloud. "Researcher for Genesis, a bio-tech firm in Seattle."

"You may be interested to know that the *Seattle Times* calls her a 'key researcher in a ground-breaking genetic treatment,' " I supplied. "Maybe you'd like to see how Margaret

Featherman's disappearance is being reported back home in Seattle." I handed him my envelope stuffed with Ralph Ames' faxed material. As Alex Freed scanned through the articles, his initial frown deepened. At last he finished reading and handed the faxes back to me.

"It's a big story," I told him. "If Christine Moran breaks this part of it before you're ready, the FBI's whole investigation—not only here but all over the country—is going to blow sky-high."

Alex nodded. "I can see that. If you'll excuse me, Mr. Beaumont. I'd better get on the horn to our supervisor and see what she wants us to do about this."

"Right," I said, backing toward the door. "Don't let me stand in your way. But while you're at it, you might pass word along to Todd Bowman that Naomi Pepper's daughter, Melissa, is employed at a Kinko's in downtown Seattle."

"What's that supposed to mean?" Alex asked.

"Just give him the information," I said. "He'll know what to do with it."

I showed myself out. Back at my stateroom, I held my ear to the door, trying to determine from the outside whether or not Naomi Pepper was there, but I heard no sounds at all coming from inside. When I let myself in, the room had been cleaned, but no one was home—a situation for which I was supremely grateful. My toe was hurting like hell. The first thing I did was help myself to a couple of Advil, then I sat down and peeled off my loafers, sighing with relief once my toe had some breathing room.

One glance at the telephone told me there were messages

waiting. Taking up pen and paper, I prepared to write them down. It turned out the first message wasn't for me at all. It was for Naomi.

"Mother, do not call me at work again," an angry young woman hissed in my ear. "You have absolutely no right. I'm remembering all those times you bitched me out for telling lies. How dare you call me a liar! The hell with you, and the hell with Harrison and Margaret Featherman! I don't give a shit about what happened to her, or what happens to you, either!" End of message. So much for mother-daughter relations.

I sat for a long time with my finger poised indecisively over the phone pad while an operator's voice droning in my ear instructed me to press 3 for delete or 7 for save. Melissa Pepper's message clearly was intended for her mother. By rights, I shouldn't even have heard it, but now that I had, there was a decision to make. Did I want to inflict the insult of Missy's angry words and tone of voice on her mother? Would it be less hurtful for Naomi to hear what it said secondhand from me, or would she be better off listening to it herself? In the end, I decided it was best to press 7 for save. The message would be there waiting for Naomi whenever she returned to the room and whether or not she wanted to hear it.

The next message was a hang-up. I heard someone breathing for a few seconds, but in the end, nothing was said. Not much of a question there. I erased that one without giving it another thought.

The third message was from Beverly Jenssen.

"Jonas," she said with a slightly hesitant quaver in her voice. "I'm so sorry about what happened this morning. I shouldn't have been so cranky. And I'm sorry to have to bother you again so soon, but would you please come down and see us as soon as you can? I'm worried about Lars."

Without hitting save or delete, I slammed down the phone. I shoved my now-throbbing foot back into my loafers and raced out the door. I didn't bother with the elevator. Instead, I hobbled down two flights of stairs, wincing all the way. *Why didn't I switch to tennies?* I wondered.

When Beverly answered my frantic knock, she put a silencing finger to her lips. "Shhhhh," she said, letting me into the room. "I finally managed to get him out of bed. He's in the bathroom now, taking a shower."

"What's the matter?" I asked. "Is Lars sick?" Looking at my grandmother, it was difficult not to be derailed by the bloom of purple bruise that covered half her cheek.

"I don't know if he's sick or not," she said worriedly. "But I can tell you, he's never been this way before."

"What way?" I asked.

She thought for a minute before answering. "Old," she said finally. "Lars never acted old before, but this morning he didn't want to get out of bed. He said he didn't feel like it. He wouldn't go up to breakfast, either, and he wouldn't let me order anything for him from Room Service—not even one of those little pots of coffee, and you know how much Lars likes his coffee. He's acting like he doesn't care if he lives or dies, Jonas. That scares me to death."

"I suppose all of this is because of what happened to Mike and Lucy Conyers, isn't it?" I asked.

Beverly nodded. "I think so. I believe Lars blames himself because he didn't manage to catch Mike when he could have.

You know how hard he tried, but he feels he should have done more. I was hoping you could talk to him, Jonas. Sort of man-to-man. You know him better than anyone else does. You've been his friend for a long time—a lot longer than I've been his wife."

She was right about that, of course. Lars Jenssen's and my joint history was years old. When I came back from Ironwood Ranch, the treatment center in Arizona, and ventured warily into my first AA meeting at the Denny Regrade's old Rendezvous, Lars was the first person who came to talk to me afterward. He offered to buy me a cup of coffee and chew the fat for a while. Later, when I asked him to serve as my AA sponsor, he agreed without a moment's hesitation. He had seen me through some dark times, including one colossal slip and the loss of both my ex-wife, Karen, and my partner, Sue Danielson. After living without a father all my life, I knew Lars was probably the closest I would ever come to having one.

"I don't know what I can do," I said dubiously, "but I'll be glad to try."

"Good," Beverly said, reaching for her sweater. "I'll go see what the Wakefield girls are up to and give you two a chance to talk. You men will do better if you have a little privacy."

"We don't need privacy," I objected. "You're his wife, Beverly. Don't you think you should stay?"

"No," she said. "It's better if I leave."

She started for the door. The sound of running water emanating from the bathroom told me Lars was still in the shower and taking his own sweet time. "What did Lars say about your eye?" I asked as Beverly hurried past.

She stopped and looked up at me. "That's the reason I called you," she said.

"What do you mean?" I asked.

"He didn't say a word."

I was surprised. "You're telling me Lars saw your face and he didn't say anything?"

"Not a peep," she said. "And believe me, that's not Lars."

"No," I agreed. "You're right. Something must be wrong."

Beverly reached up and gave me a quick peck on the cheek. "Much as I hate to admit it, you were right this morning, Jonas," she added. "It was stupid of me to get on that treadmill and wind it up so fast that I couldn't keep up. But just because it was a dumb thing to do doesn't mean I liked hearing you say so."

"No," I said. "I suppose not."

"So be careful when you talk to Lars. We're very good at pointing out other people's shortcomings, but we both have short fuses when someone else draws attention to one of our own."

"Thanks, Grandma," I said. "I'll try to bear that in mind."

I sat down on the love seat and waited for the bathroom door to open. When Lars came out, I was shocked to see him. He had aged ten years. His legs and arms, showing beneath the hem on his terry-cloth robe, looked more like sticks than they did flesh and bone. When he saw me, he shook his head.

"Ya, sure," he said disgustedly. "That's women for you. What a tattletale! I shoulda known Beverly'd call you first t'ing."

Most of the time Lars managed to keep his Scandinavian accent under control. Today that clearly took too much effort.

"What's the matter, Lars?" I asked.

He looked away from me, out through the glass door on the lanai, where lowering clouds and misting rain obscured even the smallest hint of shoreline. He was quiet for so long that I wondered if he had heard or even remembered my question.

Finally he turned back to me. "It's yust no good," he said. "No good at all."

"What's no good?"

"The power of life and death," he said somberly. "That should be up to God and nobody else."

Here was Leave It To God's ugly philosophy rearing its head once again, but I was pretty sure Lars Jenssen wasn't a card-carrying member of an anti-progress terrorist movement or a hired-gun hit man, either.

"You did the best you could," I said quietly. "You almost saved Mike Conyers. It's not your fault that you couldn't hang on to him. Nobody could have done more."

"You t'ink so?" Lars asked, then he sighed. "The way I see it," he added, "there's a whole lot more I shoulda done."

19

B EVERLY JENSSEN LEFT Lars and me plenty of room
for our "man-to-man" chat, but I think she would
have been disappointed had she been a mouse in the corner
and able to hear it. Because, other than those few veiled ref-
erences to Mike and Lucy Conyers when Lars first came out
of the shower, we didn't mention them again, either directly
or indirectly, for most of the afternoon. If that's not man-to-
man, I don't know what is.

That doesn't mean, however, that we didn't talk. We did.
We talked about glaciers the entire time the *Starfire Breeze*
was sailing around Glacier Bay without her passengers getting a close look at anything but a few close-up ice floes covered with seals. As far as I could see, the clouds never lifted,
the rain never stopped, and visibility didn't improve.

Cruise-ship brochures usually picture blue-ice glaciers set against sunny skies, but viewing glaciers, even in the summer, comes down to the luck of the draw. The U.S. Park Service limits the number of cruise ships that can be in Glacier Bay National Park on any given day. If the *Starfire Breeze's* assigned day meant her passengers couldn't see squat, that was too bad for us. We wouldn't be allowed a second chance to come back and try again.

So rather than seeing glaciers, I listened to Lars Jenssen tell stories about glaciers. "Used to be, before all the halibut fleet was refrigerated, we'd go climb up on glaciers or icebergs and hack out some ice before it was time to go to the fishing grounds. Stuff's so hard it's hell to cut, but it lasts for danged ever. Even in the middle of the summer, we could take a load of halibut from here to Seattle and never have to worry about running out of ice or having to stop along the way to buy more."

"Isn't cutting ice off glaciers dangerous?" I asked.

Grinning, Lars looked almost like his old self. "It is if you stand too close to the edge," he said.

"What about floating icebergs? Aren't those dangerous, too?"

"Best advice is don't run into 'em," he said. "It's just like running into rocks. Nobody ever mentions it much, but as far as I'm concerned, hitting skim ice is way more dangerous than hitting icebergs."

"Skim ice?" I asked. "What's that?"

"In the spring, freshwater melt freezes and forms a razor-thin layer on top of the salt water. It's so damned thin, you don't even see it. But if you go running through it long enough, the ice can cut clear through the bottom of your boat. Next t'ing you know, your boat doesn't have a bottom. You'd better be in your survival suit and have your lifeboat released."

"Did that ever happen to you?" I asked.

He shook his head. "Not to me personally, but it did to a good friend of mine, Tommy Olsen. Had a boat called the *Reckless*. We looked for old Tommy and his crew that whole spring and summer, but we never found any of 'em. Part of the *Reckless* washed up on shore later. That's how the Coast Guard knew what had happened. It had been cut in two at the waterline. Poor old Tommy. Left behind a wife, a son, and two little girls. They must all be grown by now."

Lars lapsed into somber silence. I wondered if this Alaskan cruise and its accompanying trip down memory lane wasn't too hard on him. Over the years I had heard Lars tell stories about his life in the halibut fleet, but those tales had all been filled with fun and high jinks and more than a few drunken brawls. The one about Tommy Olsen was tinged with ineffable sadness. It seemed as though some of those old ghosts from the fleet were weighing Lars down almost as much as he was being haunted by what had happened to Mike Conyers.

Hoping to lighten his load, I tried changing the subject. "It's a shame the weather's so bad. I'd like it to break up enough for us to get at least a glimpse of a glacier."

Lars shook his head sadly. "It's nothing," he said. "If you've seen one glacier, you've seen 'em all."

His dour response told me Beverly's assessment was right. Not only was Lars Jenssen depressed, he was acting every one of his eighty-seven years.

"Have you had anything to eat?"

"Naw," he said. "Wasn't hungry."

I finally convinced Lars to go upstairs to the Lido Deck, where I persuaded him to try some of the buffet's lunchtime offerings. What's that old saying about you can lead a horse to water but you can't make him drink? Lars allowed the servers to dish up food, but once we sat down at a table, he wasn't interested in doing anything more than sliding little piles of spaghetti and meatballs around on his plate. I was sitting wondering what I could do to cheer him up when the perpetually cheery voice of the cruise director came over the loudspeaker.

"Captain Giacometti regrets that today's weather has been so uncooperative. We will of course remain in Glacier Bay as long as possible in hopes that visibility will improve. However, as a consolation, the captain is pleased to announce two special tango contests to be held later on this afternoon and evening in the Twilight Lounge. First-seating diners may participate beginning at five P.M. The contest for second-seating diners will begin promptly at seven. Those wishing to participate should sign up with the purser's desk in advance."

I understood what was going on. The ship's crew was gamely trying to make the best of a bad situation by setting up impromptu events to keep people occupied while they weren't looking for glaciers. It was true some disgruntled passengers had turned surly. Even sitting in the Lido Buffet, I had overheard grumbles and mutters of complaint, especially from people who, due to the Mike Conyers incident the previous day, had missed out on a planned trip on the White Pass excursion train. Now they were missing out on viewing glaciers as well. It occurred to me that the proposed tango contest would do little to settle those folks' ruffled feathers.

Then, shortly after the tango contest announcement ended and through the din of clattering tableware, I heard my own name being broadcast through the loudspeaker. "Mr. Beaumont, Mr. J. P. Beaumont. Please call the purser's desk for a message."

Not again, I thought. *At this rate, I could just as well be back on duty and wearing a beeper.* Lars, however, gave no indication that he had heard the announcement or cared whether or not I responded.

"Wait right here," I told him. "I have to go check on something."

He nodded absently and waved me away. I hurried to the nearest house phone, which was in the wood-paneled elevator lobby. When I spoke to the purser's desk I was directed to contact Marc Alley, in Bahia 626. Marc answered his phone after only one ring.

"Where are you?" he asked as soon as I identified myself.

"Up in the Lido Buffet," I told him. "The opposite side from where I saw you this morning. Why? Is something the matter?"

"Yes."

"What?"

"Just wait," he said. "I'll come show you."

I went back to the table, where I found Lars sitting and staring off into space. "Marc Alley is coming to join us," I said. "I hope you don't mind."

"Marc Alley?" Lars asked with a frown. "Who's he?"

"The other guy who was out on the platform with you and Mike Conyers yesterday—the guy who got knocked down. He had stepped outside hoping to get a picture just as the back of the train went into the tunnel. In all the hubbub of what happened, I don't think the two of you were ever properly introduced."

"Oh," Lars said. "All right then."

Marc showed up a few minutes later. As he approached the table, he caught sight of Lars and started to back off.

"It's okay," I said. "Lars Jenssen is my grandmother's second husband. Lars, this is Marc Alley. Marc, meet Lars."

Lars held out his enormous, liver-spotted hand. After a moment's hesitation, Marc took it and gave it a shake. Then he pulled out a chair and sat down.

"From the sound of your voice, I'd say this is something urgent," I ventured.

Marc nodded. "But are you sure . . . ?" He inclined his head ever so slightly in Lars' direction. "Maybe we should discuss this in private."

"Lars has been around," I said. "Whatever it is, I'm sure he can handle it."

Marc reached into his jacket pocket and pulled out a familiar bright-yellow Kodak picture envelope. "After I talked to you this morning, I decided not to wait until after I took the rest of the pictures to have the film developed," he said. "I had the photo shop print the ones I'd already taken. Here, look for yourself."

He passed a stack of color prints over to me. I sifted through them one at a time. Some of the pictures were taken on board the ship. Others showed views taken through the windows of the White Pass and Yukon train. The next-to-last shot was a crooked one that showed the rough rock surfaces of a tunnel along with an out-of-focus view of the steep tree-and-rock-covered terrain just outside the tunnel's entrance. But it was the last picture in the stack that was the real stunner.

In it a stark white face stared into the camera's lens. Red-eye effect gave the face an unearthly appearance, like that of a monster dreamed up in the crazed mind of a horror-movie director and then crafted by a special-effects whiz. I was so astonished by what I saw there that I blurted out the words before I could stifle them.

"Why, it's Lucy!" I exclaimed. "Lucy Conyers. What the hell was she doing out there?" But then, of course, I came face-to-face with the answer to my own question—the only answer possible. Under the cover of darkness, Lucy Conyers had stepped out onto the platform for no other reason than to shove her husband off the train.

Without a word, Lars Jenssen reached out a hand and lifted the picture from my fingers. He held it up to his eyes and studied it wordlessly for the better part of a minute. Then, nodding, he handed it back to me.

"Ya, sure," he said. "I knew it." And then he looked away.

"Wait a minute. You knew it?" I demanded. "Are you telling me you saw Lucy at the time it happened? You saw her out there on the balcony?"

He nodded.

"But if you saw that—if you knew she was the one who did it—why didn't you say something?"

"You haven't been there, Beau," Lars answered quietly. "You don't know what it's like. I've been through the same t'ing myself, with Aggie—through times when I wanted to put her out of her misery. When I wanted to put us both out of our misery. I know exactly what Lucy was up against—what she was going through. I understand why she did what she did. Once you've been there—really been there—you realize nobody has the right to tell her she was wrong."

"Murder is wrong," I insisted. "But I can understand why you didn't want to be the one to turn her in."

"It's like I told you," Lars said quietly. "I don't like having the power of life and death over someone—never did. It's too big a responsibility."

That's when I realized that earlier, when Lars had been talking about having the power of life and death, he hadn't been thinking about losing his grip on Mike Conyers and letting the man fall to his death. No, he had been agonizing over what he knew Lucy Conyers had done and whether or not he should turn her in because of it. For him it was more complicated than a simple matter of right or wrong.

I didn't doubt for a minute that Lars Jenssen had lived through exactly the same kinds of temptation with Aggie. The difference between him and Lucy Conyers was that Lars had resisted them. But he must have come close at times—close enough to realize that he, too, might have found himself sitting in a jail cell and under investigation for murder. No wonder he hadn't been himself. No wonder Lars Jenssen had been acting "old." If I had been in his shoes, I would have felt sick and old, too. This wasn't a situation that came with easy, one-size-fits-all answers.

Marc Alley had listened to this whole exchange in dead silence. "Does this mean I wasn't the target after all?"

His question made my face flush with shame before I even managed to reply. After all, I was the one who had gone around proclaiming Lucy Conyers' innocence to anyone who cared to listen. It burned me up to think that I had been so wrong about her while Sonny Liebowitz had been dead-on right. Sonny was someone I didn't care to see ever again. I didn't want him close enough to me for the creep to rub my nose in my error, which, being the kind of guy Sonny was, he would be hell-bent to do if he ever had the chance.

I'd had more than my fill of people like that. Detective Liebowitz was a near clone of my old nemesis back at Seattle PD—the supreme jerk of the universe, Detective Paul Kramer. It had been Kramer's promotion to Captain Larry Powell's place in homicide that had been the straw that broke this camel's back. When Kramer moved his smirking face into Larry's fish-bowl office and planted his wide butt in Larry's leather-backed chair, it was only a matter of time before Detective J. P. Beaumont was on his way out. Permanently.

"Mike Conyers was an Alzheimer's patient," I explained to Marc. "Taking care of him must have been too hard on Lucy, his wife. From looking at this, I'd say she reached the end of her rope somewhere along the track as we wound our way up the mountain to White Pass."

"I do remember seeing her," Marc said, nodding. "I remember her crying in the car after it all happened. She seemed very upset. But she also seemed old to me—too old and not that strong."

"Desperation makes you strong," Lars replied. "Sometimes, you yust don't know your own strength."

I felt as though Lars and I owed Marc Alley the courtesy

of a more detailed answer. "You see," I explained. "Lars' first wife had Alzheimer's, too. It was after Aggie's death that he married my grandmother."

Marc nodded. "I understand," he said. "Alzheimer's is a terrible disease for everyone concerned, but I still don't know what I should do with this picture."

"You'll have to turn it over to the proper authorities," I said.

"Why?" Lars asked.

"Because this is a murder investigation," I explained. "It's against the law to withhold evidence or information, and you have to admit, this is pretty compelling evidence. The picture puts Lucy Conyers out on the platform right at the time Mike went over the rail. Look on the back of the photo. It's even timed and dated. The picture doesn't actually show Lucy giving Mike a push, but any first-year prosecutor will be able to make that case and have it stick."

"But what about Lucy's lawyer?" Lars asked. "Can't she do something?"

"At this point, I'd say the best Carol Ehlers could go for would be a negotiated plea agreement. Now that you mention it, the sooner, the better. Once this picture falls into Sonny Liebowitz's hands, things will only get worse."

Lars started to get up, then dropped back into his chair.

"What about Beverly?" he asked hollowly. "What about Claire and Florence? What's going to happen to them when they find out about what Lucy did? They all think of her as a friend. They're not going to want to believe this."

"They may not want to believe, but they will," I assured him. "They're all big girls. They'll be able to take it. And remember, Lars, my grandfather, Jonas Piedmont, may have died of a stroke rather than Alzheimer's, but he was sick for a long time. He was in a wheelchair, unable to take care of himself, and totally dependent on Beverly for years before he died. Beverly may never have said anything to you about it, but I'm sure she's lived though the same kind of hell you and Aggie did, and Mike and Lucy Conyers, too, for that matter. I'd be surprised if she hadn't been subject to the same kinds of temptation."

Lars looked at me. "You t'ink so?"

"I know so."

He nodded. "All right, then," he said. "I'll go find Beverly and tell her what's happened. You call that lady lawyer."

I nodded. Meanwhile, Marc Alley had been gathering up his scattered pictures. "Mind if I tag along?" he asked.

"By all means," I told him. "After all, they're your pictures."

We went back down to the Capri Deck. When I opened the door to my stateroom, I was a little concerned about whether or not Naomi would be at home. Not that she shouldn't have been. Not that we were doing anything wrong. It was just that the situation would have been awkward, and I was happy not to have to deal with it.

Again I cursed myself for not having brought along my cell phone. Once again it seemed to take forever to put through a ship-to-shore phone call. Once the call went through, however, Carol answered on the second ring.

"Carol Ehlers here," she said.

"This is Beau," I said. "J. P. Beaumont."

"Good to hear from you. Don't worry. Things are fine."

"Things aren't fine," I told her. "In fact, I'd say they're anything but fine." For the next several minutes I explained the damning details of the photo.

"The picture really is time-dated?" Carol asked when I finished.

"I'm afraid so."

"And it's clearly Lucy Conyers in the photo—Lucy and nobody else?"

"No mistaking her," I said. "It's Lucy, all right."

"It's a good thing I'm still here in Skagway," Carol said. "I'll go talk to Lucy right away. I was visiting with the prosecutor a little earlier, and he was hinting around about a plea bargain. Charging sweet little old ladies with murder doesn't win popularity contests. I'll try to convince Lucy that we should take the deal before things get any worse—because you're absolutely right. As soon as that picture ends up in Sonny's hands, things will get worse. If we can put a plea agreement in place soon enough, there's no reason it should ever have to."

"Good," I said. A wave of relief washed over me. The weight of responsibility was out of my hands and into Carol Ehlers' capable ones, and that was fine with me. I suspected it would also be fine with Lars. Still, despite what I had said earlier, I was worried. I suspected that hearing about Lucy Conyers' planned guilty plea wouldn't go over well with Beverly Jenssen, or with her friends Claire or Florence Wakefield, either.

I hung up. "So what do I do with the picture?" Marc asked, holding up the envelope.

"Keep it for right now. We'll give Carol Ehlers time to

work things out. When we get into Sitka tomorrow, I'll call her again and see how she fared in the plea-bargaining department. If they've got a deal, then you don't have to do anything with the picture. You can keep it or burn it or do whatever you want. If Lucy decides to plead innocent and go to trial, then it's a whole new ball game. You'll have to send it along to the proper authorities."

Marc nodded. "Does this mean I don't have to worry anymore—about someone coming after me?"

I shook my head. "It doesn't mean anything of the kind. It turns out what we initially thought was an attempt on your life, wasn't. I think it's safe to say that Lucy Conyers wasn't a member of Leave It To God, but that also doesn't mean that the LITG threat has gone away. On that score, nothing has changed."

"So I should still be careful?"

"By all means. And that reminds me, Marc. Please don't tell anyone else about what's been going on. The fewer people who know about it, the better."

He nodded sheepishly. "I realized telling Christine was a mistake as soon as the words were out of my mouth, but there was no way to take them back. By then the damage was done. It's just that I needed someone to talk to right then, some way of getting the load of worry off my chest. Christine happened to be handy and sympathetic."

"I certainly understand your need to confide in someone," I said, "but try not to tell anyone else."

"I won't," Marc said determinedly. "I've definitely learned my lesson."

Just then I heard the sound of a key card in the lock. I had thought I'd be able to hustle Marc out soon enough to get away clean, and I almost did. With another minute or so, he would have been out of the cabin and everything would have been fine. But just then Naomi Pepper walked into the room. She stopped in the doorway.

"Am I interrupting something?" she asked, looking questioningly from Marc to me and back again.

"Oh, no," Marc said quickly, "I was just leaving." If he was surprised that Naomi had a key to my room, he didn't let on.

"You don't have to leave on account of me," Naomi told him.

"That's all right," he said. "I need to be going anyway."

Marc let himself out of the room. Naomi had obviously been out on deck. She went into the bathroom to hang up rain gear, which was still dripping water, and with her hair wet and windblown. When she came out, her hair was still damp, but it had been combed into a semblance of order.

"Was that about the picture?" she asked.

"How did you know about that?"

"I was out on deck all afternoon with your grandmother and her friends. They were all determined to catch at least one glimpse of a glacier."

"Did it work?"

"It did, actually. Just a little while ago there was a slight break in the weather. Most of the other passengers had given up and gone inside by then, but not us. Your grandmother is one stubborn woman. We got to see a calving glacier after all, and we were still out on deck when Lars came to tell us."

"Us? You mean he blabbed it to all of you? He said he was going to tell Beverly."

Naomi shrugged. "We were all there together, so he told us, too."

"Great," I groaned. "So what did Claire and Florence have to say?"

"About the glacier?" she asked.

"No, about the picture."

Naomi shrugged. "Oh, that. Not much. They were shocked, I suppose, and sad, too, but they all—even your grandmother—seemed to take it in stride. Beverly told me later that Lars was looking ever so much better—like he'd had the weight of the world lifted off his shoulders."

"I'm sure that's how he felt," I said.

I slipped off my shoes and lay down flat on the bed, folding my arms under my head. I lay there and wiggled my little toe to see if it still hurt. It did. *Time to take some more Advil*, I counseled myself.

Naomi sat down on the edge of her bed. "I guess I owe you an apology," she said. Her back was to me, so I couldn't see her face, but I heard what sounded like genuine regret in her voice.

"What for?" I asked.

"For my nasty comment this morning. You were interfering in my family, and I'm interfering in yours. We deserve each other."

"Apology accepted," I said. "But speaking of families, that reminds me. There's a voice-mail message from your daughter."

"From Melissa?" Naomi asked eagerly. "You mean she actually called me back?"

"It wasn't a very nice message," I cautioned. "I saved it for you, but you may not want to listen to it."

"Let me guess. She told me to go to hell."

"More or less."

"You're right. I don't need to listen to it."

"Why does she hate you so much?"

"She thinks that if I hadn't divorced her father—who, it turns out isn't her father anyway—he wouldn't have gotten sick and died."

"Didn't I understand you to say that Gary died of liver cancer?"

"Right. Missy maintains that if he had still been at home with us when he first became ill, he might have seen a doctor sooner and maybe they would have caught the cancer in time to do something about it—that with early detection they might have saved him. She thinks his death is all my fault," Naomi added.

"But isn't liver cancer incurable?"

"Pretty much," Naomi said quietly. "At least that's what I was told."

"So what Melissa thinks isn't even logical. It doesn't make sense."

"Who says teenagers have to make sense?"

There was no arguing with that. "I'm sorry," I said.

"Me, too," Naomi agreed with a sigh. "And you're right. I'm not going to listen to that message. All it would do is make me feel worse than I already do."

She kicked off her own shoes and stretched out on her bed. Lying there side by side with our sock-covered toes pointing up at the ceiling, I felt a rare moment of intimacy. Naomi and I were together without really being together, and yet we understood one another in a way I couldn't possibly have explained to a third party.

"What are we going to do about dinner tonight?" I asked. "Order from Room Service again?"

"Beverly and Lars invited us to join them and Claire and Florence during the first seating. I hope you don't mind, but I told her fine. For one thing, they eat in the other dining room. Beverly said she'd clear it with their maître d'. I just don't have what it takes to go back and face down Sharon and Virginia."

"It's all right with me. Besides," I added, "I know how Beverly is. Once she gets an idea into her head, there's no stopping her."

"It's lobster night," Naomi informed me after a while. "Semi-formal instead of formal."

"So I don't need to haul out my tux."

"No," Naomi said. "But you looked quite handsome in it."

"Thanks," I said grudgingly. There's nothing like a compliment to turn any right-thinking American male into your basic monosyllabic kind of guy.

"And there's one other thing," Naomi added warily.

"What's that?"

"Beverly signed us up for the tango contest."

I sat up in bed. "She what?"

"She entered our names for the first-seating tango contest

in the Twilight Lounge. It starts at five o'clock. She said you'd won one before, years ago. She asked if I could tango, and I told her some. She says she's sure we'll do just fine." Naomi paused. "Is that true, by the way?" she continued. "Did you really win one in your youth?"

"It's true," I admitted reluctantly. "A girl from my dancing class, Denise Hughart, I think, and I were chosen to represent Rose Toledo's Dance Studio at a citywide youth dance contest at the bathhouse on Greenlake the summer I graduated from eighth grade. We won, and a picture of Denise and me showed up in the local section of the *Seattle Times*."

My family history isn't something I usually talk about with relative strangers. It hurts too much. But Naomi Pepper was dealing with her own fractured family relationships, so I doubted she'd find mine all that shocking or unusual. After all, in her own way, Naomi was as much of an unwed mother as my own mother had been.

"My parents never married," I admitted after a slight hesitation. "He was a sailor over at Bremerton. They were engaged to be married, but my father was killed in a motorcycle accident before they had a chance to tie the knot. When I made my presence known a few weeks after my father's death, it caused a big family rift. My grandfather and namesake, Jonas Piedmont, immediately disowned both my mother and me. She and her parents were estranged the whole time I was growing up. In fact, I didn't even meet Beverly or my biological grandfather until just a few years ago—long after my mother's death and just before my grandfather died as well."

I glanced over at Naomi. Instead of looking at me, she was

staring up at the ceiling. Somehow the fact that she wasn't looking directly at me made it easier for me to continue.

"My grandfather forbade my grandmother to have any contact with my mother or with me, but the whole time I was growing up, Beverly kept a scrapbook that included every mention of me that made it into the newspapers—from my truncated career in Cub Scouts and my few good mentions in Ballard High School sports, right on through my crime-fighting exploits at the Seattle PD. When I finally reestablished contact with my grandparents, the very existence of that scrapbook helped bind over some long-festering wounds. No doubt that picture of me as a gangly-legged tango winner made it into Beverly's collection."

"So that's where your initials come from?" Naomi asked. "From your mother's father?"

I nodded. "The J. P. part comes from him, from Jonas Piedmont."

"And Beaumont?"

"I was named after Beaumont, Texas, my father's hometown. I don't know anything more about my father than just that—where he was from. I don't even know his name. On the father line of my birth certificate all it says is 'deceased.' "

"Don't you wonder about him sometimes—about what he was like and what his family was like?"

"Some," I admitted, "but not enough that I've ever done anything about it."

"And what about your dance partner? Whatever happened to her?"

"Denise? I don't know. When school started that fall, I

don't remember her showing up at Ballard High School. Once we won the contest, she just dropped out of sight."

After that we were quiet for some time. I appreciated it that Naomi didn't find it necessary to say anything more. Finally, with a groan, I heaved myself off the bed.

"Where are you going?" Naomi asked. "We still have the better part of an hour to go. If we wanted, we could probably even grab a nap."

"I don't need a nap," I told her. "What I need is more Advil. If I'm going to end up in a tango contest tonight, I'd better have plenty of painkillers in my system before I put my shoes back on. I remember how to do the tango, but when I won that trophy, I was a whole lot younger than I am now. My back and feet were younger, too, and I didn't have a broken toe, either."

"Come on," Naomi said. "It won't be that bad."

"Are you kidding? By the time we finish, I'll be lucky if they don't end up sticking me in a full body cast."

20

A FTER DOWNING two more Advil, I came back to bed and lay down again. Naomi was quiet for such a long time that I assumed she had taken her own advice and fallen asleep. I very nearly did the same thing.

"Thank you for letting me stay here," Naomi said. Her voice roused me out of a doze.

"You're welcome. What was I supposed to do—leave you to sleep outside on the deck? This is Alaska, after all. It's cold and wet out there."

"What was happening was a whole lot worse than being cold and wet," she said. "I was feeling as though the whole world had turned against me—everyone but you. Even when you suspected me of killing Margaret—even when you found out about what had happened between Harrison and me—you

still treated me like a decent human being. Your grandmother's got every right to be proud of you."

I realized then that Naomi was right. Somehow the
ground between us had shifted. I no longer regarded her as a
suspect in whatever it was that had happened to Margaret
Featherman. And maybe, in that respect, I was simply following Beverly Jenssen's lead. No matter what anyone else said
or thought about Naomi Pepper—including derogatory opin-
ions from at least two of her former friends—my grandmother regarded the woman as the genuine article. Good
enough to enter a dance contest with, anyway.

At four-thirty Naomi and I didn't exactly bounce out of
bed, but we did get up. Naomi took her clothes and disappeared into the bathroom to finish drying her hair and dressing while I made do with the closet and the mirror over the
dressing table. At four-fifty, with me still limping slightly, we
appeared at the entrance to the Twilight Lounge, where Lars
and Beverly Jenssen, along with the Wakefield girls, had com-
mandeered a front-and-center table.

In the end it wasn't much of a contest. All of the other
entrants were far older than Naomi and I were. It was clear
that many of them had danced with each other for years.
Nonetheless, my Advil seemed to kick in, and I danced with
only the slightest hitch in my get-along due to my injured
toe. But it wasn't only the Advil that decided the contest's
final outcome.

As Naomi and I danced together, something magical happened. Having a pair of thirteen- and fourteen-year-old vir-
gins dance the tango is truly casting pearls before swine.
When I danced with Denise Whatever-Her-Name-Was, I had

no idea about what went on in the world or in life. The birds and bees were still pretty much a mystery to me. Back then I didn't have the first clue about women and what made them tick. By the time I danced the tango with Naomi Pepper, I knew a lot more than I did at fourteen, and so did she. When our hands touched, the air around us seemed charged with electricity. When our bodies met, it was with so much implied urgency and promise that it took my breath away. It also gave me an astonishing hard-on.

When the judges announced that Naomi and I were the winners, Naomi threw her arms around my neck and planted a triumphant smooch on my lips before we went up on stage to retrieve our trophy—a matched pair of Starfire Cruises coffee mugs. Then we had to stand, posing and smiling, while the ship's photographer did his *Starfire Breeze* photo-op duty.

As we filed out of the Twilight Lounge and headed for the dining room, Lars sidled up beside me. His color was better than it had been earlier. He seemed more like himself.

"I t'ink that girl likes you," he said, giving me one of his familiar lopsided grins. "Ya sure, I t'ink she likes you a lot."

When they opened the doors, we walked into the Regal Dining Room with Lars and Beverly leading the way. Claire and Florence insisted that we put our prizes in the center of a table set for six. I wondered what Beverly and Lars had done with their young whippersnapper tablemates who had been married a mere forty years. There was no sign of them.

Beverly had managed to whip the wait staff into shape. They graciously served a congratulatory and complimentary bottle of champagne for the ladies. I ordered a bottle of non-alcoholic champagne for Lars and me to share. That way,

when it came time for the obligatory toast, no one had to feel
left out.

Lobster with jasmine rice. Ravioli with a creamy sun-dried
tomato sauce. I'm sure the food was wonderful, but I have to
say I don't remember how any of it tasted. I was, however,
painfully aware of Naomi Pepper's smiling presence next to
me and of the disturbing effect she was having on my body.
Every once in a while, I'd catch her looking at me, too. She
appeared totally at ease, but I wondered if my face reflected
my own inner turmoil.

Somewhere in the middle of that damned tango contest,
lightning had struck, and I didn't know what the hell to do
about it. The problem was, I couldn't tell from the discreet
glances Naomi cast in my direction if the same thing had happened to her or if what I was feeling was totally one-sided.

During the pause between the entrée and dessert, I
excused myself. Under the pretext of using the rest room, I
hurried instead to the gift shop. There, feeling like a gawky,
awkward teenager, I purchased a package of prophylactics.
The two young women behind the counter were both
younger than my daughter Kelly. It was one of those times
when it would have been nice to be able to pay for my ship-
board purchases in nameless, anonymous cash, but that's not
the way cruise-ship accounting works. All purchases are
charged to the room and then paid for at the time of departure
from the ship. Refusing the simpering clerk's offer of a bag, I
stuffed my purchase into my pocket and returned to the darkened dining room just in time for the cherries jubilee parade.

When I got back to the table, I found I had barely been
missed. Lars was in the middle of one of his long-winded

yarns. "Ya, sure," he said. "We were on old Wally Torgesen's *Sea Wind* back then. We had sold off all our fish and had eight days to blow in Sitka before the next trip. Late one night somebody came up with a brainy idea. We filled the fish hold full of old tires and sailed them over to Kruzof Island. We put in just north of Cape Edgecumbe and off-loaded all the tires. Then we hauled them up the side of Mount Edgecumbe to the crater.

"It was hard work—took us all day long to do it, but we were a bunch of young turks back then with more muscles than brains. By late afternoon, we set fire to all those tires and took off. We sailed back into town yust as everybody was going crazy because they were sure the volcano was gonna blow. They were about to fly in a volcano guy from the U Dub down in Seattle when somebody finally came up with the bright idea of having a volunteer fly over Mount Edgecumbe in a helicopter to check things out. When the authorities discovered it was all a put-up deal, they were pissed."

"I should think they would be," Beverly Jenssen sniffed disapprovingly. "After causing that kind of fuss, I'm surprised you didn't end up in jail."

Lars laughed. "I am, too. As far as I know, nobody ever let on that we were the ones who did it."

The after-dinner show that night was *Pirates Aweigh*, a bad musical revue loosely based on a pirate-ship motif. Not only were there beautifully costumed dancers in need of rescue from wicked pirates, there was also a troupe of Chinese acrobats. They sprinkled the entire performance with improbable headstands and cartwheels that had nothing whatever to do with the rest of the show. But then, the physically astonishing contortions of the acrobats made no more sense than did any of the singing and dancing numbers.

By the time *Pirates Aweigh* was finally over, Beverly and Lars, along with Claire and Florence, were ready to call it a night. Naomi and I left the four of them in the elevator lobby while we headed back to the Twilight Lounge for one more bit of *Starfire Breeze* night life.

"I get the feeling the people they hire for shipboard entertainment, especially the 'writers,' aren't exactly the cream of the crop," I groused.

"Lighten up," Naomi returned lightly. "Don't be so critical. Everybody else enjoyed the show immensely."

"There's no accounting for taste," I said.

In the Twilight Lounge, Dahlia Lucas was singing once again, and her music only served to make things worse. Talk about a one-track mind. My internal struggle continued unabated. I had offered Naomi Pepper a safe harbor for the duration of the cruise with the understanding that the haven came with no strings attached. At least, I hadn't intended there would be strings. If she wasn't feeling the same urges I was, I didn't want to pressure Naomi or give her the idea that I was taking undue advantage of her precarious situation.

On the other hand, if she was interested, I worried about whether or not I could deliver the goods. As far as romance was concerned, I hadn't exactly been playing the field of late. As a matter of fact, I felt as if I was totally out of the game. When Dahlia Lucas launched into her sultry rendition of that old Judy Garland standby "What Did I Have I Don't Have Now?" it did nothing at all for what was, by then, a severe case of performance anxiety.

Talk about taking the coward's way out. When Dahlia finished her first set, I gamely suggested we stick around for the second.

"No," Naomi said firmly, making up her mind for both of us. "It's been a long day. Let's go back to the room."

"How about a walk around the Promenade Deck?" I figured a cooling-off period would do me good.

"Are you kidding? It's still pouring rain out there. Let's just go to the room."

And so we did. I unlocked the door and let Naomi go inside first. When I stepped into the room, I expected it to be in more or less the same condition it had been in when we left it hours earlier. Not completely the same, of course. I was sure Hector would have come around by then and done his evening turndown service. I expected to find the sheets folded back and for us to have chocolate mints strategically placed on our newly fluffed pillows. What I didn't expect was that the room would be completely rearranged. The twin beds had magically joined themselves back into one. The turndown service had been done, all right. Two sets of heart-shaped mints were waiting on pillows placed at the head of a decidedly king-sized bed.

"Wait a minute," I objected. "I had nothing to do with this."

Naomi turned to me and smiled. "Of course not. I came up here during intermission and asked Hector to fix it. I didn't think the two of us would fit on one of those twin-sized beds, do you?"

She walked into my arms then and kissed me again. This wasn't at all the kind of congratulatory buss she had given me earlier in the Twilight Lounge when we went up to the stage to accept our trophy coffee mugs. No, this was exactly the kind of sexy, head-spinning kiss the tango had promised to deliver—that and then some.

"Wait a minute," I objected when I came up for air. "Are you sure?"

"Of course I'm sure," she said confidently. "Sure enough that I stopped by the gift shop and bought some of these."

She opened her hand. Concealed inside her palm was a package of Trojans, the same brand I had purchased earlier in the gift shop. When I roared with laughter, Naomi frowned in annoyance.

"What's so funny?" she demanded. "Using protection isn't a laughing matter. It's one thing to ask you to go to bed with me. The problem is, I'm also asking you to go to bed with whoever Gary may have gone to bed with during those last few months before he got so sick that he couldn't screw around anymore. The man may be dead, but I still don't trust him any further than I can throw him."

"That's not why I'm laughing," I told her. "Look."

I reached in my pocket and pulled out my own discreetly wrapped package of Trojans. Naomi's mouth dropped in amazement. "You bought some, too?" she asked. I nodded. "At the gift shop?"

"That's right."

"No wonder the girls behind the counter got such a kick out of it," Naomi said indignantly. "They kept giggling and whispering. I was embarrassed and thought it was extremely rude. In fact, I had half a mind to report them for it."

We laughed about it some then together. After that we sat

down on the love seat. I don't know how long we stayed there, alternately talking and necking. It could have been an hour or it could have been three, but by the time Naomi stood up and announced it was time to go to bed, I was in total agreement. And as it turned out, I needn't have worried about my performance. Making love is just like riding a bicycle. No, it's much, much better.

Afterward, I fell asleep and slept like a baby. I awakened in watery early-morning light with the strange scent of someone's perfume and shampoo in my nostrils and with the unaccustomed sound of someone snoring gently against my shoulder blade. I felt the comforting warmth of a naked body cuddled along my back. All that was good. The telephone sat on the bedside table, inches from my face. The orange message light on the phone was blinking steadily away. That was probably bad, but at least I'd had the presence of mind to turn the ringer off.

When I reached for the phone, Naomi groaned and wrapped one arm tightly around my chest. "Don't," she said.

"Don't what?"

"Don't take that message. Whatever it is, I don't want to know about it, and neither do you."

"I've got to," I said.

"Go ahead then," Naomi said. "Just don't expect me to stay here and listen."

She got out of bed, wrapped herself in a robe, and disappeared into the bathroom. I called the voice-mail number and found there were three messages. One was from Lars and Beverly. They would be going to breakfast early in the Regal Dining Room, and did I want to join them. Later they would be going into Sitka, where Lars was anxious to show me some of his old stomping grounds. They both hoped I'd agree to come along on the trip.

The second message was also from Beverly and Lars, only this one was meant for Naomi. They invited her to breakfast and then to come on the trip to Sitka as well. In other words, the jig was up. In leaving a message for Naomi, Lars and Beverly had no doubt figured out that the two of us were staying in the same stateroom.

They were bound to find out sooner or later, I told myself. *I suppose it could just as well be sooner.*

The third message made no sense at all. It was the from someone named Michael at the purser's desk who had left the message on the voice-mail system at 1:43 A.M. "A woman named Dulcinea called," the taped voice said. "No message. We offered to put the call through to you in your stateroom or to voice mail, but she said that wasn't necessary. She said she'd be seeing you tomorrow—make that today—in Sitka."

After those three messages finished playing, Melissa Pepper's saved message came back on. I ended that one without listening to it again. I had pulled on a pair of pants and was sitting on the end of the bed still puzzling over the third message when Naomi emerged from the bathroom. Her hair was brushed and pulled back from her face. When she sat down next to me, there was a hint of mouthwash and newly applied perfume in the air.

"Good morning," she said, snuggling up beside me.

"Good morning."

"Who was it?"

"Beverly and Lars want to know if we'll join them for breakfast in the Regal."

Her eyebrows went up. "They know I'm staying here?"

"They do now. They left one message for me and another for you. I'm sure they're smart enough to notice that it's the same room. They also want to know if you'll go along on a trip into Sitka. So do I."

"But what about . . . ?" she began.

"Todd Bowman? Call him and ask him. All he said was you had to have his permission."

"But it seems so stupid—like having to get a pass from your teacher to go to the bathroom."

"Ask him," I urged.

"All right," Naomi said after a pause. "I will."

"The last message must be for you instead of me," I added. "Who's Dulcinea?"

Naomi shrugged. "What are you doing, checking up on my liberal arts credentials? Dulcinea is Don Quixote's girl-friend—you know, as in Cervantes. Sancho Panza is his side-kick and Dulcinea is his idealization of Aldonza, the whore. She's the focus of Don Quixote's romantic love, his ideal woman."

"She's not someone you know?"

"Of course not. Why?"

"Never mind," I said. "It's nothing. Do you want to go to breakfast or not?"

"Do you want a truthful answer, or do you want me to lie?"

"Truth," I said.

"Wouldn't you like just one more quick roll in the hay before we go out to face the world?"

"Is that a trick question?"

It wasn't, and we did. By the time we showed up in the dining room, Lars and Beverly were already finished with breakfast. I was glad to see that a combination of time and deftly applied makeup were working their magic. Beverly's black eye was far less apparent.

Naomi and I had coffee and juice and hoped the looks on our faces didn't give too much away. Lars greeted us by asking if we had caught sight of Mount Edgecumbe—the seat of his youthful triumph—as we came up Sitka Sound. We both admitted that we had been too busy just then to be doing any sightseeing.

"Damned horny kids," Lars muttered under his breath. I hope I was the only one at the table who heard him.

"What about the meeting then?" he asked. "Have you heard about that?"

"What meeting?" I returned.

"Word's gotten out on board about Mike Conyers and that other woman, the one who fell off the boat."

"Margaret Featherman?"

"Right," Lars answered. "That's the one. Anyway, people are upset and worried. Their kids back home are worried, too. Since two passengers have already died on this cruise, people are starting to call the cruise-ship office because they're afraid their parents may be in danger. So the captain has scheduled a meeting in the theater in twenty minutes to give whoever wants one a briefing on what's been happening. It should be over before we put in to Sitka."

I glanced questioningly in Naomi's direction. She shook her head. "You go if you want," she said. "Whatever I don't know isn't going to hurt me."

"Right," Beverly agreed. "We'll let the men sort those things out. That's what we have them for, isn't it?"

Twenty minutes later, Lars and I were seated in the plush velvet seats of the *Starfire Breeze*'s Starlight Theater. It was just as well everyone hadn't come along. By the time the cruise director stepped to the microphone to introduce Captain Giacometti, the place was jammed with a standing-room-only crowd.

"I'm sure you're all concerned about what you have heard, and it is true, there have been some unfortunate happenings on this cruise," the captain said. "Because Starfire Cruise Line is fully committed to cooperating with the authorities, the FBI has been called in to investigate. I can assure you that no one on this ship is in any danger, but in order to put your minds at ease, I would like to call on FBI Agent Todd Bowman. He will be glad to give you an overview of what has happened and to let you know what measures are being taken to see to it that nothing more out of the ordinary happens in the course of this cruise. Mr. Bowman."

Todd Bowman, looking uncomfortable, stepped to the microphone. "Good morning, ladies and gentlemen. I'll get straight to the point. On Monday evening, while the *Starfire Breeze* was off Port Walter in Chatham Strait, a passenger named Margaret Featherman fell overboard."

The words "fell overboard" made it sound as though Margaret had gone for an unfortunate little swim of her own volition. That was something less than the whole truth.

Obviously Todd Bowman's briefing was going to gloss over the gorier details.

"In the case of Mrs. Featherman, the Coast Guard has been summoned and is conducting a search. So far we have found no trace of the missing woman. Because there was a Chatham Strait black-cod opener scheduled to begin the next day, a large number of fishing vessels are known to have been in that area. The Coast Guard has been making regular announcements on Channel 16 asking for all fishing-boat crew members to be on the lookout for her. So far none has reported seeing her," Bowman continued.

Lars leaned over to me. "And they won't, either," he whispered. "Even if they did find her, they wouldn't report it. Yust filling out paperwork alone would hold them up for a whole day at least. They'd lose the time. You sure can't catch fish when you're up to your eyeballs in paper."

"Wait a minute. Are you saying someone may have found her and not reported it?" I whispered back.

"Are you kidding? They'd be crazy if they did."

That gave me pause for thought and even more reason to wonder about my mysterious phone message. Maybe Margaret Featherman really was alive. If I suspected as much, wasn't I obligated to let Todd Bowman know? Not really. Besides, Coast Guard resources were the ones being used to search for someone who may or may not have drowned.

You know nothing for sure, I reminded myself. *Mind your own business.*

"As for Mr. Michael Conyers," Agent Bowman continued. "Mr. Conyers was an Alzheimer's patient who died in what was apparently not an accidental fall from the White Pass and Yukon Railway late yesterday morning. Since that incident took place while Mr. Conyers was off the ship, the crime is deemed to have happened under the jurisdiction of the state of Alaska. It is currently being investigated by detectives from the Alaska state troopers. My understanding from them today is that a suspect has been placed under arrest with regard to that incident. Because it's not my case, I can't say anything more about it at this time, but I believe I can assure you that this was what we would term a domestic situation. No one still on board the *Starfire Breeze* is considered to be a person of interest in the Conyers case."

Bowman paused and studied his audience. "Any questions?" he asked.

I noticed that he had made absolutely no mention of the presence of any other FBI agents on the ship. That meant the Leave It To God investigation was still ongoing and still under wraps.

A man in the middle of the first row stood up. He was someone I recognized as one of the previous afternoon's vociferous complainers—someone who had been bent out of shape when the glaciers hadn't appeared on cue.

"This Featherman thing happened days ago," he groused. "Our family members back home are reading all about it in their newspapers and seeing it on TV. How come we're only now finding out about it?"

Todd Bowman sighed and cleared his throat. "It isn't FBI policy to make statements about ongoing investigations, and since we had taken over the case, the cruise line decided not to comment, either."

"Why not? Were they afraid we'd all abandon ship and demand they fly us back home?"

Todd glanced around him. I'm sure he was looking for someone from Starfire Cruises to step up and take the heat. No one did. Bowman was stuck on the podium all by himself, and they left him there to handle it. In the meantime, the man in the front row made no move to resume his seat.

"As I said," Todd said calmly, "we have no reason to believe anyone else on the ship is in any danger."

That, of course, was an outright lie. According to Rachel Dulles, there was reason to believe Marc Alley was still in danger and so was Harrison Featherman.

"If that's true, why are you still here?" Mr. Twenty Questions asked.

Todd Bowman fumbled visibly before producing a suitable answer. "As I said, we're continuing to investigate Ms. Featherman's disappearance."

With a grunt and a derisive shake of his head, the still unsatisfied guy in the front row sat back down. "Any other questions?" Bowman asked.

No one stirred for some time, but before Todd Bowman managed to make good his escape, a woman two rows from the back stood up. "I understand the Native Peoples of Alaska and many of the state's other residents are unhappy with the proliferation of cruise ships in their once pristine waters. Is there a chance this woman's disappearance is related to that? I mean, what better way to discourage tourism than to start targeting cruise-ship passengers even when they're in the privacy of their own cabins?"

There were nods and murmurs of assent all around the room, which meant the *Starfire Breeze*'s rumor mill had been working overtime. Leave It To God's narrowly focused plot against a relative handful of doctors and their patients was now being transformed into a wide-ranging terrorist movement against Alaska's multimillion-dollar tourism industry. In the hands of the media, this new concept was a real winner. When it came to selling newspapers or advertising copy, what could be better than knocking off Mr. and Mrs. Joe Blow Tourist during the course of their lifelong dream vacation to beautiful Alaska. This could come across like one of those old-fashioned Indian massacres straight out of the 1880s.

Had this all been happening in some major metropolitan area, I'm sure the FBI agents sent to handle it would have been older, wiser, and far more experienced operatives than the likes of poor Todd Bowman. He did his best to play with the cards he'd been dealt.

"I have every confidence that what's going on here has nothing whatever to do with targeting Alaska-bound tourists."

That's what he said, but I don't think the lady in the back row believed him. Before anyone else could comment, Bowman took advantage of the slight pause to bolt from the stage. End of discussion. As the audience made their way up the aisles, there was more grumbling and griping. Lars added his own complaint to the voices of dissent.

"Whole t'ing was a waste of time," he muttered. "They didn't tell us anyt'ing we didn't already know."

I didn't bother explaining that's how press conferences

work, because that's what the whole exercise had been—a press conference minus the press. I doubt there were any reporters in attendance from the *Starfire Courier*. During the course of the briefing I had looked around, more than half expecting to spot Christine Moran, notebook in hand, busily taking notes. But the *Starfire Breeze*'s resident freelancer was nowhere in evidence. Not right then. But she turned up soon enough.

When we met up with Beverly, Naomi, and the Wakefield girls in the Atrium Lobby, Christine Moran was right there with them.

"Why, hello, Mr. Beaumont," she said with a smile. "So nice to see you again."

"You two know each other?" Beverly asked.

"He seems to know darn near everybody," Lars said.

"Christine wanted to talk to me about Margaret," Naomi put in. "I told her we were going into Sitka and she's offered to come along."

I could see from Naomi's expression that the last thing she wanted to do was talk to a reporter about Margaret Featherman. As for me, I sure as hell didn't want to have Christine Moran hanging around all day while we walked around Sitka in hopes of running into the mysterious Dulcinea. Still, I was afraid that saying no might arouse more suspicions than saying yes.

"Of course not," I said with as much phony enthusiasm as I could muster. "The more, the merrier."

21

 $\int$ ITKA IS A PORT where there are no docking facilities
large enough to accommodate cruise ships. As a consequence, the *Starfire Breeze* had to drop anchor in Sitka Sound.
Some of the ship's tenders, which, in time of crisis, serve as
lifeboats, were lowered into the water. Shore-going passengers were loaded into those and then ferried over to the visitors' dock.

The storm that had blown through the day before wasn't
quite done with us yet. It was still dripping rain as we landed,
but it looked as though it might clear eventually. It was possible that whichever cruise ships had drawn lots for that day's
trip to Glacier Bay would have better glacier viewing than the
passengers on the *Starfire Breeze*.

Once the ladies' plastic rain caps were all in place, our little group started off after Lars. As a tour guide, he set a brisk pace. Even with the morning dose of Advil, I was glad I had opted for tennis shoes.

Lars was enthusiastic about showing us the sights. "That's the P-Bar," he announced, pointing to a business adorned with more than its share of neon beer signs. "The real name is the Pioneer Bar, but nobody here calls it that. There's more than one fisherman who's walked out through that door and disappeared for good. The police and newspaper reports always say, 'Was last seen leaving the Pioneer Bar.' "

"Were they murdered, or what?" Claire Wakefield demanded while puffing vigorously in an effort to catch her breath.

"Some were, I suppose," Lars said with a shrug. "Especially the ones dumb enough to come in here flashing a roll of cash after selling their fish. But most of the time it's just accidental. Some of the guys leave this place with enough of a load on that they walk right off the dock or fall off their boats. Or else they climb aboard, fire up the engines, and run smack into a rock. Believe me, there are plenty of those around here, too."

"Did you go there?" Beverly asked.

"Used to," he said. "Back when I was drinking."

Like a hen with a bunch of chicks, Lars herded us through town. We spent some time inside the old Russian Orthodox Church—a frame building that had been constructed while Alaska still belonged to Russia. He showed us the Pioneer Home where Lars' younger brother, Einar, had lived out his last days before succumbing to the ravages of diabetes. After that he took us to Castle Hill, where drooping, bedraggled gardens only hinted at their summer glory.

All the time Lars was leading us around and administering his travelogue, I tried to keep one ear trained on the low-voiced conversation between Naomi Pepper and Christine Moran. As far as I could tell, Naomi was sticking to providing only the most basic background information about Margaret Featherman. I found it interesting that Christine was pursuing those questions with Naomi rather than asking them of Sharon Carson and Virginia Metz, but it wasn't any of my business, so I didn't ask.

And while all that was going on, I still had to keep an eye peeled in case anyone—Dulcinea or one of her minions—made an attempt to contact me. After all, if the middle-of-the-night caller hadn't been trying to reach Naomi, then, barring crossed phone connections, I had to assume I had been her target. She had said she'd see me in Sitka the next day. Everywhere we went, I wondered if that would be true, and if Christine Moran would be on hand to witness whatever was going to happen. With all that going on, it's no wonder that the process left me feeling somewhat stressed.

Lars, for his part, was totally unaware that the rest of us weren't enjoying ourselves nearly as much as he was. Caught up in his reminiscences, he had no idea that his flock was running out of energy and patience both. Seeing Sitka with Lars Jenssen brought back memories of Ted Moffit, my first wife's father.

Ted was a good old boy who was blessed with boundless energy and enthusiasm. Over scores of yearly family vacations he took countless numbers of slides featuring his three children—Karen and her younger brother and sister—posed grinning in front of every American tourist icon including Arizona's Grand Canyon and Boothill Graveyard, Yellowstone's Old Faithful, and South Dakota's Wall Drug and Mount Rushmore. The collection included shots of all the stopping-off places in between—long-closed diners and motels that had died slow and painful deaths after President Eisenhower's interstate highway system came into being. Ted was a great one for summoning hapless neighbors and relatives for evenings that consisted of pie, coffee, and marathon slide-viewing sessions. He had absolutely no sense about how long people could endure sitting and nodding through endless hours of incredibly boring slides.

Lars was exactly the same way about Sitka. He wanted to show us everything about the place and then some. When he suggested our next stop would be the dock where all the fishing boats were tied up, a minor mutiny occurred.

"Not me," Beverly announced. "I'm tired and my feet hurt. I've walked as far as I'm going to walk."

Claire and Florence were quick to nod in agreement while Lars, on the other hand, looked as though the women had just broken his heart. My feet hurt too, but having had no contact with the mysterious Dulcinea, I wasn't ready to give up and go back to the ship.

"I'll stay," I volunteered. I turned to Naomi and Christine. "What about you two?" I asked. Christine had stuck to Naomi as if they'd been connected with a layer of superglue.

Something on my face must have given Naomi a hint of what I was feeling. "I'll tell you what," she said. "Christine and I will go back to the ship with Beverly and the others and make sure they arrive safely. That way, you men can take in the docks and whatever else you want to without a bunch of party poopers slowing you down."

"Good idea," Christine said. "I need to be getting back anyway."

I felt like giving Naomi a kiss out of sheer gratitude, but I knew better than that—not with Lars and Beverly looking on. "If that's what you want to do," I said as casually as I could. "That'll be fine with me."

Up to that moment the women had been lagging behind. Now, with the prospect of going back to the ship and getting out of the drizzling rain, they set off at a much faster pace. Lars looked after them, shaking his head.

"Women," he muttered in disgust. "Probably want to stop off and do some shopping."

"What's wrong with that?"

"Yust more yunk to carry home," he said.

We went down to the dock then, just Lars and I. It had been years since he had been in Sitka. Nevertheless, he recognized many of the boats moored there, calling out their names and giving me a rundown of their various former skippers and crews. Listening to him talk, I had a sense of living history. Here was someone who knew firsthand the history of Alaska's fishing fleet for over half of the twentieth century. When Lars Jenssen died, much of that history would die with him.

"You should write all this down," I told him. "Or at least record it on tape."

"Naw," he said. "Nobody'd be interested in hearing what I have to say."

We had walked as far as the last set of docks. It was when we turned around to come back that I saw it. Painted on a shed far from where even the most daring tourists would venture was a billboard featuring a scrawny knight seated on an equally scrawny horse. The picture was a reasonably good plagiarism of the one by Picasso. QUIXOTE CLUB, the sign said. Below the club name was a toll-free number, and below that were the words, "Call for free shuttle service."

"What's that?" I asked.

Lars shrugged. "The Quicksaudy Club," he returned. Lars' mangled pronunciation, an authentically Ballardese version of Quixote, was a long way from Naomi Pepper's perfectly enunciated Spanish *kee-hoy-tay* from earlier that morning.

"But what is it?"

"Whaddya t'ink?" Lars returned. "It's full of women strippers. You got no business going there."

"You know about it then?" I asked. "You've been there?"

"Everybody in the fleet's been there," he said defensively.

"What do you know about it?"

Lars sighed. "It's a long story," he said. "There used to be this place out of town a couple of miles. It was called the Kiksadi Club named after one of the Tlingit clans. In the old days when they used to allow after-hours drinking outside the city limits, it was a real booming place. Every summer they used to import lady strippers. They came up and worked the place for a month or two at a time. One of the girls told me once that she made enough money dancing in Alaska each summer that she could pay her tuition and go to school the next year without having to work a part-time job. Sort of like fishing,"

Lars added. "Used to be real good pay for what was seasonal work."

"I take it you knew some of these girls personally?" I asked. By then we had left the dock area and were walking back to the ship—strolling, really, rather than walking.

"I was drinking then," Lars said. "Anyways, one of the girls who came up one year got friendly with the guy who was the manager of the Kiksadi Club. Real friendly. So friendly, in fact, that she thought he was going to divorce his wife and marry her, but he didn't. He dumped her instead. So she got herself some financial backers, went down the road half a mile or so, and opened her own place—the one you saw on the sign back there, the Quicksaudy Club. It's spelled different, but it sounds a lot like the other one. It was easy to get them confused, and I think she counted on that. It worked in her favor."

It was only easy to confuse the two if you were a Norwegian fisherman from Ballard who was half lit most of the time. But Lars Jenssen had been sober for years. From the newness of the sign, it looked as though the Quixote Club, no matter how you pronounced it, was still a going concern.

"Ya, sure," Lars said after a thoughtful silence. "That Dulcie always was one smart cookie."

I stopped short. "Who?"

"Dulcie—the woman who runs the Quicksaudy. She was a real looker back then, but she also had something upstairs."

"Dulcie?" I asked. "That's her name?"

"Not her whole name," Lars said. "That's just what the guys in the fleet called her. I can't remember her real name."

"Dulcinea maybe?" I asked.

Lars looked at me and frowned. "You know, that may be it. How did you know that?"

So Dulcinea wasn't going to contact me; I was supposed to contact her. Desperately, I looked around, searching for a cab. Naturally I didn't see one anywhere. "How do we get there?" I asked. "How long will it take? Can we walk?"

"You want to go to the Quicksaudy Club?" Lars demanded suspiciously. "How come? Looks to me like you've got a perfectly good woman waiting for you back on the ship. Matter of fact, I've got one, too. There's no need . . . And hell, no, you can't walk. It's a good five miles out of town."

"Where's the nearest pay phone then? I'll call a cab."

"There's one back at the dock, but the shuttle's cheaper. It's free."

I turned and headed back in that direction, with Lars dogging my heels and protesting my every step. At the docks, I went far enough to be able to see the club's sign and make a note of how to contact the shuttle service. I've never dialed one of those telephone sex lines, but the voice that answered the shuttle number was sexy enough to be worthy of a 1-900 designation.

"Welcome to Quixote Club, where your pleasure is our only business," she said breathlessly while a pair of castanets clattered evocatively in the background. "If you are in need of our shuttle service, please press one now. Your call will be transferred to an operator for assistance."

I turned back to Lars. "What is this, a whorehouse?"

He glowered at me. "Not as far as I know," he said.

When the dispatcher came on the phone, her voice was

pleasant enough if not quite as sultry. "What's your loca-tion?"

"I'm down by the docks," I said. "The docks with the fish-ing boats."

"Very good. Our next shuttle will reach your location in approximately ten minutes," she said. "Our next show starts on the hour. How many people will be in your party?"

"One," I said.

"Two," Lars growled behind me. "There'll be two."

"No way," I said to him.

He shook his head. "Two," he insisted. "Either I go, too, or you don't."

I gave up. "Two," I grumbled into the phone.

"Very well, sir," the operator said. "You'll have no trou-ble recognizing our vehicles. They're all painted pink. You'll need to come up to the road and wait there. The shuttle will stop by and pick you up. And we'll need your name, sir, so the driver can verify that she's picked up the correct passenger."

"Beau," I barked back at her. "The name's Beau."

"Very well, Mr. Bow. Someone will be right there."

I put down the phone. Lars was standing behind me, shak-ing his head. "I t'ink this is a bad idea," he said. "If Naomi and Beverly hear about this, there'll be hell to pay. You can count on that."

"So it is a whorehouse then?"

"It may have started out that way," Lars admitted. "Yust at first. But I mostly went there to watch the girls and to drink single-malt Scotch. Dulcie always made it a point to have one of the best bars going. I'll bet she still does."

"Right," I said. "I'm sure she does. Now go on back to the ship, Lars. I'm a big boy. I don't need you along to hold my hand."

"Yes, you do," he said. "If you went there by yourself and got into some kind of scrape, Beverly would never forgive me." And that was the end of that.

The shuttle arrived in less than ten minutes. Most of that time Lars and I stood side by side without saying a word. When the shuttle showed up, it was a sturdy Suburban painted that distinctive shade of pale pink favored by successful Mary Kay ladies the world over. Stenciled in black on both front doors was the same silhouette image we had seen on the sign back at the docks—Don Quixote on his knobby-kneed horse.

The driver rolled down her window. "Mr. Bow?" she asked.

"Right," I said without bothering to correct her. Lars and I clambered in.

The driver was a young woman in her early twenties. She was dressed in what looked like high-class waitress gear—a tuxedo shirt, black bow tie, and black slacks. Like the girls in the cruise-ship gift shop, she reminded me of my daughter.

"Rosinante," she said.

"I beg your pardon?"

"Rosinante," she repeated. "That's the name of Don Quixote's horse. People always want to know the horse's name. I've started telling people that first thing, just to get it out of the way."

Carefully she threaded her way through narrow streets clogged with cruise passengers determined to do their last bit of Alaska-based shopping. I peered through the crowd looking for familiar faces. Riding in the back of the pink Suburban, I wasn't eager to be recognized. It made me grateful for the dark-tinted glass in all the back windows.

"Look's like the weather's clearing up some," our driver announced. "I wouldn't be surprised if it turned sunny late in the day."

That's right, I thought grimly. *Talk about the weather.*

"Where are you from?" I asked.

"Seattle," she said. "Lynnwood, actually. I have one more quarter to go at the U Dub before I get my degree in counseling. The season's winding down here. I'm headed home in a few weeks."

A hooker with a degree in counseling, I thought. *That's rich.*

"How long have you worked here?"

"This is my last year," she said.

"The girls can only work four years," Lars put in. "That's as long as Dulcie will let them stay. It's like an athletic scholarship. You get four years of eligibility."

The driver glanced at Lars in the mirror. "I haven't seen you before, but I'll bet you're one of Dulcie's old-timers, aren't you!"

"Ya." Lars nodded. "Ya, sure."

Just as Lars had said, Dulcie sounded like quite a business-woman. She cycled her girls through her system in four-year shifts. *That way she get's 'em when they're young and healthy, and sends them on their way before they get too old.*

We were out of town now—I wasn't sure in which direction—and driving through a hazy suburban landscape interspersed with patches of forest. We might have been in one of Seattle's eastern suburbs—North Bend or Snoqualmie. We passed a sign on the right-hand side of the road that said ROOKIES. A gravel driveway wound up a rise and gave way to an uneven gravel-and-mud parking lot dotted with pickup trucks and SUVs. The building situated in the middle of the lot looked like any other nondescript commercial building—one that could just as easily be either a bar or a warehouse.

"There used to be a lot more trees around here," Lars said. "And why does that sign say 'Rookies'? What happened to the Kiksadi?"

"Changed hands," our driver informed us helpfully. "The new owners decided not to try to compete with Dulcie, so they turned it into a sports bar. They have male strippers in occasionally, but only on special occasions. The girls are all down the road—with Dulcie."

"That's it!" Lars exclaimed with a grin. "She told the guy that she was gonna get even and put him out of business. Looks like she did yust that."

Half a mile farther down the road we came to a second clearing. Even in the middle of the day, there must have been thirty cars parked in the smoothly paved lot, not counting the five matching pink Suburbans lined up in reserved spots near the front door. The Quixote Club wasn't just a single building, either. Behind the main building—a two-story rambling affair that showed clear signs of regular painting and maintenance—stood a series of small, sturdily built cabins. I had a pretty good idea about what those were used for but made no comment. In the contest between the old Kiksadi Club and the Quixote Club, no matter how you pronounced the name, there could be no question that the Quixote was the hands-down winner.

Our driver pulled up to the door. "You buy your tickets from the booth just inside," she directed. "The show starts in about ten minutes. When it's over, come outside and we'll shuttle you back downtown. It'll take a few minutes to change. When things slow down like this, we have to double as dancers and drivers both."

Inside the door was a vestibule complete with a glass-enclosed ticket booth. Beyond that was another room that reeked of cigarette smoke and was filled with the talk and laughter of guys having a good time. The ticket booth was staffed by a woman who was almost as wide as the booth itself. "May I help you?" she asked.

As soon as the woman opened her mouth, I recognized the sultry voice from the answering machine. She may have once been beautiful. It was difficult to see her former beauty wrapped in the fleshy, sagging-jowled body imprisoned behind the glass, but the woman's voice alone was enough to bring Lars to attention.

He squared his shoulders, stepped up to the window, pulled out his billfold, and handed over a crisp hundred-dollar bill. For a change there was no grumbling about how much things cost. "Hi, there, Dulcie," he said. "Two, please."

The woman handed him two tickets and his change, then there was a momentary pause while she studied him. At last her eyes lit up with recognition. "Why, Lars Jenssen, you old devil! What on earth are you doing here? So you finally decided to come check up on me, did you? Why didn't you call ahead and let me know?"

I couldn't quibble with Dulcie's genuine pleasure at seeing Lars again. If he had come to what he called the Quicksaudy Club for just the dancing and drinking, as he claimed, then I was a monkey's uncle. But then again, anything that may have transpired between Lars and Dulcie was years in the past. It was no more my business than what was happening between Naomi Pepper and me was his.

"Where the hell have you been?" Dulcie asked.

"On the wagon." Lars' answer was a little sheepish and delivered with far less bravado than he might have used in the course of an AA meeting.

"Good for you," she returned. "What else is new?"

"My wife passed away a few years ago, but I got remarried," he continued. "My new wife, Beverly, and I are here on our honeymoon. We came in on the *Starfire Breeze*."

"Well, it's good to see you again. And we've got plenty of O'Doul's, or Sharp's, if that's what you're drinking these days. And who's this?" she asked, nodding in my direction.

"My new grandson," Lars said. "His name's Beau—Beau Beaumont."

So here it was, contact at last—the moment I had been waiting for. But Dulcie never missed a beat. She beamed at me. "Glad to meet you, Beau. I'm Dulcinea Wadsworth. Most people call me Dulcie."

The outside door opened and two more paying customers got in line behind us. "The show's about to start," Dulcie said, "so why don't you go on inside. My table's the one to the right of the door. It's marked 'Reserved,' but go ahead and sit there anyway. If anyone objects, tell them I said so—as long as you don't mind sitting in the back row, that is."

"The back row's fine," Lars said. "I already told you, I'm married now. Besides, a man my age can't afford to get too excited."

Leaving Dulcie Wadsworth to collect her other admissions, Lars and I stepped inside and took two of the four seats at a table marked RESERVED. I was careful to leave the chair next to me empty in case Dulcie planned to use the cover of darkness to explain the message she had left for me earlier.

It was just before noon, so I was startled to see that the room was more than half full. I was also surprised to see any number of familiar faces—including Mr. Twenty Questions, the guy who had given Todd Bowman such hell in the Starlight Theater a few hours earlier. It was clear from the way the members of the audience were dressed that most of the old duffers were passengers from the *Starfire Breeze*. There were also a few swaggering, flannel-wearing youngsters. These were fisherman off the fleet, I supposed.

Young or old, all of the attendees were intent on having an uproarious boys' day out. They were drinking, smoking (an activity discouraged on the ship in anything other than the designated smoking lounges), laughing, and having a good time. Except for the bartender and three overworked cocktail waitresses, there weren't any other women in sight.

"What'll you have?" the cocktail waitress asked once she worked her way over to our table.

"O'Doul's," Lars told her.

"Tonic with a twist," I said.

"That'll be ten dollars each," she said. "Cash only, no tabs, no credit cards."

Dulcie Wadsworth had a fine business sense, all right. And

from the looks of things, the Quixote Club was raking in the
dough.

Several more customers came in after we did. Then, just
before the lights dimmed, Dulcie herself entered the room as
well. She swept past the place I had left for her. Instead, she
eased her wide girth onto the chair next to Lars and then
leaned over and gave him a peck on the cheek.

"It's so good to see you again," she said. "You're looking
well. Sorry to hear about your wife."

Lars nodded. "It was Alzheimer's," he said.

"She was sick for a long time?"

He nodded again. Dulcie reached over and patted his arm
sympathetically. On her hand were several oversize rings,
including a door-knob-sized emerald surrounded by a mound
of sparkling diamonds. "I wish you and that new wife of yours
years of happiness," she said. "You certainly deserve it."

The cocktail waitress returned with our drinks. "Did you
already pay for those?" Dulcie asked.

"Yes," I told her.

"Give them back their money, Kristin," Dulcie ordered
the waitress. "Lars is an old friend of mine. Their drinks are
on the house."

Without a word, the cocktail waitress nodded, handed us
back our money, and then hurried off to deliver the rest of her
tray of drinks while she could still see to do it. When the
lights dimmed, a woman stepped onto the small stage that was
positioned just to the right of the bar. It was difficult to tell
how old the dancer was. She was dressed as a ragged old charwoman complete with a cap on her head and a dust mop in her
hand. The outfit reminded me of those old charwoman com-

edy routines Carol Burnett used to do on TV, except Carol Burnett never used to take anything off. This one did—all of it—and I have to admit, it was pretty impressive. By the time the ugly duckling had turned into a beautiful and almost naked swan, money—paper bills in the form of tens and twenties—were raining down around her head.

As the audience applauded and roared its approval, I felt a hand on my leg just above my knee. I looked up and there, sitting next to me, was Margaret Featherman. Without a word, she put a finger to her lips to silence me. Then she beckoned for me to follow her outside.

If the United States Coast Guard was still out searching Chatham Strait for Margaret Featherman, they were looking in the wrong damn place.

22

WITHOUT A WORD, Margaret led me through the vestibule and over to a door that I had assumed led to a closet of some kind. Instead, the door opened onto a steep stairwell. She led me up the stairs and into a large and comfortably furnished living room complete with a massive log-burning fireplace. In one corner of the room was a home office complete with computer, printer, and a set of file cabinets, while at the other end was a rough-hewn refectory table. In front of the fireplace sat a coffee table made from a gnarled slab of polished root, and under the burl-wood table was an enormous bearskin rug made from an amazingly large grizzly. It was a room I felt immediately at home in even if it was situated smack on top of a whorehouse.

It wasn't until we were both inside the room that Margaret turned and faced me. That's when I saw the bruises on her face. Green and yellow marks that began above her eyes and covered both cheeks made Beverly's accident on the treadmill look minor in comparison.

Margaret nodded. "I know," she said. "The bruises are ugly as hell, but that's what happens when you hit the water wrong. I'm just lucky I wasn't knocked out cold. If that had happened, I'd be dead by now. Hello, Mr. Beaumont," she added. "How are you?"

"Fine."

"You don't seem especially surprised to see me."

"I'm not. I heard your voice in the background on the phone the other night. At least I thought it was you."

A look of concern passed over her face. "Did you tell anyone?"

"No, not without knowing for sure. I waited to see if you'd call back. You didn't."

She sighed. "I'm glad you didn't tell," she said. "The fewer people who know I'm still alive, the better."

"What do you want?" I asked. "And why did you contact me instead of your friends or a family member? They're all worried sick about you. They think you're dead. And as far as I know, the Coast Guard is still looking for you. When they find out you're safe and sound, they may very well charge you for the cost of that search."

"It's all right," she said. "I can afford it. I've been using Dulcie's computer to keep an eye on the market. If the Coast Guard sends me a bill, I'll be able to pay."

"You still haven't said what you want with me."

"I want to offer you a job."

"A job? What makes you think I want a job?"

"You're a retired cop. You're on your uppers enough that you're putting in your time as a cruise dance host. It crossed my mind that you might appreciate a regular dollars-and-cents paycheck or two to tide you over until you land yourself a rich widow."

A lot had happened since that morning when Naomi and I had met up with Margaret Featherman on her way to the gym. Naomi had moved beyond the dance host rumor, but as soon as Margaret mentioned it again, I went all defensive and came out swinging. "I'm not interested in rich widows," I told her curtly. "Or rich divorcées, either, for that matter. And I'm not in the market for a paycheck. I'm fine without one."

"That's too bad," she said. "I was really hoping I could talk you into helping me."

Margaret Featherman was anything but the kind of person who could appeal to someone's better nature—assuming I had one of those. But she was a survivor and a fighter—traits that forced me to grant her a certain amount of respect. She had also piqued my curiosity.

"What kind of a job?" I asked.

"You're a former homicide detective," she said. "I want you to find out who tried to kill me. I may be big news right now, but that's only because people think I'm dead. At the moment I'm sure there are a whole lot of people working like mad to find the person who killed me. But once they figure out I'm still alive, they'll lose interest. There's far more riding on a homicide investigation than there is on an attempted homicide."

I had to admit there was some truth in what she said. In

terms of parceling out resources, law enforcement agencies expend far more energy and focus on cases where the victim actually dies than they do in situations where, by virtue of luck or the advances of medical science, the potential victim ends up pulling through.

In spite of myself, I felt myself being sucked in. Rachel Dulles had asked me to look out for Marc Alley's well-being, and I had agreed to that, but it hadn't appealed to me nearly as much as what Margaret Featherman was offering me now—the chance to get a killer off the streets. Even though I had pretty well made up my mind to say yes, I decided to play hard to get. Margaret was in the habit of always getting her own way. I wanted her to have to work for it.

"Before I say yes or no," I told her, "I want you to answer some questions."

"Like what?"

"Like who sent you the draft copy of Harrison's new will?"

Beneath the ugly bruises, Margaret's skin turned chalk-white. "Melissa Pepper," she said.

I had been right about the Kinko's connection. "Why?"

Margaret shrugged. "Who knows? To hurt me, maybe?"

"And how did she come to be in possession of it?"

"Harrison gave it to her," she answered.

"And why did he do that?"

"I don't know. Maybe he's sick and dying, or maybe he just thinks he is. But the will makes it pretty clear. Melissa said Harrison told her that she's really his daughter, not Gary Pepper's. And that in the event of Harrison's death, she's to receive a portion of his estate equal to Chloe's. They each get twenty-five percent, while the other fifty goes to Leila and her new brat. Melissa said Harrison wanted to encourage her to 'get her life on track.' That's how she put it.

"Since she evidently didn't know about any of this before, I have no idea why, after all this time, Harrison would have tracked Melissa down to give her the news. Missy Pepper's been screwed up for years—since long before Gary Pepper died. My best guess is that the idea that one of Harrison's offspring isn't living up to her potential is driving him crazy. He's something of a perfectionist."

"So you talked to Melissa?"

Margaret nodded. "She called me that afternoon, after she sent the fax. She called on my cell phone. It was a number I didn't recognize, but I answered because of the IPO. I thought it might be something about that."

"Why did she call you?"

"To ask me if it was true or not." Margaret paused. "The little bitch," she added. "Why didn't she ask her mother, instead?"

I could have told Margaret that Melissa Pepper hated her mother, but I didn't. When no answer was forthcoming from me, Margaret continued. "As soon as I got off the phone with Missy, I called Naomi and gave her hell about it. She claimed she knew nothing about the will, but she must have. And the will isn't the point. I couldn't believe she had betrayed me that way with Harrison. I asked her why she had done it. All she could say was didn't I understand? She had wanted a baby so desperately. All she wanted was a baby. She said, since I had Chloe, I probably didn't know what it was like, but I did, of course. I understood far better than she could have imagined."

"What do you mean?"

"It's not fair," Margaret objected. "If you're not going to help me, there's no point in my telling you any of this."

"I'm leaning in that direction," I said. "Tell me anyway."

"I had an abortion," she said.

"So? It's not the end of the world. Lots of women have abortions."

"It was an illegal abortion." As Margaret spoke, the words she loosed in the air were so brittle they might have been flying shards of glass.

"A botched illegal abortion," she added. "It was after Chloe was born but before *Roe v. Wade*. Harrison made me do it. The miracle is that it didn't kill me. It almost did, but I couldn't have any more children after that. Chloe was it."

"But why get an abortion in the first place? You and Harrison were married then. Didn't you want more than one child?"

"We did want more, but when we found out I was pregnant, Harrison wanted me to have the fetus tested. Amniocentesis wasn't nearly as sophisticated back then as it is now, but it was enough. The test showed my baby, a little boy, would have had Down syndrome. Harrison didn't want that. Not him. He only wanted perfect children, you see. Now he'll have three: one, Chloe, who, in his estimation, is perfect in every way and worships the ground he walks on; and Melissa Pepper, who has her sights set on being a grade-A loser and who says she hates him anyway, at least that's what she told me on the phone. As for the third one, who knows about him?"

"You say Leila's baby is a he. Are you implying that they've already had this fetus tested, too?"

"That's what Melissa told me. It's no surprise. Of course Harrison had Leila's baby tested. He isn't a person who leaves such things to chance. If there'd been anything wrong, I'm sure he would have disposed of that baby the same way he did mine, the son of a bitch!"

I have one of those little ELPH cameras—the tiny ones with a built-in flash and autofocus. Jeremy and Kelly gave it to me last Christmas, probably so it would be easier to have a camera around when it's time to take pictures of little Kayla, my granddaughter. When I turn the camera on and line it up to take a picture, it whirs and the picture moves into focus. And that's what happened for me right then with Margaret Featherman. The focus shifted, and I saw her and her overweening anger against her ex-husband in an entirely different light.

"That's why you went back to school, isn't it?" I said. "That's why you got yourself a Ph.D. in genetics, and it's why you've been at Genesis ever since, working on the patch."

She nodded. "I had to do something. From the beginning, Chloe adored her father, and she didn't want to have anything to do with me. And the truth is, I was so angry right then—with Harrison, with Chloe, and with the unfairness of it all—that I probably wasn't much of a mother. But the two of them absolutely closed me out—two against one. It's always been that way. When I finally figured that out, I decided the hell with it. That's when I went back to school. It was a way of making some small good emerge from my own terrible tragedy. I've spent almost every waking moment since trying to salvage something from my life and to find a way to keep the same thing from happening to someone else."

"Is it going to work?" I asked.

"The patch? I don't know," she said, shaking her head. "I believe it will, and looking at the way our shares are selling, it sounds as though the investors believe it will, too. It's a patented process, and if it turns out to be successful, it could have applications in other possible birth-defect situations as well as Down syndrome. The problem is, Genesis has always been a small, closely held company. In order to do all the required testing, in order to get FDA approval, we needed a massive infusion of capital, which now we seem to have."

"Thanks to you."

"No," she said. "It's not thanks to me at all. It's thanks to a little boy who never got to take his first step or feel the sun on his face or smell the rain in the desert or open a stocking on Christmas morning. I never saw him or held him or touched him. Harrison even refused to give the baby a name. To him our child was never a baby, just a fetus. There wasn't a funeral or a casket or a marker in a cemetery with his name on it. I gave him a name, though. In my heart I've always called him Alton James, after my father."

It was only a matter of minutes since I had followed Margaret Featherman out the door of the Quixote Club and up the stairs into Dulcie Wadsworth's apartment. If anyone had told me that within that time I'd end up feeling so sorry for the woman that I'd have a lump in my throat, I would have told them they were crazy. And I would have been wrong.

There were tears—real tears—in Margaret's eyes as she told me about her lost child. Her grief was still right there, concealed under the brittle surface of her anger—the armor she used to keep other people from getting too close. As long as she maintained the tough facade, no one saw a second layer beneath it, the all-consuming hurt. In fact, most of the time, I'll bet even Margaret failed to remember it. It's called self-delusion. I might not have recognized it either, if I weren't something of an expert at it myself.

We fell quiet for a moment. From the bar below we felt rather than heard the steady thrum of bass booming through the Quixote Club's loudspeakers. Dulcie Wadsworth had soundproofed her apartment well enough that none of the music leaked into the living quarters, but there was no way to shut out the thumping vibration.

"Maybe I'm wrong in thinking Naomi's the one who wanted me dead or hired someone to kill me," Margaret continued at last. "I can't see any motivation. And the same thing is true for Harrison as well—no motivation. But I still need to know who did it. Will you help me?"

"Tell me what went on when this so-called waiter burst into your room. Try to remember everything that happened, everything that was said."

Margaret looked at me appraisingly. "You know about him?"

I nodded. Instead of asking how I knew, she shuddered slightly and shifted gears. "He came in right after Naomi left—seconds after. That's why I thought at first that she had let him in. The guy looked like someone from Room Service. He was carrying a tray with a covered dinner plate. I thought someone had ordered a treat and sent it to me as a surprise. So even if Naomi hadn't left the door ajar, I probably would have let the guy in myself because he looked legitimate. He put the tray down on the table, but then, when he removed the cover from the plate, that's when I saw the gun on the plate—a gun and a roll of duct tape. He picked up the gun and aimed it at me.

"I said, 'What are you, crazy? Put that thing down before somebody gets hurt.' Instead, he waved the gun at me and said, 'Pick up the tape.' That's when I realized it wasn't a man at all. It was a woman dressed as a man."

"Was she wearing one of the ship's uniforms?"

"It looked like it, but I can't say for sure. For all I know, the damned thing could have come from a costume-supply shop."

"What happened next?"

"She told me to pick up the duct tape and cover my mouth. I thought she was going to shoot me. I was scared out of my wits, but I did as I was told. And all the while I kept backing up—trying to get away, I guess. Trying to put some distance between me and the barrel of that gun. I'd had the door to my lanai open, and when I came to the sill, I stepped over it and just kept backing. By the time I finished covering my mouth, I was right up against the rail. I was so frightened by then—my hands were shaking so badly—that it was all I could do to put the last piece of tape on my face.

"That's when she told me to jump. I wanted to argue with her, but my mouth was taped shut, and I couldn't say a word. She said, 'Jump,' again, and then she said the strangest thing. She said, 'Now it's between you and God.' Then she punched me in the shoulder. The next thing I knew, I was over the rail and falling."

"Damn," I said.

"What's wrong?"

"I was right. The FBI *is* protecting the wrong Dr. Feather-man."

"The FBI? What are you talking about?" Margaret demanded.

"Have you ever heard of an organization called Leave It To God?"

"Never. They sound like a bunch of oddballs."

"They're a long way beyond odd," I told her. "They're cold-blooded killers. They've presented the FBI with a list of targeted doctors—the ones who are most involved in developing cutting-edge life-saving procedures. Two of those doctors on Leave It To God's list are dead so far—both victims of as-yet-unsolved homicides. So are two of those doctors' patients. The FBI looked at the list and assumed all the names on it belonged to physicians. When the name Featherman turned up, they decided Harrison Featherman fit the bill and had to be the target. I doubt they even considered the possibility that Ph.D.s would be on the list."

"Or women," Margaret added. "The Attorney General may be a woman, but that doesn't mean that the guys who work for her—the ones in charge of running the FBI—aren't a bunch of male chauvinists."

When she said that, it sounded as if the old hard-edged Margaret Featherman was back—the tough nut I had met in the dining room the first night of the cruise. And right at that moment, hard-edged was probably a good thing. Margaret needed to be tough about then.

"We have a few things going for us," I said.

"Like what?"

"You're not dead, for one. You've actually seen the person

who tried to kill you, and you can probably identify her. All we need is a little time and luck, and maybe we can find her."

"What do you mean, 'we'? I want to hire you so I won't *have* to do anything. You don't expect me to give her a second crack at me, do you? She made a believer out of me. She meant to kill me, and she would have if I hadn't gotten the duct tape off and wasn't such a good swimmer. Even so, I never would have made it to land. The shore was too far away and the water was too cold. It's nothing but pure luck that a fishing boat showed up when it did. They appeared out of nowhere. I started splashing water so they'd see me, and when they seemed to be within hearing distance, I yelled my head off. The guys on board plucked me out of the water, dried me off, warmed me up, and brought me here."

"See there?" I said lightly. "That's Leave It To God's whole idea. They left it up to God, and God saved you. Obviously you were meant to live."

"Somehow I don't find that idea especially comforting."

"Once the fishing crew pulled you out of the water, why didn't they call the Coast Guard and let them know you were safe?"

"I bribed them," Margaret responded.

"With what?"

"With money—or the promise of it anyway. I gave them an IOU which I fully intend to honor as soon as I get back to Seattle. I told them I was sure my husband was the one who had tried to kill me—my husband and his girlfriend. It must have sounded plausible enough. I convinced them that if they took me back to the ship, the killers would simply try again."

"And they believed you?"

"They must have. They brought me here, didn't they? They told me that if I didn't want to go to the cops, Dulcie Wadsworth was the only person they could think of who could help me. And she did. She gave me a place to stay. And when I told her about you, she said she'd figure out a way to bring you here. She did that, too.

"I asked her how she was going to make it work since I didn't think you'd ever been in Sitka before and that I doubted you'd know anything about it. She said, 'Honey, I'm going to give the man a clue. If he isn't smart enough to figure it out on his own, then he won't be smart enough to help you, and we'll need to find someone else.' "

I was listening to her, but only half. With the other part of my brain, I was trying to come up with a plan. Leave It To God was a shadow organization. But if we could manage to bring down one of their operatives without alerting the entire organization that we were on to them, we might be able to penetrate their communications network and clean up the whole mess. As far as I could see, there was only one way to do that.

"I want you to come back on board the ship," I said.

Margaret looked stricken. "You what?"

"I want you back on the *Starfire Breeze* long enough to see if you can spot the killer and point her out to me."

Margaret was shaking her head before I even finished making my pitch. "Oh, no," she said. "Not on your life. How do I point her out without her seeing me?"

I thought about Antonio Belvaducci and his darkened room lined with security monitors, the ones showing what was going on in public areas all over the ship. The woman who had attacked Margaret Featherman had been careful to keep her face hidden from the lens of the nearest camera as she burst into Margaret's room, but she wouldn't be so careful as long as she thought her victim safely dead. With Margaret out of the way, her killer's identity was safe.

"The *Starfire Breeze* has a state-of-the-art security system," I explained. "When you went over the side, one of the video cameras caught you falling, duct tape and all. That's how we knew what had happened to you wasn't suicide and it wasn't an accident, either. Those videotapes are kept intact for the duration of the cruise. Whoever did this is either a passenger on the ship or a member of the crew. You'll be able to find her because her face is bound to be there. All you have to do is keep looking, and you don't have to do that looking in public, either. I'll talk to Captain Giacometti. You should be able to watch those tapes in the privacy of the ship's security room. There's no way the killer can get to you there, unless she really is a member of the crew."

"She's not," Margaret Featherman declared. "I'm sure of that."

"How come?"

"Because I didn't decide to come on the cruise at all until just three weeks ago. I heard Harrison was going to be on board, and I decided I had to be, too. Just in case the IPO went through the roof, I wanted to be here so I could zing him about it. And I wanted my friends along as part of my cheering section. We were already booked for Reno, but I canceled those reservations and booked us all on the *Starfire Breeze* instead."

"You're saying you and your friends were last-minute additions to the cruise?"

"That's right. It's late in the season, and the cruise line had rooms that were going begging. They gave me a great price."

"In other words, if you're the target, the killer has to be someone who signed up for the cruise after you did. That narrows the field some. Where's a telephone?"

"What do you want a phone for?"

"To call the ship and talk to the captain."

Margaret shook her head. "I don't know about that. It seems dangerous to me. What if the woman finds out I'm on board? What if she sees me and comes after me again?"

"She won't," I said. "I'll talk to the captain. If he can't figure out a way to ensure your safety, we'll forget about the whole thing."

"Maybe I could stay in your cabin," Margaret suggested.

It was a good enough idea but one that wouldn't fly. "No," I said. "That'll never do."

That was all I said. There was no sense in telling Margaret Featherman that I was already taken and by Naomi Pepper herself. Finding that out would have made Margaret mad all over again, which would have been a shame. My admiration may have been grudgingly given, but I was just beginning to like her.

23

ONCE DULCIE WADSWORTH'S PHONE was in my hand, I rethought my initial intention. I spent my entire career at Seattle PD being accused of Lone Ranger-ing it. And so, I decided to be a team player. I *tried* being a team player. Instead of calling Captain Giacometti first, I called the *Starfire Breeze* and asked for Kurt and Phyllis Nix's stateroom. No answer. Rachel Dulles wasn't in, and neither was Alex Freed. I didn't leave a message. Then, because I really was trying to do the right thing, I even tried asking for Todd Bowman. No deal there, either. When I asked to speak to Captain Giacometti, I was told he was unavailable. Since I had started at the top of the chain of command, that left me no choice but to go down.

"What about First Officer Vincente?" I asked.

"If you can tell me what this is about . . ." the operator began.

"I can tell you it's urgent," I said. "A matter of life and death." Which was technically true. The fact that Margaret Featherman wasn't dead had far more to do with pure luck than it did anything else. Or maybe, LITG was right, and God was the one who had put that fishing boat in the right place in Chatham Strait at just the right time.

I waited on the phone for a very long time. "First Officer Vincente," he said. "May I help you?"

"I don't know if you remember me. My name is Beaumont, J. P. Beaumont."

"Oh, yes," he said. "I remember you quite well. You are the FBI agent who is not an FBI agent, correct? The one who was allowed improper access to our security tapes."

This wasn't going the way I wanted. "That's correct," I admitted.

"What can I do for you, Mr. Beaumont?"

"I need to ask you a favor."

"I don't think so, Mr. Beaumont. You are in no position to ask a favor of anyone; now, if you please—"

"I've found Margaret Featherman," I said.

He stopped dead. "You what?"

"Margaret Featherman, the woman who went overboard," I said. "I've found her."

"Is she alive or dead?"

"She's very much alive."

"Thank God. That is wonderful! How did this happen? Who located her, the Coast Guard?"

"No, Mr. Vincente. I found her. And I must swear you to secrecy. No one can be allowed to know she is still alive."

"But that is absurd, Mr. Beaumont. Out of the question. Surely we must tell her family, notify the FBI, let the Coast Guard know."

"You are aware, of course, that there are two entirely separate FBI investigations being conducted on board the *Starfire Breeze* at this time, correct?"

Vincente paused. "Yes," he agreed warily.

"And that one of them deals with a plot to kill one of the doctors on board."

"Yes," he said. "I am aware of such an investigation."

"What you don't know and what the FBI doesn't know is they're protecting the wrong doctor. Leave It To God wasn't after Harrison Featherman at all. They were after his former wife."

"But how do you know this?"

"Because of what the killer said to Margaret Featherman before she was shoved overboard. The perpetrator is still on board your ship, and we've got to catch her before she gets away and before her compatriots know she's been compromised."

"Mr. Beaumont, I don't understand why you're telling me all this. Surely, the FBI investigators are the ones—"

"I've already tried calling them," I said. "I don't know where they are. All I know is, they're not answering their phones, and time is of the essence. I want to bring Mrs. Featherman back on board. I want to smuggle her down into the security room and see if she can spot the woman who attacked her on any of Antonio Belvaducci's tapes."

"The first thing is to notify the Coast Guard so they can call off the search."

"No!" I insisted. "That's exactly what you mustn't do—not until we get our ducks in a row."

"Our what?"

Idiomatic English strikes again. "We have to have everything in place," I said. "That's all." I could tell from the silence on the other end that I had his attention.

"What is it you wish me to do?" he asked.

"First let me ask you something. What happens if someone boards the ship without having swiped their key when they disembark?"

"An alarm sounds," First Officer Vincente replied.

"That's what I was afraid of. Look, I'll come back to the ship in a little while. If you can, have an extra key card made for Mrs. Featherman and have it swiped as though she had left the ship in an ordinary fashion. Then I'll use that to bring her back on board. She can go straight to the security screening room and get started viewing tapes."

First Officer Vincente considered my proposal for some time. "All right," he agreed finally. "I suppose that will work. And if the FBI agents have returned by then?"

"We tell them what we have and turn the whole operation over to them."

"Very well, then. Captain Giacometti is not on board this afternoon, so this is my decision. I suppose that will be all right. How soon will you be back at the dock?"

"Say half an hour?"

"All right then. I'll deliver a pre-swiped key card to the security officer in charge of loading passengers into the tenders. The card will be in an envelope with your name on it. Ask him for it when you get there."

"Thanks," I said, putting down the phone. Having sold the program to First Officer Vincente, I might have danced with glee, but right then the door at the top of the staircase opened and Dulcie Wadsworth waddled into the room, followed by Lars Jenssen—an irate Lars Jenssen. He glared from me to Margaret Featherman and back again.

"What's going on?" he demanded.

Dulcie went straight to Margaret. "Is everything all right?" Dulcie asked.

Margaret nodded. "I think so. Mr. Beaumont here has made arrangements for me to go back on board the ship. He wants me to look at the ship's security tapes to see if I can identify the person who attacked me."

Lars' jaw dropped. "This is the woman who fell off the ship?"

I nodded. Dulcie turned to me. "Are you sure that's such a good idea—taking her back on board the ship, that is? Won't it be dangerous?"

"If the killer finds out she's still alive, it might turn dangerous," I agreed. "If the attacker realizes Margaret could possibly identify her, she may try coming around and taking another crack at it. That's why time is so important. Once Margaret is on board the ship, I've made arrangements for her to be taken directly to the security monitoring room. As long as she's there, looking at tapes, she'll be safe enough. The problem is getting her from here to there without anyone recognizing her."

Frowning, Dulcie Wadsworth looked Margaret Featherman up and down. "What size are you again?"

"Eight or ten," Margaret replied. "Depends on the cut."

"Wait here," Dulcie ordered. "Let me see what I can do."

While Dulcie made her way back down the stairs, I turned to Lars. "This is Margaret Featherman, Lars. Margaret, this is Lars Jenssen, my grandmother's husband."

He held out his hand. "Glad to meet you," he said. "My wife has a shiner, too, at the moment. Had an accident on a treadmill. Not nearly as colorful as yours, though," he added.

Having exhausted his effort at small talk, Lars turned to me. "I didn't even know you were gone," he grumbled. "I thought you were sitting right there the whole time enjoying the show along with the rest of us. Then, when the lights came back up, you were nowhere to be found. Dulcie said not to worry. She said she knew where you were, but I've got to tell you, it gave me a scare. I didn't know what to think."

That's what he said, but I had a pretty good idea what he was thinking. He thought I had left the show early for only one purpose. He thought Margaret and I had been involved in the same kind of activity he and Dulcie had been up to for years. I was sure he'd be only too happy to report my assumed transgression to Beverly without making mention of any of his own.

"Yoo-hoo," Dulcie called from downstairs. "Margaret, come down here for a minute. I think I've found something that will work nicely."

While Margaret hurried to answer her summons, Lars continued his dressing-down. "You had no business yust going off like that without saying a word about it."

The irony wasn't lost on me. I may have been the one person in the country right then with a chance at putting Leave It To God out of business, but here I was being chewed out by

Lars as though I were some errant schoolboy. We were long-term friends, but I had reached my limit.

"Right," I bristled right back at him. "You can show up at a whorehouse in your old stomping grounds where the local madam-with-a-heart-of-gold treats you like some kind of visiting dignitary, but if I disappear for half an hour in the same establishment where you're evidently a regular customer, you go ballistic and call out the National Guard."

"It isn't," he said.

"It isn't what?"

"It isn't a damned whorehouse," Lars declared.

"Really? I say, if it looks like a duck and quacks like a duck and walks like a duck . . ."

"It is not a whorehouse," Lars said again, his voice rising.

"Have it your way," I told him. "But I'm not a kid, Lars. I don't need watching every minute, and I don't expect to have to ask your permission to leave a room for five minutes. That's not the way things work."

At that, Lars marched off across the room. There he stood, brooding and silent, staring out the second-story window, and I made no effort to follow him or talk him out of it. A few minutes later, Dulcie came huffing back up the stairs.

"I think we've about got it handled," she said. "You'll be surprised."

"Good," I said. "Thanks."

Lars said nothing.

Dulcie cast a concerned look in his direction. "Is something the matter, Lars?" she asked.

"Damned-fool kid. He's got the idea in his head that this place is some kind of whorehouse."

"Isn't it?" I asked.

Dulcie Wadsworth's eyes narrowed, and her cheeks flushed with anger. "Whatever makes you think that, Mr. Beaumont?"

"Well," I said lamely. "There are the girls—"

"They're dancers," she said, cutting me off. "That's what they do—dance. And the ones who come to the Quixote Club thinking they're here to do anything more than dance lose that idea in a hurry or they get sent packing. When I came to town years ago, Sitka was a wide-open after-hours kind of place. I happen to know from personal experience that there were plenty of men who were ready to take advantage of naive young women—the ones dumb enough to fall for their sad stories.

"But that's not what the Quixote Club is all about. I don't operate that kind of establishment, Mr. Beaumont. My girls sign contracts. The contract lays out in black and white all the dos and don'ts. If the girls stick to the rules, they can make more money dancing here for three months than they could working a year at most jobs back home. And when they do go home, it's with the understanding that they're to return to school and complete their education. Four years is all they can work for me—four years and that's it. If they want to go after a graduate degree, they have to find some other way to pay for it because by then it's time for them to step aside and give other girls—other younger girls—the same kind of chance they've had."

I remember how, in one or another of those old fairy tales, someone talked about having their ears boxed. By the time Dulcie Wadsworth finished her tirade, that's exactly how I felt—as though I'd had my ears boxed. I felt them turning beet-red. It didn't help that during her speech Dulcie Wadsworth had walked up so close to me that her ponderous breasts thumped against my chest for emphasis as she went along. And I have no doubt Dulcie could have taken me in a fair fight.

"Any other questions?" she finished.

"No, ma'am," I said. "I don't think so."

"Good then." With that she turned back to the door, which she had left open. "How's it going, Margaret?" she bellowed into the stairwell.

"Fine," Margaret called back. "I'll be up in a minute."

Lars turned away from the window. "I'm sorry about that, Dulcie," he said.

She waved aside his apology. "Don't worry about it, Lars," she said. "Your grandson isn't the first man to make that mistake, and I doubt he'll be the last."

There was a creak on the stairs. I looked back toward the door as an old woman stepped into the room. She had a widow's hump that left her so bent over that her face was totally concealed. Her peroxide-blond hair was covered by a white-haired wig arranged in an armor-plated pageboy. She was dressed in an outfit—a silk, nautically themed sweat suit—that looked as though it might have come straight from the *Starfire Breeze* gift shop. In fact, it was almost a duplicate of the one Rachel Dulles had been wearing the first time I saw her.

"What do you think?" Margaret Featherman asked. "Will this do?"

I was impressed. "You could have fooled me," I said.

Lars nodded. "Me, too," he said grudgingly.

"You have to watch out that you don't undo the Velcro," Dulcie warned Margaret. "The outfit comes off easily. That's the whole idea. It isn't designed for street wear."

"I'll be careful," Margaret said.

"Now, how do we go about getting back to the ship?" I asked. "I told First Officer Vincente that we'd be there within half an hour."

"No problem," Dulcie said, picking up the phone. "I'll have someone bring the car around."

That car turned out to be another Suburban. Instead of the standard Quixote Club pink, this was one of the shiny black ones favored by the FBI and Secret Service. It came complete with a deluxe full-leather interior and heated seats. I didn't see how many miles were on the odometer, but it smelled brand-new.

The driver was the same young woman who had driven Lars and me to the club earlier. If she had danced a number in the show, there was no sign of that now. Dressed once again in her driving togs, she hurried around the Suburban, opened the door for us, and helped a stooped and frail-looking Margaret Featherman into the middle seat. I followed Margaret. Once seated, I turned around in time to see Dulcie Wadsworth envelop Lars Jenssen in a smothering bear hug. She gave him a smooch that left a bright smudge of red lipstick on his cheek.

"It's so good seeing you again, Lars," she said. "Come again soon. Don't be such a stranger."

"Doubt I'll be back again," Lars muttered with a shake of his head. "Don't travel as much now that I'm not fishing. You know how it is. I'm not as young as I used to be."

Dulcie laughed. "None of us are."

"But you've done a good job here, Dulcie," Lars added. "A real good job."

"I couldn't have done it without help," she said, hugging him again.

I thought about that kiss during the better part of the ride into town, which only took a few minutes. It was mid-afternoon by the time we were back at the dock. I left Margaret and Lars to get out of the car while I hurried over to the crewman, Security Officer Angeleri, who was checking passengers prior to their boarding the tender. As soon as I told him who I was, I expected him to hand over an envelope. Instead, he waved me aside. "Please wait until I finish loading this tender, sir," he said.

Simmering with indignation, I wanted to argue with him about it, but I couldn't. There were far too many returning passengers milling around on the visitors' dock and clambering into the tender. It was no place to make a scene, especially in view of the fact that Lars, trying to be helpful, had escorted the decrepit and shuffling Margaret right up to where I stood. I consoled myself with the thought that at least the two of them made a believable-looking couple.

It didn't take all that long to load the tender, but the time passed slowly, especially since I wanted us to be on the tender rather than standing on the dock waiting for the next one. At the time my biggest fear was that we'd run into someone we knew—someone who would recognize Margaret Featherman or Lars Jenssen or me. The last thing we needed was for someone like Claire or Florence Wakefield to show up. They'd take one look at the convincing old lady Margaret Featherman had turned into. Then they'd go straight to Beverly and blow the whistle.

While we waited, I recognized several of the guys who had been with us in the audience at the Quixote Club. In preparation for returning to the ship, they had all shucked their high spirits. To a man they seemed subdued and as intent on being invisible as Lars and I were. Even Mr. Twenty Questions made it a point to avoid eye contact. He didn't acknowledge us, and we did the same.

"Now then," Security Officer Angeleri said finally when the fully loaded passenger tender pulled away from the dock. "You are to go to the far end of the dock. First Officer Vincente has another tender waiting there. It will take the special passenger to the crew gangway. That hatch leads directly to crew quarters. An officer will be waiting there to escort her to the screening room."

"Her," I objected. "What about us? We need to be with her."

"I don't know about that," Security Officer Angeleri returned dubiously.

"You go on the crew tender," Lars said. "I'll wait for the next one here."

Another flurry of passengers approached. The chance of avoiding a scene did the trick. "All right," Angeleri said, giving in. "Go."

Margaret started off toward the end of the dock. Before I could follow her, Lars tapped me on the shoulder. "Not a word to Beverly about Dulcie," he whispered.

I couldn't have agreed more. "I'll keep quiet if you do," I

promised. "As long as you don't say anything about Margaret."

Lars nodded. "Ya, sure," he said. "Fair enough."

"And you'd best wipe that lipstick off your face before Beverly gets a look at you," I told him. "If she sees that, she'll figure out for herself that you've been up to something."

Guiltily, Lars scrubbed his face clean, and we let it go at that.

Margaret Featherman and I were the only passengers to ride the specially designated crew tender out to the ship. When we left the pontoon docking platform and stepped onto the ship, First Officer Vincente was waiting just inside the gangway. The look he gave me was anything but friendly, but when he saw Margaret Featherman, he frowned and hesitated.

I could understand his consternation. He hadn't expected me to be on the tender along with Margaret. Not only that, I'm sure that in her absence, Margaret's picture had been circulated among the crew. Even I had to admit that the aged, white-haired woman standing in front of him bore little resemblance to the handsome middle-aged woman whose image had most likely been captured by the ship's ubiquitous photographers.

"This is Margaret Featherman," I said. "And this is First Officer Vincente."

As if to put Vincente at ease, Margaret whipped off her wig and held out her hand. "I'm glad to meet you," she said. "Thanks for all your help."

Relieved, Vincente, too, offered his hand. "But of course, Mrs. Featherman," he said solicitously. "I am most happy to meet you. It is my great pleasure to welcome you back on board. Captain Giacometti wishes me to inform you that he is pleased as well. The entire crew of the *Starfire Breeze* is at your disposal and will do everything possible to assure your continued safety. To that end, once you are finished viewing the tapes, Captain Giacometti is pleased to offer you the use of his quarters until this matter is settled."

"I appreciate that very much," Margaret said.

I appreciated it, too, but not wanting Vincente to send me packing, I decided to practice being seen but not heard. To that end I kept quiet.

"Now, if you will come this way," First Officer Vincente added, "I will show you to the security screening room."

I more than half expected First Officer Vincente to tell me to get lost, but he didn't. I followed them down the corridor and slipped into Antonio Belvaducci's darkened screening room. Once again I did my best to stay out of the way while First Officer Vincente made introductions and issued orders.

Antonio listened carefully, nodding as Vincente posed the problem. By the time the first officer had finished, Antonio was smiling broadly. "I have just the thing," he said. "There is only one video camera every passenger must pass by," he said. "That is the one mounted just inside the ship at the top of the gangplank. In Seattle, passengers start boarding at one o'clock in the afternoon. The ship sails at five. So there will be four hours of tape to view, but that is not so very difficult, and it will approach the problem in an orderly fashion."

"Very good," Vincente said. "The sooner, the better."

Antonio pushed a rolling desk chair in Margaret Featherman's direction. "If you would care to take a seat, I'll cue up the first tape for you."

Margaret took the offered seat while First Officer Vincente excused himself and left. I found another chair and settled in to wait.

The process took the better part of two hours, and I had a hard time sitting still. Twice I got up and tried calling Rachel Dulles and Todd Bowman. The fact that there was still no answer in either of their cabins was cause for worry, but I didn't see any sense in leaving them a message—not until I had something substantial to report. Not that finding Margaret Featherman alive wasn't substantial.

The real reason I didn't leave a message may have had to do with ego. Once a detective, always a detective. Officially it may have been the FBI's case, but I was in on it now. I had no intention of letting go, not until I was good and ready—not until I had the whole thing sacked and bagged.

As for my being a team player? Screw it! This time I didn't see how anyone could fault me. After all, how could I be a team player if they hadn't let me on the team in the first place?

Time passed. Boredom, the fast-paced tour of Sitka, and the humming quiet of the darkened room all went to work on me. Somewhere along the way I must have dozed off in the chair. At four-fifteen, sixteen-fifteen according to the clock on the screening room's wall and halfway through the boarding tape, Margaret Featherman's excited voice startled me awake. "There she is!"

Jumping from my chair, I stood over Margaret's shoulder and peered at the screen. And there, walking up the covered gangplank, was someone I recognized—Christine Moran, the reporter who had interviewed Marc Alley; the person I had last seen walking back toward the ship with Naomi Pepper, the Wakefield girls, and my grandmother.

"You're sure that's her?" I demanded.

"Of course I'm sure," Margaret snapped. "That woman tried to kill me. How could I possibly forget her face?" Margaret turned to Antonio Belvaducci. "Now that I've spotted her, how do we find out what her name is?"

· "I already know her name," I interjected. "It's Christine Moran. At least that's the name she's going by on board. She claims to be a journalist. She's here supposedly covering the neurologist meeting; at least that's her cover story."

"So what do we do now?" Margaret asked.

"*We* do nothing," I said, putting the emphasis on the "we" part. "You do exactly as First Officer Vincente suggested. You go to Captain Giacometti's quarters and put your feet up. I'll notify First Officer Vincente." I turned to Antonio. "Where's your phone?"

Antonio pointed. "A list of pager numbers is posted beside the phone," Belvaducci said helpfully. "Dial his number and First Officer Vincente will call back."

I glanced at the clock. It was less than two hours prior to the *Starfire Breeze*'s scheduled 6 P.M. departure time. Doing as I was told, I dialed the phone and then paced the floor and waited. I wanted to try calling Rachel Dulles and Todd Bowman again, but I didn't want the phone to be busy when Vincente called back. But then, instead of calling, he simply appeared in the doorway.

"What has happened?" he asked.

"Mrs. Featherman has located her attacker," I said. "Her name is Christine Moran. I've met her. She's on board masquerading as a journalist."

"Very well," Vincente said at once. "As the officer in charge of security, I will gather a crew of men and take her into custody. Meantime, Mr. Beaumont, would you please be so good as to contact the FBI agents on board and let them know what has happened. I am sure they will handle the situation from here."

He left and I turned back to Margaret. She was still sitting in front of the screen. In the dim light of the shadowy room, I saw her shoulders heave. She was crying.

I walked over to her and placed a hand on her shoulder. "What's wrong?" I asked.

"I don't know," she said, sniffling. "It's not like me to break down and go all to pieces. What's the matter with me?"

"It's relief," I told her. "Sometimes that'll get you just as much as anything else. Now, do what First Officer Vincente said. Go to Captain Giacometti's quarters and get some rest."

Any other time, I would have expected an argument from Margaret Featherman—out of sheer perversity if nothing else. Now she simply nodded. "I will," she said. "But you'll call me when all this is settled?"

"I will," I told her. "But in the meantime, be careful. We're not out of the woods yet."

24

Belvaducci summoned a crewman, who came and collected Margaret Featherman. Before I left the screening room, I once again used Antonio's phone. This time when I reached Rachel Dulles' and Todd Bowman's voice-mail recordings, I left messages for both of them. Now that we knew Christine Moran was our target, someone with the right credentials needed to take charge of the situation. The two messages were pretty much the same.

"This is Beau Beaumont. I've located Margaret Featherman. She's alive and well and under wraps back on the ship. She's identified the woman who attacked her. Her name is Christine Moran, who's supposedly a journalist here covering the neurological symposium. Please contact me as soon as you get this. I'll be in my stateroom, Capri four-five-four."

Minutes later, when I unlocked the door to my room, I heard the sound of the television set playing inside. That meant Naomi was home. When I first caught sight of her, she was sitting on the love seat with her eyes glued to CNN. She hurried to the door as I stepped inside the room.

"Beau," she said breathlessly. "You're not going to believe it!"

"Believe what?"

"What's happened! Marc Alley heard that somebody found Margaret," she said. "Not only did they find her, she's supposed to be all right. She's somewhere in Sitka."

"She is?" I asked. My heart fell. Being on board the *Starfire Breeze* was almost as bad as living in a small town. It was hard to believe that someone had already turned loose the ship's gossip mill. I had tried to be so careful in bringing Margaret aboard. I wondered who it was on the visitors' dock who had seen through the elaborate disguise and recognized her. However it had happened, the word was out. *Damn!*

"When did you hear all this?" I asked.

"Marc Alley came by just a few minutes ago. He came to tell you about it," Naomi continued. "He said he was talking to someone who just came from that bar Lars pointed out to us earlier this morning. What did he call it again? The P-Bar, I think. Anyway, there was some young guy in there talking about how a few days ago the crew of the boat he was on found a woman swimming for her life out in Chatham Strait. He said she promised all of the crew a sizable reward if they'd bring her to shore and drop her off. He said she was going to put money into the boat's overstock or gross stock. I forget exactly what he said."

"Gross stock," I told her. "That's the income a fishing boat takes in. It's divided up among the crew."

Naomi nodded. "So they brought her here, to Sitka."

Despite the serious argument that had transpired between Naomi Pepper and Margaret Featherman the last time the two women saw each other, Naomi was clearly overjoyed to learn Margaret was alive and safe. I, on the other hand, was appalled. If Naomi knew about Margaret and if Marc knew about Margaret, then it was only a matter of time until Christine Moran knew about Margaret as well.

Since the *Starfire Breeze* was anchored offshore in Sitka Sound, I wasn't worried that she'd get away. I was concerned that the FBI would miss out on the chance of nabbing her with the goods. I wanted them to nail her before she had a chance to ditch any incriminating evidence that might link her to others in the organization. Catching Christine Moran was one thing, but putting the Leave It To God organization out of business and behind bars was far more important.

"How long ago was Marc here?" I demanded, trying to conceal my dismay.

Naomi shrugged. "Not that long. A few minutes. I tuned in to CNN to see if anyone else had heard this. And, sure enough, they said that there were unconfirmed reports that missing genetic researcher Margaret Featherman had been found alive in Alaska. What do you think of that?"

How much worse can it get? I wondered.

Without answering, I moved past Naomi and reached for the phone. I knew Marc Alley's stateroom was on Bahia Deck, but for the life of me I couldn't remember the number. "Marc Alley, please," I said to the ship's operator.

"Beau," Naomi said. "What's the matter? You look upset."

I was upset, and the longer Marc's phone rang without him answering, the more upset I became. My phone rang the moment I put the receiver back in place. "Hello."

"Mr. Beaumont," First Officer Vincente said. "I'm so glad you are there. Miss Moran is not in her room."

"Is she off the ship?" I asked.

"Not according to the computer. She came back aboard several hours ago. I have secured her room by changing the lock to a special code that can be opened only by me or Captain Giacometti. That way, if any incriminating evidence was left in the room, she will not be able to return and retrieve it. The problem is, until we have copies of Ms. Moran's photo made from the videotape, my security watchmen have no idea what Miss Moran looks like. You said you had met her, correct?"

"Yes."

"Will you help us find her?"

"Of course. Where do you want me to meet you?"

"At the purser's desk," he said. "We'll go through the public areas of the ship one at a time."

"I'll be right there."

I put down the phone and turned around to find a white-faced Naomi Pepper sitting on the love seat staring at me. "You already knew about Margaret being alive, didn't you!" she said accusingly. "You just let me go on and on when you already knew all about it."

"Please, Naomi. I'm sorry. There wasn't time to explain when I first came in the door, and there's even less now. I've got to go. If I don't, the woman who attacked Margaret just might get away with it."

"Where are you going?" she demanded.

"To the purser's desk. I'm supposed to meet First Officer Vincente and his crew there."

Naomi shook her head in exasperation. "Oh, all right," she said. "Go!"

Once again I didn't bother with the elevator. I bounded up the stairway two steps at a time, ignoring my injured toe as best I could. I was taking a shortcut to the purser's desk through the Pizzeria when I saw Marc Alley and Christine Moran seated together at a table. Marc was talking animatedly while Christine listened in such dead earnest that it made my blood run cold. I knew at once that he was right in the middle of telling her the same story he had told Naomi. First Officer Vincente might be only a few hundred feet away from me at the purser's desk, but at that moment, for lack of ability to communicate with him, he could just as well have been light-years away.

What I wouldn't have given right then for my trusty cellular phone so I could have summoned him. I was about to turn back and go in search of a house phone when Marc Alley saw me and waved—frantically.

"I was looking for you, Beau," he called across three tables. "You've got to come hear this for yourself. Somebody's found Margaret Featherman. I was just telling Christine all about it. She's been following this story from the beginning, so it's only fair that she should get the scoop."

I always try to stay away from playing poker with the

boys—it's hard to win when your face—for good or ill—
betrays the kind of cards you've got in your hand. All my life
I've attempted to avoid the kinds of situations where lying
would be necessary since my face always blows my cover.
When I was little, all my mother had to do was look at me and
she knew exactly where I'd been and what I'd been up to, and
it was the same thing now. When Christine Moran's eyes met
mine across the checkered tabletop, a charge of electricity
flashed between us. It was similar to what had passed between
Naomi Pepper and me while we were dancing the tango, only
this was done without any physical contact whatsoever. And
it was far more dangerous.

I knew, and Christine Moran knew that I knew.

Now that the Mike Conyers situation had been sorted out,
Marc Alley seemed to be in enormously high spirits. "Is that
great news or what?" he was saying enthusiastically.

"It's great," I agreed lamely. "Wonderful. Who found
her?"

I was well aware of who had found Margaret Featherman,
but for Marc's sake I had to appear surprised—surprised and
interested. And, no matter what, I had to find a way to carry
on a convincing conversation—one that would last until First
Officer Vincente figured out I wasn't going to make it to the
purser's desk and came looking for me.

"The crew of a fishing boat called *Miss Piggy*," Marc
began. "They were headed down Chatham Strait for a black-
cod opener and—"

Christine reached for her purse and made as if to stand up.
"I'm sorry to interrupt, Marc, but I'd better go call my editor

and see what he wants me to do about all this. If you two will excuse me . . ."

I looked at Christine's purse, a small clutch-style number. It was made of leather and looked expensive.

During the cruise I had noticed that most of the women on board had abandoned their purses while they were on the ship. As long as they had their precious key card, there was no need to carry money or any other form of identification. I understood instinctively that there was some important reason Christine Moran was carrying hers. It came down to two possible choices. Either she had a weapon inside it, or she was using it to carry around something important, something she hadn't wanted to leave in her room, even in the comparative security of a room safe.

The purse wasn't large. It was big enough to carry a small weapon and too small for a large one. No matter what, I was determined not to let Christine Moran walk away with whatever was inside it.

"Don't go," I said, trying to sound sociable. "Stay for a while and let me buy you a drink."

It helped that Christine's back was to the wall. Marc was on one side of her and I was on the other. Unless one of us moved, Christine Moran was stuck where she was.

"Really, Mr. Beaumont, I have to go," she objected. "I have a job to do."

"So do I," I returned.

Another charge of electricity passed between us. Marc frowned and shot me a puzzled, questioning look of his own. "A job?" he asked. "I thought you were retired."

"Off the team but not out of the game," I said.

Christine Moran understood exactly what I was saying. Marc was still mystified. "What do you mean?" he asked.

"I mean the three of us should just sit here for the time being and wait until First Officer Vincente comes this way. I'm sure he and some of the crew are looking for us right this minute. And with that security camera up there . . ." I pointed and waved, hoping that the exaggerated movement might somehow catch Antonio Belvaducci's attention. ". . . I'd guess it won't be all that long before he finds us."

"Yes, Christine," Marc said. "Please stay."

Christine's jaw tightened. "You can come with me if you like, Marc," Christine said. "In fact, it might be better if you did. Whatever it is your friend here has in mind, I'd rather not be a part of it."

Her right hand slipped into the purse. When it came out again, I caught a glimpse of the blued-steel barrel of a weapon. Not a large one, but at such close range, size hardly matters. Marc saw it too, about the same time I did.

"Christine—" he said.

"Let's go," she urged. "Just you and me. As for you," she added, glaring at me. "If you make a single move to follow us, you know what'll happen."

Naturally I wasn't wearing any kind of weapon. None. No shoulder holster. No ankle holster. Nothing—not even a slingshot. The only thing I had going for me was my mouth— the power of persuasion and all those summers I spent in my youth selling Fuller brushes door-to-door.

"You don't want to do that, Christine," I warned. "If you do, things will be a lot worse than they are right this minute. At the moment, all anybody has on you is one count of attempted murder in the case of Margaret Featherman. If you force Marc to leave the table at gunpoint, believe me, it turns into a whole other ball game."

Christine tucked the purse under one arm and then tugged at Marc's shoulder. "Come on," she said. "Let's go."

Staring at the gun, Marc started to rise. "Don't fall for it," I warned. "She's bluffing."

Abruptly, Marc sat back down. Now he looked away from the gun and stared at me. "Christine's the one who did it?" he asked. "She's the one who threw Margaret overboard?"

I nodded. "And what's she going to do now, Marc, shoot us? Then what? We're moored in the middle of Sitka Sound. Do you think she'll go over the rail and swim for it? I doubt Christine's as good a swimmer as Margaret Featherman is. Margaret swims a couple of miles every day before she goes to work at Genesis. How about you, Christine? Just how good a swimmer are you? If you jumped over the side of the ship and left the decision to God, do you think He'd help you make it to shore the same way He helped Margaret? You left it to God, and Margaret Featherman came up winners. How about you, Christine?"

I was deliberately taunting her, trying to draw Christine's attention away from Marc and get her to focus on me. My mouth moved and the words flowed across my lips in that bell-like crystal clarity and utter calm that occurs only when you're scared out of your wits—when time slows and expands until every heartbeat seems to take a minute and every breath lasts a year at least. I was a trained cop who had spent a whole career working in law enforcement. If I was that scared, what about Marc Alley?

But maybe having spent all those years looking his next grand-mal seizure in the eye had allowed Marc to find his own calming clarity. He eased back into his chair and pushed the back of it inches closer to the wall, making it that much more difficult for Christine to get past us and break free.

"That's why you attached yourself to our group this morning as we left the ship, isn't it," I continued. "Marc had told you I knew something about what was going on, and you thought if that was true and if I had heard anything about whether or not Margaret had been found alive, the first person I would share that news with would be Naomi Pepper. That's why you were so eager to interview her, right?"

Christine said nothing, but I didn't expect her to reply. Mine was a rhetorical question. I already knew the answer.

Suddenly, out of the corner of my eye, I spotted a flurry of movement. Two uniformed crewmen entered through one of the Pizzeria's two entries while two others, led by First Officer Vincente, entered via the other. None of them seemed to be armed, but as they converged around our table, seven to one seemed like pretty good odds to me.

"I'd put the gun down if I were you, Christine," I told her. "I'd put the gun down and raise my hands in the air."

Meanwhile First Officer Vincente walked up to the table looking totally unperturbed. "You are Miss Moran?" he asked.

She nodded.

"Please put down your weapon and come with me," he said. "I am placing you under arrest."

"You can't arrest me," she said. "I'm an American citizen."

"As first officer, I am the ship's chief security officer, madam," he told her. "Under maritime law, all ship passengers come under the captain's jurisdiction. As the captain's designated security officer, I am in charge. The fact that you are an American citizen has nothing to do with it. There are several FBI agents due back on the next tender. Once they arrive, I will be happy to turn you over to them. In the meantime, you will please come with me."

The mention of the FBI was too much for Christine Moran. Exploding into action, she made a break for it. She shoved Marc's chair out of the way and sprinted along the wall toward the nearest exit. One of First Officer Vincente's security crew brought her down with a flying tackle. The gun spun away in one direction, while the purse, which she had clutched under her arm, went flying the other way. It skittered away across the marbled floor, scattering contents as it went. While two members of the security crew subdued Christine Moran and wrestled her into a pair of handcuffs, another crewman went across the floor gathering the purse and everything that had fallen from it. He brought the collection of loose items back to the table where Marc and I were sitting and dumped them in a heap on the marble tabletop.

The pile contained the usual kinds of female survival stuff—a comb, two tubes of lipstick, a compact, some wadded Kleenex, several pens, a small bottle of prescription medication, a change purse, and a set of car keys. The last item the sailor retrieved appeared to be a small leather wallet, but it was too thin to be a wallet—too thin and too flat. And when he dropped it onto the table, it landed with a distinctly unwallet-like clatter.

Using the tip of one of the pencils, I raised the leather top. Under it was an electronic organizer—a PalmPilot. Not the keys to Rebecca, perhaps, and not a little black book, either, but I was pretty sure that organizer would contain the phone numbers and codes that would give the FBI all the access it needed to Leave It To God. And since it seemed unlikely that PalmPilots come complete with that old *Mission Impossible* ability to self-destruct, I figured Rachel Dulles and Alex Freed were going to have a blast.

First Officer Vincente looked at the organizer. "What is that?" he asked.

"It's her database," I told him. "Which means it's really a home run."

Vincente looked at it and smiled. "A home run," he agreed. "With bases loaded."

25

I**T'S POSSIBLE THAT** by the time the second seating came around that night, Margaret Featherman was once again installed as reigning royalty at her table for six in the Crystal Dining Room. I have no idea whether or not that happened. After being debriefed by a roomful of at first guarded, but eventually appreciative FBI agents, I returned to my stateroom, where Naomi Pepper and I opted to order dinner from Room Service. She may have been mad at me earlier, but by dinnertime, Naomi was pretty well over it.

"So this is what it's like to be involved with a police officer," she said thoughtfully, spearing a chunk of almond-crusted red snapper. "Every once in a while you cops just leap up and go racing off like that without a word."

"That's pretty much it," I agreed. "Usually, there's no time to hang around giving long-winded explanations."

"Or even short-winded ones," she added. "It all sounds very exciting, but I suspect it would take some getting used to. Are you planning on going back to work anytime soon?"

"I don't know," I said. "Being a dance host on the *Starfire Breeze* seems to offer plenty of excitement. And you never know. It's always possible that you might hook up with a rich widow—or an enticing not-quite-rich and not-quite-divorced widow."

"Who happens to like to tango?" she asked with a smile.

"You bet," I told her. "And who has the trophy coffee mug to prove it."

We went to bed early that night, without waiting for Hector's turndown service. The DO NOT DISTURB sign was prominently displayed on our door and the telephone ringer turned off. The only hazard with going to bed that early is waking up early as well. I awakened well before sunrise. The first thing I saw in the gray dimness of the room was the telephone— with its voice-mail light blinking away. Rather than call for messages from there, I eased my way out of bed doing my best not to disturb a peacefully sleeping Naomi. I went in the bathroom, closed the door, and used that phone to dial in for messages.

The message from Lars had been left a mere twenty minutes earlier. "If you get this anytime soon, meet me in the Lido Buffet for coffee. I'll be there for an hour or so."

Naomi was still sleeping when I came out of the bathroom. I jotted a note on the notepad, left it on my pillow, then

I tiptoed out into the corridor. I spotted Lars sitting at a table in the middle of the noisy room.

After pouring myself a cup of coffee, I sauntered over to his table and helped myself to a chair. "What's up?" I asked. "And where's Beverly this morning?"

"She and the Wakefield girls went for a massage," he said. "Beverly's never had one, and she refused to go by herself. Early morning was the only time all three of them could get in together. After that, I guess they're going to have their hair fixed. Again. It's another one of those formal nights," he added grumpily.

"Beverly deserves some fun now and then," I said. "I know for a fact you've had yours."

It was an uncalled-for dig, and Lars responded with a noticeable wince. "It's not what you t'ink," he said. "Not now."

"Isn't it?" I said.

Of course, having just crawled out of a luxuriously warm bed that came complete with a delectably willing woman, I wasn't in any position to cast aspersions.

"Maybe it was at one time," he said. "Back in the old days, when I was fouled up on booze a lot of the time, I us'ta go to the Kiksadi Club, and not just for the drinking, either. But that was between Aggie and me, and we got it all settled, long before Aggie got sick. By then, it was all water under the bridge. But I did stay friends with one of the girls," he added. "Friends and nothing more."

"With Dulcie Wadsworth."

"Ya," he said. "The guy she was mixed up with was a real bad character. And what he did to her was all wrong. That's why, when she wanted to go into business for herself, I helped her do it."

"You were one of her financial backers?"

"The financial backer," Lars said. "The bank turned her down flat. Believe me, it's been a damned fine investment over the years—best one I ever made. The money's come in real steady."

"Does Beverly know anything about your investment?" I asked with more than a slightly sarcastic emphasis on the word *investment*.

"No," he said. "And she's not going to know—unless you tell her."

"Come on, Lars. You two are married. You can't keep that kind of thing secret. If nothing else, it'll turn up when it's time to do your income taxes."

"No, it won't," he said. "It's all paid off now. There won't be any more money coming in from the Quicksaudy Club."

"Why not?"

"Because Dulcie bought me out several years ago—lock, stock, and barrel. Where do you t'ink I got enough money pulled together to move your grandmother into Queen Anne Gardens?"

"From Dulcie buying you out?" I asked.

"Where else?" he returned. "And another t'ing," he added. "Whatever Dulcie did before, the Quicksaudy Club never was a whorehouse, either. Understand?"

Lars looked at me defiantly through his rheumy old blue eyes. I think if I had disagreed with him right then, he would have taken a swing at me and punched me out on the spot— smack in the middle of the Lido Buffet.

"Yes," I said. "Now that you put it that way, I guess I do understand. The Quixote Club never was a whorehouse and never will be."

"Right," Lars said with a smile. "Not as long as Dulcie's around. She's a fine woman, Beau. Not as fine as your grandmother by any means, but still very nice."

There was a faraway look in his eye when Lars said that, and it crossed my mind that it was probably a good thing for Lars that he had divested himself of all financial interest in the Quixote Club. As a man I could afford to be philosophical about such things. I doubted very much that Beverly Piedmont Jenssen would be.

No wonder Lars had wanted to have coffee with me so bright and early. He didn't think she'd be philosophical about it, either.

"Don't worry, Pop," I told him, giving Lars a playful whack on his scrawny, bony shoulder blade. "Your secret's safe with me."